WHEN THE
STARS
THREW DOWN THEIR
SPEARS

WHEN THE STARS THREW DOWN THEIR SPEARS

The Goblin Wars: Book Three

KERSTEN HAMILTON

Houghton Mifflin Harcourt
New York • Boston

www.hmhco.com

The text of this book is set in ITC Founder's Caslon.
Book design by Sharismar Rodriguez

The Library of Congress has cataloged the hardcover edition as follows:
Hamilton, K. R. (Kersten R.)
When the stars threw down their spears / by Kersten Hamilton.
p. cm.— (The goblin wars; bk 3)
Summary: Teagan leaves her flesh and bones behind to join Finn
in hunting the uncanny creatures that have spilled from Mag Mell into Chicago,
realizing that she must destroy the Dark Man and his minions
once and for all to save her remaining loved ones.
[1. Goblins—Fiction. 2. Magic—Fiction. 3. Imaginary creatures—Fiction.
4. People with mental disabilities—Fiction. 5. Irish Americans—Fiction.
6. Zoos—Fiction. 7. Finn MacCool—Fiction. 8. Chicago (Ill.)—Fiction.] I. Title.
PZ7. H1824 Whe 2013 [Fic]—dc23
2012029195

ISBN: 978-0-547-73964-9 hardcover
ISBN: 978-0-544-22771-2 paperback

Manufactured in US
DOC 10 9 8 7 6 5 4 3 2 1

4500478060

This book is for you. Listen to your glimories. Follow them home.

PROLOGUE

SOMEONE hadn't made it into lockdown. Teagan didn't know the girl Kyle was holding off the floor by her hair. She was screaming and twisting, trying to get away. Kyle tickled her belly with his claws. "I've been waiting for you, Tea!"

Finn reached for his knife that wasn't there; Abby whirled and grabbed a whole bucket of flatware from the salad bar.

"Dumpster Boy!" she shouted, and threw the whole thing at Finn. The flatware spilled out of it as it tumbled. Finn snatched a spoon out of the air, and his hand flicked toward Kyle. The spoon seemed to blossom from the dent at the base of the Highborn's neck, even as the rest of the flatware rained to the floor.

Kyle let go of his hostage's hair to grab the spoon with both hands, but before he could pull it out, Angel had the girl, and then Leo was right against the Highborn's back. It was only when Kyle arched that Teagan realized that Leo had a knife in his hand. Kyle went down so violently that the knife was pulled from Leo's grip.

The girl he'd been holding ran screaming from the room.

Leo stepped back. "When you get to Hell, tell them Leo Gagliano sent you."

Teagan felt the tears welling in her eyes as she stared at Kyle's motionless form.

"Tea," Finn said as she walked past him. "Don't cry. Two worlds are better off without Kyle in them."

"Yeah, right," Abby said. "That's like telling her not to be Teagan Wylltson. You're welcome, by the way."

"For?" Finn asked.

"Passing the silverware? I told you I was psychic."

"What?"

"I said if we ever got attacked in a restaurant we'd be safe, right?"

"This is a cafeteria, Gabby. And you said if Tea was attacked, she'd be safe."

"So, she's safe."

Teagan shut out their bickering as she knelt beside Kyle. He turned his face toward her as the pool of dark blood spread around them. She could feel the life seeping out of him. He didn't have the strength to move again, but even through his beast-mask of a face, Teagan could see the fear. Kyle was afraid of dying. She couldn't pretend she wasn't glad his life was over. Glad he wouldn't hurt anyone else. But the fear in his eyes was unbearable.

Teagan took his hand, careful of the claws, and held it in her own, pressing her palm to his. Kyle's eyes widened in surprise.

Leo pulled a handkerchief from his pocket, took the spoon from Kyle's other hand, and wiped it down.

"What are you doing?" Finn asked.

"Prints," Leo said. "Any security cameras, Angel?"

"I'll have Jing take care of it," Abby said.

"Who's this Jing?" Leo asked.

"I'll introduce you sometime. Right now you should take Finn and get out of here. The cops will be here any minute."

Kyle's eyes clouded, and Teagan felt the last flicker of life drain away. *Like it had drained from her mother.* Aileen Wylltson had never opened her eyes as she lay dying. But her face had been . . . peaceful. Teagan's lips moved, silently forming her mother's poem:

> *Selves—goes itself; myself it speaks and spells,*
> *Crying* Whát I do is me: for that I came.

"You should get away from that thing, Tea," Leo said. "It's probably got diseases."

"Leave her alone, Leonardo," Abby said. "Tea does what she does."

Teagan closed her eyes. *Tea does what she does.*
I may be Highborn. But I am not *like my family.*
What I do is me: for this I came.
If I am any creature of yours, Almighty, she prayed, *help me speak and spell something other than this into creation. Give me the courage to live what I am.*

"Are you praying for him? That's rich."

Teagan looked up. Isabeau had come into the room.

"For myself," Teagan corrected.

Finn started toward Isabeau.

"Finn," Teagan said. "Wait. I want her to carry a message. Tell Mab I said no more."

"No more games?" Isabeau laughed. "Oh, there's plenty more coming. Have you heard about your little chimp friend yet?"

"I heard." Teagan pulled Leo's knife from Kyle's body. Leo reached for it, but she waved him away.

"What are you doing?" Abby asked.

"What I came for." Teagan stood up. "Tell Mab I won't allow her to hurt my family and friends."

"*You're* challenging Mab? By yourself?" Isabeau scoffed.

"She's not by herself, is she, goblin?" Finn said.

"You mess with her, you mess with us," Abby agreed.

Isabeau pushed her shades up on top of her head, and her oil-puddle eyes looked blankly at Teagan. "You know this means war."

"Then let there be war," Teagan said, and threw the knife like she meant it.

PART I: GLIMORIES

ONE

THE world *tilted* as the blade flipped end over end toward Isabeau. Teagan had felt the shift before, when her little brother had changed her future with a song.

Now she felt the ripple of change spread as if she had dropped a stone into a still pond; it hit Finn, Abby, the Gagliano brothers . . . Isabeau. The shock waves rebounded off each of them, coming back from every direction and passing through her, crossing one another.

Suddenly, the coppery scent of Kyle's blood was so thick in the air she could taste it. She felt the heat leaking from his body beside her, heard the Doppler shift of the sirens outside racing toward them, and sensed the faint electrical field generated by every beating heart in the room.

Leonardo, Michelangelo, and Donatello Gagliano glowed like tiny LEDs behind her; their cousin Abigail was brighter, but Finn Mac Cumhaill hummed like a high-power line. She had felt the blood pounding through his veins before, felt his heart beating, and she felt it again now—even though they were separated by fifteen feet. She felt the adrenaline in him. *This isn't telepathy. In telepathy, you can read thoughts. I'm reading the electrical impulses in his body.* She felt his muscles move as he lunged toward Isabeau.

"No!" Teagan shouted. Isabeau, the bilocate, had no electric hum. The form standing before them was only her soul, wrapped in cold matter that would explode when the iron blade pierced it, sending her back to her sleeping body in Mag Mell. If Finn was touching her, he would be pulled into Mag Mell with her.

Finn caught Isabeau's arm as the knife hit—hilt first, thudding against the girl's fashionable pink jacket and clattering to the cafeteria floor.

"Lame," Angel said. The other Gagliano brothers shuffled their feet uncomfortably.

"Shut your mouth, Michelangelo." Abby glared at him. "Tea's only done this, like, once before. And that time, she was throwing silverware at a box."

"Gabby's right." Finn scooped up the knife with his free hand. "It was a good throw. Your release was a little too quick is all. If you'd held it a fraction of a second longer, you'd have nailed it."

"So you could tell it wasn't going to stick?" Abby said.

"Anybody could see that." Leo pointed at Kyle's still form. "What's happening to his face?" Death was reshaping Kyle, flattening the muzzle, retracting the bloody claws.

"What the hell?" Donnie said. "He looks just like a normal guy!"

"Tough luck for you," Isabeau said. "How *do* humans feel about murdering teachers?"

"Shit," Leonardo said. "The cops already have this place surrounded."

Isabeau turned to Teagan. "'What I came for.'" She repeated Teagan's words, clearly puzzled. "*What I came for*'?" She shook her head. "What does that even mean? You're standing in a high school cafeteria in a hoodie that hangs to your knees and pink—what are those, pajamas?—declaring war on the Queen of the Sídhe."

Teagan fought the urge to shove her hands in her pockets and pull Finn's hoodie close around her. The confidence she'd felt the second before she'd thrown the knife had drained away along with the adrenaline rush, or had been washed away by the ripples, and the smell of Kyle's blood was starting to make her sick.

The truth was she had been running for her life since the goblins had first appeared, and Isabeau knew it.

"Pathetic," the goblin girl said. "The cops are coming, Fear Doirich is going to kill you if they don't, and none of you have any idea what to do next."

"We'll improvise," Finn said. "One problem at a time."

Isabeau tried to brush his hand from her arm, but he held on. "Is this the army you plan to lead to war, Teagan? One Irish Traveler and four Italians?"

"Five Italians," Donnie said. "You remember our brother Rafe? The one you were sucking face with before you framed him for murdering the lunch lady?"

"Shut up, Donnie." Leo started to pace. "I'm trying to think here."

"One Italian who can't think, three who are useless, and a tasty gangster wannabe. And you have the *lhiannon-sídhe* and his girlfriend, don't you? I suppose he'll inspire a poet to write a song about you when you're dead. Oh, wait. I forgot. He's going to be dead, too, as soon as Fear Doirich catches up with him. None of you have any idea what you are messing with."

"Mab wanted me to kill Fear Doirich," Teagan said. "Why?"

The goblin girl's smile froze. "You really have been to Mag Mell."

"And back," Finn said. "We're that clever."

Isabeau snatched for the knife Finn was holding, her hand moving unbelievably fast. Finn was faster still, and his arms were longer. He held it up out of her reach.

"Does Fear know what Kyle ... what I was doing here?" she asked.

"I'd say he noticed what Kyle had done to Teagan."

Leo kicked the body. "The perv did something to you, Tea?"

This time Teagan did shove her hands into the hoodie pockets.

"Nothing that kicking him will change. He infected me with a retrovirus." A little bit of gene therapy engineered to burn away her genetic inheritance from her father. To make her pure Highborn.

"Shit." Leo rubbed his knife hand on his jeans, as if that

10

could clean off any residue left from touching Kyle. "I knew it had diseases."

"Please." Isabeau reached again for the knife and melted against Finn, forcing him to hold her up.

"Tea," Abby said. "Did you just growl?"

"Of course not." Teagan cleared her throat. "That was just a...a..."

"A what?" Donnie asked. "A burp?"

"I don't know." Teagan flushed. "A . . . noise."

She knew perfectly well that Isabeau's body wasn't warm, that it didn't feel like flesh against flesh. It didn't feel as *good*. But that didn't stop the bilocates from indulging their appetites.

"Let me go, Mac Cumhaill," Isabeau purred. "I've got to get back to my body before the Dark Man finds it. You have no idea how vicious he can be."

Finn pushed her upright but didn't release her arm. "Tell us, then. What happens when you swear a blood oath to a fallen *aingeal*, then break it?"

"Quiet," Teagan said, tipping her head to listen.

Footsteps at the end of the hall. Cautious footsteps.

"I just want to—" Isabeau managed before Finn clapped his hand over her mouth.

"Officer Fiorella is coming," Teagan said.

Donnie headed for the cafeteria entrance. "Fiorella does something other than give D.A.R.E. lectures and flirt with student teachers?" He pushed the door open a crack and peeked out, then pulled it closed. "Tea's right. He's at the end of the hall. You could hear him? Seriously?"

"I told you," Abby said. "She's got, like, superpowers. So what do we do, Tea?"

One problem at a time. Teagan took a deep breath. Leo Gagliano had just killed a teacher. That was the most immediate problem.

"Get rid of the body before Officer Fiorella comes through that door." Teagan knelt beside Kyle and started rolling up his shirtsleeve. "Bring her over here, Finn."

"Whatever you're doing, do it faster," Donnie said. "Cop's coming."

"You wouldn't dare." Isabeau hissed. "You wouldn't *dare* send Mab's son home like this."

"Oh, she would." Finn dragged Isabeau across the floor toward Teagan. "It's a shame I don't have my kit. I could use a bit of duct tape right now."

"Duct tape?" Leo had stopped pacing.

"The most useful stuff in the world," Finn assured him.

"What are you two doing?" Abby asked.

"Improvising." Teagan unbuckled Kyle's Gucci belt and pulled it off.

"Stop kicking." Finn held Isabeau's arm against Kyle's while Teagan wrapped the belt around them both and pulled it so tight it cut into the flesh. "You wanted to go back to Mag Mell. You're going."

"Wait!" Abby said as Teagan and Finn backed away. "Isabeau, where's Molly?" The bilocate had been staying with Molly's family as a foreign exchange student, and Molly hadn't been in class.

"Dead," Isabeau said flatly.

"Goblins lie." Finn stood up. "We won't know where Molly's been until we find her."

"You'll find her body," Isabeau said. "Kyle killed her."

"Where?" Leo demanded.

Isabeau shrugged. "Go look."

"Fiorella's almost here," Teagan interrupted. "We're out of time."

"Back up," Finn told the Gaglianos. "Get as far away from her as you can."

Teagan followed Finn as he started away from Isabeau and Kyle. Officer Fiorella was just outside the door.

"Now!" Teagan said.

Isabeau screamed as Finn whirled and threw the knife; it pierced the hand she threw up to protect her throat. And then whatever gave the goblin girl's soul substance in this corner of the multiverse came apart. Violently. Teagan was in midstep when the shock wave hit. It threw her forward into Finn and almost knocked him off his feet. Isabeau's scream echoed inside Teagan. She knew exactly how it felt to be at the center of that disruption in space and time—it was how she had gotten back from Mag Mell, dragging Finn with her.

It hurt. A lot.

"Don't be feeling sorry for her," Finn said, setting Teagan upright. "There's no time for it."

She nodded, looking around to make sure everyone else was all right. The Gaglianos had been farther away, but apparently not far enough. Abby was helping Angel to his feet.

Kyle and Isabeau were gone. Leo's knife lay in the middle of a pool of Kyle's blood. The red spatter on the ceiling tiles would be from Isabeau.

The scream and the explosion must have frozen Officer Fiorella in place, or he'd have been through the door already.

"Ew," Abby said. "You've got . . . stuff on your back, Tea."

"Stay sharp." Finn pulled the hoodie off over her head. She could feel the tension building in his body again. He was expecting more trouble. "Don't tell the cops anything they don't already know. Mamieo will send someone for us." Teagan nodded again. Her mom had ended up in a mental hospital once because she told the truth about goblins.

Finn tossed the hoodie into the pool of blood just as Officer Fiorella burst through the door.

He didn't look anything like the friendly, joking officer who teased students at his D.A.R.E. presentations. His gun was out, and the hand that held it was shaking. Teagan had seen the eyes of frightened animals dart from opponent to opponent the same way his were now.

"Who screamed?"

"Calm down, Fiorella." Leo had his hands on top of his head, his fingers laced together. "It's all over. Everyone's fine."

"The rest of you, put your hands on your heads," Fiorella said. "Where I can see them."

Finn put his hands on top of his head but he moved closer to Teagan as well, not quite touching her, but close enough that the electricity arced between them. The tension in his body was almost painful, and now Teagan understood why.

14

Officer Fiorella was shaking, and he couldn't decide where to point his gun.

"Leo Gagliano?" Fiorella said, turning it toward Leo. "You graduated three years ago." Fiorella knew only the jocks or the bad kids. That he still recognized Leo couldn't be a good thing. "What are you doing here?"

"I'll tell you." Leo's voice was gentle. *He's done this before,* Teagan realized. His body language was submissive. Respectful. "Where do you want me to start, Officer?"

"How about you start with the dead kid down the hall?"

Teagan's heart sank. Cade and Jing had stepped in and tried to help because they were Abby's friends. Her friends. Finn had told her this would happen if they let civilians get involved.

"He's dead?" Leo asked.

"His guts are on the floor."

"Jing is with him," Abby said. "He won't let Cade die."

"The mighty Jinghez Khan was crying like a baby." Officer Fiorella looked like he wanted to cry, too. "Cade's a mess. If he's not dead, he will be."

"An animal can survive evisceration," Teagan said.

Officer Fiorella turned to her, and suddenly she was looking right down the barrel of his gun. She felt Finn move beside her, ready to get between them.

"Who are you?" Fiorella demanded.

Her mouth was suddenly very dry. "Teagan Wylltson."

His eyes flicked to the knife in the pool of blood. "You cut open animals, do you, Ms. Wylltson?"

"She works with the vet at the zoo," Abby said. "You know you've got an attitude? It's like we're the bad guys or something."

Fiorella studied Teagan for a moment longer. "I remember you. I let you into the science fair once. What are you doing mixed up with this?"

"She was in the wrong place at the wrong time," Leo said before Teagan could answer. "There was another girl here, too. She ran."

Officer Fiorella turned back toward Leo. "You're telling me what's going on?"

"Jack the Ripper was teaching the freaking psychology class," Abby said, pulling out her cell phone.

"Hey!" Fiorella swung toward her. "Put it away, and get your hands back up."

"I get a phone call," Abby protested, raising her hands. "Right?"

Donatello sighed. "He hasn't arrested anybody yet, Abby."

"She a friend of yours, Leonardo?" Fiorella asked.

"Our little cousin," Leo said.

"A Gagliano who's never been arrested?" He studied Abby. "What are you, the white sheep of the family?"

"She's a good kid," Leo said, his hands still on top of his head. "Let me tell you what's going to happen, Abigail. When the rest of Chicago's Finest come through that door, they're going to take us down to the station to have some pictures made. Then Krueger's gonna show up in his fancy lawyer suit with all kind of reasons why they can't keep us, and we'll go home."

"That's true," Officer Fiorella said. "So why don't you give me a break and tell me what happened here before anyone shows up?"

"She told you," Leo said. "Jack the Ripper was teaching psych class. You need to look into background checks, Fiorella. The guy didn't even have a home address and you let him walk in here and teach?"

"How do you know he didn't . . . ? Never mind." Officer Fiorella shook his head. "So, you didn't like his lesson plan?"

"Did you see the sick stuff he wrote on the board?" Abby asked.

Leo frowned at her. *"Shut it, Abby."*

"So, *you're* going to keep talking to me instead, right, Leo?" Fiorella asked.

"Right. The guy they let teach—Bullen wasn't his real name. He wasn't even a teacher. He killed the cafeteria lady and pinned it on our brother."

Officer Fiorella's eyes narrowed. "You have proof?"

"None you'd like. So he frames my kid brother, like I said. We show up to talk to him about it. I meet my cousin Abby, and she tells us the teacher just slashed Cade open with his claws—"

"Claws?"

Leo shrugged. "There's a classroom full of kids that saw it, Fiorella. Ask them. I wasn't there. Like I said, Abby tells us what was happening and we corner him down here. He's got a hostage—a girl—but she gets away. Then he and this evil chick named Isabeau explode."

"Explode."

"I swear." From the expression on his face you'd think he'd just walked out of church. "They explode."

Angel and Donnie were completely focused on their older brother. *Getting their story straight.* The police were not going to get one word out of them that hadn't already come from Leo's mouth.

They all heard the doors slam at the end of the hall, and the sound of running feet. Six of Chicago's Finest came through the cafeteria door with their guns out. Fiorella put his gun away.

Teagan could feel Finn relax. It really was over now; no one else was going to die.

Finn glanced at the clock on the cafeteria wall. "Less than thirty minutes from incident to arrival. Impressive."

"No talking," one of the officers said. "Keep them separate until we've taken statements."

"These two," Officer Fiorella was saying, pointing at Leo and Finn, "aren't students here."

An officer took Teagan's elbow and led her toward the door; his partner did the same with Abby.

The officer steered her to the side of the hall so they wouldn't disturb the bloody footprints on the floor.

Cade's blood.

They walked past locked doors with black paper taped over the small windows. Full lockdown. The students and teachers huddled against the walls inside the classrooms knew by now it wasn't a drill even if no shots had been fired. They were probably texting furiously, trying to figure out what was going on.

The door to the AP Psychology class where Kyle had been pretending to teach while he waited for Teagan was wide open. She stopped. Paramedics were working on Cade. They wouldn't be working if he were dead, would they? Jing was standing behind them, his arms wrapped around himself, rocking on his feet. Officer Fiorella was right. He was crying.

"Oh, my god," Abby said.

That's what happens when you get civilians involved. Teagan could almost hear Finn's voice. She hadn't called the Gagliano brothers or asked Jing or Cade for their help. Abby had. But it was her fault Abby was involved.

The officer pulled gently on Teagan's arm. She followed him toward the front doors of the school, praying that the paramedics knew what they were doing. Because if they didn't, a boy who'd just tried to help because he was a friend would go into shock and die before he reached the hospital.

A crowd of people had gathered on the other side of the police line in front of the school—parents responding to texts. A column of smoke reached into the sky.

"What's burning?" Teagan asked the officer.

"The library park," he replied. "You from that neighborhood?"

"Yes," she said. The park was where she had left Finn's guardian angel, Raynor Schein; her own father; Gil, a wounded phooka; and Joe, the North American Green Man, all facing a seething wall of shadow men at the doorway to Mag Mell. Demons, Father Gordon would call them. The Dark Man's offspring.

The officer put his hand on top of her head so she wouldn't

19

bump it getting into the back seat of the patrol car he'd led her to. Then he shut the door, but he didn't get in the front. She was alone, watching the smoke rise.

Abby was taken to another car, and Finn, his hands cuffed behind him, put into a third. The paramedics loaded Cade into an ambulance as the press arrived. The Gagliano boys still hadn't appeared when the authorities started evacuating the school, teachers leading lines of students out of the building and down the street.

Teagan tried the door handle. Locked, of course. It was maddening to be sitting in a police car, unable to find out what was happening to her friends and family.

Her little brother, Aiden, wouldn't have needed to hear what was going on; he wouldn't have had to try to figure it out. To Aiden, the world had a sound track; he heard not only the *cantus firmus*—the Song of Creation—but also the songs of everyone around him.

She wasn't like Aiden, though. *Give me the courage to live what I am.* Not a Highborn, no matter what Fear Doirich and Mab might call her. Not a goblin, no matter what anyone might think.

She was a tyger. Her father had seen it when she'd found him in Mag Mell, even before Kyle's retrovirus had burned all of her DNA from his side away. Dehydrated and half out of his mind, he'd looked into her and quoted Blake's poem. *Tyger! Tyger! burning bright . . .*

Fierceness coiled tight inside her, a *need* to put an end to what Fear Doirich and Mab were doing. To protect her family.

She leaned her head against the seat in front of her. The only problem was, she was still Teagan, tyger or not. Wanting to stop them wouldn't get it done any more than wanting to throw the knife had made it fly straight and true.

Isabeau had been right. She had absolutely no idea what to do next.

She huddled in the car for at least half an hour, while more officers poured into the school and more reporters arrived. They were kept out of the school, but busied themselves interviewing students in the parking lot. Finally, the Gagliano boys were led out, put in cars, and driven away, cameras flashing the entire time. The officer and his partner finally got into the car with Teagan.

"Buckle up," he instructed, and watched until she did.

Leo was not quite right. She wasn't photographed or fingerprinted when they reached the station. She was simply led down a long, quiet hall with stained dingy carpeting to a room that had nothing in it but a table and three chairs. She looked around the room for a two-way mirror—she was sure she had seen that on TV—but there wasn't a mirror of any kind. Only a window, which looked out on an alley full of weeds.

It was a shabby, cold room. Teagan ignored the chill and went to the window, pressing her face against the glass and trying to see the smoke in the distance. Raynor and Joe had stopped the demons. If they hadn't, it wouldn't be smoke pouring out of the park. It would be something much worse. Chicago was simply not ready to meet the creatures of Mag Mell.

She was going to have to get Gil back there as quickly as possible. Even if phookas didn't have disgusting habits, her house was already too full of refugees from Mag Mell. There was Lucy, the sprite that had built her nest in Aiden's hair; their aunt Roisin; and Grendal, Roisin's *cat-sídhe* friend . . .

A big black bird landed on the ledge outside the window and peered in.

. . . and Thomas, the *lhiannon-sídhe* shape shifter who changed into a raven.

The bird tipped its head, peering up at Teagan with a beady eye.

"Is Dad all right?" Teagan asked.

The raven's beak gaped, but she couldn't hear the caw through the glass. Teagan looked around the room for a piece of paper, anything she could write on to communicate, but there was nothing.

She started to sign in ASL, then shook her head. Thomas wasn't Aiden. He wouldn't understand ASL.

"Dad," she said loudly, pressing her hand against the glass. "Is Dad all right? What happened at the park?"

"Are you . . . talking to that bird?"

Teagan whirled around. A man and a woman were standing in the open doorway watching her.

TWO

I 'M Detective Deneux." The woman's voice was almost monotone. "This is Detective Gilkyson."

Deneux bore an uncanny resemblance to an aging bloodhound. Her lower eyelids drooped, her cheeks sagged, and the corners of her mouth fought against the weight of wattles beneath her chin.

Detective Gilkyson was at least forty but trying to look younger, like the narcotics officers who sometimes came to school dressed like students. His blond hair stood straight up, and his blue eyes were open so wide it looked as if he were in a constant state of shock. He was carrying two Styrofoam cups.

"Were you talking to that bird?" Detective Deneux asked again.

The raven gave Teagan one last look, lifted its wings, and flew away.

"I'm worried about my dad," Teagan said honestly. "He works at the library, and I heard there was a fire."

"So you were talking to yourself?" Detective Gilkyson suggested. "Lots of people talk to themselves. It's okay. That's perfectly normal." He held out a cup of liquid the color of the carpet stains. "Coffee? It's black. Budget cuts."

"Thank you." Teagan took the cup and wrapped her hands around it, hoping some of the warmth would seep into her.

"Have a seat, Miss Wylltson," Detective Deneux commanded. "We'd like to ask you a few questions. We'll start with why you were at school in your pajamas. Isn't there a dress code?"

Teagan sat down without answering. Detective Deneux pulled up a chair across from her, and Detective Gilkyson set the other coffee in front of Deneux and started pacing.

"Tell me what happened," the female detective said.

"I'm not sure I should talk without—"

"A lawyer?" Detective Deneux shook her wattles. "You don't need a lawyer unless you've done something wrong. You haven't, have you?"

"No." Teagan turned her cup, wishing she'd watched more crime dramas. "I'm a minor. Are you supposed to be talking to me without a parent present?"

This time it was Deneux who didn't answer. She just opened a folder. "All of your friends talked to us. They said that Isabeau and Mr. Bullen exploded."

"Yes." Teagan was sure they had. Leo had told Fiorella that much. Gilkyson stopped pacing and turned his wide eyes on her.

"Where's the chunks?" he asked.

"Chunks?"

"You surf YouTube, don't you?"

"Not much."

"So, you never watched the video of the whale exploding? In Florence, Oregon."

"No," Teagan admitted.

"They had a dead whale on the beach. It was stinking up the neighborhood, so the highway department decided to get rid of it by blowing it up. They loaded it up with dynamite, and kaboom! Chunks of rotten whale raining down every-where. Destroyed a new car over half a mile away."

"Seriously?" Deneux fixed Gilkyson with a droopy stare. "People would be so dumb as to think that when you blow something up it just disappears?"

"The video's on YouTube," Gilkyson assured her.

"So, Miss Wylltson." Deneux turned back to her. "We know you're not stupid. *What happened to Mr. Bullen and Isabeau?*"

A uniformed officer poked his head through the door. "Excuse me, Detective?"

"I said I didn't want to be disturbed," Detective Deneux barked.

Teagan looked at Detective Gilkyson. "I want to make a phone call." If she could call home, at least she could find out if her dad was okay.

Gilkyson's cheeks pinked and his eyes slid away from hers. He shook his head.

"Shut the door!" Detective Deneux snapped.

"Sorry, Detective," the officer said, as the door opened fur-ther.

"Did I hear Miss Wylltson asking to make a phone call?" A man stepped through the door, and the police officer shrank away from him. Teagan could see why. Abby had implied for years that her family had Mob connections. If Leo shoving a blade into Kyle's back hadn't convinced her it was true, this man would have. He wasn't otherworldly evil like Kyle or Isabeau. He exuded pure *human* evil.

Detective Gilkyson gawped. "This kid can afford Krueger and Kline?"

Teagan was sure her family couldn't afford the suit Mr. Krueger or Mr. Kline, whoever she was looking at, was wearing. Surely this wasn't the person Mamieo would send.

"Of course she can't," Detective Deneux said. "He's the Gaglianos' lapdog. He makes inconvenient things disappear. Don't you, Krueger? You have as much blood on your hands as any of them."

The lawyer lifted a hand and examined his nails, as if checking for traces of dried blood.

"I'm too well acquainted with the law to break it," he said when he'd finished admiring his manicure.

"To get caught, you mean," Deneux corrected.

"When you catch me, Detective, we'll discuss it. Until then, you can hold the door for us on our way out. That is if you accept my representation, Miss Wylltson?"

"She doesn't."

They all turned this time.

"Good lord," Detective Deneux said.

"Cripes," Detective Gilkyson said. "Will somebody shut the door? And lock it?"

"Don't bother," the newcomer said. "Ms. Wylltson is going right back out through it. The name's McGillahee, Seamus McGillahee. I'm her lawyer."

Teagan blinked. Seamus McGillahee's boyish face made Detective Gilkyson look positively ancient. And she'd never seen a plaid jacket before, not outside of a commercial for a used car lot.

"Mamieo called you?" Teagan asked.

"Technically," Seamus McGillahee said, "she called my partner, Mr. Kelly. He has a work-related headache this afternoon—"

"A hangover," Detective Deneux clarified.

"I see you know Mr. Kelly. He was working all night and asked me to come down and sort things out." He held out a card, and Mr. Krueger took it.

"Doyle Kelly and Company?" Krueger's brow creased. "I assume you are the company?"

"No," Seamus McGillahee said. "I've only recently joined Mr. Kelly's practice. My understanding is that he considers the Almighty to be senior partner in the firm."

"The Almighty? As in God?" Detective Gilkyson asked.

Teagan frowned. Mr. Kelly did sound like someone Mamieo would know. Hangover and all.

"I'm not responsible for the eccentricities of my employer." Seamus shrugged. "If there is an Almighty, he's a silent partner. I'm the one taking care of Mr. Kelly's clients."

"You're a joke." Mr. Krueger flipped the card toward the trash can, but Seamus snatched it out of the air and tucked it back into his breast pocket.

"How old are you?" Mr. Krueger demanded.

"Old enough to pass the bar."

"He's legit," the uniformed officer said. "We checked before we let the Mac Cumhaill kid out."

"Finn's out?" Teagan asked.

"Your cousin is waiting in the lobby with Mamieo and your father," Seamus said. Teagan stood up, but Mr. Krueger moved smoothly between her and the door.

"Not so fast. My clients and very good friends requested I take this case." He looked Seamus up and down. "I assume you sell cars when you're not practicing law?"

"I have a minivan I could part with if you're in the market."

"An Irish Traveler," Mr. Krueger said in disgust. "Is thieving, embezzling, and cheating up your alley as well as selling cars?"

"I'll admit to being half Irish," Seamus said. "But there's no law against that in the city of Chicago, and no rule against it in the Bar Association. As to the rest . . . I've never, ever been caught doing anything of the kind."

Detective Deneux's laugh was an unhappy marriage of bloodhound's bay and terminal cough.

"He's apparently acquainted with the law as well, Krueger," she said when she'd recovered. "You are two of a kind."

Seamus turned to Teagan and smiled. "Are you ready to go, Tea? You don't mind if I call you Tea, do you?"

"I can leave?" Teagan looked at Detective Deneux, who didn't answer.

"You're not under arrest," Seamus said. "You could have

28

walked out of here at any time. The cops didn't tell you that, did they?"

No. And Krueger hadn't told her that, either. Teagan looked at Detective Deneux, and the woman shrugged apologetically. Mr. Krueger was examining his nails again. Maybe Abby was right. She should watch more TV. She had no idea what was going on here.

"No, she can't," Detective Gilkyson said. "She was asking what happened at the park. That changes everything. We've got Homeland Security issues."

"Homeland Security?" Teagan gripped the edge of the table. *What happened at the park?*"

"Just a little fire," Seamus assured her. "No buildings involved. No injuries."

"And how do you know that, Mr. McGillahee?" Detective Gilkyson asked.

"I drove past it on my way over," Seamus said. "Aren't you overreacting, Detective? She's a high school student. Unless you have grounds for arrest, she's walking out of here."

"Miss Wylltson." Detective Gilkyson was practically gritting his teeth. "Do you know this man?"

"I've never met him before."

"Then I *respectfully* request that you wait here while I make a call or two to verify who Wonder Boy here is. I honestly am concerned for your safety."

"Fine. Why not give him a few minutes?" Seamus said agreeably. "We don't want him to worry about you."

"Why don't you walk out the door with me right now,

Miss Wylltson?" Mr. Krueger offered. "You know my clients very well, I understand. They will vouch for me."

Teagan shook her head. "Please thank the Gaglianos for me, Mr. Krueger. I appreciate the offer, but my family sent Mr. McGillahee. I can wait a few minutes, Detective Gilkyson."

Krueger nodded and left, the uniformed officer going out after him.

"*'Thank the Gaglianos for me'?*" Seamus repeated, as the door closed behind them. "You might as well appreciate being circled by sharks. The Gaglianos are not people you want to get involved with."

"My best friend is a Gagliano," Teagan said.

"Do tell," Detective Deneux said. "Isn't that interesting."

Seamus McGillahee sighed. "You don't need to tease them with such information, Ms. Wylltson. They are already interested enough. Gilkyson seems like a very thorough fellow."

"He is," Detective Deneux agreed.

"Which means we're going to be here for a little while." Seamus took off his checkered coat and settled it over Teagan's shoulders.

"Thank you. I was freezing."

He nodded, then turned to study Detective Deneux, so focused he seemed to be reading her wrinkles like tea leaves. She stared back out of hound-dog eyes.

"You're one of the good guys, Deneux," Seamus said. "But you *see* things, don't you? Things you don't dare tell anyone about. Cats that walk upright—caught from the corner of your eye, and when you turn they're gone."

Detective Deneux took a drink of her coffee, and Teagan noticed that the cup shook just the tiniest bit.

"You've never told anyone that, have you? Sometimes you hear them at night, walking on your roof, and you pretend that it's pigeons making the sound, even though you know—*you know*—pigeons don't stir in the darkness. You lock your windows tight to keep them out. And how about those shadows that slide along the walls at murder scenes where nothing else is moving? You've stumbled headfirst into a fairy story."

"And the singing mice are about to appear and turn me into a princess. They're a little late."

Seamus grimaced. "You need to update your video collection, Detective. It's singing frogs now, fireflies with bad teeth, and hard-working restauranteurs. And there are no singing frogs in this fairy story."

Teagan bit her tongue. There had been singing frogs in Mag Mell. They'd come out of their ponds when her little brother, Aiden, sang. And it *had* been like a Disney movie . . . until a water goblin had pulled Aiden into a pool, held him under, and tried to drown him.

"Then what kind of fairy story are you talking about, my Legal Leprechaun?" Deneux asked.

"The kind with blood and curses," McGillahee said, and his voice gave Teagan the shivers even with the jacket over her shoulders. "Mostly Irish blood and goblin curses."

"Let's start with the blood," Detective Deneux said. "Was that Irish blood at the school today?"

"No." McGillahee leaned forward. "But if you want a tip,

everything that happened, almost from the beginning—it was the Druids' fault."

"What?" Teagan asked.

Seamus raised his hand. "I know what you're thinking. *Everyone blames the Druids.* But let me make my case."

"Are there Druids at your school, Ms. Wylltson?" Detective Deneux asked.

"Not . . . that I know of." But she hadn't known there were *cat-sídhe* or Highborn in Chicago, either. She hadn't known that *sluagh,* faceless creatures that feed on the souls of the dying, lived in the sewers beneath her house. Her teachers could be Druids, for all she knew.

Seamus gave them both an incredulous look. "Of course there aren't any Druids at the school. The people of the tree are long gone from *this* world."

Detective Deneux took an aspirin bottle from her pocket, shook two pills into her hand, popped them in her mouth, and chewed. She'd finished her own coffee, and didn't hesitate to take the cup Teagan offered her to wash it down.

"What Druids are you talking about, Mr. McGillahee?" Detective Deneux asked after she'd swallowed the pills.

"I was getting to that. In the time before time, a people called the Fir Bolg lived in Mag Mell, the world-between-worlds with doorways into every corner of creation. Their children walk this earth today. Some of them can see things others can't see."

"Like cats that walk upright and shadows with nothing to cast them."

"Exactly. Like talking cats and animated shadows. It was the Fir Bolg's job to step through those doors, quiet as servants, never seen and never heard, to mend and tend creation. On this earth their favorite doorway led into Ireland, and the Fir Bolg had been given special charge to keep it until the people it was created for, the Milesians, arrived."

"These Milesians see cats?"

"No," Seamus said. "They were just people. Very smart, musical, magical people. But before they arrived in Ireland, Fear Doirich, the Dark Man, and Mab, Queen of the Highborn, came riding on storm clouds with all the Sídhe."

"And who are the Sídhe?"

"The cats and shadows," McGillahee said. "And others that are much nastier. You might be familiar with the *beansídhe*. Ugly hags that howl outside the window when someone's going to die? Perhaps when your Irish grandmother passed? They probably told you it was a dream."

"My *French* grandmothers are alive and well in Des Plaines." Detective Deneux took another drink of her coffee. "Both of them."

"Well, the Sídhe are goblin creatures—phookas, sprites, night hags—creatures Fear Doirich cobbled together from many worlds, powerful and evil. Now, I'm skipping a great deal, because I know you want to get to the Druids, and I don't know when that Homeland Security wannabe is going to come back through the door."

"Gilkyson is a bit of a twit," Detective Deneux conceded. "But it's nothing life won't cure. In twenty more years."

"When the Milesians finally arrived, the Fir Bolg came out of Mag Mell to help them fight the goblins. Amergin, a Milesian bard with a magical voice, drove the Sídhe out of Ireland. They fled into Mag Mell, locking the doorways behind them."

"And what happened to this bard?" the detective asked. "Is he playing Vegas?"

"Mab sent her sister Maeve to seduce him"—Seamus made a magical motion with his hand—"and, *poof!* The goblins spirited him away. He's only important to our story because he chased the goblins into Mag Mell, anyway."

Teagan winced. The goblins had spirited him away, but not before Maeve fell in love with the bard and betrayed Mab and Fear Doirich. The Dark Man had then tortured the lovers to death, but there was no way Seamus could have known that.

"The Fir Bolg wandered through Ireland and all of the isles and they became the Irish Travelers, scraping by as tinkers, marrying the local girls, and giving their daughters in marriage. They were assimilating, and would have disappeared as a people, leaving nothing but a legacy of second sight ... until a poor tinker named Cumhaill fell in love and ran away with a rich man's daughter.

"The rich man called on Fear Doirich to curse the lovers. They died horribly, of course. And that's where the Druid comes in."

"The rich man was a Druid?" Deneux asked.

"No, he was a war chief. But before she died, Cumhaill's

wife had a baby. He was raised in the woods by a woman warrior and a female Druid, who named him Fionn Mac Cumhaill,
and taught him to fight the goblins that killed his parents."

"*That's* the Druid you're blaming for what happened at the
school today?"

"There is a direct line of cause and effect, reaching through
the centuries," Seamus said. "If not for the training and the
magical spear the Druid gave him, Fionn would not have been
able to kill Aillen the Burner."

"In the cafeteria?" Detective Deneux asked hopefully.

"You are single-minded, aren't you?" Seamus said. "All
this happened long before the time of King Arthur. Aillen was
the demonic son of Mab and Fear Doirich. And he—"

Detective Gilkyson came back through the door, looking
like he'd swallowed a slug.

"We'll be leaving now." Seamus stood and offered Teagan
his arm as if she were a princess at a prom. "Good day, Detective Gilkyson, Detective Deneux."

THREE

WHY did you tell her ... all of that?" Teagan
asked as they walked down the hall.

"Because she'd forgotten. Fallen out of
the story and forgotten who she is."

"You honestly think she has Traveler blood?"

"I can identify a Traveler face through abrasions, contusions, hangovers, and missing teeth. Wrinkles and jowls aren't going to deceive me—there's no mistaking the look of shattered dreams and a broken heart. She looks a lot like Doyle Kelly, in fact."

Teagan stepped over a coffee stain. "You said you were half Irish."

"My father was a Traveler who went rooter for a good Scottish Protestant girl."

"He settled down?"

"For five whole years, before he left." At the change in his voice, Teagan glanced up. It was only a second, and then his smile was back. "I understand it was a personal record, and a valiant attempt. When I was little, my mother told me the *glimories* called him away."

"Glimories?"

"She made the word up. Glimories are glimpses of what once was, memories wrapped up in story and dream. Mother says they will lead us to the truth if we let them."

"Did they lead your father to the truth?"

"It wasn't glimories that called him." The hard edge was back in his voice. "It was another woman. Called him away from his family and left him to die blind drunk in a dark alley after she'd moved on. Mother never knew, but Doyle Kelly did. He's the man who made sure I stayed home and got an education. Now I go by my mother's Scottish name, and I'm proud of it."

"Deneux seemed proud of her name as well."

"So, someone left her like a cuckoo's chick in some French nest and no one ever told her. Travelers have done worse. You know I'm right about her. You saw her hand tremble when I mentioned the *cat-sídhe*, and her face doesn't lie. Speaking of faces, you're a little stunner, aren't you? Mamieo told me I'd be rescuing her granddaughter, but you don't look like a Mac Cumhaill at all. There's something—"

Teagan waited, but he just shook his head.

"You don't take after your father. I've met him."

"I look like my mom," Teagan explained. "She was a cuckoo's chick in a Traveler's nest."

Seamus snapped his fingers. "Adopted. I'd forgotten that."

"How would you even have known about it?"

"My father's family were distant relatives of the Mac Cumhaills, of course. Isn't every Traveler? I know most of the stories and do keep track of the clans. If your mother looked like you, I'll wager she gave Mamieo Ida no end of trouble."

"I don't know," Teagan said. "Mom never talked about her family or growing up."

"Not close to the Travelers, then. Well, you are lucky I'm here, Teagan Wylltson."

"Because you're part Traveler?"

"Because unlike Kelly, I'm sober. And unlike Kelly, I don't duck for cover when a Mac Cumhaill calls for help."

"What?" Teagan stopped walking. "I thought *the Mac Cumhaill* was a hero to the Travelers."

Seamus looked surprised. "You *haven't* been raised close to the Travelers. Most people feel that Fionn brought the curse down on the clans when he killed Fear Doirich's son. They consider it the original Mac Cumhaill's fault that we have been hounded through the ages. Travelers shun the family. Until—" Seamus glared at an officer who was a little too interested in the contrast between Teagan's pink pajamas and the garish coat.

"Until?" Teagan asked as the officer hurried down the hall.

"—Until they run into goblin trouble of their own. They know the Mac Cumhaill will stand between them and goblin-kind, even if it kills him. The people who come when Mamieo calls? Someone shed blood for them."

Teagan pulled the coat tighter around her. That actually explained a lot. Like the cabby who Mamieo had called once when they needed a ride from the Dunes State Park to Chicago. He hadn't spoken a word to them the whole way. It wasn't out of respect that he had come. He was paying a debt.

Teagan stopped before the door at the end of the hall. "Do you mean that when Finn was living alone on the streets, even if he'd found other Travelers, they wouldn't have taken him in?"

"Not if they valued their lives. Being born the Mac Cumhaill isn't an honor. It's a death sentence, not only for the unfortunate young man, but also for everyone around him. Goblins trouble us all, Ms. Wylltson. But your cousin will die at their hands. Violently and probably alone."

The Mac Cumhaill never dies peacefully, or old and gray. Finn had told her that himself. And it was true that almost every new creature they met tried to kill them.

"So why are you here?" Teagan asked. "What do you owe the Mac Cumhaills?"

"Nothing at all," Seamus said. "My senior partner is the one who was entangled. I'm doing him a favor."

"Your family has never called for help?"

"A McGillahee never needs help. We're incredibly lucky, usually wealthy, and can talk ourselves out of any trouble we get into."

"You *talk* your way out of goblin trouble."

"I've never had a chance to try it on a Highborn, of course. But it works with lowborn goblins. So much more reasonable than a bare-knuckle brawl. We're politicians, lawyers, negotiators, dreamers of dreams that come true . . ."

"Dreamers of dreams that come true?"

"Well, my mother was. She always expected me to be as well, but I disappointed her. My dreams were all about motorbikes, mayhem, and fast cars. She couldn't make me a dreamer of dreams, so she settled for making me a gentleman. Freedom awaits, miss." He opened the door for her and waved her through.

Finn and Mr. Wylltson were sitting together in the waiting area. Finn was leaning back against the wall, his long legs stretched before him.

Mamieo Ida looked up from where she was *twinkling* at the dried-out old desk sergeant. She'd used more than a pinch of her glamour dust, because the white-haired sergeant was twinkling back at her over his trifocals, clearly enchanted.

"There you are, m'dearie!" Mamieo said. Teagan couldn't miss the glare she threw at Seamus. She clearly wasn't amused that Mr. Kelly hadn't come himself.

Finn stood up as soon as he saw Teagan. She hadn't taken three steps before he had crossed the floor, swung her up in his arms, and buried his face in her hair. It was like being wrapped in warmth and electricity, which ran delightfully along her skin from head to foot.

"Did anyone ever tell you that you're unbearably beautiful when you get released from police custody, girl?" he asked.

"I can't say that they have. And I apparently wasn't in custody. Just too ignorant to leave on my own."

"I'd appreciate it if you would put my daughter down, Mr. Mac Cumhaill," Mr. Wylltson said. "There are others here who would like to hug her."

Finn lowered her to her feet. Seamus had snatched the jacket that fell from her shoulders before it hit the ground.

"So the Gaglianos aren't your only awkward connections,"

he observed, shaking it out. "I hope you'll consider what I've just been saying."

"And what were you saying, then?" Finn asked.

"I was explaining some family dynamics."

Teagan turned to her dad. The last time she had seen him he'd been scruffy, and wearing *his* pajamas. Now, not only was he clean-shaven, he was neatly dressed, neither of which could conceal the fact that most of his right eyebrow was gone, and the hairs that were left had curled from heat. He smelled ... singed, when he wrapped his arms around her.

"Are you all right, Rosebud?" he asked. "I'm sorry it took us so long to get here. Ida had to find her lawyer—" Teagan couldn't miss the quizzical look he gave Seamus, who was putting his checked jacket back on. He looked even younger standing next to Mamieo Ida than he had in the interrogation room. "And then he had to pick us up, of course."

"I'm okay. Are *you* all right?" He grimaced as she touched the side of his face. "What happened?"

"Let's move the reunion to my office, shall we?" Seamus suggested, glancing at the desk sergeant, who was still smiling at Mamieo. "I'm sure Mr. Kelly would expect me to get you all out of here as quickly as possible."

Seamus McGillahee's "office" turned out to be the minivan he'd offered to sell to Mr. Krueger. If the pillow and bedding he had to move off the bench seat before they got in was any indication, it was his bedroom as well.

"Generally wealthy?" Teagan asked as Mamieo and Seamus took the front seats and Mr. Wylltson climbed in back.

Seamus nodded as he started the van. "I said generally. There are exceptions."

"What happened at the park?" Teagan asked her father as she slid to the center of the seat to make room for Finn—then slid back so he could put his arm around her. It was colder in the van than it had been in the interrogation room, and having a high-power line to snuggle against was very, very nice.

Mr. Wylltson shook his head. "Raynor might understand it, but I don't."

Seamus glanced at Mamieo. "Raynor? That's not a Traveler name."

"Raynor Schein," Mamieo said, still bristling. "He's a holy *aingeal*."

"Have you been mixing your medications, Mrs. Mac Cumhaill?" Seamus asked. "It happens with people your age."

"My age?" If Mamieo's eyes could throw daggers, Seamus would have been bleeding. "*My age?* The only medication I take is a wee explosive to get my heart started again when it threatens to stop."

"I'm not sure that nitro pills work that way," Seamus said mildly.

"Oh, you're not, are you? There are saints and *aingeal* currently walking among us, Seamus, as well as those of goblin-kind."

"*Cat-sídhe*, sure." Seamus pulled into traffic, neatly cutting off a Camry. "And the occasional Highborn. But I've never encountered either a saint or an angel," he shouted over the Toyota's blaring horn.

42

"You haven't, have you?" Mamieo said. "And what if I told you there's a saint sitting in your back seat as we speak?"

Finn groaned. "Will you stop it, Mamieo? I'm no saint and I've no intention of becoming one."

"Of course you are," Mamieo said primly.

Seamus turned to look at Finn. "No, I can see it, really. You're the very picture of manly sainthood snuggled up to Tea there."

"I've been wondering, Mr. McGillahee," Mr. Wylltson interjected. "How did you fool the police into believing you are a lawyer?"

Teagan smiled. Redirect. She'd seen her dad do the same thing at library story time when the children started teasing someone. He was on Finn's side no matter what he pretended.

"I wasn't fooling anyone, sir. I know the law like the back of my hand. I failed the bar three times to prove it."

"Failing proves you know the law?" Teagan asked.

"It does when I fail by exactly the point spread I say I will," Seamus said.

Even Mamieo had apparently forgotten about the saint in the back seat. "Why would you do that, Seamus McGillahee?" she asked in astonishment.

"I had school bills to pay, and my law school friends had money. They bet me I couldn't swallow my pride and fail the exam on purpose—but I had to prove it was on purpose by calling the number of questions I'd miss. If I was one off, so was the bet."

"Why three times, though?" Teagan asked.

"Because I had no takers for a fourth, and so I was forced to buckle down and practice the profession."

"Forced?" Mr. Wylltson asked.

"I loved the idea of being a lawyer. Of fighting for justice." For an instant there was power in Seamus's voice, as if his words might catch fire in the air and burn into anyone who heard them. "But our legal system's not about justice, is it? It has nothing to do with right or wrong. It's about knowing the rules, and how to get around them. That's why it treats men like Krueger so well. He's dirty, but the law he bends will never touch him. Something needs to, though. Someone."

Mameio studied his profile. "So it's justice you want, is it?" she asked softly. "That's an older law, boyo. No politician, pope, or king can stand before it. Certainly not lawyers."

"I know." Seamus cleared his throat, and whatever had come over him was gone. He was wholly his laughing self again. "Still, I think my law degree was a step in the right direction. Just a step. The problem is my brilliant mind. I'd be good at anything."

"Brilliance can be a burden, I suppose," Mr. Wylltson said wryly.

"Laugh if you want," Seamus said. "Disbelieve me if you wish. But it does make it hard to settle on a career. I wanted to keep my options open."

"For what?"

"I don't know. I've always had the feeling that something bigger was coming. Something important was just around the corner." He sighed. "I *will have* an excellent career as a lawyer, though. The McGillahees are famous for their clear thinking

44

and cool temperaments. We excel in peaceful negotiation, but we will fight if provoked."

Mamieo sniffed. "Your future clients might feel a wee bit more confident of that if you dressed in a proper jacket, instead of that ridiculous getup."

"Really?" Seamus didn't look the least bit hurt. "Only a fool judges a man by the jacket he wears."

"Is it a game to you, then?" Mamieo said. "Are you playing at being a Traveler?"

"Trailing my coat behind me like an Irishman at Donnybrook Fair," Seamus agreed.

"What does that mean?" Teagan asked.

"It means he's looking for a fight," Mamieo said. "The boys would trail their coats behind them at the fair, and when someone stepped on them, fists would fly. Who were you daring to step on your coattails, McGillahee?"

"Mr. Krueger wasn't the one I had in mind, but he'll underestimate me if we ever meet in a courtroom. I could see it in his eyes."

"You're playing to stereotype and prejudice," Teagan said. "Using something that is wrong, rather than trying to correct it. Wouldn't it be better to change their opinion of you?"

"Please," Seamus said. "I am half Traveler. My reputation's not going to get better as long as the goblins are around, no matter what I do. When the Highborn step out of Mag Mell, it doesn't always mean death. They're often happy enough with the destruction of our hopes and dreams."

"That's who the jacket is for?" Mamieo frowned. "You're

hunting Highborn. Well, you don't need to wear a billboard to announce yourself, boyo. They'll find you."

"At the police station?" Teagan asked.

Seamus glanced at her in the rearview mirror. "You've seen them. One could be sitting right beside you on the bus, standing before the judge as your opponent in a court of law. Sitting on the bench. And there's no way you could tell it was a goblin. Kelly picked up the bottle as soon as he'd hung up the phone after Mamieo's call."

Teagan could see the muscles tighten in his jaw. Shattered dreams and a broken heart. The goblins hadn't touched Seamus McGillahee. But they had touched someone he respected and loved.

"I'm sorry to hear that about Kelly." Mamieo sighed.

"The Highborn have given him trouble," Seamus said. "I plan to give the damn goblins double in return."

"Goblins follow Fear Doirich," Teagan pointed out. "But not every Highborn does."

Seamus shook his head. "I suppose you're referring to the story of Maeve, who left Fear Doirich because she fell in love with Amergin the bard."

"Maeve's one example." Finn squeezed Teagan's hand.

"You know what I think? I think," Seamus said, "she tricked the man into going to Mag Mell, where Doirich no doubt killed him. All of the stories end that way, with trickery, betrayal, and deceit."

"What about Drogo, the bilocating saint?" Mr. Wylltson asked. "I understand that he was a Highborn who left Fear Doirich as well."

46

"I've heard that," Seamus admitted. "And I think … it's possible that the Highborn threw him out."

"Why?" Teagan said.

"Because something happened to Drogo. A 'sickness' that made him so hideous that men built a room without a window or a door to keep him in. Why would they do that? The records say it was so the sight of him wouldn't frighten the villagers."

Teagan's stomach tightened thinking of Kyle's wolflike muzzle, his canine tongue, and the incomplete shifters she'd seen feeding on phooka flesh in Mag Mell.

"Drogo lived alone in the darkness for forty years," Seamus said, "eating nothing but barley water and the Holy Eucharist they slid to him through a little slot. If he was a Highborn, there was something wrong with him. The goblins must have thrown him out. The Church in her charity took the creature in and locked him up where he could do no harm."

"I don't believe it," Teagan said. "Whatever happened to him, Drogo was *good*. We remember him as a gardener, and for how he cared for the poor. Not as a creature locked in the dark."

"Well," Seamus said, "if he *was* good, he was no Highborn."

"Seamus." Mamieo had been studying him as he talked. "There's something you need to know before you go on. The girl I took in—the daughter I adopted by the laws of our own people—"

"I'm sorry for your loss, Mamieo," Seamus said. "And yours, Mr. Wylltson, Teagan. I should have mentioned that before."

"Aileen, our Teagan's *máthair*," Mamieo plowed on. "I didn't find her wandering the streets. I stepped into Mag Mell on Samhain's Eve, and snatched her from the jaws of the Wild Hunt. I stole her out of place and time. Aileen was the orphan child of Amergin and Maeve."

Teagan saw Seamus's eyes flick to her in the mirror as the connections clicked into place, and then she was thrown hard against the seat belt as he slammed on the brakes. Horns blared as the minivan swerved through traffic to the curb.

"Get out," he said, when the van had jerked to a stop. "I won't drive your kind—"

Mamieo snatched the keys from the ignition.

"Give them back," he said through clenched teeth. "I came to help a Mac Cumhaill. Not to provide taxi service for *goblin girls*."

"She's as dear to me as my own blood." There was grit in Mamieo's voice. "Now, Mr. McGillahee, you're going to apologize."

"Certainly," Seamus nodded. "I'm sorry that you've lost your mind, Mrs. Mac Cumhaill, and"—his eyes meet Teagan's in the mirror—"that I gave aid to a filthy goblin. Give me back my keys and get her out of my van."

Finn slammed his door open so hard Teagan thought it might have damaged the hinges. "Step out with me for a moment, Seamus."

"Why would I do that?"

"You mentioned that the McGillahees would fight if provoked. I intend to provoke the bloody hell out of you right here and now."

48

"Don't." Teagan caught Finn's shirttail as he started to get out. "He doesn't understand."

"Oh, I understand," Seamus said. All of the warmth and friendliness had gone out of him. His stare was like ice. "I can take one look at you and *understand*. Warriors have gone off with goblin girls before, and I've never understood it. Now I've seen it with my own eyes. I've felt it. But I wouldn't have believed it of the Mac Cumhaill. You have to be better than this, Finn."

"Finn." Teagan touched his hand. "What if you had found out about my mother just minutes after you'd met me?"

"That's not the point. The point is I won't tolerate anyone calling you filth. Get out of the van, McGillahee."

"As you wish." Seamus opened his door.

"Gentlemen." Mr. Wylltson's voice wasn't loud, but the timbre made the air vibrate around them. Both Finn and Seamus turned to look at him. "Mr. McGillahee, we will get out of your van and walk."

"I'm fine with walking," Finn began, "but I'll teach this ignorant Scotsman a thing or two first."

"I appreciate the sentiment," Mr. Wylltson said. "I don't like to hear my daughter or my wife called filth, but ignorance is never cured by violence."

"I'm not ignorant," Seamus said through gritted teeth.

"Aren't you, then?" Mamieo leaned toward him. "Tell me, what does *glaine ár gcroí* mean, boyo?"

"Purity of our hearts," Seamus said.

"Not completely ignorant, then," the old woman said. *"Neart ár ngéag."*

"Strength of our limbs."

49

Mamieo nodded. *"Beart de réir ár mbriathar."*

"Action to match our speech."

"The motto of the Fighting Fianna," Mameio said. "You are Fir Bolg, Seamus. You have that from your father, if nothing else. Remember who you are. Something is happening that hasn't happened in a thousand lifetimes of men. Fir Bolg—your own kind—have walked in Mag Mell and come back to tell about it. Locked doors are opening, and creatures great and small are tumbling into this creation. Aren't you even a little curious?"

"Not curious enough to cuddle up with a Highborn."

Mamieo snorted. "It's a fool that judges a man's mind by the jacket he wears. Or so I've heard. Is the flesh Teagan wears —or your own, for that matter—any more than a jacket? The Almighty has been whispering it to me in the night, singing it over me as I sleep. A great mending is to come, and things are trending in the right direction. You want to cause the goblins trouble? Be a part of the mending, man. I've been pounding at the doors of the Almighty to find out how it can be done, and I have the answer." She smiled. "All we have to do is get back into Mag Mell and let the angel in. If that's done, the mending can begin."

"Oh, is that all?" Seamus took a deep breath. "Can you prove any of this?"

"Come and see." Mamieo dangled the keys in front of him.

FOUR

SHUT the door, Finn," Mamieo said as Seamus took the keys.

"Mamieo, I don't think we should go anywhere with this Scottish idiot."

"Set him an example, boyo. Get back in the car."

"Mamieo—"

"Give him time. The Almighty set about mending my heart by sending me a child out of the night. But it's taken me thirty years to get the point."

"Which point?" Finn was still holding the door open.

"That the Almighty heard a Highborn child cry in the night, and sent me looking. That was providence for the both of us. Now *I* called for help, and Seamus here is the one who answered."

"You are saying the Almighty sent you into Mag Mell because a goblin child prayed?" Seamus asked.

"Did I say she prayed? Aileen had no more idea of the Almighty that night than you do, you heathen Scot. I said she cried out for help. The difference between us was she knew she didn't know everything, and I thought I did."

"Sounds familiar," Finn said. "Are you sure you're not part Scots, Mamieo?"

"Get in the van," Mamieo snapped. "That should sound familiar too, boyo. I've said it three times."

"That police car has been past us twice," Mr. Wylltson said. "I never thought I'd be worried about the police."

Finn climbed back in, and Seamus started the van.

"I'm not asking you to believe me," Mamieo told Seamus. "I'm suggesting that if you shut your mouth and listen, you might learn a thing or two you don't know. Or you can let us out on the street and spend the rest of your life wondering."

"I'm listening."

"Good. John Paul was about to tell us what happened at the park when you started going on about your law career. The man might get the tale told if you don't interrupt."

"Fine." Seamus pulled into traffic again.

"Well," Mr. Wylltson began, "I could *feel* the shadow men's presence before I started singing."

Seamus looked at Mamieo, his eyebrows up.

"And that's not interrupting?" Mamieo said. "Put your eyebrows down, boyo, before they get stuck that way. John Paul has no second sight, but he is a direct descendent of the Welsh bard Myrddyn Wyllt, the real Merlin. Our wee Aiden, Teagan's six-year-old *bráthair*, has Myrddyn on his father's side and Amergin, the Milesian bard whose songs drove Fear Doirich and the Sídhe into Mag Mell, on his *máthair*'s, and second sight as well. That's important for you to know if you're to understand what's happening. After Aileen was killed, John Paul was taken to Mag Mell and tortured by the Dark Man."

"Fear Doirich?"

"Himself," Mamieo said.

"Cops following us." Finn was looking over his shoulder.

Seamus nodded but didn't say anything. Teagan leaned forward so that she could watch the cruiser in the side-view mirror. She knew exactly what her father meant. The police had always seemed friendly before. Helpful, even. Now they were a little scary.

"John has no Traveler blood in him," Mamieo went on, "and he's not an *aingeal* or a Highborn, and as those are the only creatures that can walk completely present in any world of creation, John Paul's body was damaged by stepping into Mag Mell, his mind almost destroyed."

"Not my mind, Ida, just a few of my memories. And I'm getting better."

"How did he get out of Mag Mell?"

"His children have Highborn blood in them, from their *máthair*, don't they? My Aileen half grew up in Mag Mell. After she died her ashes were scattered in the library park. They woke the trees and opened a doorway that shouldn't have been —the doorway Finn, Teagan, and Aiden went through to find their da. Raynor has been guarding it to keep the shadows and goblinkind from stepping into Chicago."

The police cruiser turned down a side street, and Teagan snuggled under Finn's arm again. Raynor may have been keeping the shadows in, but he was also waiting for Fear Doirich to step out. The Dark Man's spells kept the holy angels out of Mag Mell.

"Teagan and Finn went back to Mag Mell," Mamieo said. "Tea was going to drag Fear Doirich out and give him to the angel. But it didn't work out that way. Which brings us to John Paul standing shoulder to shoulder with an *aingeal* as a wall of vileness tried to roll out of Mag Mell while the children went off to deal with the nasty creatures at the school."

"He won't have to stand guard there anymore," Mr. Wylltson said. "As I said, I could feel the shadows. And just after the kids left, something came walking through the park that I *could* see."

"Hellhounds?" Teagan guessed.

"Hellhounds!" Seamus actually turned his head this time. "There are *hellhounds* loose in Chicago?"

"Watch the road, boyo," Mamieo said. "The hellhounds have been dead for weeks. Finn killed one, and Raynor killed the other."

John Wylltson shook his head. "It wasn't any kind of animal. I saw two ragged, dirty children walking toward me. I remembered that Mamieo had taken Aileen from Mag Mell as a child, and I started toward them thinking they might need help. But when I got closer, I could see that they weren't flesh-and-blood children. They were statues, like you'd find over a child's grave. I was close enough to see that they were weeping ashes from empty eye sockets when Raynor grabbed me. He covered my face with his hand and shouted for Joe to run—and then there was fire all around us."

"What were they?" Finn asked. "Why would they burn down the park?"

"I don't know," John Wylltson said. "Raynor was too busy trying to put out the fire on Joe to explain, and Joe was too busy protecting the invisible phooka."

"Joe's the Green Man who planned and planted this continent," Teagan explained before Seamus could ask. "Raynor called him to town to talk to the old willow in the park. The willow's roots had grafted onto roots of trees in Mag Mell. That's how the door opened."

"He's all right?" Finn looked worried. "I owe him. Joe helped me get into Mag Mell after your daughter broke up with me."

"That kiss in the park did not look like you had broken up," Mr. Wylltson said disapprovingly.

"It didn't, did it?" Finn grinned, and Teagan felt a blush spread all the way to her toes. "The tragedy was temporary. You know I'm the man for her, John."

Teagan caught Seamus McGillahee's eyes in the mirror, studying her.

"I know you *say* you're the man for her," Mr. Wylltson said.

"Tell me what I have to do to prove it to you. I'll do it."

"Ah." Mr. Wylltson rubbed his chin. "Now, that's an interesting offer, Mr. Mac Cumhaill. I believe I'll take you up on it."

"For heaven's sake, John Paul," Mamieo said. "The boy went into Mag Mell and brought your girl out. Isn't that enough?"

"Actually, I brought *him* out," Teagan said, but everyone ignored her.

"No, Mamieo." John Wylltson sat up taller. "It's not enough. My daughter is too young to be serious about anyone, and much too young to get married."

"A phooka?" Seamus interrupted. "You mentioned a phooka?"

"I brought him out of Mag Mell as well," Teagan said. "But—Joe was on fire, Dad?"

"Raynor put him out. Then we all had to get out of the park before the fire department arrived. Joe carried the phooka, and Raynor helped me. After he'd brought us safely to the house, he went back for his stuff. That's one fast-moving angel."

"Isn't he?" Finn agreed. "I had a devil of a time getting past him when I jumped into Mag Mell."

"Wait," Teagan said. *"Is Gil at our house?"*

"Who's Gil?" Seamus asked.

"The phooka," Teagan and Finn said at the same time.

"Joe is watching over him in the backyard, so there's no need to worry. And speaking of our house," Mr. Wylltson said, "if you turn right at the next street, and then take the next left, we'll be there."

Seamus made the turn in a calm and almost legal way, but there were no parking spaces in front of the Wylltsons' house. A group of teens were standing on the sidewalk—three boys. No, two boys and a girl, Teagan realized, as the one who'd been squatting stood and wiped her mouth on the back of her hand.

They were too similar not to be from the same family, from their long, thin legs to their multitoned hair. Red and black. It had to be dyed.

Finn turned to see where she was looking.

"Who's that lot, then?" he asked.

"I've never seen them around here before," Teagan said.

"What in the name of Peter and Paul are they?" Mamieo asked.

The girl met Teagan's eyes and laughed, her mouth a little too wide . . . a little too *toothy*. The boys had bulky torsos and mohawks—not the kind with shaved sides and spikes, but short on the sides and combed to a crest. The laughing girl had a white streak in her mottled mane.

"I don't know," Finn said. "But I'm guessing they're not from around here."

"Should I stop?" Seamus asked.

Finn reached for the door latch, and Teagan tensed. If he went out that door, she was going after him. Because whatever they were, she was absolutely sure he shouldn't face them alone, even if he was humming like a high-power line again.

"No," Mr. Wylltson said. "They're leaving." He was right—the teens had turned and were loping away down the street. "And Raynor is just inside. We'll be parked in a moment."

But they weren't. They circled the block, and this time Seamus managed to make two wrong turns on one-way streets, which would have taken them past the library if the street hadn't been blocked off.

"Is that the HAZMAT truck?" Teagan asked, sitting forward in her seat.

"Detective Gilkyson did say Homeland Security was involved," Seamus reminded her.

Not only was it the HAZMAT truck; its crew was fully suited up, as if they were dealing with dangerous chemicals or radiation. One was even carrying a Geiger counter. "Aren't they overreacting?"

Mr. Wylltson shook his head. "It was a ... *different* fire. I don't even know how to describe it."

The teens were long gone when Seamus finally made it back to the Wylltsons' street and found a parking space a block away.

They'd walked halfway up the block when they found the corpse of a *cat-sídhe* on the sidewalk. Mamieo and Seamus just stepped over it, but Teagan couldn't bring herself to. It was starting to flatten, the ligaments loosening and tissues beginning to break down. The creature's babylike hands were clenched into fists, its almost human mouth frozen in a scream, and its tongue swollen and blackened. The open sores on its belly suggested that it had died of disease, not violence. But from the look of it, something with teeth had been tearing at the corpse's already damaged belly. Teagan glanced at Finn. This was where the teens had been standing. Where the girl who'd wiped her mouth had been kneeling.

Finn took her hand, and Teagan was sure he felt her grief for the *cat-sídhe* as clearly as she felt the electrical impulses in his body.

"Rosebud?" Mr. Wylltson asked. "Are you all right?"

Mamieo and Seamus turned around.

"There's a dead *cat-sídhe* on the sidewalk," Teagan explained. "You'll have to step over it, Dad."

"I wondered what that smell was." Terrestrial bacteria apparently didn't need second sight. The dead *cat-sídhe* gave off the cloying smell of putrefying flesh.

"It's Maggot Cat," Finn said as Mr. Wylltson stepped into the street to avoid the body. "The leader of the beasties that chased us all over town."

"You don't usually see the beasties dead," Mamieo said. "They crawl into nooks and crannies to die."

"Maybe he couldn't make it to a hole," Teagan said. "He was outside our house last night when the *sluagh* showed up looking for me." Apparently, the *sluagh* didn't care whether you were dying or simply bilocating. A soul stepping out of its flesh was irresistible to them. Teagan shuddered. "If it hadn't followed Maggot Cat away, it would have caught me."

"He didn't help you on purpose. It wouldn't have followed him if he hadn't been dying."

"He was still a person."

"A person?" Seamus said.

"He had a mind and a will," Teagan explained. "He was a person."

"An evil little person with an evil little mind who tried his best to do us harm." Finn eyed the storm drain on the other side of the street. "But if the *sluagh* took his soul, I am sorry. I wouldn't wish that even on a *cat-sídhe*. You go on. I'll tuck this away in the alley, and we'll give him a decent burial when we have a chance."

Seamus shook his head. "It's a *cat-sidhe*. Kick it down the storm drain and let the *sluagh* who took its soul deal with the stink."

"Na," Finn said. "Tea wouldn't like that."

Seamus gave Teagan another look, more worried than the one he'd thrown her in the van.

"Oh, lord," Mr. Wylltson said. "Here come Lennie and Sophia." Mrs. Santini and Lennie, her eighteen-year-old son, lived just across the street from the Wylltsons.

"I'll head them off," Mr. Wylltson said. "She's going to want to talk to you, Teagan. I'm sure she's heard that something happened at school. I'll be in as soon as I can."

They left Finn to take care of the *cat-sidhe*, and Teagan and Mamieo hurried Seamus up the street.

"Welcome to the widdershins world of the Wylltsons," Mamieo said when they reached the steps. "Things are a bit . . . different here."

FIVE

SEAMUS followed Mamieo through the door but Teagan hesitated, looking down the street in the direction the teens had run. Aside from Mrs. Santini's large lavender housecoat and fuzzy pink slippers, there was nothing unsettling to be seen. Nothing otherworldly, at least. That would all be waiting inside the house.

"Keep an open mind," Mamieo was saying as Teagan came in. "I'll be introducing you to more than just an *aingeal*."

We probably should have warned Seamus about the rest of them sooner, Teagan thought. Thomas, Roisin, and Grendal were sitting on the couch watching the news about the attack at the school. Springing two more Highborn and a *cat-sidhe* on him before he'd met his angel might not be such a good idea.

She hadn't taken more than two steps into the room when Aiden popped out of a hunting blind he'd built with a blanket and two chairs.

"Look out, Mamieo!" he shouted.

Teagan saw the tripwire a millisecond before Seamus

blundered into it. A can attached to the other end of the line toppled, releasing an avalanche of marbles that bounced, rattled, and skittered across the wooden floor—along with Lucy, the sprite.

Teagan grabbed her grandmother's arm before the old woman could slip on the marbles, and almost fell herself. Lucy zipped hummingbird-like around them, trying to get a look at their guest.

Seamus batted the tiny girl as if she were a bug, sending her tumbling to the floor.

"Let her alone, you bully!" Aiden came all the way out of the hunting blind. Lucy shook herself at the sound of his voice and rose into the air, her eyes flashing a dangerous red.

"Get 'im, Lucy!" Aiden shouted. "Bomb Attack One!" Lucy skimmed the floor, scooping up a marble. Thomas and Roisin had jumped to their feet, and Grendal leaped to the back of the couch.

Lucy climbed up, carrying her marble. The high ceilings of the old house gave her a tactical advantage.

"No!" Teagan shouted as the sprite started her dive. She let go like a cross between a dive-bomber and a shot-putter, launching the marble with all her might.

It bounced off the bone at the corner of Seamus's temple. He staggered back a step, and the slick, hard sole of his dress shoe came down on another marble. His arms windmilled wildly as he went over. He landed flat on his back and threw his arm up to protect his eyes. Grendal had come off the couch to see if the sprite needed help. She didn't. She was on the lawyer in a flash, her twiglike arm reaching up his nose. Seamus screamed, and Lucy held up a nose hair triumphantly.

"Stay down," Teagan advised him. "Aiden, get Lucy off of him."

Aiden made his way through the marbles and scooped her up. "Are you all right?" he whispered.

"Yes," Seamus said.

"I didn't mean you, bad guy," Aiden said. "I meant Lucy. *You're not supposed to hit girls.*"

Lucy chittered lovingly up at her hero. As far as Teagan had been able to tell, sprites breathed through holes in their tough exoskeletons like insects, but Lucy still managed to make noises for Aiden. She finished her tirade and held out the nose hair she had harvested.

"Yuck," Aiden told her. "That's nasty." Lucy dropped the hair and rubbed her hands together.

Seamus was sitting up, his hand to his nose. There were tears in his eyes.

"That's . . . a sprite."

Mr. Wylltson came through the front door and paused.

Grendal jumped back up on the arm of the couch to stay out from underfoot. Mr. Wylltson couldn't see or hear the *cat-sídhe* or the sprite, but Grendal enjoyed following him around the house and listening to him read aloud, learning words. When Teagan had explained this, her dad had started talking to the creature, holding doors open to give his invisible guest time to get through. He was so good at pretending, it almost seemed he could see as clearly as the rest of the family, except when he talked to empty chairs where he thought it might be sitting.

"What's all this?" he asked, surveying the carnage.

"A trap," Aiden said. "Like Mom used to help me make. I need a trap for the bad guys. Then I can save everybody."

"Son," Mr. Wylltson said, offering Seamus a hand, "we do not trap guests, even for practice."

The corners of Aiden's mouth turned down. "He attacked first."

"The pratie has a point," Mamieo said. "The wee girl was just curious, and Seamus knocked her tush-over-teakettle."

"I apologize," Seamus said, still rubbing his nose. "I had no idea it was a girl."

"You're not supposed to hit people littler than you, either," Aiden said as Lucy settled on his head. The sprite immediately started weaving elaborate patterns in his hair, her eyes flashing warningly.

"Seamus McGillahee," Mamieo said, "I'd like you to meet Teagan's brother, Aiden, and his friend Lucy, the sprite. Aiden, this is the fellow who got your sister out of jail, so keep a civil tongue in your head and your marbles in your pocket."

Teagan was glad Mamieo left out the part where the lawyer tried to dump her on the side of the road. Aiden had very strong opinions about how ladies should be treated.

Seamus nodded at Aiden and turned toward the others.

"Aileen's sister, Roisin, recently of Mag Mell," Mamieo continued. Roisin curtsied. She didn't understand much English yet, but she smiled at him. Seamus didn't offer his hand, and his face went a little pale.

"Yes, I'm using your real name in front of Sídhe folk, Seamus," Mamieo went on. "We do that here."

Seamus apparently knew that some Sídhe could use the power in a name to twist and bend your will. Highborn were the worst. Highborn goblins loved to play the game of trapping people with promises. Even *cat-sídhe* could take control of your muscles, making you move when you didn't want to.

He doesn't like us, Aiden signed in ASL behind Seamus's back.

I know, Teagan signed back. *We'll have to help him like us. Does he have a song?* Whatever Seamus McGillahee's song was, Teagan was sure he wasn't a bad guy. Aiden tipped his head, considering him as the introductions went on.

"This is Grendal," Mamieo was saying. "You can see for yourself what he is."

The golden *cat-sídhe* stood up on his hind legs and blinked his abalone-shell eyes.

"Greetingsss," he said in a little-girl voice. He'd picked up quite a bit of English in the few days he'd been in the Wylltson house.

Seamus nodded again. Freckles that Teagan hadn't noticed before were starting to stand out on his face, making him look both younger and very Irish.

"And this is Thomas, who has the misfortune of being a damned *lhiannon-sídhe*."

Thomas smiled and held out his hand, and Seamus literally took a step back.

"A muse who sucks Irish poets' blood?"

"I'm reformed," Thomas said. "I don't follow Doirich

anymore." He took Roisin's hand. "Some of us never did. And the blood-sucking was … usually … figurative. It was more about torturing them to death."

Aiden signed something to Teagan that she couldn't decipher. He tended to be sloppy when he wasn't focused.

What? Teagan signed.

Aiden didn't sign back. Instead, he came over, pulled Teagan into the alcove just off the living room, and whispered, "He has *lots* of songs."

"Like?"

"'I Got Friends in Low Places' and 'We Are the Champions,' but,"—Aiden frowned—"'Tainted Love' is the loudest right now."

"'Tainted Love'? Did Abby let you listen to Marilyn Manson?"

"Who's Marilyn Manson?"

"Never mind."

"Can we look her up on—?"

"Absolutely not," Teagan said. "Where did you hear the song?"

"Beldar Conehead sings it in a movie. Lennie showed me. There was a monster, and Beldar wanted to run away." Aiden grimaced. "He wasn't a very good singer. But it's our secret code. When the *really* bad guys come, I'm going to say '*Eh-eh*' like Beldar, and Lennie will run away. If Lennie sees them first, he'll say 'Red Alert'!"

"'Tainted Love' is really one of Seamus's songs?" Teagan had to stifle a laugh. You couldn't tell it from the lawyer's face.

Aiden nodded. "But he keeps switching. He has a scratch."

Mr. Wylltson's massive collection of music was on old vinyl records, which Aiden wasn't allowed to touch. But he knew if a record was scratched, the needle bounced from one song track to the next.

"Wait," Teagan said. "You always know who's coming. You can hear our songs as we're walking up the street. You should have known we had a guest with us."

"I was trying not to listen," Aiden explained as they stepped back into the living room. "I keep hearing bad things. But I *did* tell Mameio to stop."

"I thought you were watching Aiden," Mr. Wylltson said to Thomas before Teagan could ask what bad things had Aiden worried.

"Nobody told me he wasn't allowed to build traps. It's kept him occupied all day."

"I suppose no one knew we would be having company." Mr. Wylltson turned to Tea and Aiden. "'Traps' plural?"

"What does *plural* mean?" Aiden asked.

"It means more than one."

"Yep, *plural*," Aiden said proudly. "I made lots of 'em. I was going to try them on Lennie. He was supposed to come in. Not you, Mameio."

"I headed him off at the street," Mr. Wylltson said. "That was a very good trap, son, but as I said, we have a guest right now. I need you to unmake every single one and apologize to Mr. McGillahee. And clean up these marbles."

"I'm sorry," Aiden said.

"Widdershins, Mamieo?" Seamus lifted a foot so Aiden could retrieve a marble. "*Widdershins?* This place isn't backward. It's bedlam."

"It grows on you," Thomas assured him. "Where's Finn? Is he all right? Did Kyle—"

"Finn's fine. He's taking care of something outside for me," Teagan said. "We're all fine."

"It was *Kyle?*" Thomas seemed dubious. "And you're all fine?"

"We had help," Teagan explained. "Abby and her cousins. And Kyle wasn't bilocating. He's dead."

Thomas's lips thinned to a sad line. "He was evil. But I've known him forever." The statement was probably a little more literal than if a human had said it. Thomas had been around long enough to know Shakespeare.

"I sent his body back to Mag Mell tied to Isabeau. She *was* bilocating."

Thomas sucked in his breath. "The last person to kill one of the Dark Man's children triggered a curse that's lasted for a couple thousand years."

"And I declared war on Mab."

"You what?" Mr. Wylltson asked.

It somehow sounded completely different in her own living room, without a dead Highborn at her feet and an evil bilocate in front of her.

"I declared war on Mab." Teagan put more conviction into it this time. Aiden slipped his hand into hers and squeezed. He had a worried look in his blue eyes.

"Almighty preserve us," Mamieo said, and crossed herself.

"I'm just trying to understand what I've stumbled into," Seamus said. "The Wylltson family, Mamieo and Finn, and a group of Italians have declared war on Mab, Queen of the Sídhe, and killed the son of Fear Doirich, the goblins' god."

"To be fair, Doirich started it." Mamieo sounded just like Aiden had a few moments before.

"But—war?" Mr. Wylltson asked.

"We have no choice, Dad," Teagan said. "They won't leave us alone, and we can't run. They've hounded the Mac Cumhaills for generations because of what Fionn did, haven't they? They'll hunt us to the ends of the earth and they will kill us. They will kill anyone who helps us. If we can't run, we have to fight."

"We have a little time to prepare," Thomas offered. "There was only one gate in North America, and it's closed now."

"We still have to deal with whatever creatures have already made it into Chicago," Teagan said. "And the Highborn will be coming. They'll just have to step into Ireland, like Kyle and Isabeau did, and catch a flight over."

"Some creatures definitely made it out before it closed up," Mamieo agreed.

"There were some teens on the street the first time we drove past," Teagan explained to Thomas. "They might have been Highborn. I think one of them was ... eating a dead *cat-sídhe*."

"What did they look like?" Thomas asked.

"Long legs, heavy shoulders. Not very clean. Their hair

was red and black. I've never seen a Highborn who looked dirty."

Grendal's eyes narrowed, and he growled. "Dump Dogs."

"That sounds scary." Aiden backed up against Teagan's legs, and she put her hands on his shoulders. He didn't need any more scary things in his life.

"What are they?" she asked.

Thomas sighed. "Let's just say there are some Highborn no one invites to parties."

"They came to parties," Grendal said.

"The Dogs came to your hall?" Thomas turned to Roisin and spoke in Gaelic.

Roisin's chin went up, and Grendal's tail lashed as she answered.

Thomas spoke again, and there was an edge in his voice Teagan had never heard before. Disgust. She looked to Mamieo, the only one in the room other than Thomas, Roisin, and Grendal who understood the language.

"They're ... disagreeing about the nature of the creatures we've been discussing. Roisin feels they're not as bad as Thomas thinks."

"A discussion that we should have in private," Thomas said, switching back to English. "I apologize. The group you've described is part of a clan that lives in the city dump in Mag Mell. Shape shifters."

"Like you?" Aiden asked.

"Not at all like me," Thomas said. "Mab has the bodies of her slaves thrown on the trash heap. The Dump Dogs eat them."

"Her Fir Bolg slaves?" Mamieo asked. Thomas nodded grimly.

"They eat dead *people?*" Aiden grimaced.

"Recycling, Mag Mell style," Thomas said. "Mab wouldn't waste time burying a slave. The Dump Dogs dispose of them, bones and all, but only if there is nothing small, old, or sick to tear apart instead. They prefer the blood still pumping in their meat. This pack must have made it out in the confusion before the gate closed."

Roisin studied each person's face as they spoke. She asked a question of Grendal, and he replied, the tip of his tail twitching. She shook her head, and he growled again. Dump Dogs were apparently a touchy subject all around.

"And these creatures are loose in Chicago?" Mr. Wylltson asked.

"We saw five of them at least," Teagan said.

"They're nocturnal," Thomas said. "Not at their best while the sun is up. They were probably just curious."

And a little hungry. The female had taken a bite or two of Maggot Cat, even if carrion was not her first choice for food.

"What does 'nocturnal' mean?" Aiden asked.

"It means they sleep during the day and come out at night," Seamus said. "They've probably gone off to sleep somewhere."

Aiden put his hands to his head and squeezed his eyes shut. It was his way of saying *La, la, la, I can't hear you* to the music in his head.

"Let's discuss the Dump Dogs later, shall we?" Mr. Wylltson suggested.

"So you sent Isabeau back to face Mab," Thomas said,

71

changing the subject. "I feel sorry for her. We used to get along. Isabeau was fun."

"Isabeau?" Roisin's eyes flashed. That was one word at least she understood. "*Isabeau?*" She picked up a book from the arm of the couch and threw it at Thomas's head.

Teagan didn't need any translation for that. She'd felt exactly the same way when Isabeau had snuggled up to Finn. The *sídhe* girl was clearly accustomed to bending men to her will. Roisin turned and fled up the stairs before Thomas had a chance to recover.

The *lhiannon-sídhe* started to follow her, but Grendal stepped in the way.

"She'll be back. She didn't believe that the Dump Dogs ate dead people," the *cat-sídhe* said. "I smelled it in Mag Mell, but she didn't believe. Roisin doesn't like . . ." The *cat-sídhe* scratched his head, clearly searching for words.

"To be wrong?" Thomas suggested. "I'm learning that."

"Yes," Grendal agreed. "But she'll get modified. Aileen got modified, yes?"

Teagan wondered where he had picked up that word.

"Grendal said Mom got modified." Aiden looked at his father. "Is that true?"

Mr. Wylltson looked from Aiden to the stairs, trying to figure out the context.

"'Modified' as in she changed? Yes. My wife was amazing, but"—he glanced at Teagan—"she was fierce beyond belief if she felt she was right about something. It took her some time to learn that she wasn't always as right as she thought she was."

Mamieo laughed. "You should have seen her when she

72

first came from Mag Mell, pratie. She was determined to have her own way in everything. I was that certain the girl had been raised by wild beasts."

Grendal made a sound halfway between a cough and a growl.

"What did you do?" Thomas asked when the *cat-sídhe* had recovered.

"Loved her," Mamieo and John Wylltson said at the same time.

"Fiercely," John Wylltson added softly. "I loved her fiercely from the first moment I saw her. It was the only thing to do."

"Yess," Grendal agreed, then turned and started up the stairs. They were too high for him to climb like a human would, so he hopped from step to step like a thin-tailed kangaroo.

"Did you know my wife well?" Mr. Wylltson asked the hat rack near where Grendal had been standing.

"Dad," Aiden said, "the *cat-sídhe* went upstairs."

"Of course he did." Mr. Wylltson looked at Seamus. "You can see them, can't you?"

Seamus nodded.

"Of course you can." Mr. Wylltson's face pinked.

"Did the news mention any students taken to the hospital?" Teagan asked. Her dad wasn't the only one who could redirect. She hated seeing him embarrassed in front of Seamus.

"The news was reporting that they transported *a* student to the hospital," Thomas said. "He was listed in critical condition." Teagan felt a small wave of relief. At least Cade had made it that far.

"How about Molly? Have they said anything about a girl named Molly?"

"Nobody's mentioned a Molly."

"All right," Seamus said. "I've met a very strange family; seen a couple of Highborn with relationship issues, a *cat-sídhe* and a sprite; and heard that you are all in more trouble than can be dealt with. But no holy angel. You know what I think? I think a sane man would walk out that door, and keep walking."

"That's true," Mr. Wylltson said. "Things are much more serious than I'd thought when Mamieo invited you. You don't need to be involved. I wish to God none of us did."

Seamus looked around the room. "You are all going to"—his eyes rested on Aiden, and he hesitated—"need to build traps. Really good traps."

You are all going to die. Teagan was sure that was what Seamus had started to say. He just couldn't bring himself to say it to a six-year-old.

Aiden took his hands from his head. "That's what I said!"

"The angel's in the kitchen," Thomas offered. "I'm afraid he's having a little difficulty reconciling himself to being in the same house with me."

"Because you're *lhiannon-sídhe*?"

"Because Thomas killed Raynor's brother," Mr. Wylltson explained.

"He killed an angel?"

Aiden folded his arms and frowned. "*On purpose.* But Dad says we have to let him stay because he loves Aunt Roisin."

74

"TECHNICALLY, he killed himself," Thomas said. "I was just the catalyst. Geert was a musician and a poet with a touch of melancholy, which made it simple to inspire certain thoughts."

"Come on." Mamieo took Seamus by the elbow and dragged him toward the kitchen. "I'll introduce you to Raynor."

Teagan followed them. The Wylltsons' kitchen was huge, stretching across the whole back of the house. Raynor was on his knees in the corner that had once been her mother's art studio. His blue work shirt and jeans showed evidence of living in the park for days, but his blond hair was neatly pulled into a ponytail as always, and his round glasses gave him a quizzical, wizardly air. Some of the motorbike parts he'd been collecting —the frame and rims, gas tank and handlebars—were together now, but the engine was in pieces, spread across newspaper on the floor. Tea realized this was the *stuff* he had gone back to salvage from the park. He'd been hiding the parts in the bushes and working on it at night.

"Raynor!" Mamieo put her hands on her hips.

The angel pointed a greasy finger at John Paul Wylltson, who'd just stepped through the door behind them. "He said I could."

"In the *kitchen*, John Paul?"

"He said he needs to keep his hands busy." Mr. Wylltson glanced back toward the living room, where Thomas sat. "It keeps his mind off . . . other things."

It was a large motorbike, even for such a huge kitchen. Raynor was taking up well over half of the room. Teagan was sure there were more parts now than he'd had at the park. Perhaps he'd found some kind of delivery service. She saw a box with a label from California that had definitely not been sitting out behind the library. It had just been opened.

Seamus stepped forward. "Mamieo claims you're a holy angel."

"Only the Creator is holy," Raynor said, wiping his hands on a red grease rag. "But I am an angel."

The lawyer's eyes went past him to the parts scattered over the floor, and his face paled. "My God, that's an Indian Four!"

"Just an angel," Raynor said. "We've established that. But yes, it is a 1930 Indian Four." Raynor pulled a magazine page from his pocket and unfolded it. The shiny red motorbike in the photograph had only the vaguest resemblance to the things spread over the papers, but the four massive cylinders and the lettering on the gas tank were recognizable enough.

Seamus said, "It will bring you at least sixty thousand on the open market when you've finished restoring it. Do you have a buyer?"

"I'm not going to *sell* it." Raynor took a protective step toward the frame. "I'm going to ride it."

Seamus reached out and touched the lettering on the tank. "I've dreamed about this motorbike since I was a kid."

"Lots of people dream of the Indian Four," Raynor said. "One of the most beautiful motorbikes ever made. She's got a seventy-seven-cubic-inch engine—"

Teagan edged toward the kitchen door. Once the angel got started on engines, you couldn't shut him up. Her mind was moving almost as fast as it had in the cafeteria. First, she was going up to her room to change out of the pajamas she'd worn in the park overnight. Then she'd try to call Molly, then check in with Agnes at the zoo, because Molly wasn't the only one who was missing—Oscar had been taken, too. And Agnes could check on the cultures Teagan had collected from Maggot Cat while she was at it. His corpse had been putrefying at an unreasonably fast rate. Teagan stopped. Gil was in the backyard with a cut on his throat where Mab had tried to slice it open. If Maggot Cat's condition was any indication, it was possible that an infection would be much, much worse for the phooka than it was for creatures of this world.

Teagan was sure that Maggot Cat had died because he had little, if any, resistance to the tiny fauna in this corner of creation. She wanted her phone, a shower, and clean clothes desperately. But she couldn't have them until she'd taken care of the phooka. She'd need to get her first-aid kit from the bathroom and get out the back door without Seamus following. She didn't want to explain the wounded phooka to him. Not yet. She eased out of the kitchen.

Thomas was still sitting on the couch staring at the stairs. Roisin had clearly not come back down.

"Thank you for coming to check on me, Thomas," Teagan said.

"What?" He dragged his eyes away from the stairwell. "When?"

"When I was at the police station. You landed on the window—"

"Afraid not." The shape shifter shook his head. "I was watching Aiden, remember?"

Terrific. Her dad talked to hat racks and she talked to birds. No wonder Seamus thought they were an unusual family.

"Did you see someone who looked like me?"

"Never mind." Teagan headed down the hall. "I was just getting the first-aid kit."

She took her small emergency kit—the one she carried with her if a neighbor called with a sick or injured pet—from the bathroom closet and checked the contents. There were nitrile gloves, sterile bandages, hand sanitizer, saline wash, scissors, tweezers, Q-Tips—everything she might need for a minor emergency situation with a small animal. She found a clean washcloth, filled a plastic basin with hot water, and tried to walk back through the living room and kitchen without anyone noticing her. Thomas was still staring morosely. In the kitchen, Mamieo was filling Raynor in about the police station while her dad and Aiden listened; Seamus was still mesmerized by the motorcycle. She made it all the way to the back door before she realized that she couldn't open it. Not with her hands full.

"Where are you going?" Mr. Wylltson asked.

"Just stepping out to take care of Gil's neck." Teagan held up the supplies.

"Gil?" Seamus shook himself away from Raynor's motor-bike. "The phooka?"

"Yep," Aiden said sadly. "I'm not allowed to play with phookas."

"I'll come along," Seamus said. "I've never seen a phooka."

Aiden started after them, but Mamieo caught his collar.

"I wasn't going to play with him," Aiden said. "I was just going to watch Teagan."

"We'll watch from the window," Mr. Wylltson said. "You are not allowed to go into the yard."

"Rats," Aiden muttered.

Raynor opened the door for her, and Seamus followed. The smell of burnt wood was noticeable as soon as she stepped into the yard. Joe was in the far corner, all seven feet of him leaned up against the fence, his brows drooping like Spanish moss above his round yellow eyes. He had been well camouflaged in the park, his bark-like coat as well as his skin blending into the shrubbery. Now half of his body was dark-ened and charred, his long, lichen-gray beard as singed as Mr. Wylltson's eyebrows.

Joe was indigenous to this corner of creation, made of the stuff of this world. Anyone who looked hard enough could see him, though they might mistake him for a shrub. The phooka curled at Joe's feet was a different story. Gil was as invisible as a *cat-sídhe* to those who weren't gifted with second sight.

"Welcome," the Green Man said after Raynor had introduced Seamus. "Any friend of Raynor's is a friend of mine." He turned to Raynor, more slowly than Teagan had ever seen him move. "He is a friend, isn't he?"

"I think so," Raynor said. "Shouldn't you be sleeping?"

"I'll plant myself somewhere soon. This little one needed watching. He's a long way from home."

Gil could have been a wild boy painted by Raphael, beautiful in face and form except for his long, tufted ears and his left hand. Teagan couldn't call it deformed, exactly. It was pink and perfectly formed—for a pig's trotter. Gil's human right hand was pressed to his wounded neck, and his eyes were closed but he couldn't manage to keep the lashes still. *Feigning death,* Tea realized.

"Phookas are the broken ones," she said when she saw Seamus staring at the boy's two-knuckled hand. "Twisted by the Dark Man for his own amusement." Gil was going to need some clothes. Currently, he wore nothing but a rag wrapped around his middle. Only the mild winds of May and June blow in Mag Mell. Never the winds of October in Chicago.

Joe creaked as he turned. "What happened, Tea? I persuaded Mag Mell to let you carry iron into realms where no iron belongs. I made a way for Finn to follow you." His hair shook like leaves in a gentle wind. "I thought you would bring Fear out, and Mag Mell would be well again."

"I'm sorry, Joe," Teagan said. "Things were so different from what I expected. Mab is trying to destroy Fear Doirich. The Dark Man is going insane."

"He's killing her," Joe said. "Killing Mag Mell. She was weeping. I heard the willow cry out before—" He shrugged his charred shoulder.

"I'm so sorry," Teagan said again.

Joe lifted his eyes to the buildings beyond the fence and across the alley. "Plans can go wrong. Even very good plans."

Teagan nodded. Green Men planned forests and gardens that covered continents. Gardens that might take a hundred thousand years to grow, but that could be destroyed in what must seem like the blink of an eye to them.

"I had to make a split-second decision," Teagan explained. "I chose to save Gil." Well, there it was. The lawyer's horrified look was back.

The phooka gave up his ruse and sat up. "That's not my real name."

"Well, you're stuck with it," Teagan said. "Unless you want to tell me—"

"No," Gil said quickly. "I don't. You tried to *bend* me."

Now not only was Seamus looking horrified, Raynor was frowning. He had warned against using her Highborn power to bend creatures' wills into making promises they didn't want to.

She'd thought she'd had a really good reason to bend Gil to her will in Mag Mell—and she still wasn't sure it was completely wrong. Phookas' own wills got them into all kinds of trouble. But knowing she'd destroyed his trust hurt more than she'd expected.

"What's in that bowl? Is it good to eat?"

"No. It's soap and water to clean your neck. I'm sorry that I tried to bend you, Gil."

"I like your other eyes better," the phooka said. He was jiggling like Aiden on a sugar high, but Teagan couldn't tell if it was fear, shock, or just the cold.

"What other eyes?" Seamus asked.

Teagan winced. How could she possibly explain? He already thought she was a goblin. If he ever saw her walking as a bilocate with molten golden eyes, he would probably call in an exorcist.

"Shhh, shhh, calm down, little one." Joe put a huge hand on the phooka's shoulder. "No need to get excited."

Gil was little compared to Joe, but he was still as tall as Teagan. She wondered how phooka boys felt about pastel colors, as she wasn't sure anyone else's clothes but hers would fit him. The fact that he was still sitting on the cold ground worried her.

"Can you rip open another door into Mag Mell?" Teagan asked Joe. "We could send him back."

"If I had two good arms." Joe shrugged again, and for the first time Teagan realized the other shoulder wasn't just blackened. His arm was stiff.

Raynor touched his friend's charred coat. "I'm so sorry that I couldn't—"

"No, you had to take care of the problem," Joe said. "I'd

have done the same thing if I could. A good winter's sleep and everything will begin to grow new again. Raynor..." Joe wrinkled his nose. "You smell really bad."

"You do smell bad, scary angel," Gil said.

"Oh, sorry," Raynor said, pulling out the grease rag he'd shoved in his back pocket. "I've been working."

Joe hated everything about combustion engines. He felt that they led to automobiles, which in turn led to asphalt and cement.

"If you could just"—Joe made a shooing motion at the angel and his grease rag—"take that somewhere else?"

"I'll get back to my machinery, then. Coming?" he asked Seamus.

"I'll stay a little longer," Seamus said, watching a squirrel that was peeking out of Joe's beard.

"Suit yourself." Raynor started back to the house.

The squirrel studied Seamus with bright, beady eyes, then scrambled up the beard and jumped to Joe's shoulder, where it started digging at the burnt parts, tearing away pieces of the bark coat and what looked like charcoal beneath it.

"Should it be doing that?" Seamus asked.

"Yes," Joe said, but he twisted and grimaced. "She's scratching my itches. Squirrels are *good* at scratching. I couldn't manage without them."

Teagan knelt beside Gil. Abby had tossed a handful of cornstarch on him when he'd first been pulled out of Mag Mell so she could see him. When Tea leaned closer, she could still make out traces of the powder dancing around him. Cornstarch was mixed into the tear tracks on his face and crusting the edges of the cut on his neck.

Teagan tried not to think of Maggot Cat's pus-oozing wounds as she opened the first-aid kit.

"Do you know where you are, Gil?" She wanted to be sure the phooka boy wasn't in shock.

"Yes. I'm at *Teagan's* house."

No chill swept through her when the goblin spoke her name. His voice had almost no power in it—not even as much as the voice of a *cat-sídhe*. No wonder the phookas never told anyone their real names. Without that power, they were completely vulnerable to any creature that wanted to bend them.

"What's that?" Gil watched suspiciously as she took out the box of nitrile gloves.

"Gloves." Teagan pulled one on and held up her hand to show him. "They keep my hands clean. Can I look at your cut?"

Gil nodded. Teagan tipped his head up so she could see the wound.

"I'm going to wash it with soap and water, all right?"

Gil nodded again, but when Teagan touched the soapy gauze to his neck, he screamed.

"Are you all right?" Joe leaned over them.

Teagan sat back on her heels. "Did that hurt?"

"No," the phooka lied. He wiped away a tear with the heel of his hand. "I'm not crying because it hurt," he said. "I'm not."

"Then why are you crying?" Joe asked.

"Because she left to fight a Highborn. Finn went to help her, but Raynor wouldn't let me go. I said I could help."

"You wanted to help her?" Seamus asked. "I thought you didn't trust her."

"What are you?" the phooka demanded. "I heard your name, but not what you are."

"He's a lawyer," Teagan explained. "He helped me."

Seamus looked pained, but Gil nodded.

"I don't *trust* her, lawyer." The phooka boy reddened to the roots of his hair. "I just *love* her."

Finn dropped over the back wall and landed like a cat, his soft leather boots hardly making a sound against the grass. "What was all that screaming about? I thought someone was being murdered. Joe, good to see you."

Teagan held up the washcloth. "I was just trying to clean Gil up."

"And the goblin was explaining how much he loves her," Seamus said.

"Making moves on my girl again, Gil? I won't have it."

Gil's ears drooped. "Hi, Finn. I thought you were dead."

"You did not," Teagan said. "Where were you, Finn? I was starting to get worried."

"Cooling my head a bit. And I took a look around to make sure the uglies had left the neighborhood. They have."

"You could have *gotten* dead," Gil said. "Before you came back. That can happen."

"Wishful thinking, boyo." Finn squatted beside Teagan. "Maggot Cat's taken care of. At least, it's out of the way until you figure out what to do with it. Hey, my man. Other than flirting with Tea and wishing me dead, how are you doing?"

Gil held up his trotter. "God didn't heal me."

"Yeah, I was there. Things didn't go well for you. Not at all. But we told you Fear Doirich was no god."

"I gave you to him, and he let Mab *cut* me." Gil wiped his nose with the back of his trotter. "He could fix me. But he didn't."

Seamus moved a little closer. The squirrel on Joe's shoulder flicked its tail at him, but the lawyer was more interested in the phooka than the tree man.

"What will you do in this world?" Seamus asked.

"I don't know," Gil said. "I want to go home. I'm cold and I'm really, really hungry."

"There's no harm in him," Finn said. "Once you get to know him, you'll understand."

"What do phookas eat?" Seamus seemed willing to give Finn, at least, the benefit of the doubt. "Maybe I can find something for you."

Gil looked up hopefully. "Babies! Can you find a baby?"

SEVEN

SEAMUS took a step back. *"You eat babies?"*

Finn swatted the back of Gil's head. "He's never. He says that, but he's never."

"I *would*," Gil insisted, putting both his hand and his trotter up to protect his head from another smack. "I'd rip their flesh and crunch their little-bitty bones."

"It's all talk," Finn said. "He's hunted children, of course. They all do. But the faster, stronger beasties always get them first. Gil's sort eats beetle bugs and bloody raw fish."

The phooka boy glared. "Don't *tell* him that." His eyes narrowed. "What do lawyers eat?"

"It depends on the lawyer," Seamus said, recovering a little. "Some eat hamburger, some eat caviar."

"Caviar is fish eggs," Finn explained. "It's that nasty."

Gil's stomach growled, and he licked his lips. "I want some fish eggs!"

"Do you have to talk about food right now?" Teagan asked. "I need to get this wound cleaned, and it's going to be hard enough without adding wiggling and salivating into the mix."

"Just trying to help," Finn said. "I don't want Seamus here getting the wrong impression."

"I think he already has plenty of wrong impressions," Teagan said.

Seamus ignored her. "So Teagan brought you here? Why?"

"He's not a witness on the stand, McGillahee," Finn said. "How's he supposed to know why Tea does the things she does?"

"I do know." Gil laid his ears back, and if it hadn't been for the pig trotter still protecting his head from Finn, he'd have looked completely and bashfully human. "She did it because she loves me."

"I what?" Teagan said.

"You do," Joe agreed. "Anyone can see it."

"She hunted god," Gil told the tree man. "She could have *gotten* him. But she didn't. She saved me instead." He wagged his ears happily. "I love her, too. I even know her real name. Teagan, Teagan, Teagan!" he shouted.

"Quiet down," Finn told him.

"Gil," Teagan said firmly. "I love Finn."

"I do, too," the phooka said. "A little."

Seamus raised one eyebrow at Finn, who ignored him.

"If you love us so much, why did you betray us to Fear Doirich?"

Gil flushed so dark it was visible through the soot and grime on his face. "I thought god would fix me. And when I was a man, I could save her."

"Right after you let them eat me," Finn said.

"Maybe." From the faraway look in Gil's eyes, Teagan was

sure he was imagining just that. Then he dropped his gaze to the grass and sighed. "No. We shared a nest. I'd save you, too."

"I'm glad to hear it," Teagan said.

"You shared a nest?" Seamus asked. "What does that mean?"

"Never you mind what it means." Finn flushed, even though Gil had only instinctively huddled close to him for warmth as they slept in the chill of the deep woods. Phookas slept in group nests.

"Could you both go inside?" Teagan asked. "You are disturbing my work."

"I'm not disturbing Gil," Finn said. "If people get the idea he's been gobbling up children, it's not going to go well with him."

"I can't help it!" Gil said. "I'm a *phooka*."

"Let me help you, then." Finn leaned close and looked into Gil's eyes. "You know there's a child in this house?"

Gil's ears perked up, and he inhaled. "I can smell it."

Teagan made a mental note to make sure Aiden was actually getting in the water when he said he was taking a bath. And using soap.

"Him. You can smell *him*. And you've seen the old woman staring out the window at you?"

Gil leaned over to look around Finn, then ducked back.

"The Scary One." He uttered it as if it were a title. "She's there now."

"The Scary One's my own grand-*máthair*, Mamieo Ida. And I promise you, if you so much as look at the boyo, she's going to finish the job Mab started."

89

Gil's human hand went to his throat again, but his eyes lifted to Finn's.

"Not you?" Gil said. "You won't kill me?"

"Not unless I have to." Finn ran his hand through his hair. "Teagan's rubbing off on me."

"You think?" Seamus asked. "You went to Mag Mell to fight, and you ended up rescuing a phooka. You're ready to let it run free in Chicago."

"Knowing Tea has made me think twice before I kill a creature, that's for sure."

"Can't you see what's happening? *She's part Highborn.* Teagan Wylltson is bending you."

"Na," Finn said. "And she's all Highborn. Kyle took care of that, didn't he? And I ran with her through the night of Mag Mell while her eyes glowed like molten gold, and she was just as beautiful as she is standing before me now. I ran with this one, too"—he nodded toward Gil—"and none of us knowing if we'd live to see the dawn."

"And we shared a nest," Gil said.

"You don't need to keep mentioning that, boyo."

"Boyo?" Gil asked. "What's a boyo?"

"What you'll be until you're a man."

Gil held up his trotter. "But, god didn't—"

Finn stood up and offered his hand to Gil. The phooka took it with his human hand and Finn pulled him to his feet.

"Doirich can't make you into a man, Gil. He's not the one who can do it. You are. You fight for it. You fight to be what you want to be, not what that damned Doirich twisted you into. Not what McGillahee here thinks you are."

Gil wiped his nose again and nodded.

"Now, are you man enough to stand here without screaming and crying while Tea cleans that little-bitty scratch?"

The phooka closed his eyes and tipped his head back.

"You can deal with this?" Finn asked Teagan.

"I can if Joe will hold the bowl of water."

"Of course." Joe took it.

Teagan nodded toward Seamus. "Can you deal with *that?*"

"I will," Finn said. "You hold good and still while Tea fixes you up, Gil, and I'll get you something to eat. Come on, McGillahee. We're going inside."

Gil didn't even flinch as she washed the scratch out, taking her time and doing a thorough job.

"You do love me, right?" The phooka boy lowered his long lashes as she smeared on antibiotic.

"Not the way I love Finn."

"But you love me." His ears wagged happily. "You take care of me."

"As a friend. I love you as a friend." Teagan couldn't believe she'd just said that. Abby had warned her that guys never hear the "as a friend" part when you try to tell them that. She suddenly wished Abby were here to make some bizarre comment, or even Aiden, who'd tell Gil, *"Teagan likes ugly little creatures. She even loves toads."* She sighed. She'd told the phooka the truth, and that was the best she could do. It wasn't her fault that he was humming happily to himself.

She had just finished bandaging the wound when Finn came back with a stack of sandwiches in his hands and a roll of duct tape under his arm. And, thankfully, without

Seamus—though Teagan could feel him watching from the window.

Gil sniffed the sandwich cautiously. "What is it?"

"Gooey goodness. Bread, peanut butter, and jelly. Grape jelly, in this case. It's the only thing I know how to cook."

Gil started stuffing them in his mouth.

"Finn," Teagan asked quietly as the phooka ate, "do you think Molly could just be hiding? Or at the library? She goes there sometimes to catch up on work."

Finn put an arm around her and pulled her under his chin, where she was completely wrapped in his electric embrace. She felt incredibly safe, but she knew Molly wasn't. Finn's silence was answer enough.

"I'm going to keep hoping," Teagan said.

"I've dealt with goblins too long for that."

"There is always hope."

"What's that?" Gil had finished the sandwiches and was sniffing the roll of tape.

"Duct tape," Finn said.

"Good to eat?"

"Na. It's good for fixing phookas to cinder-block walls, though."

"You're not," Teagan said, stepping away from him.

Finn took the tape from Gil, pulled off a length, and ripped it free with his teeth. "You have a better idea?"

Gil backed away from him. "I don't want to be ducked to a wall."

"I don't want to duck you to the wall." Finn shook his head.

"But Joe is sleeping, and Teagan and I have to go get cleaned up. We can't have you jumping out of the yard and running off."

Teagan looked at the Green Man in surprise—he was sleeping, still holding the bowl.

Gil backed away from Finn, his eyes huge.

"I promise, Teagan," he whispered. The word sent a shiver trickling ice-like down Teagan's spine. She felt the promise settle between them. The phooka shivered, too, but he stood taller. "I *promise* I won't leave the yard unless Teagan says I can."

"I thought you didn't want me to bend you," Teagan said.

Gil stood up as tall as he could. "That was my bending. My own promise. You couldn't make me."

Finn nodded. "It'll do." He wadded up the strip of tape he had pulled from the roll.

"I'll bring you a blanket and some clothes, Gil," Teagan offered.

"That lawyer's watching us," Gil said. "Do you think he has any fish eggs?"

"Are you still hungry?"

"Phookas are always hungry."

Seamus stepped out of the back door just before they reached it, and pulled it shut behind him.

"I don't understand, Mac Cumhaill. I can understand those." He waved at the house, clearly indicating Thomas, Roisin, Grendal, and Lucy. "They've left the goblin king, or never followed him in the first place. But this creature—he said, 'god didn't heal me.' He *belongs to the Dark Man.* It's your destiny to kill goblins. You're *the Mac Cumhaill.*"

"My destiny to kill Gil, you mean?" Finn said. "He has a name, McGillahee, just like you do. Did you ever consider that all the killing I've done—that all the Mac Cumhaills have done—came about because of a curse? Gil pulled me through the waters when I couldn't swim. He fed me raw fish when I couldn't have gone a step farther without food. I'm not going to repay that by killing him, no matter who he thinks his god is."

"He betrayed you."

"Maybe so," Finn said. "But what would you do if you'd been born with a human heart and a pig's hand? If you'd thought your god would heal you if paid him enough?"

"Mamieo's right," Seamus said. "You're playing at being a saint when what's needed is the Mac Cumhaill. This is bound to end badly."

"The Mac Cumhaill always ends badly," Finn said. "I've gotten used to the idea."

"You need help."

"From you?"

"From me. You are in over your head. You need the McGillahee touch."

"I'm head over heels, and that's a fact. There's no cure for it, and I wouldn't take it if there was. I've got something now that I never thought I could have. I've got a family." Finn started to open the door, then stopped. "You know why I'm giving you time to understand? Because the girl asked me to. That's the only reason you're still standing. Put that in your pipe and smoke it, McGillahee."

EIGHT

MAMIEO was drinking hot tea and watching Aiden construct an elaborate contraption of Popsicle sticks and rubber bands at the table. The kettle was still steaming enough to give a ghost of a whistle. Teagan wasn't sure whether the old woman just couldn't hear it, or if she was too focused on Aiden to worry about it.

John Wylltson was on the far side of the kitchen, his head bent close to Raynor's. *Probably filling him in about the Dump Dogs while Mamieo keeps Aiden busy.*

Finn moved the kettle to a cool burner, and his grandmother looked up.

"Well?" she asked Seamus. "I've shown you what I promised and more. Do you still think I'm mixing my medications?"

"Not at all." Seamus leaned against the counter. "In fact, I apologize."

Lucy came out of a blue china cup on the cabinet behind him, her eyes flashing red at the sound of his voice.

"I'd move away from the counter if I were you," Teagan suggested.

"Why?" Seamus asked.

Finn pointed up at the sprite. "She keeps valuables in that cup. M&M's, spider webs, foil, and the like."

Seamus crossed the room, getting as far away from the sprite as he could. Lucy settled in again, peeking over the brim to make sure he kept his distance.

Teagan studied her brother. He must have been more frightened by the talk of Dump Dogs than she'd thought. The emotionless expression he'd worn for months after their mom had died was creeping back. She glanced across the kitchen at her dad, wondering if he'd noticed.

"So you've come to your senses, have you?" Mamieo said. "I thought meeting a holy *aingeal* might do the trick."

"He's not that convincing as an angel." Raynor looked up, and Seamus spread his hands. "You must admit you're not what most people imagine when they think of heavenly beings."

"You were expecting something—"

"Younger," Seamus said. "Shinier. More ... *kempt*. Less mechanically minded."

Teagan held her tongue. She'd once seen Raynor with different eyes—he'd been a silhouette, dark as the moon when it slips in front of the sun during a total eclipse. A corona too brilliant to look at had undulated around him. *The fire of creation.*

"But I'm staying," Seamus went on. "It's my destiny."

"There's no such thing," Raynor said.

Teagan caught her dad's eye, and he nodded toward her brother. He'd noticed, then. Maybe that's what he'd been talking to Raynor about.

"Oh ho!" Mamieo chuckled. "Destiny, is it? And what persuaded you of that?"

"The motorbike," Seamus said.

"My motorbike," Raynor repeated.

The lawyer reached out and touched the handlebar reverently. "I told you, I've dreamed about it all my life. Not *an* Indian Four. *This* Indian four—with the little dent and the missing letter on the gas tank."

Raynor looked toward the ceiling. "Very funny."

"More peculiar than funny, I'd think," Seamus said.

"He was addressing the Almighty, not you," Mamieo said. "He's a holy *aingeal* whether you believe it or no."

"That must have been some dream," Mr. Wylltson said.

"Oh, it was. I might die without achieving it, but I can't live without trying. With great risk comes great glory. And"—he shook himself free of the Indian Four's spell—"the Mac Cumhaill needs my help."

Teagan resisted the urge to smack him. "I thought the saying was 'with great power comes great responsibility.'"

"Peter Parker has his aphorisms, I have mine. So, what do *you* think I'm here to do, Mamieo?"

"Stay one step ahead of the goblins," Mamieo said.

Seamus smiled in Teagan's direction. "I can do that."

"We're all going to have to do that." Mamieo turned to Raynor. "I'm told the gate in the park is closed for good. Joe says the fire burned to the very roots of the willow."

"It did," the angel said. "No gate will open there again."

"But it will open somewhere," Mamieo said. "And somewhere nearby, I'm thinking."

"Why?" Mr. Wylltson asked.

"Because Mag Mell wants me to sing to her," Aiden said without looking up. "So she can get well."

"She'll open the gate, all right. And try to find the pratie before—"

"Mamieo!" Mr. Wylltson warned.

"Aiden." Mamieo pressed her hand to her heart. "Would you run up to my room and get me my medicine?"

"Okay." Aiden set his construction project down. He trudged over and pulled the door to the maid's stair open, then waited for Lucy, who had come up out of her cup to settle in his hair. "I'm not a baby. I know the bad guys want to kill me."

"They're after the little boy?" Seamus asked.

"I told you on the way home." Mamieo pushed the door closed behind Aiden and lowered her voice. "He's got the blood of Amergin the bard running in him. The Dark Man hates him for it, more than he hates the rest of us put together."

And for the fact that his songs were magic in Mag Mell. Teagan started to pace. *A great mending to be done.* She did not like where this conversation was headed . . .

"Mamieo," Finn said, "you're not thinking of taking the boyo back?"

"Absolutely not," Mr. Wylltson said. "Why would you even consider it?"

Mamieo spun toward him. "To save my grandson's life, John Paul. I didn't get to this age without staying one step ahead of the goblins myself. *Thinking* one step ahead of them.

Your daughter's right. We can't run. But we can beat the bastards. This time, we can beat them."

"So Mag Mell is going to open a gate," Seamus said. "And when she does . . ."

"It will be a race. Both sides—Mag Mell and goblinkind—will be after the boyo. The shadows won't want to wait. Samhain is coming, when the walls between the worlds grow thin. They'll claw their way into this world if they can. That's why I need you, Seamus."

"*All* sides," Teagan corrected. "Mab is rebelling. She'll want Aiden, to spite Fear Doirich, if nothing else. And the Highborn won't wait for a gate to open. Kyle and Isabeau just stepped into Ireland and caught a plane over. They'll be coming that way, too."

"'*I tell you naught for your comfort,*'" Mr. Wylltson said softly.

"'*Yea, naught for your desire,*
Save that the sky grows darker yet
And the sea rises higher.'"

Aiden's head popped out from behind the door to the maid's stairs. "What song is that?"

"Pratie!" Mamieo said. "You couldn't possibly have gone up to my room and back already!"

Aiden held up the bottle of nitro pills. "Lucy went. I just sat on the steps and listened."

"You know better than to eavesdrop, son."

"It's not a song," Mr. Wylltson said. "It's a poem that your mother illustrated for me once. Chesterton's *Ballad of the White*

Horse. Winston Churchill quoted it on the radio to give the English courage when it looked as if Hitler was going to win the war."

"Did he win?" Aiden's face was very pale. "Did the bad guy win?"

"He did not," Mr. Wylltson assured him.

"I want to hear it."

"It's a very long poem," Mr. Wylltson said. "But I'll recite your mom's favorite parts. You have to understand that it is about a good king named Alfred who had lost a terrible war. His army had been destroyed. He prayed for help, and Mother Mary appeared and spoke to him. She said:

> "*'I tell you naught for your comfort*
> *Yea, naught for your desire,*
> *Save that the sky grows darker yet*
> *And the sea rises higher.*
>
> *'Night shall be thrice night over you,*
> *And heaven an iron cope.*
> *Do you have joy without a cause,*
> *Yea, faith without a hope?'*"

"What's a cope?" Aiden asked.

"A robe," Mr. Wylltson explained. "Like a priest wears."

"An iron robe would squish a priest."

"That's the point, son," Mr. Wylltson said. "Mary was saying he would feel like the sky was squishing him."

"What did he do?"

"Well," Mr. Wylltson said, "he went to find help. And he found Colan. This was your mother's very favorite part:

> *"Last of a race in ruin—*
> *He spoke the speech of the Gaels;*
> *His kin were in holy Ireland,*
> *Or up in the crags of Wales."*

"Like us." Aiden was looking even more intent. "Colan was like us." Mr. Wylltson nodded and went on:

> *"But his soul stood with his mother's folk,*
> *That were of the rain-wrapped isle,*
> *Where Patrick and Brandan westerly*
> *Looked out at last on a landless sea*
> *And the sun's last smile.*
>
> *His harp was carved and cunning,*
> *As the Celtic craftsman makes,*
> *Graven all over with twisting shapes*
> *Like many headless snakes.*
>
> *His harp was carved and cunning,*
> *His sword prompt and sharp,*
> *And he was gay when he held the sword,*
> *Sad when he held the harp.*
>
> *For the great Gaels of Ireland*
> *Are the men that God made mad,*

For all their wars are merry,
And all their songs are sad.

He kept the Roman order,
He made the Christian sign;
But his eyes grew often blind and bright,
And the sea that rose in the rocks at night
Rose to his head like wine.

He made the sign of the cross of God,
He knew the Roman prayer,
But he had unreason in his heart
Because of the gods that were.

Even they that walked on the high cliffs,
High as the clouds were then,
Gods of unbearable beauty,
That broke the hearts of men."

Teagan met Seamus's eye. It was perfectly clear by his expression that this was the part of the story he felt *she* fit. Finn might think she was unbearably beautiful, but she wasn't a god *or* a heartbreaker. Everyone else in the room was held transfixed by Mr. Wylltson's voice:

"And whether in seat or saddle,
Whether with frown or smile,
Whether at feast or fight was he,

He heard the noise of a nameless sea
On an undiscovered isle."

"I hear that," Aiden whispered. "It's inside me all the time."

"We all hear it, pratie." Mamieo put her hand on his shoulder. "And isn't that nameless sea the waters the Almighty parted when he set the worlds in place? It rushes and roars in the darkness all around Mag Mell."

"What happened to Colan?" Aiden asked.

Mr. Wylltson hesitated.

"Dad, what happened to him?"

"He died bravely in the battle. It's just a poem, son."

"Was he awesome?"

"Extremely. Because of Colan, Alfred won the war."

"Alfred won the war," Aiden said, and then nodded. "Colan's part was the Irish story. He couldn't have a happy ending. Not the kind he *wanted*. Thanks, Dad."

"Son?" Mr. Wylltson asked as Aiden walked away. "Are you sad?"

"I'm just thinking about Mom," Aiden said as he sat down and picked up his Popsicle sticks. "She used to help me make really good traps. But we didn't have a trap to stop the shadow. It just came."

"Speaking of traps, what was Doirich up to? Why did the stone children close the gate?" Finn asked. "It makes no sense."

"They didn't close it," Teagan said. "Raynor did. He stepped aside and let the fire of creation through."

Raynor nodded.

"*You* burned up our park?" Mr. Wylltson demanded. "Raynor, why? Those trees were older than the library!"

"Because of what Doirich was sending out into Chicago. They weren't stone children, John. They were constructs molded from the ashes of those who died the last time they walked this earth. You call them plague and pestilence, and they last stepped into Ireland in the year 683."

"The children's plague!" Mamieo crossed herself. "Lord preserve us."

"If I had let them weep their ashes into the air, people"— the angel pointedly avoided looking at Aiden—"would have started dying."

"Don't worry, Raynor." Aiden's head was down again. "I already know I'm in an Irish story. I'm going to be awesome like Colan so Tea can win the war. Then I'll go see Mom."

NINE

TEAGAN took a step toward her brother, but Finn reached him first. He knelt beside Aiden's chair.

"You're not going to have to fight like Colan, boyo. Just let me handle it. I'm Irish enough for the both of us."

"Nope." Aiden looked up, and there were tears on his lashes. "I've got to help Teagan. That's why I need to make traps."

Mr. Wylltson put his hand on Finn's shoulder. Finn nodded, let John Wylltson take his place, and came back to Tea's side.

"Traps? I'm not following you, son," Mr. Wylltson said.

"They're to keep Lennie safe when I'm not here anymore. He's scared. I shouldn't have sung him my song." The contraption in Aiden's hands came apart, sending rubber bands and Popsicle sticks flying everywhere.

"Song?" Seamus asked, but Mamieo shushed him.

"When did the song start?" Raynor asked, pulling a rubber band from his hair.

"After Tea went to school. After she came back from Mag Mell."

"God, I hate war," Raynor said.

The tilt. The ripples Teagan had felt when she'd thrown the knife at Isabeau had spread farther than the walls of the cafeteria. They'd reached Aiden.

The stench of burning rubber filled the room.

"Crap," Finn said, snatching the remains of a rubber band from the hot burner where the teakettle had been.

"Language, Mr. Mac Cumhaill," John Wylltson said.

"Apologies, John." Finn tossed the remains of the rubber band in the sink and ran water over it, then pushed the kitchen window open to let the smoke out while Teagan started to pick up the rest of the mess.

Mr. Wylltson pursed his lips. "Son, are *you* scared because of the song you're hearing?"

"No," Aiden said fiercely. Another tear trembled on his eyelashes. This one rolled down his cheek, and he wiped it away. "I'm *not* scared. Good guys don't get scared. They're awesome. The traps are to keep Lennie safe. Lennie and Lucy."

"But not you?" Mr. Wylltson asked. Aiden shook his head. "Good guys get scared sometimes, and do you know what they do then?"

"Tell their sidekick, then go to the base to make plans," Aiden said. "That's why I sang my song to Lennie. He crossed his heart, hoped to die he wouldn't tell anybody. Then we hid under my bed and made more traps, but it didn't help." Raynor held out his hand, and Teagan dropped the Popsicle sticks she had gathered into it.

Gil had pulled himself up by his fingertips to peer through

the open window. Finn pointed threateningly, and he dropped back out of sight.

"Aiden," Mr. Wylltson said. "Last night, when your sister was going to the park, she had a scary song. And you changed it, didn't you?"

"Song?" Seamus asked again.

"Shhh," Teagan said.

"I've been trying to change this song, too, but I'm not *big* enough," Aiden said. "I want to talk to Zoë. Because it's important."

"She'll be here on Monday for your appointment," Mr. Wylltson said. "Can you wait until then? Or do you want to call her now?"

Teagan's eyes went to Finn. He gave a tiny shake of his head.

The night before, they'd seen Zoë Giordano, Aiden's state-appointed therapist, rocking a dying baby phooka on her lap in Mag Mell. Apparently she'd been lost in the dream Mag Mell casts over those without second sight, believing the baby was a client and that she was on the job. There had been no way to bring Zoë out with them. No way to save her.

"I need to talk to her *now*," Aiden insisted.

Mr. Wylltson opened a drawer and rooted through the papers. "Ha!" He held up the card she had given them on her last visit.

Teagan handed her father the phone.

"Is she there?" Aiden asked after his father dialed.

Mr. Wylltson shook his head. "Hi, Ms. Giordano. This is John Wylltson. My son needs to talk to you. Could you call back as soon as you get this message?" He handed the phone back to Tea, and she hung it up.

Aiden put his hands to his head, as if he thought it might explode.

Mr. Wylltson tipped his own head, studying his son. "How about this. Would you let me keep your song for you for a little while?"

"You can't do that," Aiden said. "People's songs are *stuck* to them."

Teagan was suddenly aware of Seamus, leaning against the wall. Watching with the strangest look on his face.

"How do you know I can't?" Mr. Wylltson asked. "I sing the monsters away before you go to sleep, don't I?"

"Dad. You always said those aren't real. You said it was a game."

"Ah, but I sang the shadow men away in Mag Mell. And I didn't let them come into the park. Just ask Raynor."

The angel nodded. "It's true. His song kept them away until I could do my job."

"Being awesome is hard work, son," Mr. Wylltson said. "You're going to need to focus on that if you're going to help your sister. Just whisper the name of the song in my ear." Mr. Wylltson squatted down beside him. "And I'll try to keep it stuck to me instead."

"You can't, Dad. Then bad things would happen to you."

"What if I promise to give it back? I'll just keep it until you have time to talk to Zoë."

The phone rang, and Teagan answered.

"Hi, Teagan." The therapist sounded out of breath. "Sorry I didn't pick up earlier. I was in the garden with mud all over my hands. Is Aiden there?"

Finn's eyebrows went up as Teagan handed the phone to her brother. Mr. Wylltson had once wandered in and out of Mag Mell on his own—he'd thought he'd taken a nap in the park, but he'd lost four hours. Zoë must have wandered out of Mag Mell while everyone was distracted. Just walked out past them and gone about her business unaware, while the shadows gathered and the gateway burned.

Aiden turned his back to them all and pressed the phone to his ear.

"Zoë," he whispered, "I need you. I'm hearing a bad song." He listened, his curly head nodding. He looked over his shoulder at his father. "Yeah. He wants to take it . . . Okay. See ya." He handed the phone back to Teagan. "Zoë said she'll come see me tomorrow after school. She said it was okay if you wanted to take the song."

"Good," Mr. Wylltson said. "Let's try it."

Aiden hesitated. "Promise you won't tell *anybody?* Because I don't want them to cry like Lennie."

"Cross my heart." Mr. Wylltson did so as he spoke. "And hope to die."

Aiden leaned forward, his lips almost against his father's ear, and whispered. Mr. Wylltson closed his eyes, then stood up and nodded solemnly.

He started humming, so softly Teagan couldn't catch the tune, then pretended to snatch something out of the air. "Got it," he said. "You walk over there"—he pointed at Teagan—"and see if it follows you."

Aiden walked across the room, and his eyes widened.

"You did it! It stayed with you."

"Well!" Mr. Wylltson looked very pleased with himself. "I guess you never know what you can do until you try. I hope you learned something today, son."

Aiden nodded. "Rubber bands smell worse than cabbage when you cook them."

"No," Mr. Wylltson said. "That you can ask for help when things scare you."

"Yeah." Aiden looked up at him, suddenly serious again. "Good guys keep their promises, right?"

"And we're good guys," Mr. Wylltson agreed. "Good guys also clean up their messes before they go play." Her brother smiled for the first time since Teagan had come home.

"Tea already did."

"Now you owe me," Teagan said.

"Okay," Aiden agreed. "Can I go to Lennie's? Mrs. Santini is going to ask me to stay for dinner."

"Are you psychic as well as musical and militaristic?" Seamus asked.

"No." Aiden gave him a disgusted look. "Lennie's mom always asks me to stay for dinner. She thinks I'm huggable."

"Sophia Santini is a good soul," Mr. Wylltson said to Seamus, then turned back to Aiden. "But I don't think that you should leave this house."

"He is in no more danger at the moment than he was yesterday or the day before," Mamieo said. "Not yet. Sure, there are *cat-sídhe* in the alleys, *sluagh* in the sewers, and cars on the street. But there always have been."

"What about the Dump Dogs?" Mr. Wylltson asked. "They're new."

"The man has a point, Mamieo," Finn said.

"I'll walk him across the street, then, if you'll allow it, John Paul. Maybe take the *lhiannon-sídhe* with me for a look around. We'll peep in nooks and crannies, and see if there's anyplace Mag Mell might be drawn to."

"All right," Mr. Wylltson agreed. "So long as you understand that you cannot come back by yourself, Aiden. You have to wait for someone to come and get you. I don't want you and Lennie playing outside, either."

"Can I take my light saber? We're not allowed to make traps at Lennie's house."

"Yes, you may take your light saber, but ask Sophia if it's all right to use it in her house before you two start swinging it around."

Aiden pulled open the door to the maid's stairs and forgot to close it behind him as he ran up to get his light saber from its holder over his bed. Lucy had abandoned watching at the window and did one last reconnaissance of the room before she followed him up the stairs.

"So ... you're keeping ... a song ... for him?" Seamus asked. "I don't understand."

"I'm not surprised," Mr. Wylltson said. "I'm a dad. The job description boggles even me sometimes."

"Ah," Seamus said. "That is one subject I don't know much about."

"One of those things you learn by doing," Mr. Wylltson assured him. "All it takes is loving them more than you can imagine."

Aiden's voice echoed through the laundry chute—"*Aiden Is the Hero*," his own made-up lyric over the *Star Wars* theme.

"No, I meant *songs*," Seamus said.

"The boyo has the gift of music," Mamieo explained, taking the sugar bowl from the counter. "In Mag Mell, he can make things happen by singing. Here ... he hears the songs over people. Stay a bit and you'll likely see for yourself."

"I don't think he should," Finn said. "He's not prepared for it, Mamieo. All hell is going to break loose, if not today then sometime soon. He's safer away from here."

"I'll survive. Other people stumble into misfortune. McGillahees stumble into good luck. This is my story, after all."

"Is it, then?" Finn asked. "That's the McGillahee touch you were talking about?"

"Yes," Seamus said. "Things I do just have the tendency to turn out well. So, I will survive." He pointed at Teagan. "And she will, too. The angel will, of course. You, I'm not too sure about, Finn. But I'll do what I can."

"Is this about your dream?" Mamieo asked. "The one with the motorbike?"

"Yes," Seamus said.

Finn's eyebrows went up. "And a lawyer's going to survive what's coming? *A lawyer?* Don't tell me you've ever done anything like this, McGillahee. Because I won't believe you."

"Of course I've never done anything like this before. I've been in school. But I'm going to be very, very good at it."

"How can you possibly know that, man?"

"It's simple." Seamus smiled. "I'm good at everything."

"Oh, *God*." Raynor rolled his eyes toward heaven. "If you *had* to send me to the Irish, couldn't you have left the Scots out of it?"

TEN

THE song echoing down the laundry chute in Aiden's sweet soprano changed to a lyric about a shark's teeth and a body on a sidewalk oozing life. The upbeat rhythm belied the bloody words.

Mr. Wylltson frowned. "'Mack the Knife'? Who on earth—"

The kitchen door opened and Abby came in, followed by Leo, who was carrying two heavy white plastic sacks.

"Leo," Seamus guessed. "Leo Gagliano."

"Do I know you?" Leo asked.

"I've heard of you." Seamus took one of the sacks from him. "I'm Seamus McGillahee, legal counsel to the Mac Cumhaills."

"Are you trying to put someone's eyes out?" Abby asked.

"What?"

"I'm bad-fashion intolerant," Abby explained. "It's like that glutes intolerance people get?"

"Gluten," Teagan corrected automatically. "Glutes are the muscles in your buttocks."

"Whatever," Abby said. "Intolerance gives you cramps, right? That jacket's giving me eye cramps." She put her hand to her temple. "And a headache."

"We finally have something in common, Gabby," Finn said. "The man gives me a headache as well."

Aiden jumped out of the maid's stair. He had put on one of his dad's white T-shirts for a Jedi tunic, and his light saber hung from a rope belt.

"Hey, Choirboy." Abby took her hand from her head. "What's with the glow sword?"

"I'm going to Lennie's," Aiden told her. "We might have to fight bad guys."

"Hey, you tell cousin Lennie that if any bad guys show up, he should give me a call," Leo said. "That's what family's for."

"And how would you deal with them?" Seamus asked.

"The same way I dealt with the last one," Leo said. "You have a problem with that?"

"The Scottish and Italian boys are all yours, John Paul." Mamieo took Aiden's hand. "I'll just see Aiden safe across the street before I take my walk."

"Mine?" Mr. Wylltson said. "Why are they mine?"

"Because you're a man of peace, and a father besides. Me— I'm about to start knocking heads together." Mamieo paused at the kitchen door. "And there'd better be fortune cookies left for us when we get back."

"Leo," Mr. Wylltson said, "we appreciate the takeout. It was very thoughtful of you. Seamus, why don't you take off your coat and stay for dinner?"

"Maybe he doesn't like Chinese food," Finn suggested. Teagan thought he sounded a little too hopeful.

"It's Sun Wah's," Leo said. "Everybody likes Sun Wah's."

"That's true," Seamus said. "I love their roast duck."

"Yeah? Well, I didn't bring any duck. We've got braised chicken with straw mushrooms, though."

Abby took a stack of plates out of the cabinet. "The guy in the corner is Raynor, Leo."

"The one who loaned me the truck?" Leo went over and shook the angel's hand. "Would you be interested in selling it?" Leo circled Raynor, looking him up and down. "So, Abby says you're an angel."

Raynor sighed.

"I'd be onto you, even if Abby didn't tell me anything."

"How?" Seamus asked.

"I drive limos for a living. I know the streets, the flow. But when I'm driving that truck, it's like Father Gordon blessed it or something. I need a green light, I get a green light. I need a parking space, I find one. This is Chicago, right? That's unnatural."

"Brynhild is outside?" Raynor asked.

"Who?" Leo asked.

"My truck. Her name is Brynhild."

"Is that right? She's parked right in front of the house. How's that for a miracle?"

Raynor was on his way out of the room before Leo had even finished speaking.

"I guess he's really not selling." Leo pointed at the food.

"Dinner's compliments of Uncle Vito, by the way. He'd really like to know how you made the bodies disappear, Tea."

"Don't worry," Abby cut in, handing Teagan a pair of chopsticks. "It's not like, 'You eat our Chinese food, you owe us.' Vito's not like that. He's just trying to be nice because he knows you didn't talk, either. You want spareribs with honey, Mr. Wylltson?" She started loading them on a plate before he could answer.

"How does he know that they didn't talk, Abigail?" Mr. Wylltson asked as she handed him the food.

Leo smiled. "I said *some* of Chicago's Finest think the Gaglianos are evil. They'll be calling you back in, Tea—you and Finn. Vito just wants to be sure we're all on the same page."

"What page is that?" Finn asked, taking a piece of sweet and sour pork.

"The one where everybody's lips stay zipped," Leo said. "I'd personally appreciate it if you didn't mention that I put a knife in the teacher's back. I'm trying to get into school, and that's the kind of thing you don't want on your application. So"—he looked at the door Raynor had gone through—"you keep our secrets, we keep yours."

"You're applying to college?" Finn asked.

"No, Dumpster Boy," Abby said. "He's applying to Hogwash like in the movie. He's going to be a wizard."

"I believe you mean Hogwarts, Abigail," Mr. Wylltson said. "You really should read the books."

"Speaking of books." Leo glanced at his watch. "I'm late to my math tutor."

"You go," Abby said. "I've totally got this."

Leo zipped his fingers over his lips, made pistol fingers at Tea and Finn, and left.

"What was *that* all about?" Teagan asked.

"You mean the math? Zia Sophia," Abby said. "She convinced Leo to go back to school. He's going to be an accountant. And now you're going to sit down, eat, and tell me all about it," Abby said, handing Teagan a plate.

"I can't eat and talk at the same time," Teagan protested.

"Fine. Eat, then talk."

"You go ahead," Finn said. "I'll take a plate out to Gil. I expect he'll want some of everything." Abby loaded a plate for the phooka.

"Are you going to sit down?" Teagan asked as Abby leaned on the table. "There's an empty chair."

"No, I like standing."

Teagan took a few bites, then started the story with Kyle showing up at school. She'd reached the part where they were captured by the phooka band when Finn came back in.

He helped himself to a plate and ate quietly while Teagan went on, telling how they'd been captured by the phooka and chased by the Cú Faoil. About the Samhain Fair, the phooka baiting, and finding Fear Doirich and Mab. When she got to what happened when they returned to the school, Seamus leaned forward, suddenly more intent.

"Okay," Abby said when Teagan was done. "We got a few problems. First, the girl Kyle had by the hair. She's an eyewitness, but I think she was probably too scared to really see what was going on. Angel—our Michelangelo, I mean—is working on that one already, talking to her about what happened so she'll remember it the way she needs to. Second, the cops will have Finn's fingerprints on Leo's knife. And then there's the goo."

"Goo?" Seamus asked.

"A few months ago, Kyle exploded right here in this room, same as Isabeau," Abby said. "We thought someone had murdered Tea, right? So we called the cops. They took samples, you know? If they compare it to the stuff they scrape off the ceiling in the cafeteria . . . it's got to be the same, right?"

"I would think it would be similar, at least," Seamus agreed.

"You know who the prime suspect was then?" Abby went on. "Finn, that's who. So there's files. He's going to be in them. And Tea will be in them. But files get mislaid. It can happen."

"*Can* happen?" Seamus asked.

"Will happen." Abby took out her phone. "It's like Leo said. Uncle Vito doesn't want us involved. And anything that involves Tea involves me. Can you think of anything else? Anything at all?"

"Security cameras at the school."

"Jing took care of it."

Mr. Wylltson shook his head. "Jinghez Khan?"

"He's always in the computers anyway," Abby said. "All the cameras were digital, so it wasn't a problem." She tapped in a speed-dial number, then turned away from the table as she talked. "Leo, are you there yet? Whatever. Here's what we need to take care of." She rattled through the list of problems she'd just discussed. "Oh, and get somebody to watch the clubs. Any really good-looking people show up wearing shades at night, we need to know about it."

"The clubs." Seamus thumped the table. "I hadn't even thought of that. When the Highborn start drifting in from Ireland—and they will, if they have no easier way—that's where they'll go first. I think I love you."

"Yeah? Well, I don't like lawyers." Abby slid her phone shut. "Plus, you're too old for me. Your lips are totally starting to wrinkle."

Seamus blinked. Teagan realized that she was staring at his lips. Even Mr. Wylltson couldn't help looking.

"May I use your restroom?" Seamus asked. Mr. Wylltson gave him directions, and Seamus left the kitchen.

"He's going to the bathroom for a wrinkle check." Abby laughed. "Maybe I can sell him some of that new Luscious Lip Crème we've got at Smash Pad. You think school's going to be closed tomorrow, Tea? I'm not feeling so good."

"That's what happens when you stay up all night watching over your best friend's body," Teagan said. "You're going to get some wrinkles yourself."

"That would be the least of my worries." Abby leaned closer and whispered loudly. "Tea, does my butt look ... lopsided?" She turned around quickly, then turned back.

"No," Teagan said. "Why? Do you have something in your back pocket?"

"Oh, my god!" She reached behind her. "Does it *look* like I have something in my pocket? I got to go check on something."

"Bathroom's taken," Finn said. "Better go upstairs."

ELEVEN

ABBY didn't come back until Teagan was almost finished eating.

"I need to talk to you," she rasped. "It's important."

"Why are you speaking like that?" Finn asked.

Abby glared at him. "I'm *whispering*. Hello? That means it's private."

Finn leaned back. "You're calling that a whisper? It's more like a screech."

"Whatever," Abby said, smacking the side of her head as if she were trying to clear water from her ear. "Let's take a walk, Tea. I can't talk here."

"Abby, I really, really need a shower," Teagan said. "And clean clothes. If you could wait—"

"I can't," Abby interrupted. "You need me, and where am I? I'm there. This time I need you. Seriously."

"All right."

"You could bring Aiden home," Mr. Wylltson suggested. "Since you're going out."

"I've got to be going as well." Seamus headed for the door. "I've got some ideas of my own about where to look. I'll see myself out."

"You forgot your coat," Finn called after him.

"Keep it," Seamus said. "I'm changing professions. It doesn't suit a gentleman adventurer."

"Gentleman adventurer?" Finn shook his head. "The man gave us a ride home, and now he's an adventurer?"

Abby dragged Teagan after Seamus toward the front door. Outside, they ran into Mamieo, Thomas, Roisin, and Grendal coming up the steps.

"Find anything?" Seamus asked.

"Not so much as a *cat-sídhe* whisker. Though it took a bit longer than I anticipated." Mamieo glared at Roisin. Teagan looked from Roisin to Thomas.

"How did you persuade her to go along?"

"He murmured sweet things in her ear," Mamieo said.

"*Mocha latte*," Roisin said, happily holding up a cup from the coffee shop down the street. "Yum!"

"The girl went into the coffee shop and wouldn't leave without her latte." Mamieo looked even more annoyed. "You'd think she didn't want us to find those Dumpster Dogs."

"She just doesn't understand the gravity of the situation," Thomas said. "Is there any food left? I'm starving."

"Plenty." Abby stepped aside to let them pass. She changed the subject abruptly. "Seamus isn't planning on moving in, is he?" Abby asked. "Because if you stuff one more person into the house, I swear it's going to explode."

"Abby ... maybe you should move back to your mom's. You've seen what the goblins are like now. Things are going to get crazy around here. Really bad."

"I can't right now," Abby said. "My older sister moved back and took over my room. Besides, you heard what I told Isabeau. She messes with you, she messes with me. Tea ... are we in instant danger?"

"I don't think so," Teagan said.

"Good. I have a problem."

"The handsome and lovable Jinghez Khan?" Teagan guessed.

"You're crazy smart, Tea, but you're not the first person I'd ask about guy problems, you know? It's this." Abby pulled up her hair and turned so that Teagan could see the side of her neck.

"You've got a *hickey!*"

"I already said it's not a guy problem. Look closer."

Teagan turned Abby so that the light fell on it. Tiny lines, capillary-thin and blood-red, made a road-map pattern inside the bruise.

"You need to go to the doctor."

"I already went to the doctor," Abby said. "Where do you think I've been all afternoon? He thought the same thing you did, at first—asked me if I'd ever had a hickey before. I told him something bit me, but it wasn't a boy."

"Something bit you?"

"One of your polterbeasts." Abby let her hair down. "It has to have been the sprite, right? I think I sat on her."

"You *think* you sat on her?"

"I just sat down, and *wham!* I swear, nothing ever hurt that bad. It itches like crazy now, and I'm seeing, like, spots and flashes."

"What did you tell the doctor?"

"That an Irish spider bit my . . . *glute.*"

"An Irish spider? And he believed that?"

"He did after he examined the bite. Well, not the Irish part." Abby shrugged. "He said it was a brown recluse, gave me some prescriptions. Antibioticals and itch creams. Said to call him if it got worse."

"Has it gotten worse?"

Abby pulled up her shirt and Teagan saw two more blotches on her side.

"They started showing up closer to the bite. The one on my neck appeared a little while ago. But the ringing in my ears went away. That's good, right?"

"We're going back to talk to Thomas right now." Teagan grabbed Abby's arm and dragged her back up the steps. "He's got to know something about sprite bites."

"You think I've got one of those viruses like Kyle gave you, Tea? It could turn me into a bug or something?"

"You're probably having an allergic reaction. Dad had a weird rash once when they'd given him fentanyl."

"A rash like this one?"

"There were geometric lines, anyway," Teagan said. "Though his were bigger."

"Thank God," Abby said. "Allergic reaction. That's what

the doctor said, too. But I just wanted to make sure. Because I was seeing these flashes, you know?"

"I thought you said spots." Teagan pushed the door open. "Thomas?" She called. "Could we speak to you for a moment, please?"

"Don't tell him where—"

Thomas stepped onto the porch.

"Are sprite bites dangerous?" Teagan asked.

"It depends on who is bitten," Thomas said. "They can be deadly."

"Abby." Teagan pulled up Abby's hair and pointed at the rash.

"When?" Thomas asked.

"Last night," Abby said. "When I first saw the tree man, I sat down kind of fast."

"And you waited all this time to tell anybody? You're tough. I hear sprite bites hurt like the fires of Hades."

"Teagan needed me," Abby said. "And I wouldn't know about Hades. I'm Catholic."

"When you saw the tree man last night? So, that's at least twelve hours ago. The good news is you would have died already if you were going to."

"What's the bad news?"

"Sprite bites take a long time to heal."

"That's it?"

"That's it," Thomas confirmed. "Where did it—"

"Thank you, Thomas," Teagan said. "We're going to go get Aiden now."

"So I'm going to live," Abby said as they crossed the street. "Until my mother gets a look at these. Everyone knows I've sworn off guys. She's been telling people I'm going to be a nun. Zia!" Abby shouted as she opened the Santinis' front door. "It's me!"

Aiden was on the couch, clutching his light saber. His stocking feet were pulled up, and Lennie was sweeping dirt that had spilled from a fallen planter into a pile. Lucy was hiding in Aiden's hair. Her eyes flashed lavender at Teagan.

The Santini house usually smelled of rosemary and thyme, and sounded like a Rossini opera. Today, there was a distinct bouquet of boy sneakers, and *Raiders of the Lost Ark* blared from the TV.

Teagan's throat was suddenly tight. If Fear Doirich wanted to torture Aiden, all he had to do was hurt the Santinis. There was nowhere as wonderful to Aiden as the Santini house, no one outside his family he loved quite so much. And they would be completely helpless against the Sídhe. They couldn't see the creatures any more than Abby could.

Mrs. Santini stood in the kitchen door with her fists on her wide hips. She blew a piece of hair out of her face.

"Hey, Ab-by," Lennie said. "You're in trouuuuu-ble."

"*I'm* in trouble? I didn't knock over that plant."

"It was Lennie," Aiden said. "He whipped it. But we already got yelled at."

"Your mother called me, Abigail." Mrs. Santini shook her head.

"Yeah?" Abby said warily. "Why'd she do that?"

"Because Mrs. Nitti called her. She said you were seeing the doctor for a social disease."

"Mrs. Nitti wasn't there. I'd have seen her in the waiting room."

"She was in the exam room next door. Those walls are like paper. You think she wouldn't recognize your voice? She babysat you, Abigail. Your mother's heart is broken."

"I'm having an allergic reaction," Abby said.

"To a boy?"

"Zia, I swear to you—" Abby began, but Mrs. Santini strode across the floor and grabbed her face—making her mouth pucker like a fish—and looked into her eyes.

"You don't have to swear, Abigail. I know a liar when I see a liar, and"—she narrowed her eyes—"you're not lying. Lola Nitti is a sow."

"Thank you, Zia." Abby scratched at her side.

"Let me see this reaction."

Abby flipped up her hair.

"Your mother's hysterical," Mrs. Santini said, examining the mark. "One of your cousins said something about a boy at school. A soccer player."

"The Turtles tattle," Lennie said.

"If they'd had a sister, they'd have learned not to talk so much." Mrs. Santini tsked. "That does look like a love bite."

"What's a love bite?" Aiden asked.

"Never you mind, Aiden. Finish up. Then you can watch your movie. We're going to the kitchen to do girl stuff."

Lennie made a gagging noise, but his mother ignored him.

"I'm making soup." She waved at piles of chopped vegetables on the counter. "The Johnsons down the street are sick and they have those three kids. Who's going to feed them?" She pulled open a drawer, took out two large spoons and put them in the freezer, then turned back to Abby.

"So, there's no love bite. What about the boy at school?"

Abby flushed red.

"I want you to know something, Abby. Before I married Lennie's father? There was a boy. I really loved him, but I let him go. Why? My mama didn't approve." She took a deep breath. "I know what it's like, growing up with the family. If you have any problems, you come to me." She paused and looked over at Tea.

"You can come too, Teagan. Your young man saved my Lennie, and I haven't forgotten it. I never forget. Listen. I know something is going on at your house since your mother died."

Teagan opened her mouth, but Mrs. Santini raised her hand.

"You think I don't see what's happening in front of my nose? It's a neighborhood. We notice people coming and going. Shut doors and closed blinds? Your dad comes running down the street in his slippers and robe, just after the park catches fire? The neighbors are talking, but I told them to shut their face. Then he meets me in the street. Why? Because he don't want me coming over right now, that's why. Whatever's going on, you can count on us. We've been neighbors since before you were born."

"Thank you, Mrs. Santini," Teagan said.

"Especially if you need any cooking done. Or laundry."

"Laundry?"

"You're wearing your pajamas," Mrs. Santini said. "What? You're too busy to wash clothes over there? I saw you drive past in that lawyer's van, then come walking down the street. You wore that to school."

"I've been really, really . . ." What could she say? Busy? No one had done her laundry for her since her mother had died. She felt the tears start, but swallowed them down.

"So that's how it is." Mrs. Santini nodded wisely. "Sit, Abigail. Sit."

Abby perched halfway on a kitchen stool and Teagan settled on another. Mrs. Santini took one of the spoons out of the freezer and pressed the back of it to the mark on Abby's neck. "You hold it there. We'll change spoons when it gets warm."

"This will make it go away?"

"It works with hickeys," Mrs. Santini said. "It's best if they're really fresh. Rashes, I don't know about. We'll see. What's the problem with your young man, Abigail? Why can't you take him home?"

"He's not Italian," Abby said.

"So, he's what? Greek? Irish?"

"No, Zia. I mean *really* not Italian. His name is Jinghez Khan. His mom's black and his dad's Chinese." Abby's chin went up. "He's gorgeous. And smart, Zia. He's really smart."

Mrs. Santini went back to her soup. "Does this gorgeous non-Italian have a job?"

"He started a consulting company last year when he was a junior," Abby said. "Computers."

"That's good." Mrs. Santini nodded. "Like Bill Gates. Does he have a car?"

"A Boss 302 Laguna Seca."

"That new Mustang?"

"Red on black. He bought it two months ago."

"So, he has a lot of girls?"

Abby looked at Teagan for help, but she could only shrug. Jing was dating the cheerleaders. Serially, not simultaneously. But still.

Mrs. Santini stopped chopping. "This guy's some kind of Casanova? Tell me the truth, Tea."

"He says he's biding time with other girls because Abby won't date him," Teagan said. It hadn't sounded quite so ridiculous when Jing said it. *Biding time until she's mine.*

Mrs. Santini checked the spoon on Abby's neck. "See, that's too warm now. You have to keep it cold." She traded it for the other one from the freezer. "You bring him around here. I'll let you know what I think. Now, Teagan, you got yourself under control?"

Teagan nodded.

"You're having problems with Finn?"

"Not problems, exactly," Teagan said. "I love him. I just don't know if we want the same things."

"What does he want?"

"Me." Teagan sighed. "A peaceful life. Maybe to beat someone up once in a while. I think that's just a habit."

Mrs. Santini nodded. "He's a good boy. And what do you want? Your education, right?"

"Right." And to keep her brother alive, and her friends safe. To stop what was happening in Mag Mell.

"Wait a minute!" Abby said. "How come you're all, 'Does Jing have a job?' What about Finn?"

"What are you going to do with your life, Abigail?"

"I'm going to be an artist."

"So, you need someone with money."

"A famous artist."

"Yeah? So was van Gogh. He died poor. Teagan's going to be a *scientist*. She can afford a harem if she wants one. Listen." She pulled up another stool. "All this Hollywood stuff about love? They never show you what happens after people fall into bed. I'll tell you what happens. They start thinking with their brains again, that's what. About what they want in life, about their dreams. No matter how much you want that boy right now, you think about that before you do something that's going to take away those dreams.

"You could be a poor, single artist. You could be a rich, married artist. But if you marry a boy who's so full of himself that there's no room for your dreams, you're gonna wish you were dead." She wiped her hands on her apron, then put the spoon away and examined Abby's neck. "Lennie!" she bellowed. "Bring me my comb and hand mirror from the bathroom!"

Lennie appeared with the comb and mirror, and Aiden peeked around the door as Mrs. Santini took them.

"What are you doing?" Aiden asked.

Lennie shook his head. "Never ask girls that. Never, never, never." They went back to the living room, and Teagan could hear them both making gagging noises. Mrs. Santini took the comb and brushed it gently over Abby's neck.

"What are you doing now, Zia?"

"Spreading out the last of the blood. You know I'm not saying anything against this Jing. I'm just saying take your time, Abby."

Teagan nodded.

"You find someone who believes in you as much as you believe in him—that's the one you want. If I had a daughter, I'd tell her the same thing." Mrs. Santini put the comb down, ran a clean dishcloth under warm water, wrung it out, then held it to Abby's neck.

"Zia," Abby said, "what was your dream?"

"I wanted to own a restaurant," Mrs. Santini said. "I love feeding people. I got Lennie to think of now, though. I love him, but he's not like other boys. I'm never going to be done raising him." She tossed the rag in the sink. "Dreams are breakable. Sometimes you can't help what happens. I had my Lennie; he needed someone to love him." She looked up and caught Teagan studying her.

"So, I dreamed a new dream. Life does that to all of us. You think your father wanted to go on raising you without your mom? No. Stuff happens, and you gather up your love and dream a new dream."

Abby reached for the hand mirror.

"What do you think?" Mrs. Santini asked.

Teagan walked over to look, too.

"That's amazing," Abby said. The bruised look was gone, leaving only the darker lines. It didn't look anything like a hickey anymore.

"You put a little foundation on that," Mrs. Santini said. "It'll cover it right up."

"Where did you learn to do that, Zia?"

"Your mama showed me."

"My mother?" Abby said.

"We went to Catholic school, but that didn't make us saints. We weren't supposed to be dating, but…" She shrugged. "Sometimes we did. Your mother more than most of us. You know why she's screaming at you, Abby? Because she loves you, that's why. She knows what it's like to wake up in a cage because she made stupid choices. Nobody likes a cage, even if they build it themselves. She don't want that for you."

"Thank you, Zia," Abby said. "You know I love her too, right?"

Mrs. Santini patted her cheek. "I know it. Now get Aiden out of here before those boys break something else. And bring that young man over, Abby. If I like him, I'll see what I can do. And Teagan"—she rounded on her—"I meant what I said. I know something's going on." She glared at Abby. "More than anybody's telling me. We're neighbors. We can help."

"Not this time, Mrs. Santini," Teagan said. "In fact … I think you and Lennie should go to New York. Visit your sister."

"Abby?" Mrs. Santini glanced at her niece in alarm. "What's really going on?"

"It's like a war between Families," Abby explained. "Only with demons."

"Demons." Mrs. Santini sat back. "Leo said something like that, too."

"The Wylltsons are different, Zia," Abby said. "Really different."

"I live beside them for twenty years, and you're telling *me* they're different? I know they're different."

"The thing is," Teagan said, "they're coming for us. They will hurt you if you try to help us, Mrs. Santini. Please ... please take Lennie to New York."

"You let me worry about Lennie. I can protect him. And my neighborhood, too."

"No, you can't," Teagan said. "You really can't. You don't understand how bad these creatures can be."

"Creatures? I thought you said demons."

"Whatever," Abby said. "Ask Leo. He'll tell you all about them. I think Tea's right, Zia. Maybe you should go for a little while."

"And leave my neighbors and my niece to the demon creatures? You girls go home," Mrs. Santini said. "And don't worry so much. I'll take precautions. Nobody's hurting my Lennie. Go on now."

Abby motioned toward the door.

"Aiden, are you ready?" Teagan asked when she reached the living room.

"Yep." He had both of his hands behind his back.

"What are you holding?"

"A whip," Aiden said, pulling it out. "I traded Lennie my light saber." Lennie gripped the light saber as if he was afraid Teagan was going to take it away. The object in Aiden's hands was a real whip, and the braided leather showed quite a lot of wear.

"A whip won't make a very good night-light," Teagan said.

Aiden tugged on her sleeve until she leaned down where he could whisper.

"Lennie needs my light saber. He doesn't have a night-light, and he's scared. *I've* got Lucy and Finn."

She couldn't argue with that. "You'll have to talk to Dad about it."

Aiden nodded, and Lennie turned the light saber on.

"You're going to run it out of batteries," Mrs. Santini said from the kitchen door. "I'm not buying you new batteries every day, Lennie. You just turn that off until bedtime."

"Okay." Lennie clicked it off. "It's a good night-light to keep me safe?"

"Yep," Aiden said. "Bye, Mrs. Santini! Bye, Lennie!"

He held Teagan's hand and skipped down the steps to the sidewalk. Abby's phone chirped as they reached the street. Teagan could tell from the look on Abby's face that something was terribly wrong.

"Oh, no." Abby's hand went to her mouth and she nodded, then turned away from Aiden.

"What's wrong with Abby?" Aiden asked.

"We'll find out later. Why don't you go show Dad the whip and ask if you can keep it?" Teagan crossed the street and let him through the front door, then waited on the steps for Abby.

"That was Rafe," Abby said. "They found Molly . . . She's dead. She was in the river, close to where they found the lunch lady. Kyle did something to her. It happened while Rafe was locked up, so he's not a suspect anymore."

"I'm going to go take a shower," Teagan said. "And change into clean pajamas before I go to bed."

"Tea . . . are you okay?"

Teagan just shook her head. She left Abby to tell the others and went upstairs. She didn't want to see anyone, talk to anyone. Especially not Finn. Because he'd been right—there had been no hope for Molly.

Teagan sat down to take off her shoes and noticed the dark brown stain all up the side of the left one. Kyle's blood. Somehow, when she'd knelt beside him, she'd gotten one foot in his blood. If her pajamas hadn't been a little too long, everyone would have seen it. She'd worn it all day: to the police station, while she ate dinner . . . at the Santinis'.

She kicked off her shoe and started to strip off the sock, but the blood had soaked all the way through, sticking the fabric to her skin as it dried. She peeled it off and threw it in the corner, then quickly stripped and turned on the shower. She stepped in, but her knees felt too weak to hold her up. She found herself sitting on the floor of the shower while the water rained down around her.

Molly Geltz, who'd been brilliant at math and awkward in life, and who'd thought it would be totally cool to be a freegan. Dead. Teagan took a washcloth and scrubbed her ankle, crying gently at first, and then harder.

Molly had died because she was Teagan's friend. A friend like Mrs. Santini and Lennie, who was probably turning on his toy light saber right now to keep the bad guys away.

Teagan hung her head and let the water run down her back as she sobbed. She watched it spin before it went down the drain, mixing with Kyle's blood and her tears, flowing through the dark sewers until it mingled at last with Molly's blood in the dark river.

PART II: ROSEHILL

R OSEHILL Cemetery. It was the first thing Teagan thought of when she woke the next morning. She needed to go to Rosehill.

She had to blink twice before she could focus on her phone. *That's what happens when you cry yourself to sleep.* But she was done crying. She had to be. She was Highborn, and she had to start thinking like one. Thinking like her mother.

Rosehill Cemetery had a secret—a wildlife preserve along the back fence. It was exactly the kind of place Mag Mell would reach out to. And if the trees were connecting with Mag Mell, she'd have to stop them before anything else came out. Before they could kill any more girls like Molly. She could take Maggot Cat's body there to bury it, and listen to the trees.

Abby, Roisin, and Grendal had already left the room before she woke up.

She found the *cat-sídhe* in the hallway outside the bathroom door.

"Roisin's in there?" Teagan asked.

"And Abby." Grendal pulled his tail protectively around

himself. Abby tripped over him at least once a day, no matter how hard he tried to stay out of her way.

"Does Roisin understand about the Dump Dogs now?"

The *cat-sídhe* sighed. "She doesn't want to."

Teagan echoed his sigh. She remembered the dinner in Yggdrasil's hall that she had witnessed. Compared to the creatures that had come to that party, the Dump Dogs looked friendly. Roisin had been locked up in that hall for most of her life, and she'd had very few friends.

"They have been a long time," Grendal said. "What are they doing?"

Teagan considered. "Was Roisin crying this morning?"

Grendal nodded.

"Abby's Magnificent Morning Makeover, then. She's fixing Roisin's face." Being a friend. Which was just what Roisin needed. She was fascinated by all things Abby. Her shoes, her clothes, her phone.

"Fixing?"

"Abby's own kind of magic. Better life through beauty products and girl talk."

"Tea?" Abby pulled the door open. "I thought I heard your voice." Roisin leaned around her to peer into the hall, and Grendal screamed.

Roisin's hair was pulled back tightly in a ponytail, and her face was coated in white cream. Her eyes were still ringed red from crying, but the corners of her mouth turned up. Abby's magic was working, even if the Highborn girl couldn't understand a word she said.

"It's all right," Teagan assured the *cat-sídhe*. "It washes off."

"Oh, Grendal's here?" Abby looked in the direction where she thought he might be. "Tell Roisin I'm taking her to Smash Pad, okay?" she said loudly, as if Grendal were deaf instead of invisible. She looked back at Teagan. "School's closed."

Of course it was. The police would still be trying to figure out what had happened even if they had no bodies. Only they did. They had a body.

"You okay?" Abby's brows drew together. "The newspaper said they were going to have volunteer grief counselors at school on Monday."

Ms. Skinner would be the first in line to volunteer, no doubt. She had advised Teagan's parents not to take Finn in, had wielded her social worker's power like a weapon to try to have Aiden removed from the home, and she would know that Teagan was involved with the events at the school yesterday. She'd want every grisly detail. Teagan didn't even want to think about having to talk to the woman.

"You want to come in here with us?" Abby offered.

"No," Teagan said. "I want some breakfast." And to get going.

"You got an appetite. That's good. How about coming with us to Smash Pad? I'm taking Thomas and Roisin. Highborn are totally into shopping, right? Plus, I got a toenail-painting appointment scheduled this afternoon. I want someone there who can see things I can't, if you know what I mean."

"That's a really good idea," Teagan said.

"I know, right?" Abby sounded pleased. "Plus, I can get

those two some decent clothes and probably some modeling jobs. So, you're coming?"

"I need to sort some things out," Teagan said. "Maybe spend some time alone."

Abby's phone dinged. "Timer. We'll talk later, right? I need to take care of Roisin. Get this off her face."

"We'll talk."

When Teagan got downstairs, Aiden was standing in the middle of the living room. His new whip stretched like a snake from his hand to the floor. A dead snake. Mr. Wylltson, still in pajamas and robe, was looking as perplexed as his son.

"I'm better," Teagan said before he could ask. "What's wrong, Aiden?"

"It doesn't work." Aiden swung the whip like a lasso, and Mr. Wylltson leaned out of the way.

"I think you need more wrist action, son. Let me try again."

"Where's Finn?" Teagan asked as her father took the whip. She'd talk to her dad about Rosehill after she'd had breakfast.

"Patrolling," Aiden said. "Finn and Thomas are patrolling for bad guys."

"Good." She should be with them. Hunting. Teagan followed her nose into the kitchen instead. Mamieo was at the stove, cooking eggs on one burner and frying bacon on another. Raynor was sitting at the table with a cup of coffee and a crisp, new *Car and Driver* magazine.

"Good morning," Teagan said.

"It might be," said Mamieo, pointing her spatula at the

window, "if not for that." Gil was clinging to the windowsill, his nose pressed against the glass, his tufted ears alert. She could see Joe behind him, trudging slowly across the yard.

"I'm used to a quiet cup of tea and a peaceful talk with the Almighty in the morning," the old woman went on. "Not being ogled like a pasty pie."

Raynor didn't look the least bit interested in the phooka.

"I'll talk to Gil," Teagan said. The phooka boy dropped from the window and ran over as soon as she stepped out the door. Beyond him, Joe reached the wall, turned, and started trudging in the other direction.

"What's that smell?" Gil asked. "It woke me up."

"Bacon. Why are you hanging on the window? I thought Mamieo was the Scary One. I thought you wanted to hide from her."

"That was before *bacon*." Gil said the word reverently. "I just wanted to look at it."

Teagan decided against telling him what bacon was made of. He had been horrified by a plate of pigs' feet at a butcher's stall in Mag Mell. Tea still didn't understand how a creature who was mostly human—all but his ears and trotter—would shudder at the sight of severed pig parts, yet want to hunt and eat small children.

"Mamieo thinks you're looking at her. She isn't used to phookas."

"Can she get used to them? I want to come in." He looked around the empty yard, and his ears swiveled in opposite directions. "Phookas shouldn't walk without a pack."

"If you promise not to eat children, you can come inside and have breakfast with the rest of us."

"You won't bend me?" Gil asked. "*Make* me promise I won't eat children?"

"I haven't decided yet." Tea knew he wouldn't have a chance with a whole houseful of people watching him. And he'd already promised not to leave the yard. But if he hunted children after he went back to Mag Mell, wouldn't it be her fault?

Gil wagged his ears thoughtfully. "Does *Finn* promise?"

"Mac Cumhaills don't eat children."

Gil considered this. "What if he wanted to really, really bad?"

"No," Teagan said. "Finn knows that eating children is wrong. He wouldn't do it."

"He could take one bite to see what they tasted like, then let them go. That would only be a little wrong."

"Wrong is wrong. Are you going to promise?"

Gil looked longingly at the kitchen window.

"No."

"Your choice. If you don't, you can't come in and eat bacon with the rest of us."

"My choice," the phooka agreed sadly. "No bacon. No friends. Just Joe."

The tree man stopped, stared at his feet for a moment, and then started pacing again. She wished she could help him. If he had been an animal, she would have had some idea of what to do for his burns.

"Joe?" Teagan said. "What are you doing?"

"Just planning." He squatted slowly and pressed his hand to the grass. "It might storm tonight. The soil needs to be ready."

The air did smell like rain. The humidity was bringing up the smells of leaves and loam. She had a sudden flash of the joy that had filled her when she'd run with the phooka pack through the forests of the night. Hunting. She needed to find Finn and head to Rosehill, to the wild. The desire to run—maybe even to howl—was almost overpowering.

"Do you need any help?" she managed instead.

The tree man glanced at her, then did a double take. "I'll get it done. You have enough to worry about, Highborn."

"Stay away from the window, Gil," Teagan instructed. "No more peeking at Mamieo."

She stepped inside, shut the door, and leaned against it.

"Trying to keep the phooka out?" Raynor asked.

"No, he'll behave. He wasn't looking at you, Mamieo. Just the food. He's really hungry." Phookas were always really hungry.

"That's all? I'll put a plate out the back door for him," Mamieo said. "Tell John Paul and the rest that I didn't cook this breakfast to let it go cold. If they don't get in here, I'll feed it all to the phooka."

"Mamieo says breakfast is ready," Teagan announced to Aiden and her dad as she passed back through the living room and started up the stairs. Abby and Roisin were already coming down, Grendal hopping behind them.

She felt the electric tickle of Finn behind her. He must have come from the hallway. She turned.

Standing on the first step, she was almost eye level with him. He'd carried the irresistible smell of the morning in with him, caught in his hair and clothes.

"Good morning, beautiful," he said. Teagan leaned closer.

"What are you doing?" Aiden asked.

Sniffing Finn. How weird would *that* sound? She changed the sniff into a kiss on the cheek, but Finn turned just before her lips met his face. She felt a shock as their lips touched, the *wild* inside her exploding like fireworks, rocketing through her to Finn. He swayed, and she managed to get her arms around him before his knees gave way.

"Wa," he gasped. "Could you steer me toward the couch, girl?"

"Oh, my god," Abby said from behind her. "*The couch? Are you going to let them do that in your living room, Mr. Wylltson?*"

"Do what?" Finn flushed red. "Oh. I just meant . . . I need to sit down. The girl's that good a kisser."

Thomas and Mr. Wylltson were staring. Aiden's mouth was hanging open.

"What were you doing, Tea?" Abby asked. "You totally lunged at him."

"I did not lunge." *I was just sniffing him.* That would sound worse than lunging. "I just . . . caught him."

"Then why don't you let him go?"

Because he wasn't steady on his feet yet. Finn's electronics had gone haywire.

"Well played." Thomas winked at Finn and grinned at Teagan. "And well caught."

Finn groped for the banister. "I'm telling you I never meant to kiss her. Not in front of her da, that is—"

"Unhand the young man, Teagan, and step away," Mr. Wylltson said. "You are befuddling him."

"By that"—Finn found the banister and Teagan let go and backed up a stair—"I did not mean that I intended to carry on behind your back. This whole thing isn't what it looks like"— his eyes lifted to Teagan—"is it?"

"Absolutely not. No."

"I didn't think so," Finn said. "Mr. Wylltson, I'm not completely sure what just happened. I don't quite understand—"

"I was married to her mother," Mr. Wylltson said. "Which is to say, I understand completely. But there is a vast distance between understanding and approval. A great gulf, Mr. Mac Cumhaill. And she is my daughter."

"Dad." Teagan came down to stand beside Finn. "*I* kissed *him.*"

"Very true." Mr. Wylltson folded his arms. "And we will have a discussion about the relative virtues of spontaneity and restraint. But Finn was the one who offered to complete a quest."

"I did what, now?"

"On the way home from the police station, you said, in reference to being the right man for my daughter, 'Tell me what I have to do to prove it to you. I'll do it.'"

"And?" Finn looked a little uneasy.

"And that's a quest. It appeals to the romantic in me. As I

can tell that my daughter ... erm ... likes you a lot, I'm going to give you a chance to prove that you are the man for her."

"And how will I do that?"

"Get a job?" Abby suggested.

"This is between Mr. Mac Cumhaill and myself, Abigail," Mr. Wylltson said. "We'll discuss it later, Finn. You and I will have another talk as well, Tea."

"If you're done with the canoodling, leering, and lecturing"—Mamieo had stepped into the room, and her glare took them all in—"I sent the girl to call you all to breakfast."

"What's canoodling?" Aiden asked as he followed Tea toward the kitchen. "Is it kissing?"

THIRTEEN

I PUT a plate of food out the door for the beastie," Mamieo said. "Joe didn't want any."

Mr. Wylltson pulled out a chair for Teagan, and pointed Finn to one on the opposite side of the table. Raynor looked up from his magazine as Thomas sat down.

The *lhiannon-sídhe* held a chair out for Roisin, and then nodded at Raynor as he sat himself down. The angel blinked, and focused on his breakfast plate. Which was progress. As far as Teagan knew, it was the first time they had willingly shared a room, much less a table, since Raynor had fled Mag Mell with Saint Patrick.

Aiden coiled his whip and tried to hang it over his arm like Indiana Jones in the movie poster, but it just fell off.

"Leave it, pratie," Mamieo said. "Eat your breakfast, or we'll be late for school."

"Wait, wait, wait," Mr. Wylltson said. "I'm not sure he should be going, Mamieo, considering the circumstances—"

"We don't know when the creatures will be coming." Mamieo finished filling the kettle and put it on the stove. "I

151

learned a long time ago that you can spend your life waiting for the end of the world, or you can spend it living. Schooling and" —she winked at Teagan—"canoodling, marrying, and such."

Roisin asked Thomas a question in Gaelic, and he grinned at Finn as he answered in the same language.

"There will be no marrying in the immediate future," Mr. Wylltson said. "And we will not be discussing this as a family at the table."

"But I want to know what—" Aiden began.

"Son," Mr. Wylltson said warningly.

"Lennie told me a joke about how porky pines hug and kiss—"

"Son," Mr. Wylltson said again.

"Rats." Aiden started eating his eggs.

Teagan gave her father a grateful look. If they never mentioned it as a family again, it would be too soon. And it would be nice if kissing Finn did not always turn out to be a spectator sport. Especially if it knocked him off his feet.

"Moving on to the subject of school," Mr. Wylltson said.

"I'll be right there in the classroom watching over the boy, John Paul." Aiden's teacher had been threatening to quit before Mamieo had volunteered as a classroom aide. When Aiden was unhappy, he sang under his breath. And his songs bent every other child in the room. He was part Highborn, too, after all.

"But what would you do if a goblin did show up, Mamieo?" Mr. Wylltson asked. "Creatures like the ones that came after Teagan at her school?"

"I could run," Aiden said. "But I wouldn't, because then

it would get you. You're really *old*, Mamieo. I can tell by the wrinkles."

"Old age is the one thing you can't outrun, pratie, and that's a fact," Mamieo said. "But these wrinkles should give you confidence. They mean I know a thing or two about staying alive."

Aiden took her hand in both of his and examined it. He stretched the skin smooth. "Do wrinkles hurt?"

"Only when I look in the mirror."

"If it makes you feel any better, John," Raynor said, looking up from his food, "I can get to Aiden's school if they need me. I'm not tied to the park anymore."

Finn shook his head. "The place is some distance from here, not just across the street."

"It's my job to be in the right place at the right time," Raynor said. "Angels take shortcuts."

"Shortcuts?" Mr. Wylltson asked.

"Through space and time."

Shortcuts through space and time ... Teagan had heard that before. "Are you talking about traversable wormholes?"

"Where did you hear that term?" Raynor asked.

"I had a math teacher who was obsessed with the idea of space travel. Mr. Macy. He thought we would someday use wormholes to reach the stars."

Abby leaned toward Finn. "Tea's totally out of your league." She was still whispering way too loudly. "You know that, right? She's almost the smartest person at school."

Almost? Teagan smiled. *Jing.* Of course, Abby was thinking of Jinghez Khan.

"Shouldn't Tea be the one to decide that, Abigail?" Mr. Wylltson asked mildly.

"But you just said you didn't approve!"

"I said *understanding is far from approval*. They need time to sort this out."

Teagan tried not to squirm. Her father had said something like that before. Walk together a little longer before you decide about something like marriage, he'd said, just before offering to throw Finn out of the house. She wasn't sure she liked the look her father was giving Finn now. It was far too . . . *thoughtful*.

"You let me worry about giving them that time, Abigail."

Abby frowned.

"So, wormholes." Teagan was desperate to change the subject. "Raynor. You were explaining wormholes?"

"I wasn't explaining them," the angel said. "I just asked how you knew the term."

"I don't like worms," Aiden said. The eyeless creatures that insisted on crawling out of the lawn and shriveling on the sidewalk after each spring rain had made Aiden's *very scary* list years ago. Lennie had told him that's where ramen noodles came from. Aiden hadn't touched worms or ramen since.

"There are no worms in wormholes," Teagan said. "It's just a name."

"Are you *sure?*" Aiden looked around the room as if a wormhole might open and a worm pop out at any minute. "Do you *know* what's in them?"

"I don't," Teagan admitted.

"But I do." Raynor had finished his breakfast. "And in this case, your sister is right. There is nothing wiggly or damp in a wormhole. Traveling through them is like riding a locomotive down a roller-coaster track faster than the speed of light. God, I love my job."

"You can go anywhere in the world … *instantly?*" Mr. Wylltson asked.

"Anywhere in this universe," Raynor corrected. "Almost instantly. Traveling between worlds of the multiverse by wormhole is more complicated. Mag Mell, for instance, is closer than the room next door, and farther than the most distant galaxy in this corner of creation. It takes a little more time and a lot more energy to get there."

Mamieo put her fists on her hips. "Are you telling us you could crawl through one of these holes into Mag Mell and take care of Fear Doirich, then?"

"I would if I could. After Pádraig visited, Fear sang a shell around her."

"A force-field shell?" Aiden asked. "Like Violet in *The Incredibles?*"

"More like an egg," the angel explained. "Gases and water vapor can pass through eggshells, but larger things cannot."

"Hellhounds came out after us," Aiden said. "They were way bigger than you."

"Looks can be deceiving," Raynor said mildly. Thomas nodded.

"What an incredibly useful trait," Mr. Wylltson said.

"That's angels," Raynor said wryly. "Useful, useful, useful."

"So, the boyo is going to school, then?"

"I think so."

"Rats," Aiden said again.

"I've packed a lunch already."

"Did you pack Lucy's lunch?" Aiden asked.

"I'm not touching Lucy's lunch," Mamieo said.

"Me, neither," Aiden shuddered. "It wiggles."

"I'll get it." Teagan put her plate in the sink, then opened the fridge. Lucy came out of her cup when Teagan took out the mealworms. She shook some into a Ziploc bag, and then held them up for the sprite to examine.

Lucy chirped plaintively, and Teagan shook in a few more. When the sprite was satisfied with the size of her lunch, Teagan sealed the bag.

"You're not to put those crawly things in with our food," Mamieo said. "The boyo can carry them in his kit."

"My kit!" Aiden jumped up. "Excuse me, please!" Mr. Wylltson nodded, and Aiden started for the maid's stair.

"Put the whip away while you're up there," Mr. Wylltson said, then turned to Raynor. "How will you know if they need help? Do guardian angels just *know?*"

"Of course not," Raynor said. "We're not psychic or omnipresent, just really fast. They'll have to call."

"You mean on the phone?" Finn's eyebrows went up.

Raynor nodded.

"Mamieo doesn't have one."

"I'll loan you mine, Mamieo." Mr. Wylltson unplugged it from the charger on the counter and handed it to her.

Mamieo held it at arm's length and squinted. "I can't see the wee buttons."

"What have you done with your glasses this time?" Finn asked. "I thought you had a chain for them."

"My mother has the same trouble," Abby said. "Let me have it a minute." She punched in some numbers. "There. Now the Wylltsons' home number is on speed dial. Just push the top button on the right."

Mamieo tried it twice, and looked immensely pleased with herself when it worked both times.

Aiden came back with the black plastic purse he used as a kit.

"Dad," Teagan began as she checked the purse for weapons, "I need to take the dead *cat-sídhe* we found on the sidewalk to the woods at Rosehill and bury him. I'd like to look around the lake and the wildlife preserve, too."

"For a gateway to Mag Mell," Mr. Wylltson said.

Teagan nodded.

"I don't want you going there alone."

She confiscated a giant rubber band from Aiden's kit and dropped in the bag of mealworms. "Raynor needs to stay near the phone. I was hoping Finn would come with me."

"Of course he'll be going with you." Mamieo turned to look at Finn, who had put his plate in the sink and was digging through the kitchen utensil drawer. "What are you looking for, boyo?"

"A knife," Finn said. "I don't like to be without one."

"Without one? Where's the one you had from your da?"

"I've lost it, Mamieo."

"*Lost it?* That blade was forged by a tinker with the blood of the Fir Bolg in his veins. It's been in the family for generations, *and you lost it?*"

Finn pulled out a serrated knife with a black plastic handle. "Don't go on about it. I feel bad enough, but it couldn't be helped. When I stabbed it into Tea—"

"You stabbed my daughter?" John Wylltson asked incredulously. "And now you want me to let you go out with her?"

"He had to, Dad," Teagan said quickly. "It was the only way home."

Finn met John Wylltson's eye. "The world was disappearing around me—expanding like a balloon, so fast it was tearing us apart. I needed both hands to hold on to her. There's nothing in heaven or earth that could make me let go of her, not so long as she wants me to hold on. I know I'm . . ." he was clearly searching for a word and coming up blank.

"Unemployed?" Abby suggested.

"Unconventional," Mr. Wylltson offered.

"*Unconventional.*" Finn looked relieved. "That'll do. But I will never harm Teagan or let harm come to her, John Wylltson. Where there are gateways, there are goblins. Will you allow your daughter to go goblin hunting with me?"

Mr. Wylltson leaned against the back of the chair and studied Finn. "Nothing," he said finally, "can prepare a man for a question like that."

Teagan held up her cell phone. "Fully charged. Angel on speed dial. I really do need to take a look at those woods."

"I suppose if she must go looking for goblins in the woods, I'm glad you will go with her. But . . . a steak knife?"

"Oh, for heaven's sake!" Mamieo said. "Turn your backs, all of you. You, too, Raynor, angel or no."

"Why—" Finn began, but she fixed her birdlike glare on him. "Yes, Mamieo." He turned to look out the window with Teagan.

Joe was standing still in the far corner of the yard, his head down. Gil had finished the food Mamieo had given him. He ran full tilt at the cinder-block wall at the back of the yard, then straight up it, pushing off with his legs when he reached head-height to drop in a backflip to the ground before he ran the other way.

"Wow," Teagan said.

"*Pfft*," Finn said. "It's not as hard as it looks."

Gil saw them watching and did it again.

"You're not thinking of taking the phooka with us, are you?" Finn asked. "Oh, you are. This isn't Mag Mell, girl. Think what would happen if we lost him."

"Think what might happen if we leave him. Joe is falling asleep. And if Raynor does have to go somewhere—"

"You can turn around now," Mamieo said primly. When they did, she was holding a delicate dagger in her hand.

"And where'd you get that?" Finn asked.

"I had it about me," Mamieo said primly. "I don't go about unarmed, boyo."

"It took you three full minutes to find the thing," Finn pointed out.

"Was it lost?" Aiden asked.

Mamieo flushed. "It was not. But I've got the phone now, so I don't need it."

"Thank the Almighty." Finn took the knife and slipped it into his boot, then pulled Seamus's jacket off the back of the chair.

Mamieo flushed. "I'll expect it back as soon as you're home. And if you lose the wee blade—"

"I'll be careful, Mamieo," Finn assured her.

"You're not going to wear that jacket," Teagan said.

"No worries." Finn shook the ugly thing. "We'll be needing something to wrap the body in."

"You two be careful," Mr. Wylltson said. "And no—"

"Canoodling!" Aiden crowed.

"As if we'd have a chance with the phooka along," Finn said.

"Oh, you're taking the invisible boy?" Mr. Wyllton asked. "Excellent."

Teagan pulled the back door shut behind her, then had to open it again to hand in the plate Gil had left on the porch.

"You must admit, they are a cute couple," Thomas was saying to Abby. She pulled the door firmly shut again.

Joe was still standing in the corner. Either he was snoring or he'd been colonized by bees.

"We're going hunting, Gil," Teagan said. "Do you want to go with us?"

"Hunting god?" Gil asked, and ran at the wall again.

"Hunting a door into Mag Mell," Finn said when the phooka landed his flip. "So we can toss you through."

"I'll go with Teagan." Gil gave her name almost as much reverence as he'd given *bacon*.

"Stop that," Finn said.

"Teagan, Teagan, *Teagan*," Gil said.

Finn caught his arm. "You're going to have to stay with us."

"I promise to stay with *Teagan*." Gil pulled his arm away. "As long as we hunt. If I find a door I might go home, and Teagan might go with me."

"She will not be going with you," Finn said.

"She likes to run." Gil peeked sideways at her. "Highborn like to hunt with phookas."

Teagan had a sudden urge to drop everything, go to Mrs. Santini's, and take her up on her offer of advice. *How exactly do you discourage a phooka, Mrs. Santini? Yes, unfortunately I did tell him I love him as a friend.* . . . Instead, she lifted the lid of the plastic trunk where Mr. Wylltson kept his garden tools.

Should have kept his garden tools. There was a dead black widow spider, an old pair of work gloves, half a bag of fertilizer, and a hand trowel.

"It'll do," Finn said when she held it up. "We wouldn't want to carry a bundled body and shovel through the streets anyway." She shoved the trowel in her pocket.

Finn handed her the jacket when they reached the back gate.

"I might need my hands free, if we meet any uglies," he said, pushing the gate open.

Finn didn't have to point out where he had hidden Maggot Cat's body. Four *cat-sídhe* were gathered around a garbage can a few yard lengths down the alley. They'd pushed it over; trash bags and Maggot Cat's body had spilled out.

Teagan winced. "You put him in a trash can?"

IGHT on top," Finn said defensively. "It had a lid to keep the creatures off of him. This lot is good news, though."

"Good news?"

"They wouldn't be here if the Dump Dogs were about, would they?"

The *cat-sídhe* looked up as Teagan moved closer. Their fur was oily, as if they'd spent too much time hiding under cars. A few of them had patches of scaly-looking bare skin as well, and the one kneeling by Maggot Cat had a weeping sore on its back.

They appeared to have been collecting trash. One held a section of a blue silk lei, another a yellow cheeseburger wrapper. Grendal would have approved of that. He was obsessed with cheeseburger wrappers. It took Teagan a moment to figure out that what looked like yellow straw clutched in the third *cat-sídhe*'s fist was the hair of a severed Barbie head. She couldn't tell what the fourth *cat-sídhe* carried; it was small and he held it protectively in both hands as he backed away from them.

The one who had been kneeling by Maggot Cat stood up but held its ground. "Go away," it commanded.

"Yessss, go away," the others chorused.

Teagan felt her muscles start to obey, then shook it off. She was sure she would always feel the tug of their voices, but she'd learned to ignore them. It just took practice.

Gil had apparently never practiced. He ran three steps back toward the house, then turned and ran back to her, caught between the *cat-sídhe*'s command and his own promise to stay with Teagan.

"Help!" he squeaked as he ran another circle. "Help me, Teagan!" Finn caught his shirt, but the *cat-sídhe* had gone quiet.

"Teagan," the brave one said.

"Oops." Gil put his hand and his trotter over his mouth.

Finn started toward the creatures, but Teagan caught *his* shirt.

"Wait," she said. "They haven't done anything."

"Yet," he said, but he stayed put.

"Tea-gan," the brave one said again.

"Tea-gan," the others repeated. A fifth *cat-sídhe* she hadn't noticed jumped up on a box on the other side of the alley and stood like a meerkat trying get a better view.

"And I thought old Maggot was hideous," Finn said. The cat on the box was bald, except for a tuft of long ginger hair on the top of its head and a few random hairs on its tail. Its skin was a sickly gray-pink and as wrinkled as a Donskoy's. It even had the roll of hanging fat around its lower belly that was the earmark of the Donskoy breed.

One of the four in the group in front of them turned to

see what they were talking about. It yowled when it saw the pink cat. The four *cat-sídhe* dropped their trash treasures and picked up rocks, sticks, and cans to throw at the creature. At least two rocks bounced off its bare hide before it gave up and dropped behind the box.

"Pleasant bunch," Finn said. "Have you had enough of them yet?"

"I have." Gil started forward. "Get sticks and hit them."

"No." Teagan caught his arm.

"He ssssaid you would help him, Tea-gan," the brave *cat-sídhe* said.

"He came too late. But I might not have been able to help him even if he'd come sooner. I'm sorry."

"Who said she would help?" Finn let go of Gil. "Maggot Cat?"

The *cat-sídhe* looked at one another.

"*Bill Bailey,*" the brave one said.

"Bill Bailey," Teagan repeated. There was something familiar about that. "What's *your* name?"

"*Pfft.* They're not telling you *their* names, girl," Finn said.

"No," Gil agreed. "They won't tell you anything."

The cat hissed at Finn and ignored Gil, looking directly at Teagan.

"Peter, Augustus, Alonzo, or James," it said, pointing at each of his companions and then himself.

Teagan blinked. Kyle may have changed her DNA, but nothing could change the fact that she'd been raised by a librarian and an artist. The creature was quoting T. S. Eliot in a context that almost made sense.

"'*All of them sensible everyday names*,'" she said, finishing the couplet.

The *cat-sídhe* murmured to one another, peering at her and nodding as if she'd given them a secret password.

"What is this about, then?" Finn asked.

"'The Naming of Cats,'" Teagan said. "From T. S. Eliot's *Old Possum's Book of Practical Cats*." Apparently aging detectives were not the only creatures who could find glimpses of what once was, memories wrapped up in story or dream. "Dad liked the book. Mom liked the Andrew Lloyd Webber musical, *Cats*, better."

"You're kidding me."

"No. She took me five times."

"I meant about the poem thing. You're telling me the beasties read books?"

"Maybe not," Teagan said. "But they might have seen the stage production."

"Is your fever back, girl?" Finn pressed his palm to her forehead. "You think the creatures gathered here to discuss the theater?"

The one called Peter looked up at him. "Break a leg," he said.

Teagan laughed, and Finn gave her a horrified look.

"It's a joke," Teagan explained. "He made a theater joke. It means good luck."

"Marrroww," Alonzo yowled, saliva spilling from his jaw and hanging in long strands. "Maaaarrowwww!"

Finn pointed at him but looked at Teagan, his eyebrows up.

"Or maybe not," Teagan said. "It might mean something else to them."

"And you think they told you their real names, just for the asking?"

"Of course not. The cats in the poem have three names—common names, special names, and secret names that only the cat knows. But they are being friendly. They gave me sensible, everyday names to use."

"Don't go making friendly back at them," Finn warned.

"They started it." Teagan took Seamus's coat from him.

"Make her stop," Gil said. "She shouldn't talk to *twisty cats!*"

"She talks to phookas," Finn countered. "There's no stopping the girl."

Teagan walked slowly toward the dead *cat-sídhe*. The others backed away, but not too far. One crept closer as she knelt and covered the body with the hideous coat.

"Pretty," the *cat-sídhe* whispered.

"Are you kidding me?" Finn asked. Teagan ignored him and focused on the cats.

"We were going to bury *Bill Bailey*," she said. "But this isn't a good place. We were taking him to the woods."

The *cat-sídhe* reached out carefully and touched the checkered fabric.

"Warrrm?" one of the others asked in a whisper. It was never cold in Mag Mell.

"Yessss," Peter whispered back, then looked up Teagan. "Yessss. Bury him."

Teagan tucked the coat around the body carefully so that

she wouldn't have to touch it as she picked him up. He smelled worse than he had the day before, but wrapping him tightly in the coat seemed to help.

"Let me carry that." Finn made a face. "I won't have you traipsing through the streets like a goblin undertaker. It's unbecoming."

The entire *cat-sídhe* chorus went wild when he reached for Bill Bailey's body.

"I'll carry him," Teagan said. "He's not heavy."

Finn led the way up the alley. He was clearly watching for the Dump Dogs.

Teagan walked beside Gil, who kept stopping to gape at everything around him, from Dumpsters to fire escapes on the backs of buildings. The *cat-sídhe* came in a group behind them, like a funeral procession, each clutching his piece of trash. She caught a glimpse of the hairless cat dodging from Dumpster to trash pile behind them.

"Go by the park," Teagan suggested as they reached the mouth of the alley. "It's on the way." Before she stepped out onto the sidewalk, she tucked the coat under her arm so that it would look less like she was carrying the body of a child.

Gil took one step onto the pavement, then jumped back into the alley as a car went past.

"What was that?"

"Just a car," Finn said. "You came this way yesterday, didn't you? You must have seen cars."

"Joe carried me. I was hiding my eyes. What do *cars* eat?"

"Not phookas," Finn said. "Just stay close to us. You'll be fine."

"No." Gil shrank back. "I can't walk by those things."

"I'm walking by them." Teagan started down the sidewalk.

Gil followed her, emitting a horrible squeaking sound that made even the *cat-sídhe* edge away from him.

"Stop," Finn said. "Stop, Tea. He can't learn to do it himself if you force him."

Teagan flushed. She'd forgotten that Gil had promised to stay with her. She walked back until the phooka boy could duck into the alley again.

"I can't do it." The phooka swallowed a sob. "I can't! The ground is *wrong!*"

"Here." Finn reached out his hand. "You pulled me through the water, boyo. I can pull you down the street. If you want." Gil grabbed Finn's hand like a drowning man and squeezed his eyes shut.

"That's good," Finn said as Gil stepped out of the alley once more.

Gil put his shoulders back and his ears up. He took an experimental step, then hopped up and clicked his bare heels together.

"No cavorting," Finn said. "Just walk."

Gil froze as the next car passed.

"See?" Finn said. "You're fine. As soon as you're comfortable, you just let go."

"You won't let go of me?" Gil asked, as if the pavement

would sweep him off his feet and away if Finn did. "Not until I let go first?"

"I won't," Finn assured him. "Now, come on."

Gil stopped jumping at every car, but stared at the Halloween decorations on lawns and in windows. He gaped open-mouthed at a group of ghosts hung by their necks in a tree.

"This place is scary," he said, still looking at them over his shoulder as Finn pulled him away.

"Scary? You're from Mag Mell, for cats' sake. Everything there has teeth, claws, or a bad attitude."

Gil just shook his head.

They were almost to the library when Teagan saw the white minivan coming toward them.

"Don't tell me that's McGillahee," Finn said.

"It's him, all right." Teagan looked for a doorway to dodge into but there wasn't one.

"Now would be a good time to get comfortable and let go," Finn suggested.

"No," Gil said. "I'm still afraid."

Seamus did a U-turn, managing to run his front tire over the curb as he did so.

"You have a little bromance going on there, Mac Cumhaill?" he asked through the open window when he pulled up beside them. Gil edged behind Finn and peeked around him at the minivan.

"Just helping a friend, McGillahee. Ever had one?"

"Not like that," Seamus said. "Detective Deneux wants to talk to you."

"Both of us?" Teagan asked.

"Just Finn. I told her that if she kept it friendly, I'd bring him down to the station for a chitchat."

"You told her that?"

"I'm trying to help you out here. Show what a helpful, upstanding citizen you are. Is that a body wrapped in my coat?"

"It is," Finn said. "I suppose I could go talk to the cops after I'm done disposing of it."

"I'd offer you a ride"—Seamus glanced from the bundle in Teagan's arms to the *cat-sídhe* behind her—"but I just cleaned my van. I'll wait for you. Could you remind me how to get to your house from here?"

"Take the next right," Teagan said. "Then a left and a left."

"Going down to chat with the police." Finn shook his head as the minivan eased down the street. "I once worried that I might complicate your life, girl. Can you imagine that? But that was before you dragged me to Mag Mell, declared war on everyone in sight, made a lot of questionable friends, and got me involved with a lawyer."

"You can't blame Seamus on me," Teagan protested. "Mamieo called him."

Finn squinted at the turn signal that had just started blinking on the back of Seamus's van. "Is he turning left?"

"Yes," Teagan said as the van disappeared. "Yes, he is."

"The anti-Aiden," Finn said. "The man's the anti-Aiden. And don't tell me he's not so bad, Tea. I'm leading a parade of *cat-sídhe* and holding hands with a phooka. I'm stretched to my limit here. I couldn't bear hearing a good word about that idiot on top of everything else. Not one."

The library was closed, the parking lot full of police cars and black SUVs. Men and women in uniform were ducking under the yellow and black crime-scene tape that was stretched across the gateway. The thick-stemmed trumpet vines that had twined through the wrought-iron fence, hiding the park from the street, were mostly burned away. The old trees that had woken when her mother's ashes were scattered among them were gone.

Teagan adjusted the bundle under her arm, then stepped closer to the iron bars. Gil whimpered, and the *cat-sídhe* started to yowl. It wasn't the ashes or the smell that was bothering them. It was the iron. Teagan could feel cold radiating from it. She hadn't come this close to the fence the day before. Not close enough to feel it. If standing this close to the fence was painful for her, it must be agony for a *cat-sídhe*.

When she'd walked without her flesh and bones, she'd had no problem carrying Finn's iron knife. It hadn't affected her—not until it had pierced her bilocating body. Finn wrapped his free hand around a fence bar, and both Teagan and Gil shuddered.

"Look at the bench, Tea," Finn whispered. "The one you left your body sleeping on." The cement that had been the bench was melted, slumped into a glassy puddle. No wonder Homeland Security was involved. It looked like a small nuclear device had gone off.

"You kids move along," an officer called.

"Raynor did *that?*" Finn asked as they walked on down the street.

Teagan looked over her shoulder. That was what her house would look like if the angel stepped aside. Gil was right. Raynor *was* scary.

FIFTEEN

TEAGAN led the way now. She'd walked to the west side of Rosehill with her parents plenty of times before Aiden was born, but when they got there, she wasn't sure she could find the path. The chainlink fence that separated the back of the cemetery from the street was completely hidden in bushes. She was afraid someone might have mended the gap in the fence that teenagers or a rogue bird enthusiast had made, cutting and folding the chainlink back to create their own entrance into the grounds. But when she finally came across the path through the bushes, it was clearly still in use. The iron in the galvanized-steel fence wires felt like ice around her as she ducked through.

Gil whimpered, but he followed Finn through the fence, and the *cat-sídhe* came after him, scrambling through as quickly as they could, then disappearing in different directions into the woods.

"I like it," Gil said, finally releasing Finn's hand. "It smells like frog water!"

It did smell wild and boggy, but these trees were not as

old as Teagan had thought they were. They were not *awake* the way the trees in the park had been. Restless, but not awake.

"Where do we put him, then?" Finn spoke in hushed tones.

"Not this close to the path." Teagan didn't want birders to stumble across them digging a hole in a cemetery, even if all they could see was an empty checkered coat. She headed south, working her way through the thick bushes and away from the fence, and occasionally catching glimpses of the *cat-sídhe* through the brush.

There was more than the fitful slumber of trees here. Gil's ears were swiveling front to back.

"Something's scratching," he said.

Teagan stopped and closed her eyes. Yes. It *was* a scratching ... like mice behind a wall. *Like something trying to get out.* There were no old graves underfoot here, no wooden coffins ready to split and spill corruption. But it felt as if there were.

"Are you hearing something?" Finn asked.

"Not with my ears," Teagan said. "But there's something here." She could hear it more clearly when the wind managed to make its way through the trees. It wasn't the rustling of dry leaves, though; it was somehow *behind* that sound.

They found two ruts, a road of sorts that led past trash piles—boards and window frames collected from construction of some kind on the other side of the cemetery grounds. It looked like they had been hidden here out of sight for years.

Augustus stepped out of the underbrush and motioned for them to follow. The *cat-sídhe* had found a tiny clearing.

"This'll do," Finn said.

Teagan laid Bill Bailey down, and Peter, Augustus, Alonzo, and James stood over him like guards while Finn took the trowel and started to dig. It went quickly once he had cleared the top layer of grass and roots. The soil beneath was loamy and soft. Finn broke it with the trowel, and Teagan and Gil scooped it out with their hands until it was deep and wide enough for the small body.

Teagan laid the coat-wrapped *cat-sídhe* gently in the ground. Peter walked closer, edging past Finn and Gil, and dropped the flowered lei into the grave.

"Deuteronomy choose you," he said.

"Be chosen," the other cats echoed, dropping their treasures in after the lei. James, the one who had been secretively clutching his treasure, dropped in a fifty-cent piece.

"That's touching," Finn whispered. "Apart from the doll head, I mean. Was this bit in the book, then?"

"No," Teagan whispered back. "In the book, Old Deuteronomy is just a wise cat. In the play, he selected cats to be born again."

Peter walked over, reached up, and touched the back of Teagan's hand with the back of his own.

"Bill Bailey ssleeeps warrrrm. Thank you, *Teagan*."

"*Teagan*," the others repeated, and her name didn't pull at her or twist her. It felt like a blessing, a word full of every good wish.

"Stop saying her name, *beasties*," Gil shouted.

The *cat-sídhe* flattened their ears and hissed.

"Oh, so *they're* the beasties now?" Finn asked.

"We *hatessss* you, Mac Cumhaill," the cats spat. *"Keeee-yill!"*

"Of course you do," Finn said as the *cat-sídhe* stepped back, fading into the bushes.

"Keeee-yill, keeee-yill," echoed in the air for a moment, and then they were gone.

"The jacket was my idea, by the way," he called after them. "Come on, let's look around."

They moved east, making their way through the brambles until they reached the paved roads of the cemetery. Gil walked gingerly onto the tarmac, tiptoeing beside Teagan past tombs and mausoleums, reclining statues in glass boxes, and bronze children gazing forever into eternity.

"What is this place?" the phooka asked. "Is it magic?"

"It's a cemetery," Finn said. "A place for the dead."

"Why do dead people need stone houses?" Gil asked as he studied a miniature Greek temple.

"The houses are not for the dead," Finn explained. "They're for the living. It gives us something to set our eyes on. We're not ready to look straight into eternity. Not yet."

"Death, you mean?" Teagan asked.

"I've tried to get my mind around it. But I can't." He nodded toward a row of graves. "They've stepped away from us, that's all. We'll follow along someday, but until we do, the missing and the longing..." He shook his head. "The reaching out to touch someone who isn't there."

"Phookas don't have that problem." Gil bounced over a log-shaped tombstone.

"So they never grieve, do they?" Finn asked.

"No." Gil kicked an ancient stone sticking out of the grass. "Phookas don't like anybody enough to miss them."

"Stop that," Finn said. "Phookas might be heartless beasties, but that's no excuse to be disrespectful. This is where people bury"—Teagan felt the adrenaline shoot through him—"Dump Dogs."

His knife was in his hand faster than Gil could get behind him. The teens were lying on the sunny steps of a mausoleum, tangled together like models in a bad fashion shoot.

They sorted themselves out, and the girl stood up, shook, and stretched.

"No Dump Dogs buried here," she said. Her voice was throaty, hoarse.

"Not yet," Finn agreed. "But that could change."

The boys stood up beside her. *Hyenas*, Teagan thought. They moved like hyenas, more feline than canine. But they weren't focused. They were ... well fed and sleepy.

"Finn," she said softly, "they don't want a fight." Which was a good thing, because they gave her the same uneasy feeling she'd had the first time she'd seen them. If they did start something, three were too many for Finn to handle, and she didn't know how much help she or Gil could be.

The girl looked Teagan up and down.

"A sensitive? That can be fun at a party. I knew a boy like that once. One of your cousins. Mmmm." She wiggled. "He was *wonderful*. Since you know we're not here to fight ... I'm Saoirse. These are my brothers, Lollan and Bairre."

"If you're not here to fight," Finn said, "what are you here for?"

"No introductions?" Saoirse looked hurt. "We know who you are. Finn Mac Cumhaill and Teagan Wylltson. Your auntie Mab is looking for you, Tea." She leaned over to look at Gil. "Who is this cutie?"

Gil gulped and shook his head.

"What are you here for?" Finn repeated.

"To rescue a special friend of Bairre's. Roisin. We went by to see her, but there was a very scary fellow at your house."

"The angel," Gil whispered.

"You're no friends of Roisin's," Finn said.

"Thomas told you that, did he?" Bairre spoke for the first time. "Have you asked her? Do you know whether she'd rather be with him or with me? Or do you choose her friends for her now?" Teagan could feel his shift in focus. Anger. But still not enough to overcome his full belly.

Lollan turned his face toward the woods, scenting the wind, and Teagan hoped that Peter and his friends had gone back the way they had come.

"And what are you three doing here?" Bairre asked. "We've been friendly. Explained ourselves. How about you?"

"Minding business of our own," Finn said.

Lollan belched, then spat in the grass. "They put some nasty shit in the bodies here before they bury them."

"Been having breakfast, have you?" Finn asked.

"He's teasing." Saoirse smiled at Teagan. "He knows Thomas will have been filling your head with rot about us.

179

Probably gave you his big bad bird 'destroyed armies, toppled kings' speech, too."

"I believe he mentioned it," Finn said.

"You're awfully quiet for a Highborn," Lollan said to Teagan. "A little on the short and skinny side, as well."

"Let her alone, Lolly," Saoirse said. "She doesn't know you well enough to know you're teasing. Let me tell you something about *lhiannon-sídhe,* Finn. They are weak little parasites. They don't make songs or art or poetry. They just amplify the abilities of those who do have those gifts. I'm sleepy." She yawned, and Teagan had the impression of too many teeth, just as she had when the girl had grinned at them before. But the goblin wasn't lying; her body was so lethargic she almost seemed drugged. She turned back to the mausoleum.

"If you want to cut us up with your teeny little knife, you know where to find us." Lollan followed her, but Bairre hesitated.

"Tell Roisin I haven't forgotten my promise," he said.

"What promise was that?" Finn asked.

Bairre laughed. "I promised to take care of her and her cat. Tell her I haven't forgotten."

SIXTEEN

THE adrenaline didn't drain from Finn as they walked on through the cemetery.

"That's why your little friends disappeared so quickly," he said. "They knew those creatures were about."

The sound of a lawn mower starting up somewhere on the grounds made Gil grab his hand, but Finn shook him off.

"I want both hands free in case I need them."

"That's just a little engine," Teagan explained to the phooka. "It's louder than a car, but not as scary."

"Yes, it is," Gil said.

"Not as scary as the beasties we just met, then." Finn glanced back the way they had come.

Teagan turned to look, too. *Those* were the creatures Roisin was crying over? There was something about the Dump Dogs that was more frightening than any other creatures she had met aside from Mab and Fear Doirich himself. Something *wrong* about them.

She felt a ridiculous amount of relief when they reached

the towers and crenelated walls that marked the gates of Rosehill, as if the barrier could somehow keep the creatures in. Finn let Gil take his hand again as they walked down the street.

"Are we going to talk to Roisin or Thomas?" Teagan asked when they reached the street. "Or . . . both?"

"We have to talk to both of them, don't we? And Raynor as well." Finn glanced over his shoulder. "Those three mean trouble for us all."

"Roisin can't be waiting for Bairre," Teagan said. "She and Thomas are promised to each other."

"No doubt," Finn agreed. "We've heard it from the both of them. I wonder if Bairre's heard it."

"Highborn games," Gil said. "She made them *both* promise."

Teagan shook her head. Roisin wouldn't . . . would she?

"I have to give them a heads-up, at least." Teagan dialed Abby's number.

"Did you change your mind about coming with us, or what?" Abby said when she answered. "Because you could still catch the bus down."

"No," Teagan said. "I met some Highborn this morning and I need to give Thomas a heads-up." Teagan looked over her shoulder. "Thomas and Roisin both know them."

"So, is it the guy Roisin was crying over this morning?" Abby asked. "What's he like?"

"You remember that creep your sister dated before she got married?"

"The one who's serving time in the state pen, or the guy that went into pharmaceuticals?"

"The one in the state pen."

"Yeah, I remember the jerk."

"I think this guy might be worse."

"What did he do?"

What had he done? Nothing. It was just a feeling.

"Tea," Abby went on before she could answer, "you get a feeling about a guy, you trust your gut."

Teagan pulled the phone away from her ear and stared at it.

"Hello?" Abby's voice was tinny and small. "Hello?"

Teagan put it back to her ear. "How did you know—"

"I told you before. I got powers. With you, I don't even need them. Why? Because I've known you forever, that's why. You meet a guy like that, forget about giving him a second chance. You don't give him a first chance. I'll have a talk with Roisin. Sometimes smart girls do stupid things before they learn better."

"Good," Teagan said. "I need to talk to Thomas. Is he there?"

"Saoirse, Lollan, and Bairre," Thomas said after she'd explained. "I do know them. Did they say anything about me?"

"Yes."

"They lie," Thomas said. "Whatever they said, it's a lie. I have sworn that I will do no harm to your family. By commission or omission, I will do no harm. I am not one of them anymore."

"You don't think they've been eating corpses, do you?" Teagan asked after she'd put away her phone.

"If they dug up a grave, they did it without getting dirt on their clothes or under their fingernails," Finn said.

"They *were* full, though," Teagan said. "And probably full of meat they ate last night."

"How could you know what the beasties were full of and when they ate?"

"Their reactions were sluggish. Probably because they'd consumed the amino acid tryptophan, which is a precursor of serotonin"—both Finn and Gil had stopped in their tracks and were staring at her—"which is converted to melatonin, the 'darkness hormone,' which lowers the body temperature and—"

"I don't understand what you're talking about," Gil said.

"She's her father's daughter," Finn said. "The man's a librarian."

"Tryptophan comes from meat," Teagan explained. "Your body uses it to make melatonin, but only when it's dark outside. Melatonin makes you sleepy. So the Dump Dogs ate meat last night."

"Well, that's perfectly understandable, then," Finn said. "Except for the part where you could tell that by looking at them."

"I could feel it," Teagan said. "I know you feel electricity too, Finn."

"Sure. From you. When we're very close, or touching. And kissing's like"—he glanced at Gil—"something we'll discuss later. But I didn't feel a thing from the uglies back there. That's what she meant about being a sensitive, is it, then? You feel the electricity in more than just me?" He sounded a little hurt.

"Yes. But not always. When we were fighting Kyle, I knew where everybody was, even those behind me. I knew which way they were going to move a fraction of a second before they actually did it. I knew the moment the impulse left their brains."

"And this started after Kyle changed your DNA?"

"Before that, but it's more focused now. When you saw the Dump Dogs, I felt the adrenaline hit your system."

Finn considered that.

"How about when . . . other things hit my system?"

"Such as?"

"Let's say I'm about to I kiss you?"

"Yes. It's like body reading instead of mind reading."

"And can you do this through the walls? Say, when I'm sleeping in the room next door?"

"Yes," Teagan said.

"Crap." Finn ran his hand through his hair. "Well, I'll be sleeping in the yard with the phooka."

"Good," Gil said. "It's scary all alone. And cold."

Finn swatted the top of Gil's head. "I didn't say we were going to snuggle. But if you were cold, you should have told somebody. I'll find you another blanket."

"Or you could just promise not to eat children and come inside," Teagan suggested.

Gil pressed his lips together and shook his head.

Teagan shrugged. "Have it your way. Why will you sleep in the yard, Finn?"

"Because . . ." His face pinked. "Let's just say that sometimes my body's got a mind of its own. I'm not sure I want you knowing what it's thinking."

"I could always do what Aiden does." She plugged her ears. "La, la, la!"

"Will that work?"

"Probably not," Teagan admitted. "But the couch downstairs would be far enough away, and more comfortable than the yard."

"Right. It's the couch, then."

"Crap," Gil said, then put up his trotter as Finn moved to swat him again. Finn dropped his hand and shook his head instead.

"Don't go using that language around Tea."

"You did," the phooka pointed out, still hiding under his trotter. "You said 'Crap'!"

Finn's face contorted. "I set a bad example *for a phooka.*"

"I'm not offended," Teagan said. "I hear worse things at school every day."

"But your da—"

"Is old-fashioned," Teagan said.

"No." Finn shook his head. "It's more than that. John Wylltson is a thinking man. I'll discuss it with him. Oh, cr . . . ud." Teagan followed his stare.

Seamus McGillahee had managed to find the Wylltsons' house after all. His office was parked just a few doors down.

"I'll tuck Gil into the backyard, then. Tell the man I'll be in shortly."

Seamus was sitting on the couch with Mr. Wylltson. There were books spread all around them. He liked to gather his favorite authors around him like a council of wizards as he considered a problem even though he knew the books by heart. He was connecting ideas, and using the physical books like pushpins to hold them in place.

Grendal was perched on the back of the couch, scratching his chin and watching.

"Why didn't you go with Roisin, Grendal?" Teagan asked after she'd said hello to everyone.

"Nnnnnot feelingsss good," the *cat-sídhe* said.

Mr. Wylltson followed her gaze. "Oh, I didn't realize he was here. I could have read aloud before Seamus arrived."

"You read to *cat-sídhe*?" Seamus didn't sound pleased with the idea.

"To Grendal, at any rate," Mr. Wylltson said. "He's acquiring English." The tip of Grendal's tail twitched.

"Learning anything?" Teagan asked.

Mr. Wylltson held up *The Art of War* by Sun Tzu.

"'I will force the enemy to take our strength for weakness and our weakness for strength, and thus will turn his strength into weakness.'"

Seamus nodded toward a leather-bound copy of *Poetics*. "Aristotle agrees. He advocates using people's preconceived ideas to move their minds any way you want them to go."

For some reason it annoyed Teagan to see him entering her father's game.

"By trailing a coat behind you?" she asked. "And daring the Highborn in the legal system to reveal themselves to the might of your mind?"

"*Touché.*" Seamus inclined his head to acknowledge the point. "The coat was ill-conceived."

"You might be surprised how well it worked out in the end," Teagan said, relenting a little. He had helped her in the police station. And he was looking out for Finn.

"Of course it did." Seamus grinned. "I believe I've mentioned the McGillahee touch?"

"*Touched* is one word for it." Finn had come in from the kitchen. "I can think of others. Let's get this interview over with, McGillahee. I told Raynor about the Dogs. He's popped over to the cemetery to have a talk with them. You might want to check on Joe, Tea."

"I thought he was asleep."

"Just napping, apparently. Oh, and your little pink friend is hanging about in the alley. McGillahee?" He motioned toward the door, and the two of them went out.

"That young man," Mr. Wylltson said as he watched them walk down the street toward the van, "has a great deal of potential."

"Finn?" Teagan asked.

"Seamus," Mr. Wylltson said. "He actually *is* as smart as he thinks he is. That's rare. He's got two parts of the equation. He's got a great brain, and he's looking for his courage. But I'm not sure about his heart."

"Are we discussing Seamus McGillahee, or the Tin Man, Scarecrow, and Cowardly Lion rolled into one?"

"I wonder," Mr. Wylltson mused. "Someone wounded that young man. He's hidden his hopes away. Seamus has big dreams, so big he doesn't dare believe they can come true." He turned away from the window. "What was that about Dump Dogs?"

Teagan explained as briefly as she could.

Grendal growled when she mentioned Bairre's name and scratched at his chin again. Teagan frowned.

"So he is Roisin's friend?" she asked the *cat-sídhe*.

"Nnooobody'ss friend." His tail lashed.

"Did you eat breakfast this morning, Grendal?" she asked.

"Nnooow," the *cat-sídhe* said. "I wassssn't hungry."

"And you said you were tired. Would you mind if I felt your chin?"

"It itches," Grendal said.

"Is Grendal sick?" Mr. Wylltson asked.

"I'm not sure." Teagan sat down on the couch close enough to reach the *cat-sídhe*.

"I'll go check on Joe," Mr. Wylltson said. "I won't be much help here."

The *cat-sídhe* tipped his head up, and Teagan worked her fingers through his thick fur until she could feel the skin beneath. It was covered in what felt like tiny scabs and was hot to the touch. Mange. It felt like mange.

"Have you touched any other *cat-sídhe* since you got here?" she asked.

"Yess," Grendal said. "The dead cat."

It had to have been yesterday.

"And that's the only *cat-sídhe* you've touched since you've gotten here? You're sure?"

"Yess."

It was too soon for mange to have developed. But lethargy and loss of appetite, coupled with the scabbing skin—it had to be mange. And it could kill him.

"I don't want to *itch*." He looked miserable. "I have to take care of the pretty kitty."

"You have a pretty kitty?"

Grendal put his hand to his head, as if he were confused.

"Yggdrasil's . . . kitties."

Teagan sat back. "The tree had kittens?"

"Two kittens." Grendal looked frustrated. "I took care of two . . ." He thumped his head with his fist, as if trying to shake the words loose. "Sssomething iss wrong with my thinker."

Teagan had no idea whether or not mange could affect the brain. She'd never spoken with a mange patient before. But something was befuddling the *cat-sídhe*.

"Are you talking about Roisin and Aileen?"

"Yess!"

"Girls. You took care of two little girls." She'd assumed that Grendal was Roisin's pet. Not her rescuer, guardian, or caretaker. She thought about her mother's fondness for cats. The *cat-sídhe* weren't the only ones who saw glimpses of their own story in Andrew Lloyd Webber's musical. Aileen Wylltson must have, too. Glimories of magical Grendal.

"I took care of Aileen until she got scary. Like you."

"I'm not scary," Teagan said as his hand drifted toward his chin. *"Don't scratch!"*

Grendal jerked his hand away and sat up straight.

"Too loud." He rubbed his ear.

"I'm sorry," Teagan said softly. "You don't want to break the skin by scratching. I think that's why the cat on the sidewalk died. He scratched himself open, and germs got into the wounds."

"What's germssss?"

"Little bugs," Teagan explained. She would check the cultures she'd taken from Maggot Cat's pus before he died, just to make sure she was right about what caused his infection. "Why did you take care of Roisin and my mom?"

"I heard the tree's whisper," the *cat-sídhe* said.

"Yggdrasil's?"

"Yggdrasil." The word sounded completely natural when he said it. "I hunted in the woods of Vanaheimr when the whisper came."

Nordic. Her dad had said Yggdrasil was the Nordic name for the world tree. She was fairly certain Vanaheimr was one of the worlds at the roots of Yggdrasil—the icy world where the Nordic gods lived. *Sleep warm, Bill Bailey.* Because *cat-sídhe* came from a very cold place.

"Have you ever heard of Old Deuteronomy?" Teagan asked.

"Nnnnoooow." Grendal shook his head.

"Do you have three names?"

Grendal opened his brilliant eyes wide.

"An everyday name, a name for your family, and a name that only you know?"

"Yess."

The *cat-sídhe* were homesick for a place they couldn't quite remember. They were filling in the blanks around their glimories with bits and pieces of a play.

"What was the tree whispering?"

"'Help. Someone to help.' I'm someone." The *cat-sídhe* shrugged. "Ssso I went. I found the kitt . . . girls and brought them to the tree. We kept them safe."

"Weren't you afraid of Fear Doirich when you went to get them? Of Mab?"

"I am a child of Bergljót, and Fróði. I am not afraid to die."

"Why were you—"

Grendal growled. "Hákon always ask questions. 'Why are you, how are you, what are you!'"

"What is a Hákon?"

"You are. Aileen was. Mab is. Curiosity killed the Hákon. That's what we say."

"Really?" Teagan smiled. "How does 'Curiosity killed the cat' sound? That's our saying."

"The words sound right," Grendal said. "But Hákon are more than cats."

"More curious?"

"Yes." Grendal's tail twitched once this time. "*Hákon hunt answers instead of mice, so they get no supper!*"

"Well, I need to go hunt some answers that will help you," Teagan said, "supper or not."

192

She found Mr. Wylltson standing at the kitchen window watching Joe rip up handfuls of lawn, shake the soil from the roots, then throw the grass over the back wall.

"What on earth . . . ?" Teagan asked.

"I asked him that," Mr. Wylltson said. "He told me he is cleaning up the abomination. Making this bit of soil what it was meant to be."

"Weedy?" Teagan guessed, turning on the faucet and lathering her hands with soap.

"He says they're all here: prairie trillium, columbine, foxglove, beardtongue, fire pink. They're not gone. Just tucked down deep. He's calling them up. We'll not only have all the goblins of hell after us, but the neighborhood association as well."

Teagan dried her hands and leaned back against the sink. "Have you ever heard of Bergljót, and Fróði?"

"The king and queen of the Nordic fairy cats," Mr. Wylltson said. "They pull Freyja the Norse goddess's chariot. Why do you ask?"

"What would you say if I told you that the invisible cat living with us is a royal prince who risked his life to save Mom and Roisin?"

"I'd say nothing could surprise me. Not after the last few months."

"And what if I said the royal prince has mange, and I need to go down to the zoo to get him some medicine?"

"I'd say no."

Teagan lowered her voice. "He has the disease that killed the cat we found on the sidewalk, Dad. It is progressing unusually fast. It will very likely be fatal."

"It is too dangerous for you to go alone."

"If I survive this school year, I'm going to college next fall. I won't have a bodyguard sitting with me in my classes."

"I remember college," Mr. Wylltson said. "If I could arrange a bodyguard, I would."

"You met Mom in college!"

"That's what I was remembering."

Something popped behind them, and a puff of air lifted Teagan's hair. It smelled like fresh grass clippings. Raynor was standing beside his motorbike.

"They were gone," he said.

"Probably to sleep off their meal somewhere quieter," Teagan said. "Maintenance had just started mowing the cemetery when we left."

"I'd like your opinion on something, Raynor," Mr. Wylltson said.

"I don't give my opinions. People always take them too seriously."

"I see your point. I was going to ask what you thought of Teagan going down to the zoo by herself. But I'll go with her."

"Then she'll have to take care of you as well as herself," Raynor said without looking up from his rag.

"I thought you never gave opinions."

"That's not an opinion. It's a fact. There are things you can't do, John Wylltson, and this is one of them. Either she can make good decisions or she can't. There is no such thing as safe. There never has been."

Mr. Wylltson looked from Raynor to Teagan.

"Okay," he said after a long moment. "You can go. You've been making good decisions for a long time now."

SEVENTEEN

TEAGAN took a skin scraping from Grendal's neck with a tongue depressor, sealed it up in a plastic bottle, then transferred nitrile gloves, hand sanitizer, and Q-Tips from her medical kit to her backpack. If the hairless *cat-sídhe* got close enough, perhaps she could talk it into letting her have some samples as well. The more information she had, the more likely she'd be able to help Grendal.

"You have your phone?" Mr. Wylltson asked as she started out the back door.

She checked her pocket, then crossed the room and gave him a kiss on top of his head.

"Be careful, Rosebud," he said. "I mean it. Anything seems strange, anything at all, you call home."

Joe was making good progress on his lawn destruction. He didn't look up as she went past. Gil was curled in a ball in the corner of the yard, fast asleep. She sincerely hoped the Dump Dogs were sleeping just as soundly wherever they were.

Teagan caught a glimpse of the hairless *cat-sídhe* out of the corner of her eye as she started down the alley. It followed her, dodging from hiding place to hiding place, peeking from behind telephone poles and piles of trash. Which was a good sign, as Finn would say, because she couldn't be completely sure the Dump Dogs were sleeping. If they were here, though, the *cat-sídhe* probably wouldn't be here. It followed her all the way down the alley.

When she reached the street, she hesitated. There were two buses she could take. One stop was a little farther away, but to get there she would pass the Black Feather coffee shop. Hákon might be more fond of answers than of mice, but this Hákon was also fond of coffee, and hadn't had any yet today. She lost sight of the pink *cat-sídhe* on the busy street, but it reappeared when she was waiting in line inside the shop. She saw it peering in the window, its hands cupped to its face.

Teagan wiggled her fingers at it, and it ducked out of sight.

She reached the counter and ordered a double latte, then stepped aside to wait. When it came, she sipped foam from the top, then settled the plastic lid on tight. The *cat-sídhe* ducked when she stepped out onto the sidewalk, but followed after her again down the street.

Teagan was surprised to find commuters waiting at the bus stop this late in the morning: three businessmen in suits and two women sitting on the bench. There was just enough room for her to sit down and settle her drink beside her while she dug in her backpack for her bus pass.

She was just pulling it out when she caught a movement from the corner of her eye. A pink-gray scabby arm reached around the back of the bench, and the *cat-sídhe*'s pawlike hand hooked around her latte cup. Teagan pretended to search while the *cat-sídhe* scooted the cup closer to the edge … closer … Then the creature popped up, grabbed it with its two little hands, and disappeared behind the bench. Apparently Highborn were not the only Sídhe who liked a little caffeine now and then. The cup reappeared as Teagan zipped up her backpack. She picked it up and shook it. There was definitely less latte in it than there had been before.

She rubbed her lips, thinking of all the times she'd left cups of coffee or cans of soda unattended only to come back and find them emptier than she'd thought they should be. She'd probably been slurping secondhand *cat-sídhe* kisses her whole life.

She pretended to take another drink, careful not to let her lips actually touch the cup, then hung her arm over the back of the bench, holding the cup lightly with her fingertips.

"You can have the rest," she said.

"What?" The woman next to her turned and stared at her suspiciously. "I don't want anything."

"Oh, no. I was just talking to a friend," Teagan said, hoping the woman would assume she was wearing a Bluetooth. It might have worked if her hair hadn't been pulled back, exposing both her ears. The woman stood up as if she needed to look down the road for the bus, and didn't sit down again.

Teagan shook the cup again, sloshing the liquid around. This time she felt warm little fingers touching hers, and then the *cat-sídhe* took the cup from her hand.

A few moments later, the creature crept around the end of

the bench without the cup. It looked even more like a Donskoy up close; a female Donskoy with huge china-blue eyes. The gray tinge to her skin was probably caused by dead layers like those she had felt under Grendal's chin, and the wrinkles from rapid weight loss. If something didn't change soon, this cat was going to die.

"Mowr?" The *cat-sídhe* asked, hopefully licking its whiskers.

"There is no more," Teagan said. "I'm Teagan."

The commuters were all studiously ignoring her now.

"I knowww," the *cat-sídhe* said. "I cha*hiss*ed you."

Surely she didn't expect Teagan to remember. A lot of *cat-sídhe* had chased them. "I had more hair," the *cat-sídhe* said helpfully. "Mac Cumhaill kicked me."

"Ah," Teagan said. "I do remember. What can I call you?"

"Gri*hiss*abella," the cat said, as if testing the name. "Gri*hiss*abella!" she said more firmly.

Grizabella. In *Cats*, she was the outcast who was eventually welcomed back.

The bus arrived and Teagan stepped back, letting the other people board first. She wasn't going to have time to take any samples.

"Are you going to be here when I get back?"

"Nowww. Put me up," Grizabella said. She pointed at the roof of the bus and made a throwing motion.

"No," Teagan said. "That would be dangerous. What if you fell into traffic?"

The last businessman to board the bus met her eye, clearly

concerned. She smiled at him, and he turned away with a better-not-to-get-involved expression on his face.

"If you meet me when I come back, maybe I'll be able to help you," Teagan said as she started up the steps. Grizabella apparently didn't want to wait. She lashed her hairless tail, then jumped up the steps after Teagan. Every seat was taken by morning commuters. The *cat-sídhe* climbed up on Teagan's shoe and wrapped her skinny arms, legs, and tail around Teagan's calf to avoid the feet around her.

Teagan held on to a bar to keep from lurching against the man behind her as the bus started. Grizabella blinked up at her, then turned to the young man sitting on the left.

"Get up," she told him. The young man fidgeted and looked uncomfortable. "Give Teagan your seat."

"Don't do that," Teagan said. "I can stand."

The young man looked at her and frowned.

"Sam?" the girl next to the young man said. "Do you know her?"

"Ssssaaam!" Grizabella said, delighted to have his name. "Get up. Nnnowww!"

Teagan could feel the power in the command even though it wasn't directed at her. Apparently Sam could as well. He stood up, threw a worried look at Teagan, and motioned for her to sit down.

"Wait," his girlfriend said. "What are you doing? I don't want to sit by a crazy girl! Do you know her, or what?"

The bus hissed to a stop, and instead of anyone getting off, four more people crowded on, pushing against Sam, who was holding them back, waiting for Teagan to sit.

"Thank you," Teagan said, and sat down. Sam's girlfriend gave him a desperate look as he was pushed down the aisle.

Grizabella jumped into Teagan's lap.

"I helped you!"

"Don't help me anymore," Teagan said, but the *cat-sídhe* leaned over and peered intently at Sam's girlfriend.

"Tell me your name."

"Don't tell me your name," Teagan said to her quickly, and then to the *cat-sídhe*, "Leave her alone."

The girl pressed herself into the corner, face away from Teagan. The other passengers were definitely avoiding eye contact as well. Fine. Since she'd been established as a mental case, she might as well try to help the creature. She took her small first-aid kit out of her backpack and pulled on a pair of purple gloves.

"What are you doing?" Grizabella asked.

"I think I can help you," Teagan said, thankful that she was wearing long sleeves. "But I don't want to catch what you have. Do you itch?"

The girl beside them made a strangling noise and jumped to her feet. "Let me out of here!"

Teagan moved her legs to let her past, then slid to the window seat, taking Grizabella with her. A baldheaded man in a business suit took the vacated seat. He settled his briefcase like an impermeable barrier between them.

"I itch all over," Grizabella said.

"May I look in your ears?"

The *cat-sídhe*'s tail twitched once. The edges of the ears were thickened and crusty, and the insides were black with oil and dirt, but Teagan didn't find any ear mites. "May I see your gums?"

"Gums?" the *cat-sídhe* asked.

"The skin of your teeth," Teagan explained. Grizabella opened her mouth and belched. Serious Dumpster breath ... with a slight bouquet of latte. The businessman beside them might not have been able to see or hear the *cat-sídhe*, but he could definitely smell it. He put his hand to his face, covering his mouth and nose.

Teagan tried not to do the same. She didn't want to offend the creature. "I am fairly sure you have mange, but I'm not sure which kind. If I get you a special shampoo, would you use it?"

The businessman finally turned to her. "Excuse me?" he said through his cupped hand.

"I'm talking to my invisible friend," Teagan said. "You can't see her, but she's riding on my lap."

"Sure you are," he shouted, rubbing his bald dome with one hand. "I don't for a moment believe that! I have had it with young people like you—"

The bus brakes hissed, and the driver stood up. "One of you two is getting off at this stop," he said. "I don't care which one. I drive a peaceful bus."

"I'll go," Teagan said. It was only a half mile to the zoo from here, and she didn't mind walking. She wrapped one arm around Grizabella, picked up her bag with the other, and managed to squeeze out past the man, who barely moved his legs. She imagined that the purple nitrile gloves had something to do with the way the other passengers got out of her way.

She set the *cat-sídhe* down as the bus pulled away.

"I need to find out what kind of mange you have if I am going to help you."

"Howwww?"

"If you let me scrape off some skin flakes, I'll take them to work and look at them under a microscope," Teagan said. "Then I'll know what kind of medicine you need. It won't hurt."

Teagan took a new tongue depressor out of her first-aid kit and scraped some skin flakes from the *cat-sídhe*'s back, then put them, along with the stick, into a large paper Band-Aid wrapper.

"That should do it." She peeled her gloves off and dropped them in the first garbage can she saw.

"Will I grow fur?" Grizabella asked.

"Yes," Teagan said. "If the medicine works. But it will take a few weeks."

"Why are you with the bad man, Highborn?" Grizabella asked as she hopped along beside her.

"The bad man?"

"The Mac Cumhaill." Grizabella spat. "He kills and kills and kills."

"*Cat-sídhe* kill and kill as well," Teagan pointed out. She tried not to imagine Grizabella squeezing a hatchling to death, sucking the breath from a baby, or whispering lewd suggestions to a street person.

"He kills ussss." The *cat-sídhe* jumped up onto a cement planter, which brought her almost eye to eye with Teagan. "You told him no."

"I don't want to kill goblins."

"Why?" Grizabella asked.

"I tricked a water goblin to her death once," Teagan said.

"Good." Grizabella nodded. "Water girls are nasssty."

"It was the most evil thing I've ever done." She could still hear the fear in Ginny Greenteeth's voice as she begged for her life, her screams as the hellhounds took her. "I hope I'll never kill anything again."

The *cat-sídhe* reached up and touched Teagan's face. "Other Highborn think you are sssick," she said, patting her cheek. "Very sssick. Because of the way you think."

Teagan laughed. "Tell me something I don't know."

"Okay," Grizabella said agreeably. "The shadowsss that came out of the park want an abode."

EIGHTEEN

HADOWS came out?"

"Yesss. But the light was too bright," Grizabella said. "Sssso they're ... melty bits and melty pieces. The Dogs put all of the little pieces in a jar and stirred them with a stick." She pantomimed stirring a cauldron. "We hear them talking, but they can't hurt us. Not without an abode."

"What is an abode?" Teagan asked.

"Sssskins and bonesss."

They needed a body? Teagan made a mental note not to leave her own skin and bones lying around where they could find them.

"Do you know where they are now?"

Grizabella shook her head as they reached the entry to the zoo.

"I don't want you to follow me inside," Teagan said. "I have friends in here that might catch your mange. But I won't be too long. If you wait here, I'll try to bring you something that will help."

"Yesss," the *cat-sídhe* hissed again. Teagan looked back

once to make sure she wasn't following her. Grizabella was perched like a ginger-tufted gargoyle atop the zoo sign, staring after her.

When Teagan was far enough away that she was sure the *cat-sídhe* couldn't overhear her, she sat down on a bench and dialed home.

"Raynor's Rescue," the angel said when he picked up. "Tell me where, I'll be there!"

"Raynor's Rescue?"

"Angel humor," Raynor said. "What do you need? You don't sound like you're in trouble."

"I was just talking with a *cat-sídhe*—"

"Of course you were. Pleasant chat?"

"Not really." She explained what Grizabella had said, and there was silence on the line. "Raynor? Are you there?"

"It's possible that some part of them made it out. I had to shield your father from the fire, so there were places . . ."

"Some *part* of them?"

"They would have become . . . less than alive."

"Less than alive, but not dead? How does that work?"

"I'm surprised that you don't know the spectrum between alive and not alive."

"If we were talking biology, I would have an idea," Teagan said. "Living creatures are in a state between birth and death. They carry on metabolic activities that produce molecules and energy needed to sustain them. But I don't think shadows work that way."

"True," Raynor said. "But we can use the analogy. Is a bacterium alive?"

"Yes. Even though it's one cell, it does everything I mentioned."

"Is a virus alive?"

"Not exactly. Viruses are more like little computer programs that take over the processes in a living cell. They borrow life."

"Exactly," Raynor said. "We've got a virus out there looking for a life to borrow. Did your *cat-sídhe* friend happen to tell you where these melty shadows are?"

"Yes. The Dump Dogs put them in a jar and stirred them with a stick."

"Terrific. Let's get off this line now in case Mamieo needs to call." Raynor hung up.

Teagan dialed Abby. She was probably in the midst of painting a rich and powerful toenail at the moment. Whoever's it was, it was not as important as this. To her relief, it was Thomas who answered the phone.

"Abby is busy at the moment, Tea."

"That's okay. I needed to talk to you, anyway." She explained what Grizabella had told her.

"I've seen something similar," Thomas said. "The shadows all fade eventually. When they reach a certain point, they attach themselves to a Highborn. It's the only way they can move from place to place."

Teagan realized she had seen it herself. Highborn with shadow men dogging their steps, melting into the ground when they stopped walking, leaping up again when they moved. Borrowing movement, if not life.

"I'll keep my eyes op—"

"Tea?" Abby had taken the phone. "I am so quitting this job. This guy gets his toe painted, right? *And then he wants me to blow on the paint to dry it.* I'm not blowing on some fat old guy's toes. Not even for art school."

"There have to be other jobs," Teagan said, trying to shift mental gears. "You could talk to Leo—"

"I tell the Turtles about this guy, they'll take him to some dark alley and use paint remover on him, you know what I'm saying? This job pays better than any of the others I've had, and if I don't save, I won't get to art school. This is killing me. You know what? I'm going to talk to Zia Sophia. I knew you'd—Wait. You called me. So, what do you need, Tea? Oops. Got a customer, gotta go." She hung up. That was okay. Thomas would fill her in.

Teagan stood and walked toward the clinic building. There was something *tickling* at her. She stopped, closed her eyes, and focused on it. A melody, muted as if it were playing inside an unopened music box.

She opened her eyes and turned, scanning for the source of the sound. The old Burr Oak. Of course. It was older than the zoo. Maybe older than Chicago. Its branches and autumn-rusted leaves drew her like a shrine would draw a pilgrim.

She hesitated before she stepped under the canopy. There was no shimmering, no scent of Mag Mell. But this tree was awake.

Dry leaves crunched beneath her feet as she walked to the trunk. She pressed her palms to the rough bark and was instantly filled with melody. The voices she'd heard all around her in the pools of Mag Mell had spoken of creation, of art and music. This song was a petition.

Teagan leaned her head against the trunk, and the music moved through her as if she were part of the tree, roots in this world, twigs laced into ... *unspeakable goodness and beauty.* She drew in her breath. The Burr Oak was holding hands with the Creator of Creation, its voice crying out for the creatures all around. Little ones, lost ones, wild ones, locked in cages. Calling out for someone to come who would make things *right.*

She took a shaky step back and forced herself to breathe. No wonder Grendal had gone to help her mother when he'd heard Yggdrasil's whisper. Any creature with a heart would have gone. Teagan wanted to step inside the tree like the dryads in her mother's books, make it her home and the prayer her own. *Make things right.*

A breeze rattled the leaves above her, singing through the branches like an Aeolian harp, sending rusty leaves tumbling down like a blessing around her. She was still shaky when she punched in her entry code and stepped into the clinic.

Agnes, the vet tech, was hunched over the computer desk, her head in her hands.

"Agnes?" Teagan said. "What is it?"

"Oscar's not coming back. He's gone."

"He's dead?" *Like Molly. The goblins had taken Molly and Oscar because of her.*

"Maybe. I don't know." Agnes said. "Not that we know of. He never arrived in Texas. The shipper lost him."

"How can you lose a live animal shipment?"

"That's what I want to know." Agnes waved at the computer. "Max was on the phone as soon as they took him. You know that senator you helped talk to Cindy and Oscar a few days ago? She was all over it as soon as she heard. She made calls. We all made calls. Nobody ordered the transfer. It was a mistake."

Agnes was crying. "He's in a box with only enough water for a couple of days. If I don't find him, he's going to die . . . unless he ended up in the hold of an airplane. Then he's frozen to death already."

"We don't know that he's dead." Teagan pushed away the thought of Molly, dead before Teagan had even made it to Mag Mell. Before she'd had a chance to do anything.

"Have you seen Cindy?" Agnes asked.

"Not yet." Teagan slid her backpack off.

"Anyone who believes that animals don't grieve . . . *shit.*" Agnes pulled a tissue out of the box on her desk. "They can die of grief."

"I was going to take care of my patients here before I visited Cindy," Teagan said.

"I've already taken care of them. I wasn't expecting you today, not after what happened at your school. I checked your cultures, too. It was *Streptococcus*. What exactly happened at the school? Are you all right?"

"I'm okay."

"I heard they found your friend Molly dead. If I believed in unicorns and glitter farts, I would think this had something to do with me," Agnes said.

"You?" Teagan asked.

"Strange things are happening in Chicago. What's the common denominator? I am. I helped Molly with a project once."

Teagan blinked. She had completely forgotten that she'd introduced Molly to Agnes the year before, when Molly needed help with a lab. "I packed Oscar up. It's irrational, I know. But I can't shake the feeling that I've done something to cause this."

"That *is* irrational," Teagan said, thankful at least that Agnes hadn't worked her into the equation. "And a little paranoid."

"I know." Agnes sat up straighter. "I was just having a minor meltdown." She tapped her keyboard and blew her nose. "It doesn't have to be fart related. Maybe one of those paranormal nutjobs I've debunked is doing this to mess with me."

"A joke?"

"A hacker must've broken into the system. They sent orders for the pickup, and once they had Oscar, they started moving him around. All they had to do is access the shipper's files. I can't find him."

The Sídhe used the Internet. Kyle had told her as much. They'd tracked her friends and found out about Oscar through her Facebook page.

"I won't quit until I find Oscar. If a hacker took him, there must be a way."

"I hope so," Teagan said. "Thanks for taking care of my patients. I need to look at a slide or two. Then I'll go see Cindy."

Teagan went down the hall to the lab. She tried not to think about Molly and Oscar as she prepared slides of the skin scrapings. Not to think about Cindy, grieving for Oscar. It didn't work. She stopped and pressed the tears away before she focused the microscope.

Both slides showed the same tiny arachnids covered in white spiky armor, crawling on the skin flakes. Sarcoptic mange, then—the contagious sort. If Aiden thought worms were scary, it was a good thing he couldn't see these eyeless little beasts. Just looking at them made her itch all over, even though she knew they rarely infested people. Revolution would kill them, and any fleas Grizabella might have as well, but it was a prescription medication.

"Is Dr. Max here?" Teagan asked Agnes when she'd cleaned the slides. "I need a prescription."

"He's downtown raising hell," Agnes said. "What do you need?"

"Revolution."

"I agree. An animal rights revolution. But I suppose *you* mean the medication. We have some samples you could take. You don't need a prescription for those."

"That would be great." Teagan took as many as she thought reasonable—Grizabella and Grendal both needed treating— and then said goodbye to Agnes, who didn't look up from her computer screen.

Next, she went to the private entrance at the back of the primate house. She felt the iron around her the moment she stepped inside. It made it a little hard to breathe.

Cindy was lying listlessly in her swing, one arm hanging in the air. Her eyes were open and turned toward the door. Her food bowl didn't look like it had been touched all day.

"Cindy." Teagan said it and signed it at the same time. The chimp sat up, then jumped out of her swing and came as close as possible.

Cindy's boy, she signed. *Bad man, bad man, Cindy's boy.*

Teagan swallowed. The bad men had taken Oscar, Cindy's boy.

"Sorry," Teagan signed. "I'm so sorry, Cindy."

When she turned to leave, Cindy went wild, screaming and bashing herself against the Plexiglas wall of the viewing area.

Teagan stepped out of the building, pulled the door shut behind her, and leaned her head on the wall. She could hear Cindy's screams through the door. If trees could cry out to the Creator of Creation, surely apes could, too. Cindy was crying out with every fiber of her being.

Oak leaves whispered on the pavement around her feet, stirred by the wind. *Send someone.*

Sarcoptic mange mites she could cure. But she had no way to fight techie goblins.

Think like a Highborn. Teagan straightened up and looked at the Burr Oak leaves. *Send someone.*

She couldn't fight goblins in cyberspace. But she knew someone who could.

NINETEEN

"Ɛʟʟ-oʜ?"

It wasn't Thomas who picked up this time. It was Roisin.

"Is Abby there?"

"Here," Roisin agreed.

"Okay, it's me now," Abby said. Things must have slowed down at the shop. "I'm teaching Roisin life skills. She's really sharp, you know? So, what do you need?"

"Jing." She glanced at the Burr Oak as she walked past it. The leaves were completely still. "Abby? Are you there?"

"Yeah." Abby's voice was tight. "He's smart, you're smart. You're, like, in all the same classes."

"What are you talking about?"

"He's, like, the school hero, you're, like . . . *Teagan*. I've always known this was going to happen."

"You think I—" Teagan shook her head. "Abby. Nothing like that is *ever* going to happen."

More silence.

"What's wrong with Jing?"

"My best friend likes him, for one."

"Yeah." Abby's voice was weak. "I do. So—"

"I need you to call Jing because I need a hacker."

Ten seconds of silence this time.

"That's it? That's all?"

"That's it. Oscar's life is on the line."

"The monkey?"

Ape. Teagan didn't even bother to correct her. "Kyle said he found my friends through Facebook, so I know he used the Internet. He either paid a hacker or there's a goblin out there who is very good with computers. They arranged to have Oscar picked up, then diverted the shipment. He's locked in a box somewhere, and we don't know where he is."

"What, like the Ark of the Covenant when they put it in that warehouse? They just *stuck* him somewhere?"

"I hope not," Teagan said. *Oh, God, I hope not.* "I need Jing to find him fast."

"Jing could totally do that."

"He has to understand—this is dangerous. He'll be messing with the kind of creatures that sliced Cade open."

"I'll call him. You need him at your house, or what? He could pick us up here. I'm *so* done with this for today."

"If he's willing to help. Don't pressure him."

"He's *Jing*, Tea. The Mighty Khan. What do you think? He's going to walk away when somebody's in trouble? HEY!" Teagan jerked the phone away from her ear. Abby never warned her when she was going to start yelling. "YOU GUYS COULD TAKE THE BUS HOME, RIGHT?"

Teagan put the phone back to her ear. "I've got to go meet a patient," she said. "I'll meet you—and Jing, if he'll come—at home."

She'd reached the zoo gate. At first she thought Grizabella had left, but then the *cat-sídhe* came around the sign, scratching at her side. When she saw Teagan's look, she stopped scratching and put both hands behind her back.

"You can fix me?"

"Yes," Teagan said. "You have mange."

"What'sss *mange?*"

"Spiders"—she was pretty sure she wouldn't know what an arachnid was—"living in your skin."

Grizabella looked down at her belly. "Nope," she said.

"They are too small to see," Teagan told her. "Invisible spiders."

"*Invisible spiders.*" The *cat-sídhe* clawed wildly at her belly. "*Eeeeeeeeee!*"

"Stop." Teagan knelt down and caught her paws. "Stop it. You're going to hurt yourself."

"Invisible is *scary!*" Grizabella's voice squeaked on the word.

"If you scratch, you're going to give yourself infections. Like Bill Bailey did."

"Ssswellings? Dead skin?"

"Yes. That's what killed him. So *don't scratch.*"

Grizabella put her hands behind her back again.

Teagan showed her the medication, and then squeezed it onto her back between her shoulder blades.

"No washing," Teagan said.

"Wasssshing?"

Of course she wasn't going to wash. She was a *cat-sidhe*. "Stay out of the rain. And don't sleep anywhere you've slept before. Don't touch other *cat-sidhe*. Not until you're better."

"The spiders will crawl on them?"

"Yes. This is just the first treatment. You are going to need at least three more, so you have to come find me."

"You touched me," Grizabella said. "With your handsss. Will the hssspiders jump on you?"

"If they do, I'll use medicine." Teagan struggled against an almost irresistible urge to scratch. She clenched her teeth, fighting to keep in her own *Eeeeeee* welling up inside.

"Sleep warm, Teagan."

"Sleep warm." Teagan waited until she was sure Grizabella wasn't looking before she poured on hand sanitizer and started scratching. Psychosomatic. But still. Her skin felt *crawly* all over.

At the next stop she saw six *cat-sidhe* riding on top of a bus headed in the opposite direction. One was gleefully plucking the feathers from a struggling pigeon, tossing them into the air to flutter into the traffic behind the bus. *Had they manipulated some poor street person into tossing them up one by one onto the top of the bus? Dropped like rotten apples from a tree? Or did they have friends in the city?*

Jing's Mustang was just pulling up to the curb when she arrived. Teagan saw Mrs. Santini's curtain twitch as he got out and opened the car door for Abby. Score one for Jing.

"Thomas and Roisin are taking the bus home," Abby said. "They didn't mind."

Jing reached into the back seat and took out a metal briefcase.

"His kit," Abby explained. "You know, like the stuff Finn carries? Only better."

"Everything a hacker needs to survive in hostile territory," Jing said.

"What have you told him, Abby?" Teagan asked.

"Everything." Abby flushed. "He asks really good questions, Tea. He listens good, too."

Jing looked down at her. Way down. He was six-four and "totally Italian," as Abby would say, even though he had no Italian ancestry whatsoever. That just meant he could have posed for Michelangelo's sculptures. Or competed in the original Olympic Games in ancient Greece. And won.

"So Abby tells me you're not human, Tea," he said.

"Do you believe her?"

Jing grinned. "I've suspected it for years. I have an *effect* on human females. And yet here we are. Friends. Just friends, after all the time we've spent together."

"You mean all the time in psychology and political science classes?"

"At the top of the class . . . and it's lonely at the top."

"Lonelier now," Teagan said. "Molly was up there with us. This is serious, Jing."

He lost his grin. "I know it. I just met your cousin, remember? I held my man Cade in my arms until the ambulance arrived."

"But you're still willing to help. To risk facing … all that, to save an ape?"

"'When bad men combine, the good must as-so-ci-*ate*,'"—Jing sounded as if he were speaking from a pulpit—"'else they will fall one by one, an un-pitied sacrifice in a contemptible struggle.'"

"Oh, god," Abby said. "That's not from an old book, is it?"

"Worse." Jing took her elbow. "From a political philosopher. Edmund Burke."

"If you quote him to my grandmother," Teagan said, "she'll love you forever. She's proud of the old Irish philosophers."

"She'd know Burke?"

"She knows of every important Irishman who ever drew a breath. Civilization rested on the shoulders of the Irish, didn't you know?"

"I believe you'll find that Chinese culture predates the Celtic world."

"I wouldn't mention that to Mamieo," Teagan said.

"You're totally going to get along with Mr. Wylltson, though." Abby waved at Mrs. Santini, who was still peeking through the curtains. "I'm going to go tell Zia that I'm bringing you over after you're done at Tea's, before she starts making calls, you know what I mean?"

Jing watched Abby cross the street.

"I am not just a good *man*, Tea. I am a *good* man. I'd appreciate it if you'd tell Abby that."

"Tell her yourself. Or better yet, show her. And I'd start by stopping flirting with other girls. Like me."

"You know I'm not serious."

"*I* know it. But *I'm* not the one you're trying to impress. Finn has a killer smile, and when he uses it on other girls, I feel like strangling someone."

"A gentle little thing like you?"

"You have no idea."

Jing looked after Abby, his brows knit.

"Jing, if you are just here to get close to Abby, you should walk across the street right now and forget the rest of it. Go impress Zia Sophia, and you'll be getting somewhere."

"I said I was a *good man*, little girl. Good men don't walk away when their friends are in trouble."

"They don't call their friends *little girl*, either," Teagan said pointedly.

"Whoa." Jing took a step back. "When did you get the scary-chick thing going on? All I meant was that you are short. You can't deny it. Stop looking at me like that. Abby's coming back—she'll think I did something wrong."

Abby was clearly relieved by whatever Mrs. Santini had said. "We've got an hour. After that, Zia expects us in her kitchen. She's going to feed you."

"That's good?"

"That's good," Abby said.

Teagan caught Jing's sleeve. "Even good men walk away sometimes. I need you to think about Molly and Cade before you get in any deeper. This is for real, and it can kill you."

"We're born with the knowledge that there is something out there," Jing said. "We hope and pray that it's all friendly. But deep down, we know it's not. Something really bad is out there. I just got a good look at one of the bastards. Whatever's happening, I'm in."

"But there's good things out there, too, right?" Abby countered. "Like Tea and Dumpster Boy." It was the first time Teagan had heard her say anything positive about Finn. "They're, like, *created* to fight the bad guys."

Teagan nodded. If she and Finn were the good guys, they'd better step up their game. So far the good guys had barely managed to stay alive.

"Speaking of, Thomas and Roisin were having issues, Tea," Abby went on. "I told them to walk by the lake before they came home. I gave Thomas my phone, in case they needed to call the angel." She looked at Jing. "The one I told you about. He can go *nuclear* if he has to."

"I'm looking forward to meeting this nuclear angel," Jing said.

"About that." Abby pushed the door open. "He's not really much to look at." Raynor was sitting in the living room.

"Where's Dad?" Teagan asked. She knew Mamieo and Aiden were still at school.

"I believe he stepped over to the Santinis'," Raynor said.

"And Finn?"

"He moved his bed into the basement. He's asleep down there. He was out most of the night, after all."

Teagan frowned. *Finn had been out all night? Hunting the Dump Dogs, no doubt. And he'd left her sleeping, safe in her bed.* She'd have to convince him that wasn't a good idea.

"Who's not much to look at?" Raynor asked.

"The angel you have living here," Jing said.

"That would be me." Raynor stood up.

Jing extended his hand. "I thought you'd be taller."

"I can see why you would," Raynor said, craning his neck to look at him. "And you are . . . ?"

"The Mighty Khan, Abby's main man."

"He wants to be my main man," Abby said. "I haven't said he could."

"So, you are applying for the position? And this"—Raynor motioned to the briefcase—"is your resume?"

"Something like that." Jing grinned. "I'm a white hat. I'm here to do some good in the 'hood."

"A white hat?"

"If you're an angel, you should have heard of us. The good guys on the World Wide Web? Today, I'm going to be a knight in shining armor."

Raynor rubbed his nose. "So you're rescuing a damsel in distress?"

"An ape, actually. But I'm hoping my damsel will appreciate it."

"Don't hope too much," Abby said. "If I appreciate, I appreciate from a distance. If you're so good, why'd you get caught in the school computers? Zia's going to want to know that. My family don't like publicity."

"Connections," Jing said. "I wanted to be on the right people's radar. I made the news and they started calling, just to find out who I was."

"What exactly were you promoting?" Raynor asked.

"My business. When I'm on the clock, people who have

222

computer systems they think can't be broken into pay me to try. After I break in, I tell them how it can be done and they fix it. It helps them keep the bad guys out."

"You always get in?"

"There is always a way."

"And when you are not on the clock?"

"Then I find missing apes to impress pretty ladies." He winked at Abby. "And I understand we're in a hurry here." He spotted the computer on the other side of the room. "I'll need to plug into your cable." He set his briefcase on the desk and pulled a battered old laptop out. "I buy reconditioned computers for burners. Like a burner phone? Use it once, and throw away. I don't know what kind of nasty surprises Tea's cousins might have left behind, and I don't want to risk any of my good systems. Do you have a password for the computer at work?"

"Yes," Teagan said. "It's *Daktari*. Capital *D,* with a *K*. We all use the same password."

Jing shook his head. "Really, *really* bad idea. Bad password, too. Get them to change it as soon as I'm done." Jing was so focused on the computer now he didn't seem to notice that they were all staring at him.

"Dead end," he said at last. "My best guess from looking at this is that we might be able to follow the trail through the FDA computer system."

"Like the guys who test drugs?" Abby asked. "*That* FDA?"

"The Food and Drug Administration has jurisdiction over research chimps," Teagan said.

Jing took a thumb drive from his pocket. "My private key,

and the keys for my friends. I need to send some e-mails. Most of my people are at school or work right now, but Ninja-Skitters and Spatzgirl might be around. I'll start with them. The FDA's not very exciting, but someone might be using it as a back door into something more interesting."

"NinjaSkitters?" Abby asked. "That sounds like a disease."

"One you never want to catch. Skitters is a social engineer. He calls people up claiming to be tech support and asks for access to their computer. Most people hear 'tech support,' their brains turn off and they do what they're told."

"Leave it to the experts, right?" Abby stepped closer. "So, Spatzgirl is, like, a klutz?"

"Spatz. Not spaz. And he's not a girl. Spatz thinks breaking firewalls is fun." He hit Send a second time, and pushed his chair back.

"Now what?"

"Now"—he took a DVD from his briefcase—"we watch a little Faust."

"I've always hated *Faust*," Raynor said.

"Really?" Jing looked surprised. "Why?"

"I'm an angel. For some reason, the story of a man who makes a deal with the devil and is dragged screaming into hell has never seemed relaxing to me."

"Ah." Jing nodded. "I was referring to Lauren Faust. Storyboarded for *My Little Pony*'s reboot season. A newer classic."

Abby squealed. "You're a brony!"

Raynor was looking completely blank.

"You know," Abby said, "bro-plus-pony. Brony, right?"

"My Little Pony," Jing said, "is a chillaxation show full of retro-goodness and sparkly social commentary. Sit and watch. You'll like it."

Mamieo and Aiden came through the front door, and Raynor used their arrival as an excuse to escape to the kitchen. Teagan glanced at the clock. *Three already.* Zoë Giordano was going to be over soon for her appointment with Aiden. Things were about to get complicated. Keeping the sprite and *cat-sídhe* out from underfoot would be difficult enough. But as an employee of the state, Zoë would likely take a dim view of hacking into the FDA's computer systems. Teagan made hasty introductions.

"Aiden," Jing said, shaking his hand. "The Choirboy Abby's been telling me about. The man with the music. Come watch a little tube with us."

"I've got to get my whip first," Aiden said, and ran upstairs.

Teagan left Mamieo, Abby, and Jing glued to the sparkly social commentary while she went upstairs to find Grendal. Aiden passed her in the hall, dragging his whip behind him.

The *cat-sídhe* was curled on Roisin's bed. He opened one eye when Teagan sat down beside him.

"You have mange," she said. "I brought some medicine that should help. You should be feeling better within a couple of days."

He shivered when she applied the medication between his shoulder blades. "Zoë is coming over to dance with Aiden. So be careful if you come downstairs." Zoë had managed to avoid tripping over Grendal or sitting on Lucy at her last visit. Still, Teagan wasn't taking any chances.

"Roisin?" the *cat-sídhe* asked.

"She's still out with Thomas. Do you need anything? A drink? Something to eat?"

"Nnnooow." Grendal yawned hugely and closed his eyes.

Teagan went down the maid's stair to the kitchen. Raynor was standing over his Indian Four.

"It's all put together," Teagan observed as she opened a drawer and took out a bag of M&M's.

"Almost." Raynor wiped a smudge from the gas cap. "Almost ready to roar."

"Aiden's dance therapist is coming over in a little bit," Teagan said, pouring candy on the countertop. Lucy zipped into the room. The sprite had incredible hearing when it came to the sound of colored candy coating hitting a hard surface. She flashed and chirped at the sight of the riches, then scooped up a chocolate and headed for her teacup. The chocolate stupor would keep her out of the way for a few hours at least.

"Zoë doesn't know anything about sprites, *cat-sídhe*, Highborn, or goblins. Aiden tells her about it, but she thinks it's coming from my mom's books. Please try not to do or say anything . . . strange around her."

"Have you ever seen me do anything strange?" Raynor asked.

Teagan looked at the motorbike.

"Lots of people do mechanics in their kitchen," Raynor said.

"TEAGAN!" Abby bellowed from the living room.

"Got to go," Teagan said. "I just wanted to give you a heads-up."

When she stepped into the living room, a white and pink Pegasus pony was frozen in midflight on the TV screen, and everyone was gathered around Jing at the computer.

"The universe must love you, Teagan Wylltson," he said. "Whatever you are."

Teagan felt Finn's sizzle before he stepped in from the kitchen. He must have just come up from the basement.

"What's all the caterwauling?" he asked. "It would wake the dead. Oh, it's you, Gabby. I should have known."

"Mind your manners, boyo," Mamieo said. "We have company."

He rubbed his eyes and squinted at Jing. "You're the man who threw the desk. Thanks for the help."

"I hear you caught up with the bast—" Jing glanced at Aiden. "Creature."

"I did," Finn agreed.

"So," Teagan asked, "did you find Oscar?"

"Not quite. Spatz knew someone who had a back door into the FDA. He is willing to trade for . . . something I have."

"Jing's on it," Abby said.

"I'm a wizard of silicon and cyberspace." Jing cracked his knuckles, then started to type. "A paragon. A master, who usually works his trade in secrecy."

"Like a superhero," Aiden whispered.

"Just like that, my little man. No record of an ape picked up on that date. No record of that shipping number. Your goblin deleted it. Deleted it from the shipper's backup copy, too."

"So you can't find him?"

"Don't talk crazy," Jing said. "Of course I can. I'm in the

system and the box went somewhere. Which means there was an arrival scan. Somebody somewhere scanned that label, found no record of it, and shoved it in the corner to figure out later. So, I check the records for that. There are all kinds of systems in place to keep shipments from getting lost forever. This would only have slowed things down a few days."

Only long enough for Oscar to die alone in the dark.

"Wait for it . . . wait for it . . . got him!" Jing put both arms up as if he'd scored a goal. "Your ape is in a shipping container at the docks. Do you want him delivered to your doorstep?"

Tea let a huge breath she hadn't realized she'd been holding. "He's a full-grown chimpanzee. He could pull a man's arm off. Probably *would* pull someone's arm off after what he's been through."

"And I thought I was here to rescue a cuddly little creature."

"Cindy likes to cuddle him," Teagan said.

"This man's a *fan* of cuddling." Jing grinned at Abby, who flushed red. "So we'll send him on home to Cindy. Lincoln Park Zoo, is it?"

"How fast can you get him there?"

"I can have him there by tomorrow morning. Special delivery. It will cost a little more, but I can divert funds from an account belonging to a very bad man"—Abby cleared her throat —"or maybe not."

"That's too long, anyway," Teagan said. "He might be dead by then."

"How about I just flag it for Homeland Security? They could have someone there right away."

"Good idea," Teagan said.

"No." Abby grabbed Jing's arm as he started to type. "Uncle Gregorio forgot his bag on the curb at O'Hare last year. You know what they did? They *blew up his underwear,* that's what they did. Because the bag was suspicious, right?"

"Right." Jing pushed away from the keyboard. "No Homeland Security."

"Plus," Abby went on, "they're already looking into the park, and maybe the Wylltsons. Give the Feds enough dots, and they'll connect them to get the picture."

"Or at least figure out who's in the middle of it." Jing leaned back. "So what do we do?"

"Can you tell if anyone is on the system at work?" Teagan asked.

"Sure," Jing said. It took him a moment to get back onto the zoo server. "Agnes Benson is logged in. You want me to drop the information in her lap?"

"Could you?"

"Maybe. If she's looking." Jing went to work again. He glanced up when Thomas and Roisin came in the door. Roisin stormed through the room without stopping to say hello and ran up the stairs.

"How many people live in this house?" Jing asked.

"All of us," Aiden said.

"John Wylltson is the only one missing," Mamieo said. "He'll be along."

"Mr. Librarian." Jing tapped a key. "I know him well."

"Is Roisin okay?" Abby asked Thomas. "She don't look too good."

229

Thomas just shook his head. "What's going on here?"

Teagan introduced Jing and explained as briefly as she could. "They just diverted the crate. I don't understand why they didn't just take Oscar and kill him."

"They enjoy torture," Thomas said.

"So they wanted him to die of thirst?"

"They wanted you to know he died of thirst. That he could have been saved, if only you'd found him."

"But the outside of the crate would be clearly marked 'Live Animal Inside.' Someone could have called."

"Never underestimate the power of human apathy," Thomas said. "Highborn goblins wager on it. Nine times out of ten, they win."

Teagan's phone rang.

"I found him." Agnes's voice was hoarse from crying. "I found Oscar. Dr. Max is on his way. I did it, Tea, and I don't have any idea how. Shit. I'm starting to believe in glitter farts. I've got to make some other calls."

"This time"—Teagan snapped her phone shut—"the goblins lose."

TWENTY

THE door opened once more, and everyone turned as Mr. Wylltson stepped in.

"Hello, Jing," he said. "It's good to see you."

"And you, sir."

"Jing just saved Oscar," Aiden announced. "With his computer."

"Just tracked a package," Jing said. "But it was amazing." He looked up at Abby. "Do I get a kiss?"

"From the monkey?" Abby shrugged. "You can ask him."

"I'd prefer a kiss from an Italian goddess."

"Yeah? I'll take you to meet Zia Sophia. If she likes you, then maybe we'll talk."

"*Talk?* Doesn't a knight-errant deserve a reward?"

"See, that's what we're going to talk about. I don't give any parts of this package"—she motioned the length of her body—"out as rewards. I'm not saying there won't be any rewarding. I'm just saying it will be mutual if there is."

"Mu-tu-al." Jing pressed his hand to his heart. "I *swear* to give as good as I get."

"Yuck," Aiden said. "Why is everybody talking about kissing all the time?"

"Speaking of which." Mr. Wylltson pulled an envelope from his jacket pocket. "This, Mr. Mac Cumhaill, contains your quest."

"His what?" Jing asked.

"His quest," Mr. Wylltson said. "Something any errant knight would understand."

Aiden ran to the door. "Mr. Seamus McGillahee," he announced, pulling it open.

"Are there currently any traps or sprites in the room?" Seamus asked.

"No," Aiden said. "I have a whip now, and Lucy's in the kitchen."

"Excellent." Seamus stepped inside. "Deneux has been chewing my ear off, Mac Cumhaill. It seems you were not very helpful during your interview."

Finn just shrugged.

"What's this about a quest, John Paul?" Mamieo asked, and Teagan winced. The old woman had been in another room during that discussion. This was not the time to bring it up.

"John Wylltson's written down what I've got to do before I can marry his daughter," Finn said.

"*Ask* her to marry you," Mr. Wylltson corrected.

"Negotiating a pre-nup?" Seamus glanced at Teagan and then at Finn. "You should never bargain with a *sídhe*."

"I'm not bargaining," Teagan said.

"But you're involved. That's enough. Maybe you should let me have a look, Mr. Wylltson—"

"No." Teagan and Finn spoke at the same time, but Mr. Wylltson looked thoughtful.

"Perhaps we should talk later, Seamus," he said.

Teagan took Finn's hand. "Dad, you can't be serious."

"Oh, I don't mean talk about this." He waved the envelope. "I'll put this on the shelf behind the change jar. Six months after we are through the current crisis you can open this envelope, Mr. Mac Cumhaill."

"*Six months!*" Abby exclaimed. "That's like half a year."

Mr. Wylltson nodded. "Exactly like. I don't believe in making important decisions in the midst of chaos. I considered making it a year—"

"Dad!"

"—but I am merciful and kindhearted. I just wanted Finn to know that I have considered it. But I do have something to discuss with Seamus. Sophia says—"

"I didn't do it," Aiden said, putting the whip behind his back. "Lennie did, but he didn't mean to. And it's not going to die."

"Is this something I should know about?" Mr. Wylltson asked.

"Mrs. Santini's potted fern," Teagan explained. "Lennie knocked it over and broke the planter. I've already talked to Mrs. Santini about it."

"He knocked it over with the whip?" Mr. Wylltson asked.

Aiden nodded. "But Finn's going to show me how to use it right."

"I've never touched one before, boyo," Finn said. "But we can try."

"I have," Seamus said. "I'm very good with a whip."

"Of course you are." Finn folded his arms. "You could drive for a living, too, no doubt. Possibly run walking tours of the neighborhood?"

Seamus held out his hand. Aiden hesitated, but Finn nodded at him and he handed the whip over.

"Someone left me one of these when I was a kid." *His dad.* Teagan could hear the edge behind his words even if he tried to hide it. "I was a big fan of Indiana Jones," he went on.

"Lennie has the hat," Aiden said. "He wouldn't trade."

"This has a nice feel to it." Seamus hefted the handle, and ran the length of the whip through his hands. "Supple. It's been broken in. I could take the wings off a fly with this."

"You're claiming you can hit a wee little fly with the thing?" Finn wasn't even trying to hide his skepticism.

"No, you can't," Aiden said. "There are no more flies. Lucy ate them."

Jing had been watching the exchange silently. "How about a penny?" He pulled one from his pocket.

"All right." Seamus rolled his shoulders, loosening up, and walked to the center of the room. Everyone moved away from him. Teagan wasn't sure whether they were worried about the whip in his hands or were fleeing the braggart. "Flip it toward the ceiling."

Jing flipped the coin with his thumb, and it spun upward. For two heartbeats, Seamus didn't move, watching the penny rise toward the top of its arc—and then he did, not pulling his arm back over his shoulder as Teagan had expected, but snapping an underhand flick. Suddenly, the whip wasn't a dead snake anymore. She saw the beginning of the movement, then it blurred and the penny *ting*ed off the front window. *Not a braggart, then.*

"Ba-daaaamn, man." Jing stepped forward and offered his hand. "That was bad. The name's Khan. Jinghez Khan."

"Seamus McGillahee." Seamus shook his hand, then coiled the whip. "Like I said, big fan of Indiana Jones."

"You should totally get the coat and hat," Abby said. "You'd rock it."

Aiden turned and looked at the door. "Zoë's coming!" he shouted.

"You hear her song?" Seamus asked.

"Yep. 'The Wonder of You,' by the King."

"Elvis?" Seamus looked disgusted.

Aiden's eyes went wide. *"You don't like the King?"*

Teagan left Seamus and Aiden to glare at one another and pulled her dad aside.

"Dad, Seamus . . . talks too much." If Seamus started going on about Druids and invisible cats, Zoë might think it was strange enough to mention to Ms. Skinner, and Ms. Skinner was just looking for a reason to declare that Aiden's environment was bad. "At the station he was telling one of the detectives . . . everything."

Mr. Wylltson frowned. "About you and your brother?"

"He didn't know we were Highborn then," Teagan said. "He knows a lot more now." Mr. Wylltson nodded as Aiden pulled open the door. Teagan saw Abby wince and look away.

235

The dance therapist generally dressed like a flower child who'd gone missing in the sixties and washed up with her retro wardrobe intact on a modern shore. Today she wore a floral peasant blouse and lime green palazzo pants over scuffed jazz shoes.

She'd tied back her gypsy hair with a hot pink scarf, showing off the smiley-face earrings that dangled from her ears. She was carrying a steel water bottle in one hand and a boom box that looked like it had been dropped once or twice in the other.

Aiden threw himself at her, and Zoë managed to catch him in a hug using the water-bottle arm.

"Seamus McGillahee!" The smiley-face earrings bobbed over Aiden's head. "How nice to see you!"

"You two know each other?" Teagan asked. Things were getting worse.

"We met just recently," Zoë said. "The children of one of Mr. McGillahee's clients were tangled in the social system, and—"

"I got them untangled," Seamus finished.

Zoë set the boom box on top of the television.

"You brought Elvis?" Aiden asked.

"How did you know?" Zoë winked at him. "Are you and Seamus friends? He could join us."

"We're *not* friends," Aiden said. "Seamus doesn't like me."

"Really?" Zoë's eyebrows went up. "Why is that, Seamus?"

"I'm sorry to interrupt," Mr. Wylltson said before the lawyer could answer. "But I just decided to make tacos for dinner. I was wondering if you might give me a ride to the store,

236

Seamus? You do have a car. And I would like a chance to discuss something with you, as I said a moment ago."

"Tacos!" Aiden shouted. "Yepper-roodle-roooo!"

"Or, you could stay and stretch with us." Zoë waved a CD in the air. "I brought the King."

"I'd be happy to give you a ride, Mr. Wylltson," Seamus said.

"Don't worry about tacos for me and Jing, Mr. Wylltson," Abby said. "I'm taking him to Zia's right now."

Mr. Wylltson handed the envelope to Teagan. "Behind the change jar. And you could start the meat. We won't be long."

"Thanks, Zoë," Aiden said after they'd all gone out the door. "Mamieo was going to make baked beets. She said so on the way home."

"I like beets," Zoë said. "But you're welcome." She popped in the CD.

Teagan took the envelope to the kitchen and put it behind the change jar, then took a chub of hamburger and a block of cheese from the fridge.

Raynor's head was bent over his work, but he was singing along with the Elvis recording under his breath. "The Wonder of You."

"Tell me what to do, and I'll help." Finn came in from the living room and glanced at the envelope. "It'll keep my mind off of things."

"You could shred the cheese," Teagan said.

"Right. How, exactly?"

She took out the grater and showed him how to use it. "Watch out for your knuckles. We don't want blood in the food."

Teagan started browning the hamburger and chopped onions while Finn grated. Aiden and Zoë had worked themselves up from "The Wonder of You" to "Jailhouse Rock" by the time Mr. Wylltson carried the grocery bags in.

Seamus backed into the kitchen behind him.

"They're doing the complete choreography," he said. "You'd think Elvis was in the building."

"She speaks Aiden." Mr. Wylltson handed the taco shells to Teagan. "And I'm glad of that."

"Do you think she has Traveler blood?" Teagan asked.

"No," Seamus said. "Not a drop."

"Done with the cheese," Finn announced. "What next?"

"We still need to shred the lettuce." Teagan handed him a head from the bag.

So it *had* just been luck that Zoë had managed to avoid stepping on the *cat-sídhe* and sprite during her visits. Or maybe she just moved so carefully that they avoided her.

"Jailhouse Rock" ended, and as Aiden and Zoë came into the kitchen for a drink of water, Teagan noticed that Gil had his nose plastered to the window again. She turned to pull down the blinds. Zoë might not be able to see the phooka, but anyone could see Joe, who was still sleeping in the corner.

Zoë stepped up behind her and put a hand on her shoulder. Suddenly she knew why Aiden loved the woman. *It was like being touched by her mom.* Little things that Teagan had somehow already forgotten flooded over her, like the smell of linseed oil and paint thinner that always followed her.

Teagan ducked out from under Zoë's hand before she

burst into tears. "Excuse me ... I ... I've got to do something." She managed to get across the kitchen and out the back door without sobbing.

"What *is* that?" Gil asked, pointing at the window as she stepped out.

"A dance therapist," Teagan said, wiping her eyes.

"I like its ears."

"Earrings. I'm sure the Highborn wear earrings in Mag Mell. I'm guessing not like those, though."

"I don't run with other Highborn," Gil said. "Just you. Please put up the cloth. I want to *look* at it." Gil frowned. "I saw it in Mag Mell. It did this ..." He curled his finger in a beckoning motion.

"She was confused. My dad saw and heard things in Mag Mell, too. But his brain just interpreted them in ways he could understand. He thought the baying of the hellhounds was storm sirens."

"So?" Gil asked.

"So Zoë probably thought you were a human. Maybe even someone she knew."

"It thought I was a man?" Gil sounded incredibly happy.

"Just don't hang on the window," Teagan said. "I'll bring you some dinner in a little bit."

Raynor had cornered the dance therapist and was talking about his motorbike when Teagan stepped back in.

"Done with the lettuce." Finn handed her a bowl of green sludge. "Is it supposed to look like that?"

"No," Teagan said. "What did you do to it?"

"Shredded it. Like you showed me."

"Shredding lettuce is different. You use a knife and cut it into thin strips."

"Ah." Finn tipped the bowl and the sludge slid to the side.

"You could be a chef, Mac Cumhaill." Seamus eyed the slime. "Open your own restaurant, perhaps."

"It will be fine," Mr. Wylltson said. "We were just going to chew it anyway. Just put a serving spoon in it and put it on the table. We're ready to eat."

"Zoë's staying," Aiden told Teagan. "Dad said she could."

Teagan collected everyone but Roisin, and they all sat down.

"Mamieo," Mr. Wylltson said, "would you bless the food?" Everyone but Thomas bowed their heads as she prayed. Teagan saw him out of the corner of her eye, staring straight ahead.

"Mamieo," Aiden asked, "how come the Almighty talks to you?"

"I've always been one of his favorites, I suppose," Mamieo said, spooning green sludge into a taco shell. "But it's more than that, pratie. When I was about your size, I had a problem with my parents. They weren't the best, you see. I was sitting in the bushes, crying my heart out. 'Almighty,' I says, 'why did you give me such a bastard for a da?'"

"What did he say?" Aiden asked.

"He said, 'Watch your language, Ida.'"

"I'm glad the Almighty mentioned it," Mr. Wylltson said dryly. "It saves me the trouble."

"The word wasn't completely accurate, I'll admit," Mamieo said. "But it did express my feelings at the time. 'Dry your tears, girl,' the Almighty says. 'I'll be your da.' 'All very fine,' I told him. 'But you must admit, you didn't give me much of a *máthair*, either.'

"'I'll be your *máthair* as well,' says he, cool as a cucumber in May. We've been on excellent terms ever since."

"That's impossible," Aiden said. "'He' means guy. A 'he' can't be a *máthair*. Dad, does it say 'he' in the Bible?"

"It does. Of course, it also says, 'He will cover you with his feathers, and under his wings you will find refuge,' and I doubt that means that the Almighty is a giant chicken. What do you say, Raynor?"

"I think I'd be crazy to get into this," Raynor said. "People have been burned at the stake for less."

"People?" Seamus asked Raynor with a raised eyebrow. Teagan glared at him.

"God is a *guy*," Aiden said with certainty.

"A guy? We're talking about the Almighty, aren't we?" Mamieo said. "The Creator of Creation. Not an old bearded gent with a god-sized winky."

"Mamieo!" Finn flushed completely red. "We have company!"

Teagan put her head in her hands. This was completely out of control.

"Oh, I don't mind." Zoë smiled. "You should hear the conversations around *my* family table. Please be yourselves."

"I couldn't be anyone else, could I?" Mamieo asked.

"No," Zoë agreed. "I'm sure no one would want you to."

Mamieo nodded. "The Creator isn't a woman, either, pratie, but something else entirely. The inspiration for both, I'm thinking."

"I'm asking Father Gordon," Aiden said.

"That should be interesting," Mr. Wylltson said. "Make sure Mamieo Ida is there when you ask Father about it. I want to hear this."

"Don't go giving them the impression that I'm in the habit of arguing with priests, John Paul." Mamieo said. "Because I'm not!"

Even Zoë looked at her in disbelief.

Mamieo sniffed. "Unless they're wrong."

"What did you do at school today, Aiden?" Teagan asked. Luckily, Zoë seemed just as interested in his playground stories as she had been in Mamieo's theology, and they made it through the meal with no more embarrassment.

"I'll take a plate up to Roisin." Thomas stood up. "If you'll excuse me?"

"I really need to be going as well," Zoë said. "Thank you for the dinner and conversation."

Teagan felt ready to collapse by the time Zoë left.

Mr. Wylltson and Seamus were finishing the last of the dishes when someone leaned on the doorbell. Aiden jumped up.

"It's Lennie," he said. "That's our secret ring!"

Everyone followed Aiden to the front door.

"Code red! Code red!" Lennie shouted.

They followed him across the street and through the side gate into the Santinis' backyard. Mrs. Santini, with a big flashlight, and Abby, who had a broom, were standing guard over a blob on the back step.

"Where's Jing?" Teagan asked.

"He left a little while ago," Abby said. "Zia and I have been discussing the situation."

"This looks like a giant owl pellet." Mr. Wylltson squatted beside the blob.

"A what?" Mrs. Santini asked.

"An owl pellet," Teagan repeated. "Owls eat mice and small animals, and digest everything but the hair and bones. They cough those up. You find them beneath owls' nests. You can break the pellet open to find out what they've been eating. Find me a stick, Lennie."

"So, we got a giant owl?" Abby looked at the eaves.

"No," Teagan said thoughtfully as Lennie handed her a stick. "Hyenas do the same thing. They swallow their victims— bones, hair, and all—then cough up what they can't digest. Let's see what this creature has been eating." Teagan broke the pellet open. She wrinkled her nose. The owl pellets she had dissected at school had all been baked to sterilize them. This pellet was fresh enough to be wet inside and smell of digestive juices. She pulled it apart just enough to be able to tell that it was formed of gray hair. Long gray hair.

"What's that?" Finn pointed at a piece of pink and white. Teagan flicked it with the stick, and it bounced toward Finn's boot. He skipped back to avoid it.

243

"Teeth," Aiden said.

Two human teeth . . . and a piece of molded pink plastic.

"It's someone's bridgework," Mr. Wylltson said.

The Dump Dogs *had* been full of meat that morning. And now that they'd cleared their bellies, they would be hungry again.

Mrs. Santini shone her flashlight out over the yard. "I heard a noise over there."

Finn followed the beam to the flower bed beneath the window. "Dog tracks." He kicked at the soft dirt. "Big ones."

The shape shifters had been looking right in the Santinis' kitchen window.

"I'm going with you tonight, Finn," Teagan said.

TEAGAN closed her eyes and tried to relax. Mrs.
Santini had refused once again to consider leaving. But she had agreed to call if she saw or heard
anything at all. And Teagan has insisted on checking every
single one of the Santinis' windows to make sure they were
locked. Now she had to stop worrying. She *had* to sleep if she
was going to hunt goblins with Finn tonight. At first, her dad
wouldn't even consider it, but eventually Raynor had reas-
sured him that not even Dump Dogs could hurt the part of
her that stepped out of her body when she bilocated, and that
Finn would be safer with her along.

She'd decided to leave her body sleeping on Finn's mat in
the basement, where it wouldn't disturb Roisin or Grendal,
with her mother's paintings watching over it from the walls.
Abby, Mamieo, her dad, and Finn were waiting for her in the
kitchen. Seamus was already patrolling the streets in his minivan, watching for any sign of otherworldly creatures.

And she couldn't sleep.

It wasn't worry about the Dump Dogs that was keeping

her awake. It was the voice of the Burr Oak crying out for someone to come and make things right, and the memory of her mother that had come with Zoë's touch.

No wonder the *cat-sídhe* caught hold of lines from poems and grown men wandered away from their families. Glimories. The *longing* for what was lost was as sharp as the blade of a knife.

Teagan threw the covers aside and stood up. There was only one way she knew of to turn off her brain—guardian angels could give the gift of sleep to those who needed it.

She padded barefoot past the clothes she'd set out to wear—clothes didn't come with you when you bilocated—to the door that separated the art gallery, with its hissing dehumidifiers, from the tiny laundry room under the stairs.

Voices were drifting down the laundry chute from the kitchen above her.

"Your grandfather and I used to go hunting together." Mamieo's voice. "All alone in the night, with the fat moon hanging over us. Ah, and wasn't it romantic?"

"It's not like that, Mamieo," Finn said. "You'll see when she comes upstairs."

"Hello," Teagan called up into the darkness. "Could you please ask Raynor to come down for a minute?"

"I'll ask," Finn called back.

Teagan was back on the mat again before the angel made it down the stairs. He looked slightly green in the dim studio light.

"Insomnia?" he asked, settling on the floor beside her.

"Yes."

"What would you like me to do? Explain the workings of internal combustion engines until you fall asleep?"

"I was hoping you could just say, 'Go to sleep,' like you did in the park," Teagan said.

"No one ever seems to love me for who I am. Only for what I can do."

"Please, Raynor. You know I need to go with Finn."

Raynor laced his fingers together and rested his chin on them. "All right. But first, we need to have the Talk."

"Dad already gave me the Talk. And if one more person mentions canoodling—"

The angel frowned. "Do you realize that your entire culture is obsessed with sex? Delightful as the subject is, there is a bigger story here."

"Then what is this about?"

"What you told the lawyer: 'With great power comes great responsibility.'"

"I was quoting a *Spider-Man* movie, Raynor."

"I know. I saw it at the Skyview Drive-In with Brynhild. I was celebrating installing a new windshield. It was amazing."

"'The Talk' is a *Spider-Man* review? I really need to go to sleep, Raynor. *I need to hunt.*"

"I'm trying to be culturally relevant," Raynor said.

"By talking about old movies?"

Raynor cast his eyes heavenward. "Couldn't you have sent one of the messenger angels? You know I'm not good at this!"

There was no sound but the dehumidifiers' hiss.

Raynor sighed. "Let me try again. I was responsible for the death of every creature in the park. I heard the trees cry out. I heard the screams of every creature that lived in them, and the cry of the Creator who loved them."

Teagan wanted to put her pillow over her head and block out his words. Had the willow's branches been laced into unthinkable beauty in the seconds before it died? Had it been whispering petitions, like the Burr Oak? And all the little creatures . . . the squirrels and mice had burned.

"They were *loved*," Raynor said. "I knew how much they were loved. If I ever took a life without understanding that, I would be one of the fallen. Choice is the greatest power any creature can have. Our choices create the future. I had to choose between the living creatures in the park and the children of Chicago."

"But . . . isn't the Almighty in control of everything you do?"

"Do you seriously believe that the Creator of Creation controls my every action? Or the actions of Mab and Fear Doirich?"

"No," Teagan admitted. "I don't."

"My choices aren't perfect," Raynor said. "They are just the best I can do. Currently, things seem to be *trending in the right direction,* as Mamieo Ida would say. In this household, at least, and that's because you are living in the future created by the choices of those who came before you. This is a long story, and one that isn't over yet. It began before Maeve chose to love Amergin, even though she knew it meant they would die. Mamieo Ida chose to step into a storm to save a frightened child. Your father chose to love your mother, even through her episodes and stay in the mental hospital—"

Teagan pulled the covers up to her chin. *If we never loved, then maybe we would never feel pain.* That's what her dad had told her. *Love anyway. It's worth it.*

"—and it will go on through you."

"Why are you giving me the Talk just now?"

"Because your choices aren't going to be perfect, either, but you've got to keep trying. Because what you have here is the best chance I've ever had to finish this. *Keep trending in the right direction.* Go to slee—"

"Raynor!" Teagan sat up quickly. "Why is it you have been ... wary of me since the first time we met? It's not just that I'm Highborn, is it? Because Aiden is too, partly, and you love him."

The angel drew a ragged breath. "I knew someone very like you once. She's living the future her choices created. It's hell."

"Mab." She saw a flash of pain in the angel's eyes. "Hell for her, or for you, Raynor?"

"For both of us. Go to sleep, Teagan."

For one moment longer she was aware of the mat and the pillow, then sleep settled over her like a weight, pushing her down until she couldn't make her muscles move. Her mind was completely alert—it was as if its ties to her body were disconnecting.

The last circuits between her mind and body shut down,

and Teagan's bilocate form sat up, stretched, then stood, looking toward the stairs to make sure the angel had gone.

She quickly put on the clothes she'd laid out by the foot of the mat, along with an old pair of shoes, then adjusted the pillow and pulled the blanket up to the chin of the body sleeping on the mat. Nothing—not cold or sound or pain—could wake it until she returned, because everything that was *her* had stepped out of it.

"Hey, Bright Eyes," Finn said, and her dad and Mamieo turned to her as she reached the top of the basement stairs.

"Good lord." Mr. Wylltson gripped the side of the table.

"Saints preserve us!" Mamieo crossed herself, and then her hand went to the pocket where she'd put her nitro pills.

Abby's mouth was hanging open. Teagan had never seen her speechless before.

She didn't have to check a mirror to know what the problem was; her eyes *were* bright. They were glowing like molten gold.

Mamieo pulled out the bottle and struggled with the cap.

Finn took it from her, opened it, and shook out a pill. Teagan glanced at Raynor. The angel was hiding in his work, exhausted from having to use so many words.

"They unsettled me the first time I saw them, too," Finn told Mamieo as he handed her the pill. "But it's Tea, just the same. As dear to you as your own flesh, remember?"

Mamieo popped the tiny pill in her mouth.

Abby still hadn't said a word, but she was shaking her head.

Mr. Wylltson came around the table and touched his daughter's face. "You're . . . cold."

"The warm me is fine," Teagan assured him. "It's sleeping downstairs. This body doesn't generate heat, or use food for fuel. I'm not sure what it's made of, but I am sure Finn's right. This is even more *me* than the part that's sleeping."

"She has no heartbeat," Finn said. "No body heat. Your da and I were discussing canoodling, Tea"—he waved at the gaping laundry chute—"you might have heard. As you can see, John, the kissing would be . . ." Finn pursed his lips, apparently searching for a word.

"It would be what, exactly?" Teagan asked.

"Unsettling," Finn said. "As we've discussed before."

Mr. Wylltson shook his head. "Raynor, you're sure Tea can't be hurt when she's . . . like this?"

"She should avoid salt in the eyes and being pierced by iron. But if anything happens to the body she is wearing now," Raynor said, "she'll just return to the one sleeping downstairs. That's the one that needs watching over. She could be trapped away from it, and it would eventually die."

"What about the *sluagh*?" Mr. Wylltson asked. "The creature that came looking for her the last time she stepped out of her body."

Raynor scratched his head. "That's a good question. I'm not sure whether it could eat her soul or not."

"I can outrun it, Dad," Teagan said. "I can outrun anything when I'm like this. And Finn has dealt with *sluagh* before."

"Several times," Finn assured him.

"This isn't all right." Abby had found her voice at last. "I thought it would be, but it isn't."

"Abby?" Teagan went over to her. "It is me, really."

"I know that, right?" Abby took her hand and frowned. "Aren't you freezing? I got a sweater that would totally go with those eyes."

"I don't need it," Teagan said. "I don't feel the cold."

"So how am I supposed to take care of you when you're like this, Tea? What am I supposed to do with this?"

"I couldn't have put it better myself, Abigail," said Mr. Wylltson. "I can't believe I'm giving my daughter permission to run wild with a boy all night. Where are you going, exactly?"

"We'll start with Rosehill," Finn said. "And if the Dogs aren't there, we'll take to the streets and alleys. I'm betting they'll be hunting street people. It looks like it's going to storm, and I know the hidey places the homeless head for on nights like this."

Teagan turned to the window. She could see Joe's black silhouette against the low clouds tinted orange from ambient city light. The rain he had promised had not arrived yet, but Finn was right. Teagan could feel the storm building.

Gil ran past the window and did his tumbling trick with the cinder-block wall.

"Not again." Finn shook his head. "No. Raynor's right here. He can peek out at the creature."

"It will break his heart if we leave without him."

"We'll go out the front, then."

"Mrs. Santini is going to be watching the street," Teagan said. "I don't want her seeing me like this."

"Does the woman ever sleep?" Finn asked.

"I don't believe so," Mr. Wylltson said. "Sophia always seems to know what's going on."

"You just want him to come along because you can't stand the idea of the creature throwing himself at the wall all night."

"That's true."

"If he tries to hold my hand, I'm sending him back." Finn leaned over to kiss the white puff of hair on top of Mamieo's head. "We'll be careful. And I'll have your daughter back before the rosy dawn, Mr. Wylltson."

"Teagan," Mr. Wylltson said, "if you do find the Dump Dogs—"

She pulled her cell phone out of her pocket and held it up. "Good."

Abby was making a strange noise in the back of her throat as they went out the door.

"That went well," Finn said, pulling it shut behind him. "Don't you think?"

Joe had finished tearing out the sod before he went to sleep. Teagan's feet sank into soft dirt as she stepped into the yard. It was going to be a lovely mess of mud when the rain came, but right now it smelled of good earth.

Gil rebounded from a flip and raced up to them.

"Eeeeeeee!" he said when he saw Teagan's eyes. "We're going to run!"

"Yes!" Teagan grinned.

"We're hunting Dump Dogs," Finn said. "The kind with big teeth. Are you sure you want to come?"

Gil nodded.

"There will be cars," Teagan warned.

"Men are not afraid of cars," Gil said.

"Keep that in mind." Finn opened the back gate. "Because I can't be holding hands tonight."

THE smell of the storm sent shivers of delight down Teagan's spine. Finn started down the alley at an easy trot, and Teagan let him set the pace. She could run all night, and Gil could almost keep up with her, but Finn's body had limits.

Grizabella was sitting on top of a Dumpster, but she jumped behind it as they approached. *Either my eyes or Finn the* cat-sídhe *killer are too much for her,* Teagan thought. Finn stopped when they reached the street, catching Teagan's arm as she started to pass him.

"*Sluagh,*" he said.

The gray-skinned creature moved spiderlike across the side of the building, turned its hungry face toward them—then dropped to the ground and dove down a storm drain.

"That's interesting," Finn said. "Maybe you don't look as tasty as the creature thought you did the other night."

Teagan laughed. When the *sluagh* had come for her before, it had thought she was dying. It must have thought it could catch her soul, helpless and confused as a newborn, to feed on.

That might have worked in the first moment she'd stepped out of her body. But not now.

They picked up the pace as they left the alley. There were very few cars on the street, but Teagan turned her eyes away from the drivers, and Gil hid behind Finn every time one passed. They even saw Seamus McGillahee's van once, prowling like a great white elephant. If he saw them, he didn't stop.

"What would he do if he found the Dump Dogs?" Finn asked.

"The same thing we would do. Dial Raynor's Rescue."

"See, that's the thing." Finn started trotting again. "Raynor can't just keep toasting the neighborhood, can he? And without that fire or his truck to run over the creatures with, he's not that much help. I'm the one who has to deal with the Dogs."

Teagan didn't comment. She'd told her dad they would call. And when she called, Raynor would come.

It was a relief to reach the cemetery, where she didn't have to worry about drivers being distracted by her eyes. The cold iron was barely a tingle as she ducked through the fence.

They walked through the woods silently, alert for any movement in the bushes. Aside from the rustling of mice in the leaves, there was nothing. When they reached the manicured lawns, Teagan hesitated in order to get her bearings. She'd been in Rosehill after dark only once, when she'd taken a Haunted Chicago tour with Abby.

There had been nothing in the cemetery that night but moldering bodies and scary stories. But there was something here now. The *scratch, scratch, scratch* she'd heard when they'd buried Bill Bailey was louder. It was all around her in the dark air, moving when the wind shifted.

"Do you hear that, Finn?" she asked.

"I hear the wind in the bushes."

"No," Teagan said. "That's not it. Something's digging in the air."

"That makes no sense."

"I hear it, too," Gil said. "It's scary."

Teagan turned in a circle. "I can't figure out which direction it's coming from."

"I'll keep my ears open," Finn said. "Let's get going." They had more than three hundred acres to search, including the woods.

They spread out, keeping just within sight of one another, and ran through the dark shadows of the tombstones and mausoleums, over the graves of Civil War soldiers.

"Tea," Finn called when they had covered half the cemetery.

Gil had stopped to stare at the statue of the little girl emerging from the filled-in fountain at the Vehon monument.

"A baby Greenteeth," he whispered.

Teagan took a step toward the statue. The goblin woman she'd called to her death had certainly never looked like that. She could just make out the writing on the wall behind the statue: *Until the Day Breaks and the Shadows Flee Away.*

Scratch, scratch, scratch.

Teagan held her breath and focused. If she didn't find out what was making the noise, it would drive her mad.

"Who did that to her?" Gil was still staring at the statue.

"Is that what's bothering you?" Finn asked. "She was never a real girl, boyo. Just a stone statue."

Gil continued staring until they pulled him away.

"The Dogs aren't here," Finn said at last. "We need to take to the streets."

"But *something* is here." Teagan eyed the towers of the gothic castle that served as the front gate. The offices were in the thick walls, and probably the night watchman as well. But she *had* to know what the scratching was before they left. "I'm going up."

"Not a good idea," Finn said. "Rain's coming. I'm surprised it's not pouring on us already."

"I *need* to."

Finn leaned back and looked up at the crenelated top of the wall.

"Let me go first, then," he said. He made it about ten feet up before his foot slipped and he turned and jumped to the ground. "It's no good for climbing, Tea. The edges of the stones are all weathered round."

"I'm going to try," Teagan said. "My fingers are smaller than yours. I might be able to find a grip."

The old limestone blocks were so weathered that she could use only her fingertips and toes, but she started working her way up the wall.

"How are you doing that?" Finn called softly so the night watchman wouldn't hear.

Teagan twisted to look down at them, but she didn't answer. Finn was standing with his hands on top of his head; Gil was trying to climb the stones after her, despite his trotter. He couldn't make it more than two feet before he fell and got up to try again.

When she reached the top, she found that the wall was higher than it had seemed when she was climbing, but she wanted to be higher still.

Teagan jumped from crenelation to crenelation until she reached the tower. She saw Finn and Gil following along on the ground, looking up at her. She waved and started to climb again.

When she reached the top, she groped over the edge and felt the tingle of a cold iron rod. She gripped it, hoping it was anchored well enough to bear her weight as she pulled herself over. It was. Finn's face was a pale oval in the darkness below her when she looked down again. Gil just wouldn't give up. He was still trying to climb and falling back.

Teagan stood on the parapet, one hand gripping the iron rod for balance. She leaned out over the emptiness, spreading the fingers of her free hand and letting the wind blow through them.

Suddenly her hair started to rise, and the air around her turned sweet. Ozone. Electrons were rising from the earth below her, reaching for the opposite charge in the clouds above. *Iron rod*, she thought, but not quickly enough. The lightning poured down like a river of fire, tracing the path the electrons had made through the air. *Through her.*

In a millisecond she was filled with light and joy. With power. She let go of the rod and held the lightning inside her.

She could feel her hair moving, and she knew it wasn't the

wind. She stretched out her hand and saw Saint Elmo's fire light her fingertips like candles.

And beyond her fingertips . . . shadow men. She could see them in the darkness all around her, scratching at the wall between the worlds with their knifelike fingertips.

"Got you," Teagan said.

"Samhain," the shadows sighed. "Samhain comes!"

The wind tore at her. Teagan grabbed the iron rod again, and the charge passed from her into the metal and down, then slammed through her again as the return bolt went back to the clouds, and down again—three full strokes, the darkness around her frozen in place, and then the vision was gone and Finn's arms were around her.

"T EA!"

"I'm fine." She laughed out loud.

"You can't be fine."

"I'm better than fine." The lighting had left a spark in her. It felt like *joy* still bouncing around inside. "How did you get up here so fast, Finn? I didn't think you could climb that wall."

"I had motivation, didn't I? I thought the lightning was going to strike you, girl."

"It did," Teagan said. "It was wonderful."

"You mean I hurried up here for no reason?" He glanced over the side. "Getting down might be a problem."

"Not for—" Teagan felt her hair start to rise again.

"Lightning!" She shoved Finn down. He flattened himself on the rooftop.

Teagan jumped up on the crenelation, trying to draw the bolt, but it struck the flagpole on the center tower instead, and then thunder roared.

Finn staggered to his feet.

"LET'S GO!" he shouted, pulling her down beside him.

"Why are you yelling?" Teagan asked.

Finn slapped his ear with the palm of his hand. "SO I CAN HEAR MYSELF OVER THE RINGING." He scooped her up and half lifted her over the side. "DOWN YOU GO."

"I won't leave you up here," Teagan said.

"WHAT ARE YOU TALKING ABOUT, GIRL? I'M SENDING YOU DOWN FIRST SO YOU CAN CATCH ME IF I FALL."

Teagan started working her way down the tower more slowly than she might have, because Finn was following her. The lightning had moved to the south, out over the city, and a few fat raindrops hit her by the time she reached the lower wall.

She waited until Finn was beside her and then they both ran, jumping from crenelation to crenelation until they found a tree close enough for Finn to jump to a branch. He climbed down, dropped out of the tree, and turned to catch her as she followed.

"WHAT HAPPENED UP THERE?" Finn bellowed.

"We've found the place where the gate is opening. But it won't be tonight." Now she understood what Raynor had been saying about Mag Mell being right next door, and far away. The shadows had been very close . . . and still a long way off at the same time.

"WHAT?"

She repeated herself, shouting this time, and Finn nodded.

Gil staggered out of the dark. He was hiccupping and there were tears on his face.

"I'm sorry, I'm sorry," he said, wrapping his arms around Teagan. She could feel his body shaking.

"What's wrong, Gil?"

"I promised to stay close to you. It hurt so bad, but I couldn't climb. I tried to, but I couldn't do it." The phooka hadn't been persistent; rather, he'd been bewitched by a promise into trying to do the impossible over and over again.

"*I'm* sorry." Teagan patted his back. "I'm so sorry, Gil. I didn't even think." This was the second time she hadn't thought of the promise that bound him to her. Apparently, Hákon hunted answers instead of taking care of their friends.

"I THINK HE'D BETTER STOP HUGGING MY GIRL!" Finn must have read her lips.

A light went on in an office window above them, and they all ducked.

"Back the way we came," Teagan whispered, motioning so that Finn would understand. She was done hunting answers. It was time to hunt Dump Dogs. They didn't stop running until they found the gap in the fence and squeezed through.

"What happened up there, then?" Finn asked, his voice not quite as loud as it had been.

"We don't have to worry about shadows tonight," Teagan said as they walked down the street. "When the gate opens, Rosehill will be the place."

"How do you know?" Finn asked.

"Because I saw the shadow men when the lightning struck me."

"You looked like a *bean-sídhe*." Gil's ears were still drooping. "All green and glowing."

Even now the spark was moving inside her. The Stormrider equivalent of an adrenaline rush, she supposed. Whatever it was, it felt good.

Teagan laughed. "I can't believe how fast you got up there, Finn."

"I tried to climb," Gil said. "I tried to come help you, too." He held up his trotter. "I hate this. *I hate my broken hand!*"

"If you hug her again," Finn said, "you might have two broken hands."

Teagan looked down the street. The rain had been all promise and few drops, but the clouds had lowered and the air was still moist enough to make halos around the streetlights. She wanted to hunt. The Dump Dogs were out there somewhere, but if choices created the future, this Hákon was going to choose a future with friends she hadn't driven insane or physically damaged by neglect. They could take a few minutes to make sure Gil was all right.

"You can do some things Finn can't do." Teagan patted the phooka's shoulder, but she met Finn's eyes over his head. Finn's eyebrows went up, and then he nodded. He got it.

"He cannot," Finn said.

"Yes, he can."

"For instance?" Finn asked.

"He can run all night and all day."

Gil's ears twitched.

"I'd forgotten about that," Finn said.

"He can swim."

"I'd forgotten that as well."

"And that flip he was doing in the backyard was very cool."

Gil grinned. He ran straight up the wall in front of them, did a flip, and landed in front of Teagan.

"I saw something like that in a free-running competition last year," Teagan said. "It's amazing."

"Free running?" Finn asked. "Is that what you call it? I just call it staying alive—with style. That was pretty good, boyo. But if a Dump Dog was chasing you down the alley and you came to a brick wall like this one, you'd bounce right back at it with that move, wouldn't you?" Finn ran at the wall, jumped up and bounced off of it and executed a perfect side flip. He ended up running parallel to the wall.

"I call that a flip-switch. I don't know if you should try it, though. One mistake and you'll break your neck."

Gil ran at the wall, bounced off, and tucked into a side flip. He over-rotated and staggered when he landed, but it was still very good.

"Oh ho, so it's a competition, then," Finn said.

Gil held up his trotter.

"Fair enough." Finn curled his fingers into a fist. "I'll use one hand, and one fist. We'll be even."

"Wait," Teagan said. "I want to try it. Show me again."

"Didn't you hear what I just told the phooka?" Finn asked. "This move can paralyze you."

"I'm nearly indestructible right now," Teagan said. "Remember?"

Finn nodded. "You learn the standing side flip first. Unless you have that down, and nice and high, you shouldn't even try a flip-switch off the wall. I'll show you how, then spot you." He did a standing side flip. "Did you see? Arms and legs tucked and you twist like you're a whirligig with a pin through your middle." He did it again. "You've noticed the boyo rotates to the left? That's because he's right-handed, so turning that way is more natural. You should try that first." He stood behind her and put his hands on her waist. "Jump when I say jump. You're going to tuck and rotate, but not until I tell you. Jump!"

Teagan launched herself up, and Finn held her in the air. "Tuck and twist." He rotated her until he could drop her on her feet.

"Okay. Now I want to try it alone." She did, and almost landed on her head. She might be indestructible, but Newton's laws of motion clearly still applied.

"I can't watch this," Finn said.

"Nearly indestructible," Teagan reminded him, and tried again. By the seventh time, her side flip was as good as Gil's. "Now the wall."

She ran at the bricks, bounced up, and rotated, staggering only a little more than Gil had on landing.

"I did it!" The spark the lightning had left in her spread through her body.

"Finn didn't see," Gil said. "He covered his eyes."

Finn glared at the phooka. "I was watching through my fingers. Now are we ready to hunt?"

"Oh, yes!" Teagan said.

"Let's run!" Gil agreed.

"Then let's take it up a notch. If you're man enough."

And Finn ran, not just down the street but jumping up steps and stairs, vaulting over walls, and landing in rolls.

Gil was adapting to the cement and straight lines, using the moves he might have used running and jumping through the forest, adding butterfly twists and flourishes that had Teagan convinced that he was a physical genius, as well as a showoff.

She tried to imitate the phooka because they were nearly the same size, but his movements were almost inhuman, so she followed Finn instead, learning as she went.

Finn would do a trick, and Gil would equal or better it. This wasn't climbing a rock face, where you needed two hands. It was more about speed and control, and the phooka gained more confidence with each block they traveled.

Finally, Finn left street level, bouncing up a series of not-so-obvious steps, from a decorative fence to an air conditioner to a window balcony and on, all the way to the roof of a building. He wasn't cheating—he used just one hand. But Gil was left in the street, looking up.

"That's not fair," Teagan called up after Finn. In Mag Mell they'd had to climb a tree to save their lives. Gil had clung to the branches and edged out along the limbs, holding on with his one good hand. The phooka was scared of heights.

Finn just held up the fingers of one hand and wiggled them, clearly saying, *I did it one-handed, then, didn't I?*

A car went past, and when Gil turned to watch it without flinching, Teagan realized that he had made enormous progress since this morning, when he had clung to Finn's hand as they'd passed. *Men are not afraid of cars.* He had been afraid to walk on hard, flat surfaces. Now he was treating the street and the walls around it like a playground. *Because Finn did.* He was measuring all things manly against the Mac Cumhaill, and he wanted desperately to be a man.

"You don't have to—" Teagan said, but Gil jumped to the

top of the fence. The next jump was faster, more confident. Teagan shrugged and followed him. When she reached the rooftop, the phooka was grinning like an idiot, and so was Finn.

"I did it!" Gil laughed. "*I* did."

"Let's go, then," Finn said.

Following Finn, the phooka seemed to lose all fear. He made amazing leaps between buildings, landing and rolling on the roofs. The first time Teagan jumped from the rooftop of one store to the next, clearing the five-foot gap cleanly and rolling, she realized that she hadn't really had fun since her mother died. Not this much fun.

With enough effort she could learn any sequence of movements, and she had the advantage of never getting tired, so she could keep working on it while Gil and Finn rested or stopped to watch the lightning in the distance.

Seamus in his great white whale was patrolling their neighborhood, so they hunted through the shopping district. There were more people out and about at night than Teagan had ever imagined: bakery workers, security guards, maintenance workers, prostitutes, and cops.

The Dump Dogs would have no trouble finding someone confused or alone here. There were drunks outside of bars, and street people of all ages huddled under doorways and overpasses. She was surprised at how many of them Finn knew. She had spent the last three years in high school; he'd spent them watching over the people of the night. It definitely wasn't the kind of job Abby had in mind. No dental.

When the sky began to lighten, they started working their way home again.

"Maybe the lawyer found them," Gil said when they reached the library. "With his *car*."

Finn touched Teagan's arm. "Tea. They're back. Your ghosties, I mean."

She turned to see two old people, a man and a woman, standing hand in hand under the amber glow of the streetlight in front of the library. The old woman wiggled her fingers at them as if to say hello. The old man had a book tucked under his arm. Teagan didn't remember if he'd worn glasses before, but there was a pair perched on his nose now.

She knelt down to check her shoelaces.

"Get ready," she said softly when she stood up.

"What are we doing?" Finn asked.

"We're going to outrun those two," Teagan said. "I can do it in this body."

She hadn't been able to before. No matter how fast she went, the ghosts had stayed right with her, never seeming to take anything but shuffling steps. And then they'd smile ... and disappear.

"We're going to outrun the old people?" Gil tipped his head and studied them. "They don't look very fast."

"I think they're ghosties," Finn said. "They've been following Teagan around."

"And they're scary," Teagan added.

"Old people aren't scary," Finn said. "Not even ghostie old people. Are you scared of old phookas, Gil?"

Gil scratched his head. "Phookas don't get old."

"Neither does the Mac Cumhaill. Maybe that's why we're not afraid of these two." He waved at them, and the old lady smiled. "She looks familiar."

"Of course she does. You've seen her twice now. Stop encouraging them. Ready?" Teagan stood up. "Now!"

She sprinted past the library gate and down the street, pushing herself to the limit. She ran until she could hear Finn pulling in air in great gasps behind her, and then looked over her shoulder. Gil was running beside Finn, and the old couple was just a few feet behind them, still smiling, still taking their tiny shuffling steps.

Teagan stopped and turned to face them, Gil skidding to a stop beside her, and Finn leaning over with his hands on his knees. The old couple looked at each other and smiled.

"I hate it when you do that," Teagan said to them. "So just stop, okay? And ... thank you for saving me from the *sluagh* the other night. But would you please just leave me alone?" She took a step toward them and they were suddenly one step farther away, and then they vanished.

"It's the dawn," Finn said. "I promised to get you home, girl."

The sky *was* rosy as they made their way back up the alley to the Wylltsons' backyard.

Joe was still motionless, so they crept past him quietly.

"That was good," Gil whispered. "Now I will sleep."

"You're not the only one," Finn whispered back. "Good night, boyo."

Raynor looked up when Tea and Finn came in the door. For an instant, Teagan was sure he could smell the ozone clinging to her or see the spark the lightning had left inside.

"Your bike's all together," Finn said. "That's amazing."

"You can get a lot done when you don't sleep," Raynor said. "All it needs is gas. What have you been up to, Tea? Playing with electrons? I should have warned you about that."

W HAT'S wrong with Tea?" Donnie asked as she
slid into the stretch limo. "She sick or something?"

He'd twisted around to look at her from the front seat.
Leo, in his full chauffeur's uniform, waited until Abby climbed
in behind Tea, then shut the door.

"Take a look at her." Rafe was in the back with Angelo.
"You can see what's wrong. You party, you pay. Know what I'm
saying?"

"Shut up, Rafe," Abby said. "It's not like that. Could we
stop at the Feather?" Abby asked when Leo got back in. "I
want coffee."

Why was everyone shouting this morning? Teagan blinked
and felt it in slow motion—her eyelashes swooshing down
before her lids banged shut. She had to force herself to pry
them open again. Colors were too bright. And shiny things—
like people's faces—had halos. Raynor should *definitely* have
warned her about this. Her backpack had seemed almost
too heavy to carry out the door. Her biology and psychology
books felt like bricks.

I will not experiment with electrons ever again, she told herself. *Never, ever again. I will stick to safe levels of sizzle. Like kissing Finn.*

Leo pulled up beside the curb outside the Black Feather.

"Don't get out," Abby said as he started to open his door.

"It's a habit," Leo replied. "You wear the uniform, your body just makes the moves."

Teagan had given Raynor and Seamus a rundown of the night's doings before she'd stepped back into her body, explaining about the lightning, about the shadows and Rosehill. Seamus had headed out to park his van close to the cemetery and keep an eye on things, and Mr. Wylltson had gone with him. No one had seen any sign of the Dump Dogs. They could be halfway to New Jersey by now...but they probably weren't. Not if they really were friends of Roisin.

At least Finn had gone to bed before she'd stepped back into her body and felt the full effects of her electron hangover. She wouldn't want him to see her this way. Not even Abby's Morning Makeover had helped. Abby had finally given up and called Leo for a ride.

Teagan leaned her head back, closed her eyes, and tried to ignore the Turtles' talk. Leo was giving Rafe explicit instructions about exactly what he was allowed to say at school that day.

How far away had the shadows really been? They had seemed miles away, years away, but that couldn't be true. Samhain was coming, when the walls between the worlds grow thin. Was it Mamieo or Raynor who'd told her that? If she was wrong and the doorway opened today, Seamus would see them, and her dad could hold them back with his songs until Raynor arrived.

Abby returned with an armload of coffees.

"Bada-bing!" Rafe said when she handed him a cup. He began to drink, then stopped in mid-slurp as they approached the school. "You know that idea you had, Abby? The one about Leo dropping us off? Probably not so good." There were news vans parked outside the school, and reporters were interviewing students going in. Of course. She'd have thought of it earlier if her brain had been working. Today was not the day to roll up like a movie star in one of Abby's uncle's stretch limos.

Everyone but Leo slid down in their seats as they passed the school.

"I'll drop you around the corner," he said. "If anything happens, anything at all, you call me. I'll get there."

"Chillax," Abby said. "I got everybody on a calling tree."

"*Chillax?*" Leo looked at them in the mirror. "You hear that from Jing, Abigail?"

Abby shrugged. "You don't like it, talk to Zia Sophia."

"I worry," Leo said. "Jing was holding up the wall of the building when we went past. Waiting for someone?"

"Of course he was. And don't worry so much. Anything happens, you'll get a text saying where to be. *Crap!*"

"What?" Teagan asked. The coffee was actually helping. She could almost look directly at people.

"I left my phone in the bathroom when I gave up on fixing your face. Give me yours, Rafe."

"Why would I give you my cell phone?"

"Because I need one." Abby held out her hand.

Leo nodded. Rafe made a face, but he handed his phone over.

Abby's the first one you dragged home. That's what Raynor had said. The Mac Cumhaill, *lhiannon-sídhe*, an angel, and ... Abby. What other girl in school could call for a limo because her friend needed a ride? Could tell her cousins and boyfriend that Teagan was not human, *and have them believe her?* Or could expect the most expensive lawyer in Chicago show up if she needed him at the police station?

Abby wasn't normal. She was some kind of ... Mob princess. Maybe not the kind with money and bodyguards, but definitely the kind with Family connections. Just like she'd always said. Of course, she'd also said that she was psychic, and that God was Italian. Teagan took another sip of coffee.

Leo pulled up to the curb out of sight of the reporters, got out, and came around to open the door for them.

"You guys be careful," he said, helping Abby to the sidewalk. "All of you."

"You worry too much," Abby said. "But thanks for the ride."

Jing was still leaning against the front of the building when they got there. He wore slacks, a green T-shirt tight enough to show off his biceps, and a matching pair of Oakley shades on his face. Abby would approve of the look, but it made Teagan shiver. Kyle and Isabeau had worn sunglasses to hide their eyes when they bilocated.

The fan club gathered around Jing parted when he pushed himself away from the wall.

"Ab-i-gail," he said, coming down the steps. He didn't even look toward Teagan until Abby had given him a kiss on the cheek.

"Zia Sophia was really that impressed?" Donnie asked.

"Of course she was," Rafe said. "She's female, right? And he's the Mighty Khan. Irresistible to all womankind."

"All but Tea." Jing glanced at her, did a double take, then pulled his Oakleys off and slid them on her face. He tipped her chin up as he adjusted them.

"Better?"

"Yes," Teagan admitted. The halos were completely gone.

"Good. I don't want you giving Abby a bad reputation. Everybody knows you two hang together. Where you go, she goes. And wherever you went, it looks bad."

"Just point me toward class," Teagan said. "I'll try not to ruin any reputations."

"Class? Don't you have an appointment with the grief counselor?"

"Not if I can possibly avoid it." Teagan headed for the door.

"How about you, Jing?" Abby asked. "Are you going to talk to them?"

"Already been. It was suggested I talk to her if I wanted to play in the game tomorrow. She said she'd be seeing you today, Tea."

"She who?"

"One of the volunteers. Ms. Skinner. Said she knew your family."

Teagan groaned. Seven hours. All she had to do was avoid the social worker for seven hours and she could go home, crawl out of this body, and let it sleep off whatever she had done to it.

She managed to avoid Skinner all morning, and took the extra precaution of skipping lunch, buying a bag of trail mix from the vending machine instead and eating it surreptitiously in the library.

There were plenty of rumors flying around about what had happened in the cafeteria. Half the student body had seen the Gaglianos taken from the building by the police. She saw Rafe walking down the hall with a fan club of his own. Apparently he was keeping his mouth shut with such flair that everyone knew he knew . . . something. And of course everyone knew he had been a person of interest in the lunch lady's murder.

Sixth period was the most difficult to get through. Mr. Diaz was back, looking almost awake. The classroom had been scrubbed by professional cleaners to remove every trace of Cade's blood, but Teagan could smell the chemicals. No one, including Mr. Diaz, talked about anything but what had happened to Cade and whether or not he would live. Class was almost over when an office aide showed up with a note.

"Ms. Wylltson"—Mr. Diaz held up the slip of paper— "your presence is requested."

Teagan packed up her books, heaved the backpack onto her shoulder, and followed the aide down the hall to the classroom that had been repurposed for grief counseling. Ms.

Skinner was sitting on the edge of the teacher's desk with a smug look on her face.

"Teagan, I'm so glad to see you!" she said, as if this had been Teagan's idea. "I was afraid you wouldn't come by."

Teagan took off her backpack and slid into one of the desks. Molly's. This had been their calculus classroom last year. "You sent for me."

"Could you take off your sunglasses?"

"No," Teagan said. "My eyes hurt."

"I want to help you, Teagan." Ms. Skinner sounded almost sincere. "And your brother. I know you don't believe me, but I do. Your family wasn't like this before your cousin showed up. I know he was on school property during the incident. He had something to do with Cade's injury, didn't he?"

"No," Teagan said.

"Several students said he was in the room, Tea." She sat down at the desk beside Teagan's, so that their eyes were level. "You know I was his social worker before he ran away? Things *happened* at the homes where I placed him. Terrible things. Did you know that he was implicated in the death of his own parents?" She tapped her pink-nailed fingers on the desktop. "What am I supposed to do? How can I convince you that I only want to help?"

Teagan looked past her out the window, then did a double take when she saw Seamus McGillahee's coat. It was almost too bright to look at, even through the Oakleys, even with the dirt stains. Saoirse was wearing it. Lollan and Bairre weren't with her. She held up a quart jar full of dark liquid.

Ms. Skinner must have seen Teagan tense, because she turned to look, too. "Who's that? Is she a student here?"

The liquid was too viscous to be water or even oil. It stretched like a slug toward the sidewalk as Saoirse tipped the jar. *They'd put the melty shadow pieces in a jar and mixed them with a stick . . .*

The slug reached the sidewalk, puddled, then stood up the way Teagan had seen shadow men do in Mag Mell, only this one wasn't man-shaped. It looked like three creatures had been fused together at the back. Three heads facing different directions, multiple limbs in the wrong places.

Saoirse dropped the jar to the sidewalk and watched it shatter. She blew Teagan a kiss through the window, then turned and walked away.

"Is that a friend of yours?" Ms. Skinner asked.

"No." Teagan pulled her cell phone out of her pocket. The screen was blank. She'd had it in her pocket last night when the lightning struck; it was fried. The shadow was lurching toward the window.

"Loan me your phone," Teagan said. "This is an emergency."

"Broken glass is not an emergency." Ms. Skinner had turned back to her. "Though we should let the janitors know."

The shadow didn't bother with the window. It stuck one head through the wall and turned a black featureless face toward Ms. Skinner. The two other heads came through after it, then one arm and a leg, apparently attached where the other arm should be. It put a hand and a foot against the flat of the wall and pulled itself into the room.

"You are acting very strangely, Teagan. I think"—Teagan grabbed her arm to pull her away from the thing—"I think that you should not touch me."

Ms. Skinner shook her off and backed right into the shadow. Her face contorted, and for one instant Teagan could see the panic in her eyes. She made a couple of jerky movements and then smiled at Teagan. Only it wasn't Ms. Skinner behind those eyes anymore. Her hands ran up and down her sides and groped her own breasts.

"Nice abode." There were more than three voices speaking as one. Many more. Her face pulled up in a grotesque smile.

And then Ms. Skinner was back.

"Oh, my god." She leaned against the desk. "My god. Help me."

But it had her again, cavorting its abode around the room like a marionette, then pulled her cell phone out of her pocket and dialed, jabbing the keys like a zombie.

"This is Bernadette Skinner," she said to whoever was on the line. "I need a child picked up immediately. He is in imminent peril." A pause. "Yes, danger. What do you think peril is? They are going to do terrible things to him." Her eyes opened wide, and her pink fingernails dug into the flesh of her cheek and raked down, leaving deep, bloody scratches. "Terrible things." The multiple voices were back, just for a second, and then she coughed. "Excuse me. I had a frog in my throat." Her eyes turned to Teagan. "Bring Aiden to my office. We'll go from there."

"No!" Teagan shouted.

"The address for the pickup is—"

Teagan picked up her backpack by the shoulder strap and swung it at Ms. Skinner's head. No one was picking up Aiden. If they did, he would disappear like Oscar had.

Ms. Skinner staggered when it hit her, and the phone spun out of her hand. Teagan hit her again, and then dove for the phone. Ms. Skinner caught her from behind, but Teagan butted back with her head and felt the crunch of bone. The clawing hands loosened and Teagan jerked free, put a desk between them, grabbed the phone, and began pushing buttons frantically.

"Raynor's Res—"

"Raynor, I need you!" Teagan shouted.

Air puffed as Raynor appeared, and Teagan could smell Mamieo's muffins. If Mamieo was baking, then Aiden was home. He was safe.

"What's the problem?" Raynor asked.

Ms. Skinner took one look at him and screamed, her mouth opening so wide that her lips split at the corners.

"Oh, I see." Raynor stepped toward her, but the woman backed away.

The angel lunged, and this time she didn't move fast enough.

"Come out of there," he said.

"No," the voices rasped.

He picked up Ms. Skinner and moved her sideways so fast she was nothing but a blur. It took the shadow a millisecond too long to follow. It trailed behind her like dark vapor, and the angel caught what looked like a foot. He set Ms. Skinner down and started reeling the shadow out of her like a spool of dark yarn, wadding it up as he went.

Ms. Skinner alternated between sobbing, clawing for Teagan, and babbling nonsense words.

It took fifteen minutes at least before Raynor pulled the last of it—the bit that had been in her head—out.

"I need to dispose of this," he said. "It takes a little time to go where I'm going and get back. Call Seamus. Make sure everything is quiet before I leave."

"What about Skinner?" Teagan asked as she dialed.

"She'll be fine in a few minutes. Mentally, I mean. The broken nose and lacerations will need to be dealt with. I'd give it five minutes before I called 911, just to make sure her brain is back."

"Nothing happening here," Seamus said when he picked up.

Raynor nodded, and the air popped as he disappeared.

Ms. Skinner leaned over the teacher's desk, blood dripping from her mouth and nose. She was still clearly dazed and confused. She was going to be in a lot of pain when the shock wore off.

Teagan opened her backpack. She hadn't taken the medical supplies out after she'd ridden the bus with Grizabella, and she couldn't just leave a person bleeding like this. Even if it was Ms. Skinner.

Awareness was dawning in the woman's eyes. "Oh, my god," she said. "Oh, my god. *The child is in imminent danger.*"

"Not anymore." Teagan wiped the blood from Ms. Skinner's mouth with a sterile gauze pad.

"Yes he is. That was *me* calling the office." Ms. Skinner's hand went to the scratches on her cheek where her own fingernails had dug gashes in her flesh. "It did *this* because I was trying to help. They are after Aiden right now. That *thing* told me what the Dogs are going to do to him. I fought so hard to dial that phone. Oh, god, I tried so hard!"

PART III: WARRIOR BARD

L OLLAN *and Bairre hadn't been with Saoirse.*

Teagan punched redial. Finn, Mamieo, Thomas, and Roisin should be at home with Aiden, even though Raynor was gone. The Dump Dogs weren't going to be able to get in the house. No one answered. She tried the phone her dad had given Mamieo. Still no pickup. She dialed Abby's phone, just in case someone was upstairs and heard it ringing in the bathroom. "Ell-oh?" Teagan could have wept with relief. Roisin was laughing, so nothing bad had happened yet.

"I need to talk to Mamieo," Teagan said. "Can you give her the phone?"

"*Mac Cumhaill,*" Roisin said. "*No!*"

"Yes, I need to talk to her." This time Roisin spoke several sentences that Teagan didn't understand.

"Dump Dogs," Teagan said. "Tell her the Dump Dogs are coming."

"*Mocha latte!*" Roisin was giggling again when she hung up. Teagan punched the off button in frustration. *If Roisin wouldn't pay attention, Seamus would.* She dialed his number again.

"I tried your home phone and no one answered. Something's happening," Seamus said when he picked up. Teagan could hear her dad's voice in the background. He was singing the songs that had kept the shadows at bay when they'd tried to pour into the park. *The gate was open!* "Where's the angel?" Seamus asked. "We need him."

"He ... stepped out for a little while." Why hadn't she asked how long it would take? "I'm not getting an answer at home, either, but I got a hold of Roisin. It sounds like they're okay. Take care of my dad. We'll be there soon."

"Police," Ms. Skinner gasped. "Call the police!"

"No," Teagan said. "What could they do against the things the shadows told you about?"

Ms. Skinner just shook her head. "Call the police!"

Teagan took a step back. The social worker was going to call for help as soon as she had the strength. And when she did, Officer Fiorella would arrest Teagan.

"Ms. Skinner ... I'm sorry I hurt you. But I was trying to save Aiden, too. And I've got to get to him now." Teagan left the woman weeping and ran down the hall to the room where she knew Abby would be. She always took art during last period to wash everything else that had happened during the school day out of her brain.

"Excuse me?" the teacher said when Teagan burst into the room. "Do you have a pass?"

"No," Teagan said.

"You can't just come in here—"

Teagan ignored the woman. She'd just beaten up a social

worker. That probably ruined any chance she had of graduating, much less getting a scholarship. Springing Abby from class early was not going to matter.

"Abby, I need you."

Abby was already out of her desk and moving.

"I said you can't just barge into my class!" the teacher shouted after them as they went out the door.

"I'm totally going to fail that class anyway," Abby said. "She's into cubism and avant-garde crap, so she hates my stuff."

Teagan stopped at the corner of the hallway and peeked around.

"So, what's happening?"

"I just beat up Ms. Skinner. She's in pretty bad shape, and she's going to call the police." She couldn't sit in the police station again, and Seamus was a little too busy at the moment to come and get her.

"You beat up the Skinner?"

"I shouldn't have. She was trying to help. The Dump Dogs are after Aiden, and the gate at Rosehill is open. I need to get home, Abby, but first I have to get out of the school before Officer Fiorella catches me. Do you think Jing—?"

Abby was already punching the number into Rafe's phone. "He'll meet us by the Mustang," she said before he'd even picked up. "Tea. Walk normal. You look like some kind of fugitive."

Teagan kept waiting for the alarm to sound, for the school to go into lockdown, for Officer Fiorella to come around the corner. But nothing happened. The halls were almost empty.

Fortunately, the news crews had gotten all the interviews they needed that morning and had packed up and gone off to find something more exciting to film than the front of a high school. Jing's Mustang chirped as he unlocked it from halfway across the lot, and Teagan and Abby were in by the time he got there.

"Things like Kyle are after your baby brother?" he asked.

"Yes," Teagan said. "We just need to get there. Have you texted Leo, Abby?" Teagan asked.

"Rafe doesn't have numbers in his phone. He keeps all the numbers in his brain or something. What an idiot."

"Get me there, Jing," Teagan said. "Please get me there, fast."

Jing was a better driver than Raynor, and that was saying a lot. The Mustang moved through traffic at twice the speed of the cars around it, weaving from lane to lane, somehow avoiding every red light.

"Timing," Jing explained. "I know the light cycles and adjust my speed for them." He slowed when they reached the residential streets, but not much.

"That looks like trouble," he said before they reached the Wylltson house. Teagan leaned forward. Even from here she could see that the front door was hanging open.

"No. No, no, no!" Teagan didn't bother waiting for him to park.

She jumped out of the still-moving car and ran for the steps. Jing must have abandoned it in the street, because he and Abby were both right behind her when she reached the front door. Jing grabbed her shirttail.

"Slow down. We don't know what we're walking into."

Aiden's toys were scattered all over the floor, but that was normal. Finn was standing in the kitchen door. He had blood on his hands, and that *wasn't* normal. His face was an emotionless mask.

"You all right, man?" Jing asked. "You hurt?"

"Mamieo," Finn said.

Abby started for the kitchen, but Jing caught her. Teagan pushed past him. Finn had covered Mamieo's face and torso with an apron. Taking in the amount of blood on the walls and floor, Teagan was glad he had. The back door was hanging open, and her brother's whip was lying in the middle of the room.

"Aiden?" Teagan said.

Finn shook his head. "Can't find him. The phooka's gone as well."

"Where's Choirboy?" Abby asked when Teagan went back into the living room.

"We don't know." Teagan took the stairs two at a time, with Abby and Jing right behind her. Neither Aiden nor Roisin were in their rooms. There was no sign of Grendal, either. When they'd finished searching the upstairs, Teagan went back to Aiden's room one last time and checked under his bed.

"Nothing?" Abby asked. Teagan shook her head.

"The only blood is in the kitchen." Jing put his arm around Abby. "The boy could be all right."

Teagan shook her head again. The shadows had shown Ms. Skinner just what the Dump Dogs were going to do to her brother. And now they had him.

291

She checked the closet where Aiden had once hidden from Ms. Skinner anyway, then went down the maid's stairs all the way to the basement. It wasn't just the silence that told her he wasn't here. There was no trickle of bioelectricity in the room. No life.

When she came up into the kitchen again, Finn was kneeling beside his grandmother, holding her wrinkled hand to his lips.

"Most of the blood's hers." Finn adjusted the apron. "But not all of it. Mamieo found her knife. She got it out plenty fast." He rubbed his thumb across the back of the wrinkled hand.

"Where—" Teagan caught herself, but he knew what she'd been about to ask.

"I'd stepped out to walk around the neighborhood." Finn's voice was as emotionless as his face. "Just stepped out to look around. Raynor was here when I left. Where's he gone, then?"

"I called him," Teagan said. "There was a shadow man at the school. He took it away." Saoirse had tricked her into calling the angel away so that her brothers could ... do this. Skinner had fought the shadow man to try to stop the Dump Dogs. And Teagan hadn't figured it out. Not in time. "It's my fault, Finn. Not yours."

"It's the fault of the goblins who did it." Finn laid Mamieo's hand gently across her chest. "And the one who set them on us. We can't go back and undo things that are done. Not me with my walk or you with your calling the angel away. I'm just trying to think where to look for the boyo, Roisin, and her cat friend. When's Raynor getting back?"

"I don't know. It's bad, Finn. The gate is open."

"Your da is keeping the shadows in?"

"Yes."

"Oh, my god." Abby had made it past Jing into the kitchen. She was throwing up in the sink when Teagan stepped onto the back porch. Joe might have been any other shrub, motionless in the corner. Fast asleep.

The soft dirt was crisscrossed with Gil's tracks, and smaller tracks as well. Aiden. He'd come out the back door. Dog prints overlaid the little-boy prints. The Dump Dogs had come out the back door after him.

Teagan followed Aiden's footprints until they ended in the middle of the yard. One small sneaker lay in the dirt. Something had hit her brother hard enough to knock his shoe off. The dog prints went on toward the gaping back gate. Teagan followed them, but the alley was empty.

She went back to the yard and sank to her knees beside the shoe . . . and felt the electric tickle of life behind her. Not three lives—Finn on the porch, Abby and Jing still in the kitchen. Five. No, six. Six lives, and one was as small as a bug.

Teagan scrambled to her feet and ran to the garden box.

"What are you doing, girl?" Finn asked as she pulled it open.

Gil and Aiden were huddled nose to nose, their arms around each other and their eyes squeezed shut. Lucy was tangled in Aiden's hair. Finn lifted them all out.

"Didn't you hear us out here?" Teagan asked.

"We thought you were the bad guys," Aiden whispered. "Is Mamieo all right?"

Teagan picked him up and hugged him tight.

"Is she all right?"

"No," she said. "She's not."

"She saved me, Tea." Aiden started crying. "They came in as soon as Raynor disappeared. I had my whip, but it wouldn't work."

"Shhh," Teagan said, but Aiden wouldn't shhh.

"Mamieo found her knife really fast. She cut one of them, and she said, 'Run, boyo!'"

"The Scary One fought them," Gil said. "I saw one bite her, but she bit it back. She kept fighting so the boyo could get away, but he's not fast enough. So I caught him and put him in the box."

"Gil." Finn turned to the phooka. "You saved the boyo?"

"*Men* don't eat children," Gil said. "You can trust them, because they *choose*."

TWENTY-SIX

TEAGAN glanced at the back gate. If the Dump Dogs hadn't found Aiden, why had they gone?

"Choirboy!" Abby came out the back door and scooped Aiden out of Teagan's arms.

"Mamieo's not okay, Abby," Aiden said.

"I know, baby boy." She pulled him close. "But she'd want you to be okay, right? She—"

A *cat-sídhe* screamed from the front of the house.

Abby clutched Aiden. "What was *that?*"

"Grendal," Aiden whispered. "Is he crying because of Mamieo?"

"Let's go," Teagan said as the *cat-sídhe* screamed again. "We need to get out of here and find Dad."

"I'll bring Choirboy." Abby let Aiden hide his face in her hair, while Lucy flitted around them, chirping.

"Don't let the boyo see." Finn went up the steps.

"He's not looking." Abby followed Teagan. "You close your eyes, too, pig-boy," she told Gil. "You can hold my shirt while we go through the kitchen."

"He knows what *dead* looks like, Abby," Aiden said. "He's a phooka."

Abby heard the *cat-sídhe*. She was talking to Gil. Teagan had to ask her about that as soon as she had time to think. Jing clearly didn't see or hear Gil or Lucy, but he towered protectively over Abby, locking the back door once they were inside.

Abby stooped and picked up Aiden's whip as they went through the kitchen, keeping the little boy's face buried in her shoulder as she did.

"You're gonna want the whip, right?"

"No, I'm not." Aiden's voice was very small. "It doesn't work."

When they reached the living room, Teagan followed Finn to the window and looked out. It *had* been Grendal screaming.

Saoirse, Lollan, and Bairre were between the house and Jing's car. Saoirse was holding Grendal up by his tail. He looked barely conscious, as if she'd slammed him against the light post. And he wasn't crying out anymore.

Lollan and Bairre were in their four-legged form. They were hyena-like, but larger and more powerful. These were the creatures that Mamieo had faced with her little dagger. They hadn't gotten past her—not while there was breath left in her body. Even from this distance, Teagan could see the blood on their muzzles and guess why they'd run to find Saoirse instead of sniffing out Aiden's hiding place. One had a rib-deep wound on his side and the other had a gash across his face. Mamieo's knife had taken an eye.

"That's what happened to your grandmother?" Jing asked.

"Yes," Teagan said. "Those are goblins. We've got to get past them. If we wait for the police, we'll be separated. The goblins will be able to take us one by one."

"Nobody's taking Choirboy," Abby said fiercely.

"We need the car," Finn said. "But if I can't handle this, you all go out the back and run. Get Aiden to his da at Rosehill. That's where the angel will go if he doesn't find us here. Watch over them, Jing."

"I'll do my best. You have anything I could use as a club, Tea? I don't do knives."

"Can you use this?" Abby held up the whip.

"Not like the lawyer-man did. But I might be able to strangle one with it."

"My old softball bat's in the closet," Teagan said, and followed Finn out the door.

"Get back inside, Tea." Finn spoke softly, and she was glad he couldn't feel her fear the way she felt every fiber of his body getting ready for his final fight. "You've got to take care of Aiden, girl."

"No." She was afraid of the Dump Dogs. But she was more afraid of what would happen to Finn. "Let's try to talk with them."

"After what they did to Mamieo?"

"We've got to stall. Give the angel time to get here."

Teagan knew she wasn't shaking on the outside as she walked down the steps. But she was on the inside, and crying out more desperately than the Burr Oak had. *Send help, send help, send help. Let Raynor get back in time.*

"Where's Roisin?" Teagan asked Saoirse, amazed at how

calm her voice sounded. The stench of carrion was very strong. It was probably coming from the coat Saoirse was still wearing.

"I told you, she's a special friend of Bairre's."

The Dog with the damaged face whined and licked blood from its chops. Teagan saw Mrs. Santini's little Metro coming down the street. It slowed to get past Jing's car. Things were getting worse.

"Roisin unlocked the front door for us," Saoirse said. "All we had to do was promise to bring Grendal back safely." The girl swung the dangling *cat-sídhe* back and forth. He wasn't dead. Teagan could feel the life in him—but it was a very small spark. "To take care of him. She thinks she's smart enough to play goblin games with us. We promised we'd bring him back safely. We never said he'd stay safe after he got here. There's more than one way to *take care* of someone, isn't there?"

Teagan felt hot, sour bile rise in her throat. Roisin had been with the Dump Dogs when she was on the phone. She'd known what they'd done to Mamieo. And she'd been laughing.

She heard a car door slam, and from the corner of her eye she could see Lennie getting out of the car and Mrs. Santini waddling toward them, a blue and yellow plastic toy in her hand.

It felt as if a cold fist was squeezing Teagan's heart. It was so painful, she was tempted to look over her shoulder to make sure no shadow man was standing behind her, reaching into her chest. There was nothing she could do to stop what was about to happen, but she had to try.

She felt Saoirse tense, preparing to toss Grendal into the

air, and Bairre and Lollan's muscles bunch as they got ready to jump for him and tear him to pieces.

Teagan moved a fraction of a second before the goblin girl did. It gave her just enough of a head start to get her arm between Lollan's leap and the flying *cat-sídhe*. She felt the Dump Dog's fangs slide like razorblades along her arm, and then she was falling, curling her body around Grendal to keep the dogs off of him. Finn had moved almost as fast as she had; she saw the flash of Mamieo's blade in his hand, and heard Bairre cry out.

Lollan turned toward her—and then he collapsed, his body a mass of jerking static. The jolt of electricity that surged through the thin wires running from Mrs. Santini's toy gun to the Dump Dog was enough to scramble his neural transmissions.

Teagan struggled to her feet, Grendal in her arms.

Jing had come out the door, the softball bat in his hand.

"I don't know who the hell you are," Mrs. Santini said to Saoirse, "but this is a Taser X3. That means I got two more shots. Control your animals, or you're going down next. Then I'll ask my big friend here to beat the hell out of you while you can't move."

Saoirse snarled at Jing, but she moved away.

Mrs. Santini released the trigger, and Lollan staggered to his feet, yelping as the barbs at the ends of the wires pulled out of his hide.

"Come on." Saoirse turned and ran. Bairre and Lollan followed her.

"We got leash laws, lady," Mrs. Santini yelled after her. "You don't like it, stay out of my neighborhood!"

Blood was running down Teagan's arm and dripping from her elbow. Finn pulled off his bandanna and twisted it into a rope.

"Put the *cat-sídhe* down for a minute," he said.

"No." Grendal was dying. She could feel the slowing, the dimming in him. But she felt his little fingers tighten around hers as well, and his head rubbed against her. He was saying thank you.

"Then hold it with one hand, girl. I've got to stop the blood."

Teagan hugged Grendal with one arm, and put her forehead against his while Finn wrapped the bandanna around her arm and tightened it.

"Hákon," Grendal whispered. *"Good hunting, Hákon."*

"Good hunting, Fairy Cat." She knew he couldn't hear her. "Sleep warm."

"What cat?" Mrs. Santini said.

Teagan just shook her head.

"Let me drive you to the hospital, Tea."

"It's not too bad, Mrs. Santini," Teagan said. "It's on the outer arm, no veins or arteries involved. It's already almost stopped bleeding."

"What were those things?" Jing asked. "Hyenas?"

"Basically," Teagan said.

Sirens started in the distance. Ms. Skinner had called the police, and they'd figured out Teagan wasn't in school.

Mrs. Santini was still watching Teagan. "You still think you've got a cat?"

"The cat's invisible," Finn explained. "We've got them all over. You know what? I think you should get Lennie out of here."

"I'll take care of my Lennie. You fix Teagan. Are those hyenas coming back?"

"Yes." Teagan's arm was starting to hurt. Thomas came around the corner at the end of the street, a tall white cup in his hand. *Mocha latte. Roisin had sent him out for a coffee.*

"Roisin!" He dropped the cup and started to run.

"Your girlfriend let them in," Finn said grimly. "They killed Mamieo, and now Roisin's gone away with them."

Thomas shook his head. "She just asked me to walk to the Feather for a mocha. She would never have done this."

"You can ask them yourself." Finn pointed. "They went that way."

Thomas stripped off his shirt.

"What are you —?" Mrs. Santini asked.

He didn't bother with his pants. The transformation was fast, as if he stepped out of his clothes and into his raven form. Then he shot into the sky and after the Dump Dogs. Mrs. Santini looked from the pile of clothes on the ground to the bird disappearing in the distance.

"Abigail—" she began.

"Zia," Abby interrupted, "you totally saved our lives, but you've got to get out of here."

"I'm not going anywhere," Mrs. Santini said. "This is my

home. My neighbors. Aiden's like a brother to my Lennie."

"They killed Mamieo Ida," Teagan said flatly. "At least keep Lennie inside. We're going to go get Dad."

Mrs. Santini picked up the clothes Thomas had dropped. "LENNIE," she bellowed, "GET INSIDE THE HOUSE! You're going to get your dad, Tea? Tell him anything the Wylltsons need, the Santinis are there."

"So what do we do?" Abby asked as Mrs. Santini waddled toward her house.

"We stick with Mamieo's plan." Teagan wiped her bloody hand on her jeans.

"What was the plan?" Abby asked.

"Those of us who can," Finn said, "are going to Mag Mell to find a way to let Raynor in. Get in the car."

"In it?" Gil gulped.

"It's either that or stay here," Finn said. "We've got to go."

"It's my impression," Jing looked around, "that you are all talking to an . . . invisible person."

"He's a phooka," Abby said, as if she'd been seeing them all her life. "Tea told me about him. My psychic powers are totally increasing." Jing just nodded.

Teagan took Grendal's body up the steps and laid it down beside the front door. She'd take care of him when they got back.

"Holy crap," Finn said, and Teagan turned to follow his stare.

If they got back. A dark supercell hung in the sky to the northwest, over Rosehill Cemetery.

"Get in the car," Finn said again.

"It's the shadows," Aiden said as Teagan settled him on her lap. "They're looking for my song."

Abby looked over her shoulder from the front seat. "Then don't sing it."

"I can't sing it." Aiden shook his curly head. "Dad has it."

"Well, we better tell him not to sing it either," Abby said, "'cause that looks bad."

"I'm not seeing anything," Jing said.

"There's, like, a tornado," Abby said. "It's huge."

"So which way do you want me to drive?" Jing asked.

"To Rosehill Cemetery," Teagan said.

"Toward whatever it is you're pointing at?"

"If John Wylltson can't hold them in, we're all of us dead anyway," Finn said. "And the man might need some help. He's got no one with him but McGillahee."

Jing drove straight through the front gates of Rosehill, past a parked tour bus. Haunted Chicago Tours. Just what they needed, a busload of civilians involved.

There were a few cars, and people standing over graves or taking pictures of a tomb. Jing parked the car. Teagan noticed he brought his baseball bat with him as they walked across the grass between the tombstones and monuments to where Mr. Wylltson was standing. The gate the shadows had clawed open shimmered between Mr. Wylltson and the lake.

As they got closer, Teagan could hear that he was singing *The Litany of the Saints* in Latin, as if he had the whole choir of St. Drogo's standing with him. It was a song that could go on forever. He sang both the call and response, as if he were lead and choir rolled into one:

*"Omnes Sancti et Sanctae Dei, intercédite pro nobis.
All ye holy Saints of God, make intercession for us."*

Aiden dodged past Seamus and wrapped his arms around his dad's legs. Mr. Wylltson picked him up, but kept singing.

"Can your dad see those things?" Abby asked.

"No," Teagan said. "He just feels them."

Jing moved closer to Abby. "I'm feeling something myself. Something evil."

"Well, Saint Finn." Seamus looked a little pale. "Are you ready to intercede?"

"My Mamieo has just been killed, McGillahee. I'm not in the mood for your foolishness."

Mr. Wylltson looked from Finn to Teagan's bloody sleeve, and his eyebrows knit.

"The Dump Dogs came looking for Aiden," Finn explained, "and Roisin let them in. Mamieo wouldn't let them have the boyo. Roisin's gone off with them."

A bright blue '57 Chevy pulled up behind the Mustang, and the Turtles piled out.

"The mighty Khan is with us," Rafe said. "Excellent."

Jing shook his head.

"Got your text, Abby," Leo said. "We got here as fast as we could." He lowered his voice as if Mr. Wylltson couldn't hear him. "Why the concert? What's going on?"

"All I know is, if he stops singing, those *things*"—Abby pointed up at the roiling shadows—"are gonna pour into Chicago like a plague or something. The angel's the only one who can stop them."

304

Donny squinted at the sky, but Leo nodded. "So where's the angel?" he asked.

"We don't know," Finn said.

"So you texted us." Leo looked at Abby.

"I didn't text anybody."

Mr. Wylltson had closed his eyes as if he were praying. His arms tightened around Aiden, but his song never faltererd

Something was wrong. Teagan looked from the Gagliano boys to the storm.

Roisin had Abby's phone.

"Was anyone else on the text tree?" Teagan asked.

"Just Zoë," Abby said.

"You think we need a social worker?" Rafe asked.

"*You* need a social worker, Rafe. I figured if something happened, Choirboy would need her. Guess what? Something happened. He needs her."

"You should have told us there were so many of them," Rafe said, glancing over his shoulder. "We'd have brought a few more soldiers."

Apparently Zoë was not worth waiting for, because the trap had been sprung. Teagan recognized a few of the tourists and mourners, now that she was looking closer. One was the man who had been with Kyle and claimed to be her relative after her mother died.

"Is that Isabeau?" Jing asked.

It was. She was dressed in a tight A-line dress with a feathered fascinator on the side of her head.

"The Jackie O. look," Abby said. "Retro, but she's got the curves to make it work."

"Oh, yeah," Rafe agreed.

"Shut up, Rafe," Leo and Angelo said.

Leo squinted at the sky and shivered. "Why's it so cold here?"

"Maybe Abby should text the weatherman and ask," Rafe said. "Hey, Isabeau!" The Highborn girl ignored him.

The Highborn who had offered to buy Finn when they were in Mag Mell was right behind her, and there were many, many more walking across the grass toward them. They must have come the same way Kyle and Isabeau had after the gate was closed—stepping into Ireland and catching flights over. And then they'd just taken the tour bus.

It could have been the same crowd she'd seen in Mag Mell at the phooka baiting. Some of the beautiful and well-dressed people—those who were shape shifters—started shaking off their human forms, eager for blood sport. There were hyenas, wolves, and scaly, fanged creatures that Teagan had never seen before. A few were incomplete shifters like Kyle had been, retaining some of their human form even as they grew muzzles or claws. A couple that was apparently not part of the Highborn group turned and ran. Gil stepped closer to Teagan, and Seamus's smile had disappeared.

"So nice to see you, Tea," Isabeau said. "My mom and dad are back together, by the way. Mom's pissed." She nodded toward the Highborn around them. "She sent us to find the shits who killed her son." Then she nodded toward the shimmering gate beyond Mr. Wylltson. "The shadows are Daddy's. He's not angry. Just . . . *mad*."

"Like, what?" Abby said. "Insane mad? Because that"—she waved at the cloud of shadows—"is just overreacting."

"Sprite bite give you second sight?" Isabeau asked. "That's the only way a dirty human can get it, but it only happens if the bite doesn't kill them. You're one in a million, Abby. Enjoy it for the last ten seconds of your amazing life." The Highborn who had already shifted began to surge forward.

Then the air puffed, and Raynor was standing beside Teagan. The Highborn stopped. Mr. Wylltson stopped singing as well, but the shadows didn't fall. They apparently didn't want any part of the angel after what had happened at the park.

"Tea, come here," Mr. Wylltson said. He reached out with the arm that wasn't holding Aiden and put it around her protectively, then looked from the shadows to the goblins. The smell of fire had come with Raynor, as if he'd been sitting on the rim of a live volcano.

Isabeau grinned and tipped her head. "Been to hell and back, Raynor? I thought you might miss the party, but Mother said you would get here. She's just so *good* at this."

"A trap," Raynor said. "That's what the pathetic mess at the school was about."

Leo edged closer to the angel. "You can deal with this, right? Abby said you dealt with stuff like this at the library park."

Raynor didn't answer.

The cold hand was on Teagan's heart again. *A trap.* The shadow men and Highborn were just the bait. Raynor was the teeth.

Mab had sent Isabeau and the others here just in case Raynor didn't make it back. But he did, and now he had to decide: step aside and burn the shadows and Highborn—and Finn, the Gaglianos, Jing, and the Wylltsons along with them— or let the supercell loose on Chicago. There was only one choice the angel could make—they were all going to die here. Mab just wanted Raynor to experience the pain of having done it himself.

Mr. Wylltson cleared his throat.

"Night shall be thrice night over you," he said.

"What's the crazy man talking about?" Isabeau asked.

"And heaven an iron cope."

John Wylltson put his hand on Aiden's curly head, and looked directly into the angel's eyes.

> *"Do you have joy without a cause,*
> *Yea, faith without a hope?"*

He was asking Raynor to remember the conversation they'd had in the kitchen. Remember the one thing that Mab couldn't know—that John Paul Wylltson was carrying the song Fear Doirich had sent to mark his Aiden. The angel's lips pressed into a grim line. He looked up at the supercell, then nodded.

"Only as long as you can keep them occupied, John," he said. "Only that long."

"Thank you." There was relief in Mr. Wylltson's voice. "Kids, Raynor is going to leave. When he does, I want you to run. All of you. Those of you who know Mamieo's plan, go into Mag Mell. And those of you who don't, get to your cars and get as far from here as you can, as fast as you can." He looked toward the shape shifters, and Leo turned to follow his glance. The Highborn were edging forward, angel or not. It would take them only a few seconds to cover the distance once Raynor was gone. *To tear her father to pieces.* "It's possible that I will be able to buy you enough time."

The Gagliano boys had turned toward the cars.

"Leo?" Rafe asked. "You coming?"

"Do what the man says," Leo ordered, his eyes on the shape shifters. "I got a job here."

Mr. Wylltson pried Aiden's arms from around his neck and handed him to Teagan, then gripped Finn's shoulder. "Take car of them."

"Dad," Teagan said, "I—"

"Get into Mag Mell," Mr. Wylltson commanded. *"Now run!"* Air popped again as the angel disappeared. Then Mr. Wylltson's Welsh tenor rose, clear and strong:

> *"The Minstrel Boy to the war is gone,*
> *In the ranks of death ye will find him."*

"No!" Aiden screamed as Teagan turned and ran for the shimmer.

She had gone only a few steps when the shadows fell from the sky.

"Wait!" Isabeau screamed behind her, apparently understanding at last. *"Wait!* I can't run in this dress!"

The shadows passed around Teagan like bats, touching her skin like a veil, but they didn't stop or reach inside. Aiden had been right. They were looking for his song. The one her dad was singing.

Teagan looked back. Jing was almost to his car, clearing a path through the Highborn with the bat, and Angel and Donnie were behind him. But Abby wasn't with them, and Leo and Rafe weren't running. They were standing between the Highborn and Mr. Wylltson. Leo had his knife out, and Rafe had a gun in his hand. Not a plastic thing like Mrs. Santini had been carrying, but something that a movie mobster would carry. The Highborn started forward. Teagan heard a shot, and saw a shape shifter go down. Then another shot, and another.

"Go, Tea!" Finn yelled, pulling her away. "Don't let it be for nothing."

There were others running past them—Highborn who had figured out what was about to happen, and were running for their lives.

> *"His father's sword he hath girded on,*
> *And his wild harp slung behind him;*
> *'Land of Song!' said the warrior bard,*
> *Tho' all the world betray thee."*

She could hear pain in her father's voice, and she glanced back once more. The place where John Wylltson stood was nothing but seething shadows, but impossibly, impossibly, he was still singing. They must be reaching inside him now, like they'd reached inside her mother. Twisting, tearing.

"One sword, at least, thy rights shall guard,
One faithful harp shall praise thee!"

His voice was breaking, and it was still too far to the gate. She wasn't going to get Aiden through it. But suddenly it wasn't one voice behind her. It was two—someone was harmonizing with John Paul Wylltson, a female voice lifting over his. *Zoë.* The dance therapist had somehow made it after all, through the chaos of Highborn. Her dad's voice was growing weaker, and Zoë's sounded like it was in an echo chamber.

"The Minstrel fell! But the foeman's chain
Could not bring that proud soul under;
The harp he lov'd ne'er spoke again,
For he tore its chords asunder—"

And then Teagan's feet were on cobblestones as the sky turned bright behind them. Raynor had returned, and she knew her father was dead.

P EOPLE *will die.* That's what Raynor had said. This is war. This was what Finn had been trying to save her from by running after they met. *The wrong people will die.* Her dad. Mamieo. Abby ... no, Abby was right beside her.

"Oh, my god," Abby was saying. "*Oh, my god.*"

There were Fir Bolg and Highborn, phookas and lowborn goblins all around them. The smell of cooking flesh hung in the air between colored tents and wooden stalls.

"Samhain Fair." Finn was on the other side of her. "We've got to get out of here. Now."

He was right. Teagan took a step. She couldn't collapse, because Aiden would be killed here just as surely as he would have been at Rosehill. Taking care of her brother meant moving. Thinking. Not collapsing in shock and grief.

The crowd was larger than it had been the last time Teagan had been here, with more Highborn walking among the phookas and Fir Bolg slaves. The reason was less than fifty feet away—a small redheaded girl in a cage. *Samhain is coming,* Teagan realized. *Everyone gathers to hunt a girl child through the woods.*

They apparently put the child on display before the hunt.

Two massive phookas, one with the head of a bull and the other with the legs of an elk but the torso and head of a man, guarded the cage. A giant redheaded Fir Bolg man in a leather apron and very little else stood before them. He held a hammer in his hand. *The child's father? Brother?*

A lady in Victorian-era dress and her companion, a man wearing a suit that could have been from a sixties sitcom, turned to Abby.

"This will be fun," the woman said.

"Whips, eh?" The man winked.

Abby looked down at Aiden's whip, which was still in her hand.

"Ew," she said. "Like I'd be into that crap, you sicko."

"Don't start fights, Gabby," Finn said, stepping between them. Teagan could see Gil dodging through the crowd, and Seamus McGillahee pushing his way through to them. Some of the Highborn had made it through the gate as well, and were talking excitedly and pointing at Finn.

"The Mac Cumhaill," someone shouted. "Kill him!"

Phookas and booth-keepers, Highborn and their Fir Bolg slaves, all were staring and pointing now.

Seamus McGillahee grabbed the whip from Abby's hand. He jumped up on a stack of wooden crates and cracked it over his head.

"*Glaine ár gcroí!*" he shouted. There was power in his voice. *Purity of our hearts.*

"*Neart ár ngéag!*" the redheaded giant by the little girl's cage bellowed, catching the fire.

313

Strength of our limbs.

He swung his blacksmith's hammer underhand, hitting the elk-man on the chin.

"Beart de réir ár mbriathar!" the Fir Bolg in the crowd roared as blood gushed from the phooka's mouth.

Action to match our speech.

The crowd erupted in chaos, the redheaded man tearing apart the cage with his bare hands, Fir Bolg attacking their Highborn masters, phookas attacking everyone, lowborn goblins snatching what they could from booths and stands and running with it.

Finn grabbed Teagan's arm with one hand and Abby's with the other and dragged them away from Seamus and the crowd into the narrow space behind the booths, where phooka children played in filthy rags the last time they had been here. Gil was right on their heels.

"We need to run." Gil's ears were flat against his head. "Really fast."

"I agree," Finn said. "Can you get us out of the market? *Without* going through the phooka village?" The phooka shook his head.

"Tea?" Abby tugged on her sleeve. "We've got company."

A lowborn goblin child had crawled out from under a pile of trash and was staring wide-eyed at them. Her mouth opened to scream—and then her eyes went to Finn and her hand went to the string of green glass beads at her throat. Teagan could see the blush spread even through the dirt on the girl's face.

"Filthy Fir Bolg," she said. "You came back!"

"You know her?" Abby asked.

"We've met," Finn said. "I put a coin in her pocket. Remember, girl? We're not here to cause you any trouble. Just go on and leave us be."

She looked past him at the growing riot in the market. Teagan turned to look as well. The blacksmith had the child from the cage and was carrying her triumphantly on his shoulder; a vendor's booth was aflame.

The goblin girl smiled at Finn, then kicked trash away to expose a hole covered by a wooden grate. The smell emanating from it made it clear that if this was a storm drain, it also served as a sewer. She pulled the grate away and slipped in. Her head poked out, and she motioned for them to follow.

"I'll check it out," Finn said. He squeezed himself down the hole. The riot was growing more violent, and Teagan was afraid it would spill into the alley before Finn came back.

"Tea," he called from the darkness. "I think there's a way. Hand the boyo down."

Teagan had to pry Aiden's hands from around her neck, but once she did, he was almost limp as she handed him down. Lucy glared at her from his hair. Teagan was glad to see the sprite had made it home; she hadn't even thought about the creature since all this had begun.

Abby went next, barely managing to fit through the small opening.

"Go on, Gil," Teagan urged.

"No." Gil's ears swiveled toward the shouts and screams behind him, and he was trembling. "You hide first."

Teagan lowered herself into the sewer. She felt Finn's

hands around her waist and let go. The tunnel was arched and she could stand upright, but Finn had to stoop. The ancient masonry was damp and worn, but it wasn't dark. The fungus on the wall Finn had propped Aiden against was glowing in multicolored glory.

Gil dropped down beside her.

The goblin girl was gaping at Aiden as if he were a small saint in a niche on the wall. In the soft light she did look like the statue at Rosehill Cemetery. A baby Greenteeth.

"The light's automagical," Abby whispered. "It just turned on."

"Bioluminescence," Teagan guessed. "Luciferin exposed to oxygen and the enzyme . . ." Her voice trailed off. This Hákon didn't hunt facts. It leaked them. How could she be alive, still moving, still breathing, much less reciting rote facts about biology? *Dad is dead.* Aiden wasn't crying, but she could see the reality of it sinking into him, too, already wrapping him in silence.

Gil poked the wall with his finger, and the goblin girl slapped his hand.

"Don't break it!" she said.

"Why is there light?" Gil asked.

"Mag Mell is happy to see the boyo," Finn told him. "That's why. She tends to celebrate when he's around."

Even the air near Aiden was better—it still smelled organic, but now it was almost loamy, as if the process of breaking down the sewage had accelerated.

Gil reached for the shining fungus again, then drew his hand back when he saw the lowborn girl's glare.

"What's your name, you?" he asked her. She tipped her head, apparently considering a long list of nom de plumes before she decided on the best one for the situation.

"Peggish."

"Not her real name," Finn told Abby. "You don't tell *anyone* here your real name, Gabby, or use ours. Come on, then. If we can drop down here, others can as well. We need to move away from the drain."

Teagan picked up her brother. Lucy really didn't like it down here. The sprite had woven herself so tightly into Aiden's hair that she couldn't be seen. Probably afraid of sprite-eating spiders in these tunnels, or something worse.

The bioluminescence died behind them but bloomed ahead as they walked, lighting their way. Gil stayed close to Teagan, and Peggish insisted on walking on the other side, in the very brightest part of the light. Abby seemed to be taking it all in stride, as if she ran from riots and walked down the sewers of Mag Mell every day of her life.

The tunnel branched, and Finn chose the one on the right. They'd gone only a few feet down it when he stopped by a pile of rubble.

"I have to go back for McGillahee," he said. "If he's still alive, I can't leave him in the middle of a riot, especially not one he started to save our necks. You wait here and keep your ears open for anyone coming down the tunnel. If it's me, I'll whistle like so"—he gave a low, two-toned note. "And if it's not, or I don't come back, you take the boyo on. I'm thinking he'll be safe if we can get him to Yggdrasil."

Teagan settled herself on the blocks of stone, never letting go of her brother. Finn reached out to brush the hair out of her eyes and tuck it behind her ear.

"I don't have the words," he said, "to tell you how sorry I am about your da. About Mamieo. About them all. If I were the saint Mamieo thought I was, I'd have been crying out to the Almighty from the moment I met you, asking the Creator of Creation to keep you safe. But I don't have words. All I've had from the beginning is my hands and my heart and my will to protect you." He caught her tear on his fingertip. "I wish to God I was a saint, girl, and my prayers could end this now." He kissed the top of her head. "I'll be back."

Gil followed him as far as the branch in the tunnel, then squatted down to keep watch, but Peggish followed Finn away.

"Gabby," Teagan said when he had gone, "how did you get here?"

"Gabby?" Abby looked offended for a second, then nodded. "I get it. No real names, right? So, I was seeing all this stuff." Abby shrugged. "So I thought I would try to follow you." Teagan nodded. The sprite bite had done more than give Abby second sight, then. Because she shouldn't have been able to walk in Mag Mell. Not in her right mind. "I told Jing if he ever wanted to see me again," Abby went on, "to get his butt out of there. I love him, T—Rosebud." She suddenly sounded very lost. "I figured that out right after we started running in opposite directions."

"I saw him almost to his car," Teagan said. "I think he made it."

"Of course he did." Abby was trying to convince herself.

"He's the Mighty Khan, right? But, Rosebud"—there were tears in Abby's voice—" . . . your dad."

Teagan nodded. "Gabby . . . Leo and Rafe didn't run. They were standing with him, holding the shape shifters back. Zoë was there, too. At the end."

Teagan felt Aiden stir in her arms, but she couldn't hide it from him. He must have heard Zoë's voice as clearly as she had. Abby put her arms around them and they sat that way— Teagan's arms around Aiden, and Abby's arms around them both, and all of them crying—until they heard Finn's whistle in the tunnel.

Teagan sat up and wiped her face on her sleeve. If she was going to keep Aiden alive, and stay alive herself, she'd have to be as tough as Finn. He'd shut his emotions away when he'd found Mamieo's body, focusing on the problems at hand.

"Our faces are totally going to pucker, right?" Abby said. "I'd hate it if Jing saw me like this."

Seamus came around the corner first, with Finn and Peggish right behind him.

"You've been in Mag Mell less than ten seconds and you start a riot?" Finn was saying.

"And I survived it," Seamus pointed out. He had Aiden's whip coiled in his hand. "It's the luck of the McGillahees."

"You're not supposed to use your real name here," Abby said.

"I'm well aware of goblin ways," Seamus said. "I'll still go by McGillahee."

"What was that you yelled?" Abby asked.

"The motto of the Fighting Fianna," Seamus explained. "I just reminded the Fir Bolg of who they were meant to be."

"He has them all convinced that *he's* the Mac Cumhaill," Finn said.

"What is this light?" Seamus asked.

"Don't ask Rosebud," Abby said. "Because she'll tell you. Just *accept* it."

"It's Mag Mell herself." Finn touched the wall. "Celebrating the boyo's existence. It's his song that can heal her. Right, boyo?"

Aiden just stared ahead, tears trembling on his lashes.

"You cry if you need to, Choirboy." Abby squatted down beside him. "But remember, you're not alone. I came all the way here to stay with you, right? I'm like the first Italian ever to walk in Mag Mell."

"The second," Finn corrected. "Zoë was here."

"Yeah?" Abby said. "But she was crazy. I'm normal."

"That's debatable, then, isn't it?" Finn sounded almost like his old self. *How could he be, with Mamieo and her father lying dead?* Because violent death was a part of the Mac Cumhaill's life.

Teagan brushed away her own tears with the palm of her hand. She had to turn off her heart and keep moving. She focused on the pain in her arm, on the dark, to hold her tears back as they started through the tunnels again. It seemed like they had been underground for hours before Teagan finally saw daylight ahead.

The sewage spilled into a stream in the middle of a wood. For all the time they had been underground, they hadn't gotten very far. She could see the city walls and hear the battle raging behind them.

Lucy came out of Aiden's hair and spun joyfully up and up into the light, executing aerial loops and curlicues.

"Someone's happy to be home, at least," Finn said. Gil seemed almost as happy. He raced into the woods. Peggish splashed in the filthy stream.

"Get out of here," Teagan told the girl.

Peggish turned to her and hissed.

"Get out of here!" Teagan shouted.

"What are you doing?" Abby asked. "She helped us, right?"

"Rosebud's trying to save the creature's life," Finn said. "With us is the most dangerous place this girl could be. Go on, Peggish. You've got to go."

The goblin girl shook her head, but Finn picked up a stick and waved it threateningly. She gave him a hurt look and climbed back into the sewer.

"Crap." Finn threw the stick down when they were sure she had gone. "I hate being the Mac Cumhaill."

Teagan carried Aiden upstream from the sewer, until the smell of the lavender breeze was stronger than the stench of sewage, scrubbed the slime off him with clean water, then checked her arm. It wasn't bleeding anymore, but the walk through the sewer tunnel couldn't have been good for it.

Abby scrubbed her face and hands. Seamus and Finn had somehow managed to come through the entire tunnel without getting coated with slime.

Seamus was looking around at the woods. A woolly

squirrelephant peered back at him, trumpeted a warning, and its whole herd came out of the underbrush and ran up a tree.

"This . . ." There was a look of complete wonder on Seamus's face, like the expression Abby had when she watched Jing. "I've never felt anything like this."

"I have." Finn met Teagan's eye. "You've finally found something worth fighting for, McGillahee."

"Worth dying for." Seamus shook his head. "And I have no idea where to begin."

"It's begun," Finn said. "There were no shadow men in the market, were there? Not even the puddly kind. John Wylltson called them all out of Mag Mell, and Raynor . . ." His voice trailed off.

"Now we find a way to let him in." Teagan wiped Aiden's tears away. Letting in the angel who had killed her father—who would have killed Aiden and Finn—was the only way they were going to survive this time.

Teagan dried Aiden's hands with the last clean patch of his shirt and checked his shoes. His feet were dry, at least, even if everyone else's were sodden. She set him down, and primroses sprung up from the bare ground and bloomed at his feet.

"That's *draíocht*," Abby said to Seamus. "Irish magic. Choirboy told me Mag Mell is full of it."

"I know what it is. I never thought I'd see it. Not like this."

"The first thing to be done," Finn said, "is to get the boyo to Yggdrasil, where he'll be safe. Then we'll have time to figure out the rest. Aiden, do you know the way?"

"How could he know the way?" Seamus asked. "He's a child."

Aiden took a step away from him and backed into Abby.

"And you're an idiot." She put her hands on Aiden's shoulders. "You don't know who Choirboy is. You never bothered to find out. You've got your own little prejudice going on, right? So you never bothered to get to know him. Choirboy could find his way *anywhere*. He can save this whole place! That's the point."

"Gabby," Tea said gently, "McGillahee saved us in the market."

"Whatever. He was saving himself, too. Those people fought for him because they thought *he* was the Mac Cumhaill, right?"

TEAGAN studied the dense underbrush around them, then glanced up. Even through the cloud cover she could tell the sun was west of noon.

Finn turned to Aiden. "Do you think you could sing to Mag Mell so she'll open the way?"

Aiden shook his head, and Teagan frowned. Aiden hadn't spoken since they'd arrived in Mag Mell. She knew her brother had a place inside where he locked himself away with his music when the world was too much to bear. He'd stayed there for months after their mom died, and stopped making up his own songs, stopped talking to strangers.

Finn squatted in front of him, but Aiden's eyes slid away from his, toward the stream.

Finn looked at Teagan, and she shook her head.

"What's going on?" Abby asked as Finn stood up.

"Mag Mell's not like the Earth we're used to," Finn explained. "Paths here are twisty. They might lead one place today and another tomorrow, or walk you round in circles. You'll not be finding your way here, not unless she wants you to. She'll show us the way if Aiden sings."

"Mac." Seamus nodded toward the wall of greenery. It was moving. Mag Mell wasn't waiting for a song. The trees and bushes beside them were shifting, making a path.

"That's the way to Yggdrasil?" Finn asked as if Mag Mell would answer.

"Wherever it goes, it's probably safer than where we are now," Teagan said when there was no response. "Peggish can't be the only one who uses that drain." Lucy apparently agreed with her. The sprite hovered over Aiden, her tiny dagger in her hand, as Finn led the way. He was walking as warily as a hunted wolf, his boots making almost no sound on the forest floor. Aiden walked behind him, then Tea and Abby, and finally Seamus, Aiden's whip in hand, bringing up the rear. Gil didn't bother with the path, but paced them in the woods.

Teagan had seen both fir forests and oak woods in Mag Mell, but the woods they were walking through now were clearly rain forest. Ferns taller than Aiden lined the pathway, and smaller ferns grew even from the branches of trees above them.

She could sense Gil under the canopy, now on one side of them, then on another, scouting. She could feel other creatures as well, woolly squirrelephants and mice, swat-bats, and, once, several winged monkeys sitting in the treetops. But mostly she was aware of the trees themselves, awake and prayerful, holding everything around her in their electric net.

Grief. The rain forest was full of grief. She didn't know whether it was the trees' or her own. Suddenly, there was what sounded like a massive explosion, and Teagan grabbed her brother as the ground shook.

"What the crap?" Finn had his knife in his hand. The forest had gone briefly still, but then the little animals started moving around them again.

"It's all right," Teagan said. "Whatever it was, it's over."

A misting rain started to fall, and she grimaced. So much for Aiden's dry feet. Drops gathered on foliage above, collecting until they were too heavy for the leaves to hold, and splashed down on them. The sun came out long enough to light apologetic rainbows in the mist, then disappeared behind curtains of drizzle again.

"Mood changes much?" Abby said, wiping raindrops from her face.

The second time they stopped to let Aiden rest, Teagan leaned against Finn, and he put his arm around her. Abby was sitting beside Aiden, pointedly looking the other way to give them space. Seamus was studying them.

"Ignore the man." Finn buried his face in her hair. She could feel his heart beating, the electric fire of his body filling her senses, a living shield between her and anything that would harm her. In all of Mag Mell, this was the safest place for her to be. Close to Finn. She wanted to close her eyes and stay like this forever.

"Mac," she said, "Mab's been one step ahead of me the whole way. I've made too many mistakes."

"We both have, haven't we? I was out walking when the Dump Dogs came." The edge of grief seeped into Finn's voice. "If I hadn't gone . . ." He shook his head. "I said before, there's no point in what-ifs. We just have to pick ourselves up and try again, don't we?" His arms tightened around her. "When it comes to choosing between me and the boyo, I want you to choose Aiden."

"What?" Teagan pushed away and turned to look up at him.

"I'm saying that Raynor's not the only one who might have to make hard choices. I've lived with them all my life, but they're new to you, girl. Sometimes you don't have time to think it through. Barely time to act."

"All right," Teagan said. "But if it comes down to choosing between *me* and Aiden, I need to know you'll do the same thing. Choose Aiden."

Finn nodded.

She felt him tense as something moved in the bushes.

"It's Gil," she said before the phooka stepped out.

"I'll carry the boyo." Gil looked over his shoulder. "We should hurry faster. There are phookas in the woods, and they're hungry. They're not here yet."

"I'll carry him," Seamus offered. "I'm stronger."

Gil glared at him. "Lawyers can't run."

"Try me," Seamus said.

"Let me guess," Finn said. "You're very good at running."

"I am, in fact." Seamus squatted down so that he could speak to Aiden, but the little boy's eyes slid sideways again. *It hurts,* he'd told Teagan once. *Sometimes it hurts to look in eyes.* But even when he couldn't look in eyes or speak, he could talk with his fingers.

Aiden, I love you, Teagan signed.

327

Seamus looked from Teagan to Aiden—and started signing.

What Abby said was right, and I'm sorry. Your father welcomed me, even though I was an idiot, and wrong about you and—his hands hesitated as he looked at Teagan—*possibly your sister.*

"What's he saying?" Finn asked.

"He's apologizing," Teagan said. "He's actually very good at it."

Abby rolled her eyes. But it was true. Seamus was eloquent in ASL.

"I was saying"—he stood up—"that I have been wrong about Choirboy, and might have been wrong about Rosebud."

"What was that?" Finn cupped his hand to his ear. "We didn't quite hear the last bit, McGillahee. Speak up."

"I said I was *possibly* wrong about Rosebud." He looked at Teagan again. "I apologize."

"So, what convinced you?" Abby asked.

"I spent all day talking to their father," Seamus said. "And then I saw the man lay down his life for them. John Wylltson was a better man than I am, and he was no fool. Not even about those he loved."

"Shhh." Teagan put her finger to her lips. She could feel the band of phookas making their way through the woods, scavenging the way Gil's pack had when they'd first encountered them, but there was an excitement building in them, too. Excitement for the hunt.

She motioned for everyone to get down, and even Abby sank into the ferns without speaking. The phookas passed close enough that Teagan could hear their voices as they called to one another about Samhain and the Great Hunt, bickering over who would taste the child. *They would be disappointed this year.*

Aiden put his hands over his ears and squeezed his eyes shut. He'd always believed that if he couldn't see monsters, they couldn't see him. Now he was trying not to hear them as well.

They crouched beneath the dripping ferns long after the voices had faded.

Finally, Gil stood. "They didn't smell us because of the rain."

"Not just mood changes, then," Finn said softly. "Mag Mell's hiding us."

Aiden was still blocking out the monsters. Seamus touched his shoulder, and the little boy opened his eyes.

If you let me carry you, Choirboy, he signed, *we'll get away from them faster.*

Aiden nodded, so Teagan helped him onto Seamus's back. The lawyer bounced a couple of times to settle him, and then Finn started out again, with Abby and Seamus behind him and Teagan and Gil bringing up the rear.

They walked without speaking, fast enough that she had to trot to keep up. The woods were changing around them as they went—the trees growing larger, more ancient. The ferns were larger as well, arching over Finn's head. If the beetles and slugs had not stayed the same size, Teagan would have thought they were all shrinking. And then the path led through a grove of giants, trees so large the Wylltsons' house could have fit inside a single trunk.

They passed one that had very recently fallen, its roots tearing a massive crater in the soil. This was what had shaken the forest, then—at least ten tons of tree, its upper branches falling from hundreds of feet.

Gil walked as wide-eyed as he had in the cemetery, clearly in awe of this place, while the rain still fell, hiding them from the creatures Teagan felt moving in the bushes.

She focused on the life around her. The giant trees were seeding electrical storms in the sky, pulling ions up from the water below and releasing them in the air. She could feel the storm's shadow tingling at her feet and hear the trees' muted music locked inside the bark.

When the path led close enough, she pressed her hands against one of the giants and almost fell to her knees. This tree was crying out for Mag Mell, for the fallen giants, for the creatures great and small. Mag Mell was dying. Joe had told Raynor as much after he'd spoken with the willow in the park. Teagan laid her forehead against the bark.

It was holding its grief up like a petition. She could feel the pain of Mag Mell echoed by the tree, pain over the broken ones, and longing for the Fir Bolg—the missing menders and tenders who should be helping her. And she could feel splinters of cold iron in Mag Mell's side. Teagan had brought one of them herself, and she'd told Mag Mell that she'd use it to take Fear Doirich away so that Aiden could return. The other was the knife Finn carried now. Mamieo's knife. Mag Mell hadn't even tried to stop him from carrying it in, because she was in too much pain for it to matter anymore.

Abby pulled her away from the tree and back onto the path, and they walked again, Teagan almost numb with the pain and grief of the trees piled on top of her own.

Now and then they passed another ancient one that had fallen, and all of them recently enough that the soil had not yet eroded around the holes they left. This was new, a symptom of the death of a world. The path led along the rim of a deep ravine until they reached one of the fallen giants that crossed the gap, and they walked across on a trunk as wide as a one-lane road. The rain stopped as they reached the other side.

Here, all of the trees were giants, and there was no undergrowth. The dimming light was caused by more than just the trees above them. The sun was setting, and bright floating jellies rose from the forest floor.

"I don't think she's taking us to Yggdrasil," Finn said as the path turned again.

"Have you ever been here before, Gil?" Teagan asked, but the phooka just pressed his hands to his heart and shook his head, as if he were walking in the Holy of Holies and dared not make a sound.

"May I sing a song for you, Choirboy?" Seamus asked. "I've been thinking about it while we walked."

Abby's eyes narrowed. "This isn't some Irish song, is it? 'Cause that's all he needs."

"No," Seamus said. "It's a Scottish lullaby."

"A lullaby? Like you sing to babies?"

"My mother used to sing it to me as she rocked me to sleep," Seamus assured her, and he began:

"Speed, bonnie boat, like a bird on the wing,
Onward! the sailors cry;
Carry the lad that's born to be King
Over the sea to Skye."

His voice was surprisingly good. There wasn't a glimmer of *draíocht* in it as far as Teagan could tell, but the trees went still, listening. And then they cried out with one voice: *Send him. Send the king.*

Teagan expected everyone to jump at the sound, but Seamus just went on with his lullaby. No one else had heard the cry of the trees.

"Though the waves leap, soft shall ye sleep,
Ocean's a royal bed.
Rocked in the deep, Flora will keep
Watch by your weary head.
Loud the winds howl, loud the waves roar,
Thunderclaps rend the air."

That resonated with the trees, and they begged for the storm. There was nothing left of the storm that had been building except potential, still unformed.

Seamus's song wasn't making magic or changing the world. He was just telling a story the trees had been waiting a very long time to hear.

"Baffled, our foes stand by the shore,
Follow they will not dare."

Abby glanced back at the ravine. "I like that part."

Seamus nodded, and went on.

> *"Many's the lad fought on that day,*
> *Well the Claymore could wield,*
> *When the night came, silently lay*
> *Dead in Culloden's field."*

Abby stopped so fast he bumped into her.

"Who puts dead people in songs for babies?" she demanded.

"The Scots, apparently." Finn had turned around.

"It's not that bad," Seamus insisted. "The lad born to be king got away, after all."

"Must have been a McGillahee, then," Finn said. "Born to live, while others fell around him."

"He was a Stuart, actually. Charles Edward Stuart. Also known as Bonnie Prince Charlie."

"The Young Pretender," Abby said.

Finn looked at her in surprise. "I can't believe you knew that."

"So, you knew it, too?"

"No, I didn't. I just wasn't expecting—"

"Me to know anything?" Abby glared at him. "I'm an artist, right? This famous painting by Maurice-Quentin de La Tour was supposed to be Bonnie Prince Charlie, so people paid, like, a million dollars for it, but it was his brother, Henry."

"The Stuarts believed in the divine rights of kings," Seamus said. "They thought that the thrones of England and

Scotland were rightfully theirs because of the royal blood in their veins." It was so much like something John Wylltson would have said that grief rushed through Teagan, fresh and hot.

"Were they?" Finn asked.

"Not according to history. Charlie's attempt to take them failed. That's what the song is about."

"So, Scottish people sing lullabies about dead people and failures," Abby said. "Lame."

Seamus brushed a fly away from his face and Lucy zoomed after it, snatching it from the air.

"We love the grand attempt, I suppose. The fight for a noble cause. What do *you* think of the song, Choirboy? Any *draíocht* in it?"

Aiden didn't say anything, but Finn shook his head.

"There wasn't. Even I could tell that, McGillahee. What were you expecting?"

"I don't know."

But he had been hoping for something. Teagan was sure of it.

They walked silently for a time, then Seamus spoke again.

"I still have your whip, Choirboy. Do you want to learn how to use it?"

"He tried," Abby said. "He couldn't make it work. You're not making anything better, McGillahee. You're, like, rubbing salt all over cuts."

Seamus ignored her. "I'll show you. Can we stop for a rest, Mac?"

"I want to check my arm before it's too dark to see," Teagan said. Her fingers were starting to feel tight, as if the blood was not circulating well. Finn nodded.

Seamus stood Aiden up on a tree-size fallen branch, and put the handle of the whip in the little boy's hand while Finn came over and untied the bandanna for Teagan.

"That don't look so good," Abby said. "Do they have antibioticals in Mag Mell?"

"Not that I know of." Teagan pressed a finger against the swollen flesh.

The blood didn't well, but the wound didn't look good, either. The edges were already puffy with infection. Dump Dogs' mouths must be filthy, and hiking through sewers couldn't have helped. She turned her attention to her little brother.

"Now, it doesn't matter how small you are," Seamus was saying. "I know you can do this." Teagan shivered. Seamus had power in his voice again. He pulled Aiden's hand back, then moved it smoothly forward. "That's the motion. Now you do it."

Aiden tried, and to Teagan's amazement, the whip cracked. He nodded to himself and did it again.

"Now I'll show you a trick." Seamus jumped up on the log and took the whip from Aiden. "This is a fast figure eight." The whip cracked in front of him and then behind him in the same swing.

Gil sniffed the breeze and turned wild-eyed to Teagan. She'd felt them, too, seconds before the wind shifted.

"Cú Faoil," she announced, just as they came into sight.

"What are those things?" Abby asked. "Horses?"

"Hounds," Finn said. "The fighting hounds of the Fir

Bolg. They were left in the last battle, set to fight goblins, and they've been at it ever since."

Gil squeaked as the huge beasts bounded into the clearing. A flight of sprites came with them, and Lucy rose, eyes flashing, prepared to fight for Aiden.

Finn started forward to meet them, his hands spread.

The Cú Faoil seemed to break in mid-jump, turning aside from Finn, but one of the younger males didn't manage to stop in time and knocked Finn to the ground. It pulled its lips in an apologetic smile. This pack had walked with them once before, on the other side of Fear Doirich's city. Cú Faoil's noses were not as keen as other hounds'. They clearly hadn't recognized Finn in the gloaming.

"I'm glad to see you, too," Finn assured them, and the pups gamboled around him. The alpha male watched tolerantly, but the female had her eye on Gil.

"Mac," Teagan said warningly as she started toward him.

The whip cracked before Finn could respond. "Down," Seamus said. The Cú Faoil dropped, every one of them, and looked toward him. The alpha female whined eagerly. "Good dogs. Come on." They crawled toward him on their bellies.

"You never mentioned your father's name," Teagan said. "Was it Mac Rónáin?"

"It was."

"Who?" Abby asked.

"Caílte Mac Rónáin," Teagan said, "was the hound master of the Fianna. These creatures fought goblins beside Fionn's men."

Seamus jumped down from the log, and the alpha male approached him.

"I've been dreaming of you all my life, you big, beautiful beast," Seamus said. The Cú Faoil wiggled like a happy puppy when he touched it. "I'm sorry we left you to fight alone so long. I'm back, and I'm not going to leave you again."

"I remember now," Abby said. "Thomas said this Caílte had an affair with Mab. And you were worried about . . . Rosebud and Mac? Your own great-great"—she waved her hand in the air—"whatever grandfather had a child with Mab!"

"No relation to me," Seamus said quickly. "The old man had several children by more respectable women. The Mac Rónáins were always womanizers. I, however, am a McGillahee."

"I don't think the hounds believe you," Finn said. "I'm not sure I do, either. Whatever the case, we'd best be moving. It'll be dark soon."

Seamus had to tell the Cú Faoil only once not to eat Gil. They still fawned over Finn, but bristled at Teagan and Aiden, and completely ignored Abby.

"Do you want to ride one?" Seamus asked Aiden as they started out.

Aiden just shook his head. Twilight seemed to linger longer in Mag Mell, and the light was still with them when the path disappeared at the edge of a clearing. There were a few low bushes, but their dark, clustered leaves didn't hide the pool in the center. Teagan stepped closer.

She had seen pools in Mag Mell before, had swum in

them past Yggdrasil's roots, had seen lights of other worlds, and heard the Song of Creation when she touched the water. But this pool was dark. It didn't reflect the bright jellies that drifted above it, the sky, or even Finn standing beside her, just her own reflection. Looking at it into her own eyes was ... frightening. Seamus's eyes slid away from the pool, like Aiden's slid from the eyes of strangers. Abby and Finn had stepped back as well. "We're not ready to look straight into eternity. Not yet." The words Finn had spoken in the cemetery echoed in her mind.

But the Cú Faoil lapped at the water unafraid, so Teagan knelt and touched it. A song filled her, and a rushing wildness like the roar of mighty waves on a rocky shore.

The waters the Almighty parted when he set the worlds in place?

"Gil," she whispered. "Where are we?"

W HERE are we?" Teagan repeated.

Gil took a step closer to the pool. "A place that phookas aren't supposed to be."

Abby gasped, and Teagan turned to look.

The moon had been creeping up the sky behind the giant trees, and now it came out above them, so brilliant that it washed away the stars. Teagan and Finn had seen the mountains and mares on it the last time they had walked in Mag Mell, but Abby, Seamus, and Aiden were seeing it for the first time. More time had passed here than in Chicago. It seemed like only two days ago it had been less than a half moon, but now it was full.

The dark leaves of the bushes around them caught the moon's light, and it turned each tight cluster into a silver rose.

"Oh, my god," Abby said. "This is the most beautiful, terrifying place in the universe."

"Multiverse," Teagan corrected automatically.

"Don't start, Tea." Abby didn't notice that she'd used Teagan's name, but Teagan doubted that it mattered here. "Don't start explaining how all this works. I don't care. No wonder your mom painted the way she did. She'd been here, right? All of this was inside her. All of this! God, *I need my sketchpad!*"

"It's the First Grove," Seamus said. "It must be. This is where the Creator of Creation stood when He sang Mag Mell out of the waters."

"Now, how do you know that?" Finn asked.

"How do you not know it? This world belonged to your people once, after all."

"Been a little busy all my life," Finn said.

"This"—Seamus spread his hands—"is the heart of Mag Mell. It makes sense that she brought us here. This is where Aiden needs to sing."

Aiden shrank back against Abby, shaking his curly head.

"Hey, don't worry about it," Abby said. "Nobody said you have to sing now, right? Why don't you practice with your whip? Show me how you make it crack, okay?" She led him away.

The Cú Faoil threw themselves on the ground, dividing their attentions between Seamus and Finn, who started arguing about what to do next.

Teagan sat down on the mossy bank of the pool. The last time she'd seen her reflection in a pool of Mag Mell, she'd been bilocating. She'd heard the first Song of Creation in that pool, powerful, joyful, and *right*. But she'd turned away from the sight of her own molten eyes . . . away from the hunt, choosing to be a healer instead.

Her whole body had resonated with the song when she'd dived into that pool. The roots of the ancient trees around her would be twined with those of Yggdrasil beneath the surface of this pool, too, remembering the song they had once heard, playing it back to the waters like an Aeolian harp still vibrating from the voice that had passed over it.

It would be stronger here. It had to be. *This* was where the song had entered the waters, given them borders and boundaries, separating them so Mag Mell could be born.

The desire to find out what was beneath the still surface was so powerful it dulled her grief, shoved all thought of war, all the pain in her arm, away. She touched the surface again and heard the song, this time sweet and good as it had been before, and behind it, the roar of mighty waters calling her out of Mag Mell. Out of the multiverse.

The sound of eternity. A sea without end, which raged on shores beyond the borders of existence.

Aiden's whip *cracked* and Teagan pulled her hand away.

"Good job, boyo," Finn said. "But it's a bit loud. We need to be quiet."

Gil was still standing behind Teagan.

"You said phookas can't come here?" she asked.

"They're not supposed to." Gil's ear twitched. "I'm a man."

Teagan's image in the pool was gone when she leaned over the waters again. In its place, a tiger paced a kitchen floor before a lamb.

"Next time, put a rock in the inner tube, Tea," the tiger said, in Aileen Wylltson's voice. *"It'll be more useful. You have to think your way through things, even in the midst of it."*

Teagan remembered that conversation. Finn had taken a beating in the alley behind their house. The bullies had been after Lennie, and he had stepped in, even though he had a cast on his arm. Teagan had done her best to help, smacking one of the bullies with a bike inner tube she'd grabbed from the garbage. It *would* have worked better if she'd put a rock in it.

"*Aileen! Don't encourage violence,*" the lamb said in her father's voice. "*There are civilized ways to deal with things like this.*"

"*I'd have civilized the hooligans on the spot,*" the tiger growled. "*It was the right thing they did, and you know it, John.*"

Teagan smiled. Mom had never wanted civilization. She'd wanted justice.

The tiger in the pond stopped pacing and looked directly at Teagan, its eyes molten gold.

"*Use your brain, girl,*" it said, then it turned to the lamb. "*You were saying?*" it asked politely.

"*That* The Jungle Book *should never have been illustrated. Kipling's words were meant to be imagined.*"

Teagan sucked in her breath. More than a memory, then. *This* conversation had never happened. At least not while she was listening.

"Image *is the root of* imagine," the tiger said. "*And imagination is the only way we can approach truth, because truth is bigger than our physical world. Edward and Charles Detmold did a brilliant job of imaging Kipling's words. There was truth in those illustrations. It's time to go, Dear.*" They turned and started walking away together.

"*Did you know that the story 'Tiger! Tiger!'—the one where Mowgli kills Shere Khan—was inspired by Blake's 'The Tyger'?*" the lamb asked.

"*As if all of us were like that cat.*" The tiger's tail twitched. "*I always preferred 'Letting in the Jungle,' anyway.*"

The howl of a Cú Faoil pulled Teagan back. It was the alpha male. He tipped his nose up and howled again, and something answered him from the direction of the ravine. A phooka, daring him to come and find it. The Cú Faoil all looked eagerly at Seamus. And then more phookas answered, and more.

"That doesn't sound good," Abby said.

"Yes, it does." Teagan stood up slowly. "Gil, do they leave the gates of the walled city open at night?"

"No," Gil said. "They close them up so nothing sneaks in." Of course they did. The phookas in the slum city outside the walls were free, but all those inside the city walls wore collars and chains.

"Tea?" Abby had a worried look on her face. "What are you thinking?"

Teagan smiled. Exactly what her mom had suggested.

"I'm going to let the jungle in," she said.

"What?"

"It was one of my mother's favorite stories," Teagan explained. "A wild boy named Mowgli called the elephants to a town and they destroyed it."

"Elephants?" Abby looked at the dark woods around them. "The cute little guys that hang by their tails from the trees?" She put the palm of her hand to Teagan's forehead. "Did your fever come back, Tea?"

"It's a children's story," Seamus said.

"Stop being arrogant and listen," Finn cut in. "The girl's got a brain like her da. The man loved children's stories."

"I'm speaking metaphorically," Teagan explained. "I'm

going to bilocate and lead the phookas who have gathered for the Great Hunt into the town."

"You can lead phookas?" Seamus asked.

"Yes!" Gil shivered with delight. "She didn't bend us. She asked us. When she hunted god, it was so good. Like something we were hungry for."

Glimories, perhaps? What had the phookas been before they followed Mab away?

"They'll kill the Fir Bolg as well as the Highborn," Seamus said before Teagan could ask Gil about it. "I won't allow it."

"*You* won't allow it? Nobody asked you, McGillahee," Finn said. "If we don't do something, this whole world will die."

"You said you were very good at running, Seamus," Teagan said.

"I take after Caílte Mac Rónáin in that regard."

Teagan nodded. Caílte had been the only Fianna who could keep up with the hounds.

"I need you to get through the phookas on the other side of the ravine and back to the town. Go in the way we came out, and warn the Fir Bolg. Get them off the streets. Then open the gates and get out of the way."

"They'll listen to him?" Abby asked.

"Of course they will," Finn said. "They think he's the Mac Cumhaill, don't they?"

"And after you get in and wreak havoc?" Seamus asked. "What then?"

"I'm going after Mab, and then I'll find a way to let Raynor in."

"*We're* going after her, you mean," Finn said.

Teagan looked toward Abby and Aiden, and shook her head.

"Oh, I don't like where this is going," Finn said. "You can't do this alone, girl."

"She won't be alone." Gil's ears were flat. "*I'm* going with her. Me. I can show her where Fear Doirich is."

Teagan nodded. She'd hoped he would volunteer. *We always know where god is,* the little phooka had told her once.

"Hold on," Seamus said. "Doesn't the phooka think Doirich is God?"

"I'm a man," Gil insisted.

"And what am I supposed to do while you two save the world?" Finn asked.

"I can't guarantee that all the phookas will follow me to the city. Some of them might just decide to go looking for flesh and blood instead." *For Aiden, if Mag Mell hasn't managed to wash the scent of child from the woods.*

Seamus turned to Finn. "You're really going to trust that she and a phooka boy can do this?"

"*Man!*" Gil shouted.

"You have no idea what she's capable of, McGillahee. Or what Gil's capable of either, for that matter."

"I'm afraid I do. I know the stories."

"I know Tea and Gil," Finn said, "and I'm not afraid."

Teagan took Finn's hand. "I am doing this with or without you, Seamus," she said. "The life is leaking out of Mag Mell now. Tonight. I don't have time to think of anything else. Are you going to save Fir Bolg lives, or wait here twiddling your thumbs?"

"I'll go."

"The Cú Faoil should be able to deal with any phooka bands you meet on the way," Teagan said. "They can get you there. You've got two hours."

"How are you going to judge time? Count?"

"I have the moon, and the trees as a fixed reference point. I can estimate."

"When you reach the sewer," Finn added, "if Mag Mell doesn't light your way, just walk against the flow of the water."

"You've crawled through dark sewers before?" Seamus asked.

"It's a survival skill. I learned it hunting in the underside of Chicago."

Aiden held up his whip, and Seamus took it.

"Thank you, Aiden." He whistled at the Cú Faoil, and they leaped to their feet, eager for the fight ahead.

"McGillahee," Finn called as they left the clearing. "Be careful. I don't want to have to listen to more Scottish songs about grand attempts."

"Try not to do anything heroically Irish while I'm away," Seamus replied. "I'd miss you."

"May I borrow your shirt, Finn?" Teagan asked when Seamus was gone. He pulled it up over his head and handed it to her. Teagan pulled it down over her own head, then started undressing beneath it.

"That's a survival skill we learned in middle school," Abby said. "Girls' locker rooms can be brutal."

Tea was wiggling out of her shirt when she heard the first

whip crack, loud as a gunshot, and then the sound of Cú Faoil battling phookas.

"It's started," Finn said. "And it doesn't sound that far away." The phookas must have been on this side of the ravine. That was going to make trying to sleep fun.

"Turn your backs," she said.

Finn nodded and pulled Aiden away, and Teagan found a place that looked comfortable to sleep, laid out her clothes, and settled down.

Finn and Abby were talking, their voices low, and the skirmish in the woods seemed to be over. The electric shadow of the almost-storm tickled at her from the ground below. *It's the life of Mag Mell I'm feeling,* Teagan realized. *She's trying to fight for herself, but she can't even muster a storm.* The electric field felt like a net, pulling her down into the moss. Mag Mell still could, it seemed, help her to sleep.

When she sat up out of her body, she had the spark of the half-formed storm in her. It wasn't as much as she had felt when the lightning struck, but it was enough to light green candles on her fingertips. Mag Mell was giving her all she could. Teagan felt the excitement of the hunt rising, saw Gil start to turn and Finn reach out and pull him back around. She scrambled into her clothes.

"Okay," she said. "I'm dressed."

Aiden looked at her wide-eyed when they finally turned around.

"You're glowing green," Abby said. "That's new."

"It's that thing she has with electricity." Finn looked up. "Should we be moving back?"

"No," Teagan said. "No lightning here, just potential."

"You're totally going to regret this in the morning," Abby said.

"I just overdid it last time." Even if she did live to regret it, she wasn't going to refuse Mag Mell's gift tonight. "Aiden? You know this is just me, right?"

Aiden looked from her to her sleeping flesh and bones.

"Here." She held out her hand. He took it, and frowned. She should really have explained this to him before she stepped out of her body.

"It's cold," Finn confirmed. "But she's every bit your sister."

Aiden dropped her hand and walked over to her flesh and blood. He felt her cheek, then pressed his ear to her chest.

"So, what are you going to do now?" Abby asked, as Aiden went on checking Teagan's vital signs.

Teagan looked at the moon. It hadn't moved very far up the sky since Seamus had left.

"Wait," she said reluctantly. "I fell asleep a lot faster than I thought I would."

THIRTY

FINN sat on one side of her and Abby on the other, silent as knights keeping vigil while the moon crawled across the sky. Aiden built traps around her sleeping body using stones and sticks. Gil couldn't sit still and paced the clearing, stopping every few feet to scent the wind. Aiden had finished half his wall of sticks and had started covering her body with leaves by the time Teagan stood up.

Gil raced over. "Time to go?"

Teagan nodded.

"Give us a minute," Finn said, making a shooing motion at Gil.

"Come on." Abby nudged the phooka boy over to examine Aiden's work.

Finn looked at Teagan for a long moment, then picked a silver-leafed flower from the bush beside him and tucked it into the buttonhole of her shirt.

"Come back to me, girl." His voice was husky.

"Keep Abby and Aiden safe for me." Teagan touched the leaf petals. "This doesn't get you out of a real date with real flowers."

"And canoodling?" Finn asked.

"Definitely canoodling," Teagan promised.

"That beats breaking up before you run off," Finn said, and then was serious again. "Is this going to work?"

"I don't know," Teagan admitted. "But it's not just the best idea I have. It's the only idea I have."

Finn pulled her into his arms and rested his chin on top of her head.

"I thought I was unsettling like this."

"Very," Finn said. "I'm just not ready to let you go."

Teagan hugged him back, listening to his heartbeat. "When will you be ready?" she asked when his arms didn't loosen.

"Never. I'll never be ready to watch you walk away. I don't know what to do with myself while I wait."

"Abby's going to pray for us," Teagan suggested.

"I've never had time for that," Finn said. "What's the sense in saying, 'Hoy, Almighty, there's a goblin now, about to squeeze the life out of a creature. Thy will be done.' I'm standing right there. I know very well what needs to be done, so I get on with it, don't I? I'll get it done or die trying."

Teagan laughed, and he held her out at arm's length and looked at her. "I'm being serious here, girl."

"I know. It's just that . . . Mamieo was right. You're a saint."

"I'd be a saint or a martyr or make an ass of myself if it would save you and the boyo. If it would let Raynor in. I'm willing to pray my heart out if it will get you back safely, but I only know Mamieo's prayer and one other, aside from blessings over food."

"Mamieo's prayer," Teagan said. "Mamieo's prayer will do."

Finn pulled her close again, and she closed her eyes. "*I do not ask for a path with no trouble or regret,*" he prayed. "*I ask instead for a friend who'll walk with me down any path. I do not ask never to feel pain. I ask instead for courage, even when hope can scarce shine through. And one more thing I ask: That in every hour of joy or pain, I feel the Creator close by my side. This is my truest prayer for myself and for all I love, now and forever. Amen.*"

Teagan nodded. "What's your other prayer?"

"Help!" Finn said.

"Just 'Help'?"

"That's it. Your voice lacked the proper note of desperation, though. I suppose it's hard to achieve when you're not in the midst of it."

"In the midst of—?"

"My life," Finn said, finally letting go. "My entire life. Godspeed, girl. The Almighty keep you safe."

Teagan kissed Aiden before she and Gil slipped into the woods. The moonlight was plenty bright for her eyes, and apparently for Gil's as well. She tried to keep the excitement that bubbled inside her quiet. She didn't want to call the phookas yet—not until they'd crossed the ravine—so they followed the path Mag Mell had left, Gil jumping fern fronds and switch-flipping off giant tree trunks in his excitement.

He stopped when they found what was left of the band of phookas Seamus and the Cú Faoil had met. The creatures had been on the pool side of the ravine, closer even than Teagan had imagined. She couldn't tell how many there had been—six, maybe seven. She had seen what Cú Faoil could do before, but it still sickened her. A dog-headed man, his grizzled muzzle belying his massively muscular build, lay split open on the path, his war club still in his hand. Teagan knelt and took it from him.

Gil looked at the bodies strewn around them, and the corners of his mouth turned down.

"Enkidu," he said. "My name is Enkidu."

Teagan stood up slowly. The last time she'd walked in Mag Mell, he'd said he wanted to tell someone his name before he died. He'd lied, of course, not giving his real name. But this time, he was telling the truth. She could feel it. He was preparing himself for death.

"Enkidu."

Gil shivered when she said it. Enkidu was the wild hunter from *The Epic of Gilgamesh*. Phookas had to have glimories of that story. Why else would a phooka yearning to be a man call himself Gil after the human in the tale?

There had to be a history behind the phookas, just as there was behind the *cat-sídhe*. The hunters were ... more broken. Were they being punished, like Eógan, the fiddler Thomas had asked Fear Doirich to turn into a tree?

This time it was Teagan who shivered. *If Hákon hunt answers instead of gods, they will not only miss supper. They will fail.*

"Thank you for telling me your name," she said as they crossed over the ravine on the fallen giant. "Now, let's run!"

She felt the spark leap up stronger as her feet hit the ground. The electric wind lifted her hair, and she felt the Song of Creation in it. The joy of the hunt flashed through her like adrenaline, and she threw back her head and howled with the excitement of it. Gil laughed beside her, and urgency bounced back from the ancient trees. *End it now,* they cried. *It must end now, or all is lost.* She glimpsed the first band of phookas through the underbrush—they stood still, watching her come.

She reached out with everything in her, with the excitement of the hunt, and the urgency of the trees. Mag Mell could not quite muster lightning for her, but this was enough. The electric charge amplified her cry ten thousand times. *Mab. Hunt Mab with me!* A jackal-man burst from the bushes and ran beside her, and then they were all running with her. She had called a single pack to run with her the last time she was in Mag Mell. This time, she was reaching every phooka in the woods.

The rhythm of the running rose in her like poetry, and she fitted Blake's words to it in her mind.

> *Tyger! Tyger! burning bright*
> *In the forests of the night,*
> *What immortal hand or eye*
> *Could frame thy fearful symmetry?*
>
> *In what distant deeps or skies*
> *Burnt the fire of thine eyes?*
> *On what wings dare he aspire?*
> *What the hand dare seize the fire?*

She jumped a bush as Gil had done earlier, giddy in the moonlight, and saw phookas all around her now. Still more were racing to catch up with them, bouncing off of trees and flipping as they ran.

And what shoulder, and what art
Could twist the sinews of thy heart?
And when thy heart began to beat,
What dread hand? and what dread feet?

Blake had gotten that part wrong. There were no sinews in her, no beating heart. Just the fire of Mag Mell, captured by the poetry's meter that moved her feet.

What the hammer? what the chain?
In what furnace was thy brain?
What the anvil? what dread grasp
Dare its deadly terrors clasp?

When the stars threw down their spears,
And watered heaven with their tears,
Did he smile his work to see?
Did he who made the Lamb make thee?

Teagan leaped high in the moonlight. "*Yes!*" she shouted to the trees. "He smiled!"

"He smiled, he smiled!" the phookas echoed.

The Song of Creation was resonating with their cry. Mercy had married Justice, and she was their child—hunter *and* healer. *That* was her symmetry, the balance in her. And it was fierce, and fearfully *good*.

More phookas picked up the words, as if it were a crazy battle call: "He smiled!" They bugled, trumpeted, and howled their joy at the thought.

Tyger! Tyger! burning bright
In the forests of the night,
What immortal hand or eye
Dare frame thy fearful symmetry?

They'd run for an hour when Teagan saw the orange glow ahead of them. The goblin city was burning. She hoped Seamus had gotten the Fir Bolg out of the way, because there were more phookas running with her than she had imagined lived in all of Mag Mell, and they hadn't reached the phooka camp outside the city gates yet.

When they did, phookas spilled out of their tents and shacks, or threw down what they were doing, caught up in the fervor of the hunt. If Seamus didn't have the gate open, they were going to crash like a wave against the wall and start tearing one another apart in their frenzy.

She heard the crack of his whip before she saw him—silhouetted by the flames of a burning building as he did his Indiana Jones impression in the open gateway. And then he was moving. It looked almost like a dance as he worked the whip, and she saw that he was holding back a horde of Highborn shape shifters who wanted to close the gate.

"Get out of there, McGillahee!" Teagan shouted. She wasn't sure he could hear her, but he must have heard the rising roar of the phookas at her back. He turned, jumped directly into the flames, and disappeared—just before the phookas crashed into the Highborn.

Enkidu kept moving, dodging past shape shifters, using the walls of buildings to bounce away from them.

Teagan was relieved to see no living Fir Bolg slaves on the streets. There were bodies, though, of both men and women. Things had not been going well for them before Seamus arrived.

They came around a corner and she saw a plaid jacket. There was no time to wonder how the Dump Dogs had gotten home. She had two seconds before Saoirse saw them. There were at least eight new Dump Dogs with her. Thomas had said it was a large family. Saoirse was the only one in human form.

"That way." Teagan pointed, and Enkidu turned down the side street as the Dump Dogs started after them. She sprinted down the dirt road by Enkidu's side, sure she could outrun them. But one, much faster than the rest, was gaining on Enkidu. Teagan could see the street opening up in front of him, and the arena, with its post for phooka baiting.

"Flip-switch," she called to the phooka boy, and sprinted ahead just far enough to get past the pole ahead of him.

The Dump Dog was on his heels when Enkidu ran straight up the post. Teagan came back around it to the right, swinging the war club hard as Enkidu flipped to the left.

It connected solidly with the Dump Dog's side, and she heard and felt ribs break. The Dog screamed, but Teagan whirled and went up the wooden bleachers after Enkidu. He leaped, caught a balcony railing one-handed, and swung himself up. Some of the Dump Dogs shifted to human form to follow, but they couldn't keep up with him, even though he had only one hand.

"Come down!" Saoirse called. "We just want to talk to you."

Teagan ignored her and focused on following Enkidu to the rooftop. He was headed for the center of town, a place that seemed to have been designed for free-running. The wood and stone buildings were attached to one another, or very close together. Even the streets were narrow enough to jump with a running start. The Dump Dogs couldn't keep up.

"Fear Doirich," Enkidu said at last. Teagan pulled him down so that they would be less apparent against the orange sky. The Dump Dogs would doubtless find them soon, and she wanted to study the situation before they arrived.

The place to which Enkidu pointed wasn't a palace, as far as Teagan could tell. Just an ornate building, not even as tall as the one they were on. Three people stood on a balcony in the moonlight, watching the distant fires. Mab, Fear Doirich, and—Teagan's heart sank. Thomas. It was Thomas, and he was dressed like a princeling in silver and black.

Fear Doirich wore the same circlet on his head that he had worn when she'd first seen him, walking in the dead garden. The undulating shadows that had followed him through the market were missing, though. Finn had been right. The shadows were gone from Mag Mell.

"I think we should—" Teagan began, but Enkidu was already moving.

"Maaaab!" he bellowed as he leaped from the rooftop. Teagan could either follow or let him die.

He landed on the balcony, and Teagan dropped beside him. Thomas took one look at them, turned, and ran through the door.

"Stop," Mab said, and Teagan could feel the power in her

voice, reaching out to bend them, take control. The Highborn's eyes were solid black. Mab was bilocating, either preparing for violence to come or just back from the riots. Teagan was glad. Mab's flesh and bones looked too much like Aileen Wylltson's. Without them, the resemblance vanished. The features were all the right sizes and shapes, and all in the right places, but where Aileen had been fierce, this thing was vicious.

"Full of lightning, aren't you, niece? Too bad Mag Mell is too weak to give you more. It might have helped." She looked at the war club Teagan was clutching and laughed. "What do you think you can do with that? Pound me to death? We're indestructible when we bilocate, you know." Her black eyes widened. "Oh, look, dearest."

Fear Doirich was looking—at Teagan, not at Enkidu.

An insane, *ravenous* look flashed over his face. He opened his mouth, as if he were going to sing one of the songs that twisted creation—then turned sideways and disappeared. A wormhole. She had never seen Raynor use one, but she was sure that was what the Dark Man had just done.

"Well, that's that," Mab said. "And you even brought the little swine back for slaughter." She pulled the knife Finn had dropped in the market from a sheath at her side. "Thank you for this. It certainly is a step up from the bronze blade I had before. It's been helpful in carving my way out of Mag Mell. Iron is as bad for her as it is for us. But it's useful. How's Raynor, by the way? Insane yet?" She laughed. "I think killing Finn would have done it. He loves that boy."

"He loved you," Teagan said.

"I don't want love. I want sacrifice. *Come here, swine.*"

"*I am not a swine!*" Enkidu bellowed as he charged her.

Move, Teagan commanded her feet as Mab's knife hand swung up. This was no different from defying the *cat-sídhe*'s voices, only harder. Much harder.

Enkidu head-butted the Highborn in the ribs just as Thomas came out the door he'd run through—dragging Mab's flesh-and-bone body behind him by the hair.

The knife arm started its downward arc, and Teagan swung her war club. It smashed into the back of Mab's hand. She might not have been able to break the bones, but the force of the blow knocked the dagger from the Highborn's grasp, and it clattered onto the stones of the balcony floor.

Mab tried to shove Enkidu away and go after it, but Teagan dove, reaching it first. Mab was fighting desperately to free herself from the phooka now. She grabbed his head and started to twist.

Teagan didn't have time to stand up. She rolled over and stabbed the dagger through Mab's foot. The shock wave pressed her into the paving stones and threw Enkidu into the balcony railing. It ripped Mab's flesh and bones away from Thomas, leaving hair in his hand.

Thomas was on his feet before Teagan gained hers, grabbing up the Sídhe queen's body again. Mab was in it now, but not quite able to move. Teagan knew exactly how it felt—five slow heartbeats before your soul settled in again. The awareness came back into her eyes, and the Highborn managed a gasp as Thomas lifted her body and threw it over the balcony. Teagan heard the impact, like a melon hitting the cobblestones below.

Teagan helped Enkidu to his feet. She didn't want to look down. But she had to make sure. She leaned over the railing beside Thomas. The Dump Dogs had found them. Saoirse, her face wet with Mab's blood, looked up and grinned. Unlike Lollan and Bairre, she hadn't bothered to shift before she started to feed.

And then the phookas poured into the street, and the Dump Dogs disappeared beneath them as a hand pulled Teagan away.

"Thomas?" Teagan asked, realizing whose hand it was. "What are you doing here?"

"Looking for Roisin," Thomas said. "I knew Fear Doirich wouldn't kill me as long as he thought I was useful in finding Aiden."

"And were you?"

"Not very," Thomas said. "But then, he wasn't useful in helping me find Roisin, either."

"Where's he gone?" Teagan asked.

"To kill your brother." Thomas touched the flower Finn had laced through her buttonhole. "Moon roses only grow in one place. I'll help Aiden if I can." The *lhiannon-sídhe* shifted, and lifted into the air on a raven's wings.

The First Grove. Fear Doirich was already there. Teagan grabbed Enkidu with one hand and shoved the knife into her own belly with the other. The world exploded around her.

EAGAN'S eyes were open, and there was nothing but green leaves above her. One heartbeat ... two ... by the fifth she could hear Aiden's screams ... and Abby's ... and rising above them both, Fear's voice, singing three distinct notes at once, the lower two discordant, and the third twisting a melody. Enkidu brushed the leaves from her face, then held his finger to his lips.

Teagan nodded, and he pulled her to her feet. Aiden's leaf blanket had saved her life. The phookas that she now saw kneeling, hands over their ears, heads bowed before their terrible god, must have come looking for Aiden, but they would have been happy to find her flesh and bones as well.

Fear Doirich stood on the bank of the pool, holding her brother up by one foot. A battle raged in the air above him, dark sprites fighting a single wood sprite—Lucy, fighting for her life, and for Aiden's.

A dying phooka lay on the ground between Teagan and Fear, its belly sliced cleanly open. *Mamieo's knife.* Finn had certainly killed that one, but she couldn't see him anywhere.

She had to turn to see Abby, still screaming, struggling to

361

free her feet from the ground. Fear Doirich had planted her like he had planted Eógan.

The only phooka still moving was the wolf-headed man on the ground before Doirich, the handle of the Dark Man's scepter pierced through its shoulder like a spear, pinning it to the ground. It was less human than any of those who knelt before the Dark Man, and clearly less devout. It snarled and snapped and tried to lunge toward him, but the Dark Man's words wrapped around it, and its mortal flesh changed, responding to Fear Doirich's song, moving to his will. Now the legs it kicked were not human, but goat legs.

Teagan started toward Fear Doirich, and the phooka on the spear looked past the Dark Man and saw her.

"Hard-choice time, girl," it said in Finn's voice. He was pulling himself up the spear shaft with human hands, trying to get to Fear Doirich.

Doirich began to turn toward Teagan, and Enkidu went straight up the Dark Man's back, wrapping his arms around his head and clapping his hand over his mouth. Teagan leaped for Aiden, the force of her jump ripping him from the Dark Man's grip.

She turned and dove into the pool, both arms wrapped around her brother. She carried him as deep as she could, down to where the roots tangled together. There were wild currents in this pool, pulling one way and then another. Aiden was nearly pulled away from her when she reached out to catch a root with one hand, but she managed to hold on to his shirt.

The water closed around them, shutting out Fear's voice. It wasn't dark below the surface. It was like falling through a one-way mirror. She could see the moon in the night sky above, and it lit everything around her. The first Song of Creation was stronger here than Teagan had ever heard it. It was wild and joyful, calling order out of chaos, beauty out of darkness, forming art and music that swirled past her in the currents, then vanished. Aiden caught a root and held on.

Teagan looked around for the lights that would show her the surfaces of other pools. They were like beautiful stars in the distance—some blue, some golden, and some strangely green—but much too far away. Getting to even the nearest would be death for her in this body. Death for Aiden.

She turned to her brother, not wanting him to be alone at the end. To be afraid. But Aiden wasn't afraid. He was floating free, eyes wide, his fingers spread to the water. He was hearing the music too, and ... Teagan frowned. Something more than music, perhaps, because his fingers curled and fluttered in signs she didn't understand. Aiden was talking either to the water or to something in the water. Something she couldn't see, and he was smiling. His fingers hesitated, and he closed his eyes.

Listening.

When he opened them again, he flashed *Up* at her in ASL, then kicked away and tried to swim for the surface. He started sinking instead. Aiden was a worse swimmer than Finn. Now there was panic in his eyes. He needed air, probably more urgently than she did. And the only way to get it was to go back to Mag Mell.

Help me, Tea, he signed.

She grabbed his arm and swam for the surface of the pool.

It had moved away from them while they were underwater, and her own lungs were burning by the time her head broke the surface. She gulped in great breaths of air, while Aiden gagged and choked beside her.

Abby had stopped screaming. She was transforming faster than Eógan had, and the bark that was growing over her body had already covered her mouth. Lucy and the flight of dark sprites were gone. Enkidu was not wrapped around the Dark Man's head anymore. Two phookas held his arms while another pounded him with its fists. Finn's twisted form lay very still.

Aiden pulled himself out of the pool, and Fear Doirich turned toward them.

"My daddy gave my song back, bad guy." Aiden's voice was raw. "And my mom said to *kick your butt*." He bent and coughed up water.

Fear sang one note, and Teagan felt Mag Mell start to scream. *Fear Doirich was about to kill her brother.* She charged him like Enkidu had charged Mab, butting her head into his stomach with all her might. It knocked the air out of him, but he grabbed her hair and pulled her away, then backhanded her hard. She tasted coppery blood as she stumbled backwards, tripping over the phooka body that had been Finn. He grunted as she landed on him, and she felt a spark leap between them. It *still was* Finn. He wasn't quite dead.

Fear started his three-toned song again, and Teagan felt herself being broken by his words. Her arms and legs were becoming useless flippers. Then:

"*The Minstrel Boy,*" Aiden sang, his soprano rising sweetly,

"to the war is come,
In the ranks of death ye will find him."

Fear Doirich roared, his voice drowning out Aiden's completely. The phooka beating Enkidu stopped to watch.

"His father's sword he hath girded on," Aiden sang, and the dust of Mag Mell started lifting around him, forming a shadow belt and sword at his side.

"And his wild harp slung behind him."

Teagan saw it; an Irish harp, graven with twisting shapes like snakes. Mag Mell was dressing her tiny warrior.

"'Land of Song!' said the warrior bard,
'Tho' all the world betray thee,
One sword, at least, thy rights shall guard,
This faithful voice shall praise thee!'"

"The Minstrel fell!" The power of the Dark Man's voice knocked Aiden to his knees. Fear's voice changed, splitting in three again, the lower notes crooning sickness, singing darkness, bringing death, while the high voice mimicked Aiden's, high and sweet.

"'Neath the foeman's chains
Forged to drag that proud soul under."

Chains formed and started to wrap around Aiden.

"The harp he loved never spoke again," the Dark Man crooned. *"For he tore its chords asunder."*

For one breath, Aiden was voiceless ... and then a raven dropped from the sky. The Irish muse *shifted* before his feet touched the ground, and he put his hand on Aiden's curly head. Suddenly, Aiden's voice grew stronger than it had ever been before.

> *"No more chains shall sully thee,*
> *Thou world of love and bravery."*

Aiden wasn't singing for himself now. He was singing over all of Mag Mell.

> *"My song will make you pure and free*
> *And end your years of slavery!"*

He grabbed the end of the chain Fear's words had formed, shook it out like a whip, then brought his arm back and down. The chain flicked up toward the sky, growing as the energy wave rolled along it. The *crack* was like a mighty crash of thunder, and the sky ... shattered.

Teagan could see the dark waters and chaos all around them, and then a comet bloomed, and the thunder turned into a roar that drowned both Aiden and Fear Doirich out.

Fear Doirich's mouth was moving, but Teagan couldn't hear him over the roar of a mighty engine. *Raynor had finished the Indian Four.* Teagan saw a flash of the angel in a leather jacket, leaning forward over the handlebars. Aviator goggles covered his eyes, and a white scarf trailed behind him.

Then the motorbike collided with Fear Doirich, knocking him—*out of existence*. Out of Mag Mell at the very least, because Raynor, Fear, and the Indian Four were gone.

"Thanks, Thomas." Aiden wiped his face on the back of his wet sleeve. "That was a really good trap. Zoë gave me a song, too. I've got to sing it now." Thomas nodded and put his hands back on the little bard's head.

And then Aiden spread his arms and started to sing the Song of Creation. Teagan could feel the ground resonating with the *cantus firmus,* as if Yggdrasil's roots beneath them were vibrating with the sheer joy of a greater voice. Aiden's sweet melody tangled with it, now above, now below ... and the foundations of the multiverse shook.

The moon darkened and turned red as blood, and Mag Mell let loose an ecstasy of cloudless lightning, each bolt mending the shattered sky. Then she hid the red moon with clouds as Aiden's words changed. A ripple rolled over Teagan, as agonizing as anything Fear Doirich had done to her, but when it passed she had arms again. She wrapped them around Finn. The scepter still pierced his bare chest, pinning him to the ground, but it was Finn's chest, and Finn's own face. She covered him as best she could with her body as the rain began to fall like tears.

She could feel the life draining out of him, even as Mag Mell healed, the circuits in his body shutting down.

"Finn!"

His heartbeat slowed, and she knew the instant it stopped. Teagan thought her own heart would stop from the pain.

There was no shock as their lips touched . . . until the *wild* inside her exploded, hunting him, catching him, calling him back. Electricity arced between them, and then his heart was beating with hers, and she held him close, willing life into him.

Mag Mell's weeping was over and the gray of dawn was all around them when Finn opened his eyes.

"You're back."

"Girl"—he reached up and tucked her hair behind her ear—"you're that good a kisser."

O W." Finn's hands reached for the scepter, but Teagan caught them.

"Wait. Let me think."

"Oh, my god." She looked up to see Abby, Thomas, and Aiden standing over them. Lucy had appeared, too, and was sitting on Aiden's shoulder. His hair was a little too wet for the tattered sprite.

"Oh, my god," Abby said again. "He kept those phooka things away from us."

The phookas. Teagan whirled to look, but they were gone. A group of dirty, shaggy men had taken their place. Enkidu, the cleanest among them, was holding up ten perfect fingers to the morning sky. She was going to figure out what had happened . . . as soon as Finn was safe.

"He saved our lives," Abby was saying. "And now—" She put her hand over her mouth.

"Abby," Teagan said. "He's not dying."

"Already did," Finn rasped. "But I'm over it. Now I've just got a great bloody stick through my chest, and it hurts like hell." He turned his face away and spat blood.

It was frothy. Air was entering the lung from his chest wall.

Teagan squeezed his hand. "You've got a punctured lung. But that's survivable. *Stop wiggling.*"

"You sound like Mamieo in one of her moods." Finn was having a hard time finding enough air to force into words. "Can you unpin me, girl? I want to sit up."

"Thomas, will you help me?"

The *lhiannon-sídhe* put his hands under Finn's shoulders to lift him while Teagan gripped the scepter to loosen it from the ground and keep it steady.

"We need to leave it in until we can get you to a doctor," Teagan said when he was upright. "It might cause more damage if we pull it out here."

"You think I'm getting to a doctor?"

"Yes," Teagan said. "As soon as Raynor gets back."

Finn looked down at his chest. "He took hours last time. I don't think I'm good for it."

"I don't think it's as far." Teagan hoped that she was right. Mag Mell had doors into all the worlds of creation. "Wherever Raynor went, it's only one step away." She turned to look at the woods.

"What's coming, then?" Finn asked.

"Seamus," she said. "Cú Faoil, and one Fir Bolg."

"Get me to my feet." Finn struggled to his knees, both hands holding the scepter in place so the weight of the golden globe at the end didn't make it dip. "I don't want the Scottish idiot to see me sitting down like this."

He was barely upright when Seamus and the redheaded

giant from Samhain Market came into the clearing. The lawyer had Aiden's whip coiled Indiana Jones–style in his hand and not a single scratch on him.

The Cú Faoil snarled at the former phookas. The shaggy men picked up the weapons they had dropped, ready to fight.

"Don't let them, McGillahee!" Teagan shouted.

Seamus gave a command and the hounds dropped. Then he saw Finn, and his face went pale.

"You need a little help, Mac Cumhaill?"

"Nope." Finn swayed, and Teagan stepped under his arm to catch him, and then Enkidu was holding him up from the other side. The shaggy men had disappeared into the woods.

"Got it under control," Finn said.

"You've got a scepter sticking out of your chest."

"About that," Teagan said. "I need to break it off. He's going to be hard to move this way."

The redheaded Fir Bolg stepped forward. Teagan steadied the portion of the scepter sticking out of Finn's back while Thomas held the front. The Fir Bolg took the wooden shaft in his hand and snapped it like a matchstick.

"How did you get here so fast?" Teagan asked as the giant weighed the gold globe in his hand and smiled.

"Mag Mell seems to be functioning again," Seamus said. "Making long journeys short, and twisted paths straight. What do we do about Finn?"

There was a pop and a roar, and Raynor and his motorbike reappeared. He was wearing Fear Doirich's gold circlet like a bangle bracelet, and he smelled like the breath of a volcano again. He shoved his goggles to the top of his head and looked at Finn.

"Raynor." Abby gripped Aiden's shoulders. "Did you see Jing? I mean when you—"

The angel ignored her.

"I'm so sorry, Aiden. Tea. I would have done anything I could—" He shook his head. "Mab?"

"She's dead." Teagan didn't know any way to soften it. "I'm sorry too, Raynor."

"*Jing!*" Abby shouted. *"What about Jing?"*

"Jing's fine," the angel said. "He's at St. Drogo's. You're not dying too, are you, Finn?" Raynor sounded almost like a child. "I came as fast as I could. And I brought you something." He held up Fear Doirich's circlet. "It belonged to your family before the Fir Bolg fought and lost Mag Mell. It's yours now."

Finn looked at the thin crown of gold.

"Crap," he said faintly.

"'Crap, I'm dying, so I don't get to be king'?" Raynor asked. "Or 'Crap, it won't fit'?"

"Crap, I don't want the thing," Finn said. He was starting to look a little blue.

"Raynor, can you settle this later?" Teagan started hauling Finn toward the motorbike. "He needs to get to a doctor."

Raynor handed Teagan the crown as Enkidu lifted Finn onto the bike.

"You might consider McGillahee." Finn's voice was barely a whisper. "Mag Mell's the perfect place for him."

"Why?" Teagan asked.

"No cars." Finn was definitely turning blue. "He won't be running over anyone."

"Hurry, Raynor," Teagan said.

Raynor put his goggles on. The Indian Four roared to life— and they were gone, leaving Teagan holding the crown.

Abby was staring at Seamus. "Consider McGillahee?"

Seamus nodded. "I'm the logical choice."

"You think you're the lad born to be king. That song was all about you."

This time he grinned. "Of course I am."

"Not so fast," Teagan said. "Finn said consider Seamus, not hand a kingdom to him. Mag Mell is more complex than she was in the time of the Fir Bolg. There are wild men now, and *cat-sídhe*, the Highborn and lowborn, and all sorts of creatures that came here with Mab."

Seamus nodded. "The Fir Bolg weren't just for this world, were they? They stepped into all the worlds of creation to mend and tend."

Her dad had been right. He was the Scarecrow, the Lion, and the Tin Man rolled into one. Seamus McGillahee had the brains, the courage, and the heart to mend and tend this place. And the crazy arrogance to think he could get it done. Plus, no one else was applying for the job, and she needed to get home to Finn.

"It is yours." Teagan held out the crown. "With a few provisions."

"Provisions?"

"That you truly are mending and tending *all* the creatures

here. That even the lowborn are given a chance to choose. To change their future."

Aiden slipped his hand into his sister's. "Teagan even likes *worms*."

"I do," Teagan agreed. "I understand that choices have to be made. But if I hear that any creatures are being hunted or abused, I will come back and take this off your head."

"Whoa, Tea," Abby said. *"You'll take off his head?"*

"I'll help," Enkidu said happily.

"I didn't say I'd take *off* his head. I said I'd take the *crown* off his head."

"It was totally in your tone of voice, though," Abby insisted.

"You used that voice like Mom's, Tea," Aiden agreed. "It was really scary."

But Seamus nodded seriously. "I'll bring justice, Teagan Wylltson." The power was back in his voice, and this time it didn't falter. "On my word. I'll mend and tend them all, and Fir Bolg will step into all creation again." He set the crown on his own head. "This is my destiny."

"There is no such thing as destiny," Teagan said, looking around for the knife Finn must have dropped when the Dark Man changed him.

"Of course there is." Seamus studied his reflection in the pool. "I'm living proof of it." He pointed at his head. "See? King."

"I chose to give it to you. See? Free will."

"Keep telling yourself that." Seamus adjusted the circlet.

Teagan didn't stop to check the wound on her arm until she'd found Mamieo's knife and wiped the phooka blood from the blade. When she did check, she decided that she'd probably need a course of strong antibiotics as well as stitches. Red lines of infection were crawling up her arm.

"I left Finn's knife in the city. I'll need that one, too. Then I'm taking Aiden home," Teagan said.

"Aiden's not staying?" Seamus asked. "I thought . . ."

"Nope," Aiden said. "Lennie needs me."

Mag Mell opened the path without Aiden singing a single note, and decorated the world around him with rainbows and flowers. Seamus, the redhead, and the Cú Faoil led the way, while Aiden pulled Abby along, showing her everything. Thomas walked quietly beside Teagan while Enkidu brought up the rear, still watching for trouble. Such as shaggy men who had once been phookas. They hadn't gone far. Teagan saw them following along, peering at them from behind fern fronds.

"What are they?" she asked Thomas quietly.

"They are the *wodewose*, the wild men of the woods," the *lhiannon-sídhe* said. "Generations ago, when Mab came to their world calling them to follow her, she demanded that their leader sacrifice his little daughter to Fear Doirich. He told her that men do not kill children, and they hunted Mab through the woods instead. They would certainly have killed her," Thomas went on, "if Fear Doirich hadn't come."

"He twisted them," Teagan guessed. "Like he twisted Finn and me."

Thomas nodded. "The lust for child flesh was something extra. A little bit of Mab herself."

Men don't eat children. Finn had given the phooka a glimory without even realizing it, and Enkidu had followed that tiny glimmer until he found . . . himself.

One of the men following them stopped at a patch of edible fungus, and another bellowed and jumped on him. They started whaling away at one another with their fists.

"Aside from the hooves, heads, and fangs, and the little bit of Mab, they didn't change all that much," Thomas said.

As Mag Mell led them, Teagan thought she recognized some of the paths. She was sure of it when they came to the deep pools. Aiden was singing Disney's "Once Upon a Dream" to call out the creatures for Abby. The frogmen emerged to croak a chorus as they marched behind him.

The Cú Faoil had to snarl and snap to keep the wild men from catching a few for lunch. Lucy glared at the sprites that came to dance for Aiden, but she didn't start any knife fights. Eventually, the paths left the ponds for another place that Teagan recognized.

Aiden stood silently, looking up at a tree that had once been a man named Eógan. The fiddler had been Thomas's slave until he tried to run away. The mending had come too late. Roots that had once been toes plunged into the ground, and one branch wrapped tightly around a fiddle, pressing it to the trunk of the tree.

The *lhiannon-sídhe* touched the fiddle's strings. "You go on," he said to the others.

Teagan picked up Aiden and carried him out of the

clearing. Mag Mell led them straight to Samhain Market after that. The phooka tent village was full of dazed-looking men, women, and children, the fair a shambles.

When Teagan saw the shimmer of the gate, she stopped. She needed to go into the city and retrieve the iron knife before she stepped through. But Finn was on the other side of that shimmer, fighting for his life.

"Right," Seamus said, when he saw the look on her face. He pulled up a wooden crate. "You just sit here a few minutes. The Cú Faoil will watch over you. Tell me where the knife is, and I'll bring it to you."

Teagan explained exactly where she had left it, and sat down on the crate as Abby and Aiden paced. Enkidu sat down beside her and studied his hands, then glanced sideways at her. But he didn't say anything.

"Thomas is coming," Aiden said.

The *lhiannon-sídhe* was walking through the mess of the market, looking like a dark, sad prince.

"You're coming back with us, right?" Abby asked.

Thomas nodded. "Some things can't be mended, can't be undone. And I have done far too many such things. Toppled kingdoms, tortured poets, sent good men to their death." He took a shuddering breath.

"Killed murderesses, banished evil gods," Teagan reminded him. "Where are all the Highborn?" She suddenly realized that she hadn't seen any in the market or coming from the city.

"They've left Mag Mell, gone into the pools and away. Roisin isn't here now, if she ever was. She might have gone back to your world. I need to find her. There's a chance I can keep her from . . . doing things that can't be undone. More than she already has."

Seamus returned with the knife in a leather bag. "You don't want to be carrying two knives through the streets of Chicago," he said. "You already look disreputable enough to attract attention from the police." Teagan put Mamieo's blade in with the other.

"Well," Seamus said, "I guess that's it."

Aiden stood up. "No, it isn't."

"What?" Seamus asked.

"I want my whip back. Lennie gave it to me."

"Oh." Seamus handed it over reluctantly. "I suppose I can get another. I am the king."

"Aiden," Teagan prompted.

"Thank you for showing me how to work it," Aiden said, clutching it to his chest.

Teagan nodded. Suddenly she didn't know how to say goodbye, didn't want to form the words, so she started toward the shimmer.

Enkidu caught her hand. "You could stay, Teagan. Fear Doirich is gone. You could stay."

"I'm not going to do that. I love Finn."

"I'll miss you," Enkidu said.

Teagan hugged him. "Fir Bolg weren't the only ones meant to walk in many worlds. I'll be back."

"Promise?" he asked slyly as she let go.

"I don't have to promise," Teagan said. "I love you, remember?"

"Like a friend." Enkidu sighed.

"Like a brother." Teagan let go of his hand.

"Ouch, Tea," Abby said as they walked toward the shimmer. "That's, like, worse than telling them you love them like a friend. You know that, right?"

And then they stepped through the gate, out of Mag Mell and into what had been Rosehill Cemetery. The fire of creation had melted tombstones and slumped mausoleums into bizarre sculptures of atomic glass.

Teagan suddenly realized that she was barefoot and wearing nothing but Finn's oversize shirt. No wonder McGillahee had said she looked disreputable. Mag Mell must have moved every sharp stick and stone away as she walked, because she hadn't so much as stubbed a toe. Teagan could see police cars parked outside the gate, and people in HAZMAT suits wandering around. People with Geiger counters.

The atomic glass was cool beneath her feet, and she couldn't hold the tears back. This was where her dad had stood. Had died.

> *The Minstrel fell! But the foeman's chain*
> *Could not bring that proud soul under.*

Abby knelt and touched a puddle of metal that must have been Rafe's gun.

"Bada-bing. You idiot," she said.

Aiden patted Abby's back. "Rafe is a good guy."

"*Is* a good guy, Choirboy?" Abby looked worried, and shot Teagan a look that said *He knows they're dead, right?*

379

Teagan nodded.

"I heard them, Abby," Aiden said. "Leo and Rafe are really far away, like the stars in the water. We can't get there yet. Zoë!"

The dance therapist and Raynor Schein were walking toward them, past the police and HAZMAT crews.

"No way," Abby said. "No freaking way is this possible. She was right there with your dad."

Abby was right. *This wasn't possible.*

Zoë met Teagan's eyes and smiled.

Teagan was suddenly sure that the woman hadn't been the least bit out of her mind when they'd found her rocking a baby phooka in Mag Mell. *When she'd asked Finn to give a certain goblin child a coin so she could buy green glass beads . . .*

Three peoples could walk in any world of creation, but Zoë had done more than that. *She'd given a song to Aiden in the pool.* Zoë Giordano walked in and out of . . . death.

"Plus, why aren't the cops stopping them?" Abby asked.

"Raynor's an angel," Aiden said. "Duh."

Whatever Zoë was, Aiden loved her. He broke away from Teagan and ran to the woman. She scooped him up in her arms.

"I sang your song, Zoë! I did it!"

"Finn?" Teagan asked.

"In Saints Mary and Elizabeth Medical Center," Raynor said. "He's stable. And Father Gordon has Jing cornered at St. Drogo's, Abigail. The young man might appreciate being rescued."

"Yeah," Abby said. "Like the cops are going to let me rush right over there. They're going to have questions, right?"

"Just walk close to me," Zoë said. "Hello, Thomas. I'm glad to see you here."

The police officers and HAZMAT crews were walking right past them, not looking up. The goblins had done the same thing in Samhain Market as Zoë held the dying baby, Teagan realized.

"You'll want to go to the medical center, Tea." The dance therapist nodded toward her arm. "But let's take Aiden back to the Widdershins' and get you some clothes first."

"But Mamieo—"

"You've been gone three days," Zoë said gently. "Everything's been taken care of. John Wylltson might not have been able to see phookas, but he could see more than you might think. Like the need to have someone there for his children. Sophia knows that John is gone. She's waiting for you."

"Zia Sophia?" Abby said. "She's, like, their guardian?" *That's what her dad had wanted to talk with Seamus and Mrs. Santini about.*

"But Ms. Skinner is never going to allow that," Teagan said.

"She has recently had a life-changing experience," Zoë said. "She isn't pressing charges, by the way. A very perceptive detective named Deneux persuaded her that she wants nothing to do with Wylltsons or Mac Cumhaills. She's handed the case over to me."

They'd made it out of the cemetery without anyone questioning their presence, or even seeing them, apparently.

"Tea, you're okay now, right?" Abby said when they reached the street. "Because I'm going to St. Drogo's."

"Of course," Teagan said.

"Thomas," Zoë said. "Will you come with us?"

"No," Thomas said. "I need to find Roisin." He turned and walked away, for all the world as if he had no wings.

"Is he a good guy, Zoë?" Aiden asked.

"He's trending in that direction." The dance therapist pursed her lips. "Raynor, I don't think he should go alone."

The angel looked after Thomas.

"I work exclusively with saints," he said.

"I'm aware."

"What about Finn?"

"Finn and Tea do a pretty good job of looking after each other, don't you think?"

"Zoë. *He killed my brother.*"

Zoë just looked at him, her eyes full of love. "I know. You have a choice to make, Raynor."

Raynor hesitated for a long moment, but finally, he nodded.

"Yes, Boss," he said, and started after Thomas.

EPILOGUE

THE kitchen of the Widdershins smelled *right* again—like paint and linseed oil. Like creation. Teagan leaned over the sink to look out the window into the backyard, making sure Aiden and Lennie weren't getting into any trouble.

Aiden was squatting like a magical Christopher Robin in yellow puddle-jumpers and a raincoat in the midst of the prairie trillium, columbine, foxglove, beardtongue, fire pink, and who-knows-what-else Joe had called up. A few were already blooming, but most were just spring green. Aiden was singing to a little tree. Lennie, in size-ten puddle-jumpers of his own, was stomping a made-up magical dance around Aiden while Joe held Grizabella, her orange fur glorious and full, in his arms. Peter, Augustus, Alonzo, and James sat on the cinder-block fence. No one was safe on the ground when Lennie Santini danced.

The Green Man had slept through his autumn thundershower and all through the winter while the squirrels scratched and worried away every piece of burn from him. He'd woken once at the solstice to mumble something cryptic, then slept again until the first plants peeked out of the soil. When he'd come fully awake at last, he and Aiden had visited the parks and wild places of Chicago, causing a chaos of growth. Somewhere in their wanderings they had gathered an oak seedling. Aiden spent an hour a day singing to the little tree, and it had already put on several years of growth.

Her parents would have loved this. *Did love it,* Teagan reminded herself. Even if they were on the dark side of a one-way mirror in space and time, Teagan was sure they loved the future they had helped create. She never would have been able to stand in this room again if she hadn't been sure of that, and sure that Mamieo Ida was with her Rory. The Widdershins' was a place of life, even though death had visited.

"You still think that's a good idea?" Abby looked up from her painting. "Singing roots into Mag Mell right here in the backyard?" She brushed away a sprite who was trying to weave a ribbon into her hair. Lucy had been keeping more than chocolates in her cup on the kitchen shelf. Her three baby sprites had been obsessed with decorating Abby for weeks now.

"It will be more convenient," Teagan said. They had to think of a better solution to the problem of the woolly squirrelephants, swat-bats, and sprites leaking out of Mag Mell, though. Joe couldn't spend all his time shooing them back in.

There was a steady stream of visitors from Mag Mell to consider, too. Currently they stepped through the remaining gate at Rosehill and made their way through the streets to the Widdershins'. Enkidu spent half his time here, and Seamus brought Irish Travelers he had recruited on their way to Mag Mell or back again. The Fianna were reforming, though this time they included not only warriors but Web wizards, street-wise Travelers, and wattle-jowled detectives. It took all kinds to deal with *sluagh* in the sewers and the occasional lowborn or Highborn run amok in the streets, courts of law, or cyber-space.

Raynor had popped in just once, after Finn had gotten out of the hospital. He'd sympathized when he'd learned that Mrs. Santini had insisted that Finn move to her house—close enough to watch over Tea and Aiden, but far enough away to be proper—then he'd taken the Indian Four that he'd left parked in the kitchen, and popped out again. Thomas was apparently a great deal of work.

"I won't have to walk all the way to the gate at Rosehill in order to get to class in Ithaca," Teagan said. There were ad-vantages to being Highborn. Mag Mell had promised to open a gate for her, to make the path from her back door to Cornell short and straight. She would be able to visit Cindy and Oscar only once a month, though. Agnes's mind might have been opened to the possibility that unicorn farts were real, but Teagan couldn't tell her about any of this. Neither she nor Dr. Max was ready for a bilocate who could study all night while her body slept, or walk through any world of creation. They certainly wouldn't understand how she could keep up with her schoolwork and commute from Ithaca to Chicago every day.

The doorbell rang.

"That's Finn," Abby said.

"How do you know? More psychic powers?" Teagan teased.

Abby pointed to the white envelope that had been gathering dust behind the change jar. "Yeah. Like math. Six months to the day since your dad told you to put that envelope up there. He's here for his quest, right?"

Finn stood on the doorstep, looking more like an Irish gypsy than ever in his lace-up boots and bandanna. He had a knife in each boot now, a few more scars, and he'd added an earring and a vest for the occasion.

"Look at you!" Abby said. "All dressed up for a fight."

"Don't you have someplace else to be, Gabby?" he asked as he stepped inside. "Like out with Jing, maybe?"

"He's picking Cade up for a game. He can't play, but he still likes to be there."

"I think I hear your *zia* calling you, then." He pushed her toward the door.

"I don't hear anything," Abby said as he opened it and pushed her out. "Tea! Are you going to let him do this?"

"Yes." Teagan laughed. "Seriously, Abby. Go call Jing or something."

Finn leaned against the door. "She's like a vampire, then, isn't she? You let her in once, Tea, and she's never leaving."

"I don't want her to leave."

He took her hand and ran his finger down the scar on her arm. The electric arc that followed his touch spread nets of static over her body and shivers of delight down her spine.

As much as she hated to admit it, Mrs. Santini was right. There was no way she was going to focus on her studies with a sexy beast in the house. Certainly not with an *electric* beast that smelled and looked as good as Finn.

"Are you nervous?" Teagan asked as they walked to the kitchen.

"Na," Finn said. "I'm Finn Mac Cumhaill. I've faced hell-hounds for you, girl. Whatever it is, I'll get it done. Besides, I've already got it figured."

"The quest?"

"Our future. It's the ghosties, isn't it? The ghosties are us, come back old and gray to peep at the past."

"Why would you think they were us?"

"Mamieo said it herself." Finn winked. "Old age is the one thing you can't outrun."

"Maybe," Teagan said. "But if that's so, we become old and gray. Aren't we in an Irish story anymore?"

"I already died once, girl. Twice is too much to ask, even of an Irishman." He stopped to study Abby's canvas. "That's ... amazing."

Teagan nodded. The First Grove was so real that you could almost reach in and pluck a moon rose. The light falling on the tiger-eyed girl beside the pool looked as if it might have spilled out of a Maxfield Parrish painting.

"I think Abby's getting a scholarship, too." The Art Institute of Chicago had been interested in the work Abby had done in the past six months. Very interested. *Transcendent* was the word they'd used.

Teagan took the envelope down from the shelf above Abby's easel and handed it to Finn.

He tore it open carefully and pulled out a piece of paper.

"It's a list." He frowned and turned it over. "Front and back." Then his face went pale, and he sank into a chair.

"What? A list of what?"

"Books." Finn's voice shook. "The man's given me a list of *books* to read. There must be a hundred of them."

Teagan took the list from Finn's hand.

"A hundred and one," she said. "He numbered them. You *are* going to do it, aren't you?"

"Of course I am. I'm Finn Mac Cumhaill. I'll get it done."

"Then, why—"

"The old ghostie man," Finn said. "He was holding a book then, wasn't he? The last time we saw him. I had to be ninety years old, and I still hadn't finished reading these books."

Teagan shook her head. "You just loved them so much you were reading them again. I'm sure of it."

"I'm glad one of us is." Finn took back the paper and turned it over in his hands. "He said I couldn't ask you to marry me until I'd finished the quest. He didn't say a word about canoodling. Do you want to—"

"Yes."

ABOUT THE AUTHOR

Kersten Hamilton is the author of *Tyger Tyger* and *In the Forests of the Night*, the first two books of the Goblin Wars trilogy, as well as several picture books and many middle grade novels. She has worked as a ranch hand, a woodcutter, a lumberjack, a census taker, a wrangler for wilderness guides, and an archeological surveyor. Now, when she's not writing, she hunts dinosaurs in the deserts and badlands of New Mexico. For more about Kersten, please visit www.kerstenhamilton.com.